Book 3

of

The Ingenious

Trilogy

The Ingenious

and the End of Days

J.Y. Sam

This is a work of fiction.
Names, characters, organisations, places, events, and incidents are either products of the author's imagination, or are used fictitiously.

www.jysamofficial.com

paperback ISBN: 978-1-8382436-6-1
hardback ISBN: 978-1-8382436-8-5

Cover design by J.Y. SAM

First edition

DEDICATION

To Franco, Isabella, Marco.

SYNOPSIS OF BOOK 2:
The Ingenious and the Heart of Shattered Glass

Tai Jones' mother, Tyaishia, awakes from a months-long coma, only to find that her son is dying of a strange illness that has aged him to near death, and her father has died – so she is wracked with grief.

Professor Harald Wolff, one of the lead scientists of the abandoned Project Ingenious, is unravelling from the lingering trauma of losing his wife and son years ago in a tragic house fire, but also because Tai is dying.

Two of the Project Ingenious children are still missing, and Dr Kendra, who partnered Professor Wolff within the project, is the only person who knows their whereabouts – but he suffers from Alzheimer's, and his own cure gives him only brief and sporadic moments of lucidity. In one of those rare moments, he reveals cryptically that one of the missing children is in the Amazon jungle 'where the black meets the white', and is anxious that they get to her before their 'father' does. The Prime Minister therefore sends his chief of security, Rory Sanderson, to Brazil – together with natural genius, Calista Matheson, and her boyfriend, Jake Winters, as well as the youngest of the Ingenious children, Jemima Jenkins. Before they leave, Jemima discovers her special ability: she can discern the remaining seconds of life a person has. And is upset to find that Tai only has 3,396.5² seconds left, that is, just under four-and-a-half months.

Meanwhile, Milly Bythaway is suffering from the same disease that Karl König died from, and her physical and mental health is deteriorating rapidly as she battles terrible migraines, memory lapses, and begins drawing and writing on the walls. She swings between good and bad days; her father, Brian, is very anxious for her. The others are well aware that this genetic disease will likely affect the other Project Ingenious children. They therefore enlist Russian scientist, Dr Vassiliev, to complete the cure that Karl König was working on before he died.

The Chauffeur at last tells his story: when they were babies, he and his sister had been abandoned in a drain, and were passed from one foster home to another. The Chauffeur calls himself 'the half man' because he was born a twin, and his other half, his sister, died after taking a drug overdose. The Chauffeur stubbornly refuses to be given a name, not even by his adoptive parents, Dr Kendra and his wife Gaia, believing that only his birth mother can tell him what his real name is.

To everyone's surprise, the heavily guarded Dr Vassiliev disappears from the stately country house that he was staying in – and they wonder whether he was abducted, or whether he defected. Late at night, Mei Hui ventures beyond the grounds, into the forest, to check the timing of the security detail guarding the house, only to be chased by someone with a limp. She manages to run back into the garden, bolting the gate, and informs head of security, David O'Connor, though his guards don't find anyone.

Realising that the cat carrier is still at the house, and that Vassiliev would never leave without his much-loved Siberian molly cat, Lyubova, Milly and Mei Hui bring in Dog's five young cats to try to sniff out the missing Lyubova's whereabouts in the forest surrounding the house. They are led to a colony of feral cats, but Mei Hui is able to discern from the cats that Lyubova is not amongst them. O'Connor snorts with disbelief that Mei Hui can 'communicate' with animals, and Mei Hui's calm and wise response offends O'Connor, sparking in him a hatred for the Ingenious children. One of the feral kittens, a tortoise-shell, follows them, and Milly brings her back to the house.

One rainy lunchtime at the stately home, Tai, Tyaishia, Milly, Brian, Mei Hui, and the Professor are having lunch, when to their surprise they find that a sickly Lyubova has returned to the house. The cat searches around for her beloved Vassiliev, but he is nowhere to be found – so she goes to Tai instead. As he strokes her, Tai sees a horrific image in the cat's mind: of a mother and young son hiding under the stairs of a burning house. As Tai describes this, Professor Wolff recognises that it is exactly how his own wife and son died, and he faints with distress. It is an impossible memory, because the young cat was born in Russian many years after his house burnt down.

After a vet treats Lyubova, she goes to Tai's bedroom and settles down to sleep on his pillow. During the night – a steady drip of the cat's memories seep into Tai's dreams, revealing what had happened to

Dr Vassiliev on the stormy night he disappeared: the doctor's nightcap had been drugged by what they later discovered was the sedative, Rohypnol, making him drowsy and highly suggestible. Via a burner phone, the doctor was then directed through the forest to a road where a shadowy man is waiting next to a car. Vassiliev climbs in, with Lyubova following suit, and they are driven far away to a dark house nestled within a small copse. Vassiliev is taken inside, and Lyubova manages to get in through a broken window. Inside, the cat discovers hundreds of paintings all over the walls, and is in particular drawn to a large painting depicting Professor Wolff's burning house. But Lyubova is captured by the shadowy man, and is thrown into a sack and driven out and dumped. Amazingly the cat manages to find her way back to the stately home, soon becoming sick.

Tai pores over the cat's memory of the burning house painting, and sees that it is signed by 'F. Jaffrey' – the pseudonym of a famous 19th century painter, whose real identity had never been discovered.

Since there is an F. Jaffrey exhibition in London, Milly and Mei Hui request to go there to check out the paintings. They meet one of the guides, an art advisor who specialises in the painter's works, Mrs Parry-Johansson. She is happy to see youngsters so interested in art, explaining that at the beginning of her career, a young boy visited the F. Jaffrey exhibition regularly, and like the girls, he too was only interested in Jaffrey's works. She told them that the boy himself was an artist, sketching and making replicas of F. Jaffrey's pictures, and, curiously, he barely looked at the originals when he copied them. This was interesting because legend had it that F. Jaffrey himself was able to create his pictures without the need for the sitters to spend hours, days, and weeks keeping still before him as he painted – apparently he paid them just one visit, and was able to make the painting from memory. All this made Mrs Parry-Johansson wonder whether this boy could perhaps be a descendant of the great artist. Both Milly and Mei Hui are very excited to hear this, because the photographic memory of both F. Jaffrey, and the mysterious boy, seem to be just like the Ingenious children's abilities. The girls ask the art advisor if she knows the name of the boy. She does, it is Jeremy Fitzsimmons.

Cross-referencing his name with the image of the shadowy man's house from Lyubova's memories, they soon discover the address of Dr Vassiliev's abductor. The Professor's ninja agents are immediately sent to the location, and they capture an old man – who they are shocked to find has a hideously deformed face. They also recover Dr Vassiliev from a locked cellar. He is alive and well.

Dr Kendra and Gaia are told to evacuate Avernus, and when they go outside to leave, Dr Kendra is shocked to see a shackled Fitzsimmons being transferred into Avernus. Terrified, he runs off through the industrial estate, but is hit by a truck, and dies in his wife's arms. There is now no way of discovering the whereabouts of the last lost Ingenious child.

A shaky Dr Vassiliev tells the Professor that when he was being kept prisoner, every day the hideous man used to grab his wrists with splayed hands – and the Professor guesses that this must be the 'father' of the Ingenious children mentioned by Dr Kendra, because the children similarly need physical touch in order to be able to read minds.

The Professor decides to explore Fitzsimmon's house himself, together with Mei Hui and Milly who can help him see. The house is filled with paintings, except for one room that contains only a single, enchanting picture covering nearly the entire length of the wall: it is of a beautiful girl standing next to a stream, with a dragonfly hovering near her head. Continuing their exploration, the Professor at last finds himself in front of the burning house painting, disturbed by the melting figures of his dear wife and son, as they hide underneath the stairs.

Against his agents' advice, and filled with so many questions, the Professor confronts Jeremy Fitzsimmons. Fitzsimmons grabs his wrists, and in a heartbeat is taken back to that fateful night. He sees that Fitzsimmons is in his back garden, looking into the house, and spying on his wife, Chiara, and his 12-year-old son, Christian. They are arguing, and an enraged Christian hurls an open can of tomatoes at his mother, which splodges onto the floor near the garden door. Suddenly Chiara notices movement through the garden window. Outside, Fitzsimmons is distracted by a faint and unusual odour in the air, and just as he realises what that smell is, the garden door opens and Chiara swings a frying pan at his head. He ducks, and she misses, but the pan breaks the cracked gas pipe nestled against the door jamb. Chiara quickly locks the door, and hides with Christian in the cupboard under the stairs in the dark. Fitzsimmons keeps banging on the door, to warn them of the gas leak – and when the door breaks open, he runs inside, only to slip on the tomatoes, knocking himself out. Inside the cupboard, Chiara passes out from the gas, and a frightened Christian switches on the light – only to cause a massive explosion. Fitzsimmons wakes up to a roaring fire. He runs outside and rolls on the grass to extinguish his burning clothes. He is just about to run back in to help the mother and son, when fire engines and firemen appear, and so Fitzsimmons hides in the bushes, watching them battle the fire. Much later, a middle-aged, sighted Professor Wolff returns home, mad with worry. He runs into the remains of his smoking house only to find the burnt corpses of his wife and son. He breaks down. The intense heat and stinging smoke burn his eyes, and the image of their dead bodies is the last thing he sees.

Meanwhile, back in the stately home, Milly inspects the photos she had taken of F. Jaffrey's paintings, discovering in one of the paintings there is a tiny image hidden in the eyeshine of the sitter, of the moment the man killed his own wife – and from this, Milly, Tai, and Mei Hui themselves surmise that F. Jaffrey's descendent, Jeremy Fitzsimmons, must be their genetic father, that is, the person from whom their genius genes were taken. They ask the Professor if they can meet Fitzsimmons, and get more information, but the Professor forbids them from ever doing so.

However, behind his back, the three return to Avernus, where they manage to get past the heavy security, and enter the mysterious Jeremy Fitzsimmons' prison cell. Tai draws closer and tenderly wipes tears from his face, but the man suddenly grabs his wrist – and when Mei Hui and Milly rush to Tai's aid, Milly too is grabbed, the circle is closed, and all three teenagers pass out.

They awake inside Fitzsimmon's mind, which appears as an enormous glass heart crazed with razor-sharp cracks. The three are stuck to its surface, but manage to swivel round to peer through the cracks. They see glimpses of Fitzsimmons' memories. Inquisitive as to how he came to be involved with Project Ingenious as their genetic father, what hand he had to play in Professor Wolff's burning house, and indeed why his heart is broken, the teenagers decide to discover the answers by searching his memories.

Travelling back in time, they see his life as a handsome toddler, Jem, much loved by his mother, Anne, and his father, Max, who also has a deformed face. He and his father have a special mind connection. As Jem grows up within Oakley Hall, he is fascinated by the collected works of his forefather, Jeremy Fitzsimmons 1st, who they know to be the great F. Jaffrey. As the boy grows into a teenager, he is tormented by the fact that his face too will become hideously deformed, like his father's, and his grandfather's, and all the Fitzsimmons men before them. Jem is gifted a Polaroid camera, and after seeing how beautiful his photos are, they encourage him to paint. At 19, a handsome Jem takes a stroll along the river and meets a young lady called Georgina Whyte. Georgie invites him to tea at the house of her grandmother, Viola, who on hearing that Jem lives at Oakley Hall, realises that he is a Fitzsimmons. Viola tells Jem that she's always suspected that his forefather, Jeremy Fitzsimmons 1st, was the renowned painter F. Jaffrey. Jem makes no comment, but when he learns that both Georgina and her grandmother have always wanted to have their portrait painted, he can't resist offering to do so. He takes photos of them, and months later unveils his painting. They are stunned by its beauty and his artistry, and from it, Viola realises that her suspicions were true, Jem's forefather was the great painter, and Jeremy has inherited his talent.

Georgina and Jeremy fall in love, and in time, get engaged. Jeremy has been having surgeries on his face for what he tells Georgina is a malignant mole. Jeremy can no longer delay Georgina meeting his parents, particularly his father, Max. He explains to Georgina that his father has an unusual condition which made his face change in his early 20s – she will be shocked by it, he tells her, but she should remember that he is the best of men, and a loving father. Georgina reassures him that she will be fine, but when she sees Max for the first time, she is horrified. She also works out that the same thing is happening to Jeremy's face, and he will eventually become like his hideous father. She runs away, breaking Jeremy's heart.

Jeremy can no longer paint, and when his parents die, he lives a solitary life in a run-down Oakley Hall. Through a litter of foxes that he takes in and cares for, he explores further his own mind abilities, amazed to find that he can download the animals' memories.

He reads in various newspapers about Dr Axel Kendra's pioneering work on gene editing, with the ability to edit out diseases from DNA. He arranges a meeting with Dr Kendra and commissions him to edit out the faulty gene from his own DNA that caused his face to change when he was 23, and instead, to enhance the genius genes that give him powerful mind abilities – all within genetically engineered offspring. He demonstrates his mind abilities by downloading Dr Kendra's mind, and replaying his memories back to him at frightening speed inside the doctor's head. A dazed Dr Kendra agrees to help him, and makes enquiries with his government contacts to get the experiments sanctioned, funded by Fitzsimmons' family fortune. Hence, Project Ingenious is born.

Years later, Dr Kendra triumphantly brings baby Alpha to Fitzsimmons, though the child is sickly and malnourished. Dr Kendra explains that, with subsequent babies, they will continue to refine and improve the genetic process. But as the years pass, Dr Kendra repeatedly tells Fitzsimmons of the massive loss of life, but Fitzsimmons demands that the project continue.

In time, Fitzsimmons despairs to learn that the Ingenious laboratories have been burnt down – but he soon realises that the children were secreted away by Dr Kendra and Professor Wolff. 12 years later, bankrupt and broken, he has had to sell Oakley Hall and move into a dark stone house amongst a copse of trees. He sees the news about the seven Oxford students studying genetics, who are dying from an unusual virus that causes cancer-like symptoms – and makes the connection with Project Ingenious. He jots down the name of the medical consultant, Dr Peter Davids, his first lead to finding his precious Ingenious children.

Fitzsimmons subsequently learns about Dr Vassiliev staying at the stately home. He bribes the housekeeper to drug the doctor's bottle of vodka with Rohypnol, and manages to abduct him and keep him prisoner in his basement. He reads the doctor's mind, and discovers everything he knows about the Ingenious children – but also sees that the children are dying from a genetic mutation, and Vassiliev, commissioned to work on the cure, is himself at a dead end. So, on a daily basis, and without him realising it, Fitzsimmons uploads Dr Kendra's scientific knowledge into Vassiliev's mind, to help him complete the cure. But in doing so, it triggers within Fitzsimmons a sudden desire to purge all his pent-up feelings, and paint again. He therefore completes the painting he started of Georgina Whyte with the dragonfly hovering close-by – and revels in the catharsis it brings. Feeling guilty about the death of the Professor's wife and son, he too sets out painting that, signing it as it as 'F. Jaffrey' – telling himself that it will be his pseudonym too.

The Chauffeur rushes into Fitzsimmon's cell and pushes him away from the children. They recover in another room, where they discover that the Professor and V2 are also recovering. They share their experiences, realising with dread that as they were absorbing Fitzsimmons' life, he too was absorbing theirs.

Deep in the Amazon, a Brazilian teenager, Saffron Morales, walks alone into the dangerous jungle. In her rucksack is a sickly black jaguar cub, Sabu – the last of its species. Desperate to save him, Saffie travels to a floating sky island where, informed by a curanderos friend, special flowers grow that can heal the young jaguar of its sickness. An isolados tribesman calls Saffie 'Daughter of Mother Earth', revealing that he had been following her for some time, and knows she has a special connection with nature. As such, she should be able to brave the insect-infested tunnel that will take her to the mountain top, as well as the tarantulas that guard the flowers. He warns her to descend the mountain before nightfall, or she will freeze to death. Saffie follows his directions, and finds that the flowers are surrounded not only by the spiders but also by swarms of wasps – as she draws closer, the insects clear a path for her. She drips the nectar from the golden flowers into Sabu's mouth, grasping the bark of a tree with one hand, and clenching the cub's limp body with the other. But the cub exhales a last breath, and before she knows it, night descends.

Calista, Jake, Jemima, Acuzio the dog, and Rory Sanderson, and their two guards had arrived in Manaus to search for the missing Ingenious girl, but to no avail. But when someone gives them a lead, they travel to a nature reserve upriver, where Saffron Morales' parents, Alma and Ignacio, are already expecting them. Saffie has the ability to feel the feelings of the Ingenious children, even over a distance, but not others. And she has been writing 'A Book of You' about the Ingenious children – knowing that they were coming to find her. Saffie also knows that the last missing Ingenious child is a boy, possibly somewhere in Asia. But Saffie's parents explain they were preparing to go into the jungle to search for their daughter since her tracker had gone dead just hours ago. They set out all together to find Saffie.

A chain of events involving a praying mantis, an ogre-faced spider, an orchid bee, a tree frog, a tiny ant, and a butterfly, ends with Acuzio sniffing out drops of Saffie's blood on the sand, which leads them to the entrance of the sky island. They brave the climb, and discover on the mountain top a mound of tarantulas next to a burnt-down tree. When the spiders part, they find to their amazement a dusty Saffie and Sabu underneath them – both still alive. The tarantulas had kept them warm in the night, and they work out that Saffie must have inadvertently used her powers to save Sabu, draining the tree of its energy, in the same way that Tai had accidentally revived his mother, depleting his own energy. But Saffie struggles to believe she has this ability. Ignacio and Saffie take samples of the golden flowers, and they all make their way back. Saffie suddenly feels that something terrible has happened in London, so they hurry. Jake also proposes to Calista amidst a flutter of swirling yellow butterflies next to the river.

The last part of the journey becomes extremely difficult as the ground turns to swamp and rolling mists obscure their vision. They find themselves surrounded by huge black caimans, and one of them snaps onto the leg of one of the guards and drags him into the water. In shock, and a fit of anger, Jemima stamps into the water and screams at the caiman – and to their surprise it returns the dazed guard.

Back in Avernus, the other teenagers are excited to get to know Saffie. When they examine the dragonfly girl painting, they are disturbed to find that Georgina Whyte's ashes are mixed in with the paint. Milly's mental health is getting worse, and she is upset to find Jake's cornflowers have nearly died. A curious Saffie, wondering about her powers, tries to revive them – only to pass out.

Tai's life is ebbing, and he asks to be taken out to his beloved great oak to die. His mother, the Professor, and the others all follow him, and Tai manages to give the tree one last hug, joined by Calista, Jake, and the other Ingenious children, encircling its wide trunk. Tai collapses.

To their amazement, Fitzsimmons has escaped from his prison cell, and runs outside to grab Tai. He uses the oak's dark energy to try to revive the boy. A battle of minds ensues, as Fitzsimmons blindly draws people, animals, and insects into him to use up their dark energy, while the teenagers desperately try to hold them back. One of the ninja agents is killed in the process. At last, Fitzsimmons passes out.

Struggling to understand what had just happened, they realise that Fitzsimmons was trying to save Tai, though he didn't care who he killed in the process. The teenagers are now understanding how they are able to manipulate dark energy, and what they can do with it. Dr Vassiliev calls to tell the Professor that he has at last completed the cure to save the children – a ray of hope. Tai is put into a medically-induced coma.

That night, as Saffie Morales sleeps, she connects with a young girl, who shouts at her to get out of her head. Mei Hui also has a dream about the dragonfly girl painting: she sees the beautiful girl in the picture come to life and breathe her name.

DRAMATIS PERSONAE

Abdul Hassan – a disgusting old man catfishing as a handsome teenager called Nadir. He starts an online romance with unsuspecting 15-year-old Shamira Mahmoud.

Acuzio – Professor Wolff's male guide dog, a husky.

Agnes Whyte – mother to Georgina Whyte, love interest of young Jeremy Fitzsimmons 3rd.

Alia Pujari – 16-year-old love interest to Inder Chauhan. She goes to ballet school, and is passionate about dance. She comes from a privileged family.

Alma Morales – mother of Saffron Morales. Married to Ignacio. The couple set up an animal shelter by the Rio Branco river, in the Amazon jungle, and live there with their daughter.

Anand Amir – works at i-Nation Bionics as head development engineer.

Anne Fitzsimmons – mother to Jeremy Fitzsimmons 3rd. Married to Maxwell (Max) Fitzsimmons.

Azarin Pujari – mother of Alia, Inder's love interest.

Benjamin Jenkins – father of the seventh Ingenious child, Jemima Jenkins. He is a consultant actuary, but due to worldwide insured losses, he decides to take a year off work.

Brian Bythaway – father of Melody (Milly) Bythaway (third Project Ingenious child). His wife, Savannah Bythaway, died of cancer when Milly was nine years old.

Calista Matheson – a natural genius, who learnt computer sciences from Jake Winters within a matter of months, and surpassed even his skills. Now 19 years old, Calista and Jake are married, and have a baby daughter, Evie.

Chauffeur – Professor Wolff's chauffeur. He is deaf and mute, and communicates with the Professor through tactile sign language.

Chhaya Chauhan – mother of Inder, third Ingenious child.

Chiara Wolff – Professor Wolff's wife who died together with their son, Christian, when their house went on fire sometime after Project Ingenious ended.

Chloé Jenkins – mother of seventh Ingenious child, Jemima Jenkins.

Christian Wolff – Professor Wolff's son. He died at 12 years old, together with his mother, Chiara, when their house went on fire sometime after Project Ingenious ended.

Chu (Dr) – the psychiatrist helping Ilse Schäfer to get over the brutal murder of her parents.

Cyrena Fitzsimmons (19th century) – wife of Jeremy Fitzsimmons 1st. Her family are landed gentry, but she is disowned by her parents for marrying a lowly farmer.

D1 and D2 – agents working for Professor Wolff. D agents are intelligence operatives, in comparison to the V agents, who work in the field.

Dog – Tai's adopted female Doberman, a stray. When her puppies died, Dog fostered kittens: Olly, Pasha, Max, Treacle, Missy Mop.

David O'Connor – chief of the security detail in charge of protecting the Russian doctor called in to complete the cure to save the Ingenious children. However, after a situation with Mei Hui, an intense dislike for the children began to fester within O'Connor.

Edward Masterson (Sir) (19th century) – married to Molly Masterson (Lady). The couple had their portrait painted by the renowned but mysterious artist, F. Jaffrey.

Eligio – an Amazonian curandero, a tribal healer, skilled in the knowledge of natural medicines from the jungle.

Evie Winters (Eve) – baby daughter of Calista and Jake Winters.

F. Jaffrey – the pseudonym under which Jeremy Fitzsimmons 1st painted. His real identity has never been revealed to the general public.

Fargo, Dan (Dr) – son of eminent scientist Professor James Fargo, known for his work on gene therapies. Called in by Professor Wolff to complete Dr Kendra's cure for Alzheimer's. He is also consulted for general medical matters.

Fidelia Fitzsimmons (19th century) – daughter of Cyrena and Jeremy Fitzsimmons 1st. She is a twin with her brother, William.

Gaia Kendra – Greek wife of Dr Kendra. Changed name to Adrienn Laszlo after escaping from Project Ingenious.

Georgina Whyte (Georgie) – love interest of Jeremy Fitzsimmons 3rd, and the subject of the dragonfly girl painting, which is discovered to have her ashes mixed in with the paint.

Gerard (Gerry) – part of the special ops division, enlisted by Rory Sanderson, the Prime Minister's head of security. They accompany Calista, Jake, and Jemima Jenkins on their mission to the Amazon jungle.

Ha-Ru Kim – world famous Korean classical pianist, admired by Tai Jones, who is learning to play piano.

Ignacio Morales – father of Saffron Morales. Married to Alma. The couple set up an animal shelter by the Rio Branco river, in the Amazon jungle, and live there with their daughter.

Ilse Schäfer – Saffie Morales has inadvertently been connecting with this young German girl, whose parents have been brutally murdered. Ilse begins displaying unusual mind abilities.

Inder Chauhan – third Ingenious child (Zeta). Indian. Lives in New Delhi slums with his parents, and is known by the other slum children as The Storyteller. Inder reads and memorises the newspaper, Times of India, every day. He is slowly discovering his powers, one of which he thinks is the ability to foretell the future.

Isaiah Fitzsimmons – grandfather to Jeremy Fitzsimmons 3rd.

Jake Winters – a computer whizz, and boyfriend to Calista Matheson. His older sister, Kara, participated in Project Ingenious, but Jake has since discovered that she died during the project and was buried in a field of cornflowers. Jake is now 20 years old.

James Gillespie – ITV's top investigative journalist. He airs a programme in which he interviews a nurse claiming to have worked on Project Ingenious, a secret government project.

Jasmine – super-computer built by Calista Matheson.

Jemima Jenkins – seventh and last Project Ingenious child (Omega). English. Now 16 years old. She is a mathematics genius, and soon discovers a most unusual ability, to do with discerning the remaining seconds of a person's life.

Jeremy Fitzsimmons 1st (19th century) – the first in the Fitzsimmons family line to display unique mind abilities. He came from a poor, farming background, and married his childhood sweetheart, Cyrena. He became a famed but mysterious artist who painted under a pseudonym, F. Jaffrey.

Jeremy Fitzsimmons 3rd (21st century) – descendent of Jeremy Fitzsimmons 1st.

Karl König – first Project Ingenious child (Alpha). German. Died when he was 17 years old.

Kendra, Axel (Xeli) (Dr) – renowned scientist known for his work on mapping the human genome and identifying the genius genes. Partnered Professor Wolff within Project Ingenious. Married to Gaia Kendra. After escaping from Project Ingenious, they changed their names to Dr Laszlo and Mrs Adrienn Laszlo.

Lijun Song – governmental official in China sent to inform Mei Hui about a new road being built. He then becomes love-interest for Yin, the woman looking after Mei Hui's children.

Lyubova (Lyu-Lyu) – Dr Vassiliev's beloved Siberian molly cat. She and Dr Vassiliev have an enduring love for each other, and are near-inseparable.

Mahit Pujari – father to Alia, love interest to Inder.

Maxwell Fitzsimmons (Max) – father to Jeremy Fitzsimmons 3rd. Married to Anne Fitzsimmons.

Mei Hui Li – sixth Project Ingenious child (Sigma). Chinese. Now 17 years old. Has the ability to read hearts – how good or bad, false or genuine, a person is.

Milly Bythaway (Melody) – third Project Ingenious child (Delta). English. Now 18 years old. She has a photographic memory, is able to remember everything she reads, and can learn new languages easily. Her special power is that she can implant images into people's minds. Milly's mother died when she was nine, but managed to knit her a beanie hat before she passed, though the hat was lost forever when Milly's escape pod crashed deep in the waters of the North Atlantic Ocean.

Molly Masterson (Lady) (19th century) – married to Edward Masterson (Sir). The couple had their portrait painted by the renowned but mysterious artist, F. Jaffrey.

Peter Davids (Dr) – cancer expert consulted when Oxford University students contracted deadly virus.

Parry-Johansson (Ms) – tour guide and art advisor, specialising in painter F. Jaffrey's work.

Prime Minister (PM) – referred to by Calista as Boz, or Bozza.

Ria – six-year-old girl who lives in the same slum as Inder. She loves wearing dresses.

Robert Chambers – work colleague of Georgina Whyte.

Rory Sanderson – the Prime Minister's head of security. He is Scottish, married, and has a three-year-old son. Sceptical about the Ingenious teenagers, until an encounter with Jemima Jenkins.

Saanvi – the Pujari family's housemaid.

Sabu – the last remaining black jaguar cub. His parents died of a strange disease, which he too has contracted.

Saffron Morales (Saffie) – second Project Ingenious child (Beta). Brazilian. Now 18 years old. Has the ability to absorb the abstract feelings and emotions of other Ingenious children, even at great distance. Also has a special way with animals. The isolados tribesmen call her daughter of Mother Earth.

Savannah Bythaway – mother of third Ingenious child, Milly Bythaway. She died of cancer when Milly was nine, after knitting Milly a precious beanie hat. Milly constantly hears her mother's voice in her head, until Milly is given the cure.

Shamira Mahmoud – a 15-year-old girl who develops an online romance with Nadir, whom she believes to be an 18-year-old boy. She promises to travel to Rochdale to be with him.

Susan Wilkinson – wife of Tom Wilkinson, foster carers of Ilse Schäfer.

Tai Jones – fifth Project Ingenious child (Theta). Jamaican. Now 17 years old. He is a simple boy, but has the ability to see people's thoughts and feelings as colourful auras. Also has an unusual connection with animals. After discovering his mother in hospital in a coma, and willing for her to live, he inadvertently misused his powers to revive her, making himself old and close to death in the process.

Tahir Ekren – innocent eight-year-old son of online grooming gang leader, Yazan Ekren.

Tom Whyte – father to Georgina Whyte, love interest of Jeremy Fitzsimmons 3rd.

Tom Wilkinson – husband of Susan Wilkinson, foster carers of Ilse Schäfer.

Tyaishia Jones – Jamaican mother of Tai Jones (fifth Project Ingenious child).

V1 – male middle-aged agent working for Professor Wolff. V agents work in the field, are skilled in the ways of ninjutsu, and often referred to as ninjas. V1 was killed on the same day that agent V3 was attacked.

V2 – young male agent, believed to be in his thirties.

V3 – female older agent. V3 was attacked by thugs in an alleyway, and has since been in a coma. Milly feels responsible for her injuries, because she planted the spy camera that was discovered by the assassin Penny Thompson, which consequently led to the agents being drawn into the trap.

Vassiliev, Vadim (Dr) – stern cat-loving Russian scientist, brought in by Dr Fargo to work on and complete Karl König's cure.

Vijay Chauhan – father of Inder, third Ingenious child. He is a cobbler.

Viola – grandmother to Georgina Whyte.

William Fitzsimmons (19th century) – son of Cyrena and Jeremy Fitzsimmons 1st. He is a twin with his sister, Fidelia.

Wolff, Harald (Harry) (Professor) – genetic scientist who led Project Ingenious together with Dr Axel Kendra. After escaping from Project Ingenious, he changed his name to Johan Hindemith. He became blind sometime afterward.

Yazan Ekren – father to eight-year-old Tahir. Ekren is head of the UK-wide online grooming ring, which includes Abdul Hassan who catfished Shamira Mahmoud.

Yin – lonely widow from Mei Hui's village who was enlisted to look after Mei Hui's children before Mei Hui left China for London.

CONTENTS

'The heaven, even the heavens, are the LORD'S,

but the earth hath he given to the children of men.'

Psalm 115:16

King James Version

PROLOGUE

18 months earlier.

The young girl sat swamped in a large brown leather armchair – her expression the epitome of misery.

Opposite her was a middle-aged woman, the psychiatrist, sitting on the other side of a coffee table – a box of tissues waiting between them with a torn gash at the top, like an open wound, primed with a bulge of white. Brown eyes studied her patient, a smudge of pity in their glaze.

There was little evidence that the girl, Ilse Schäfer, had once been a happy and exuberant child. Her laughter, infectious – finding fun and excitement in almost everything: the dance of refracted rainbows from the glass prism in her bedroom window, the glossy brown of conkers collected excitedly from the park, colouring-in pictures with pretty pastels, and the joy of making her rather serious parents laugh so hard from her playful antics that their bellies ached.

But now, three weeks after her 10th birthday, the slight, brown-haired girl sat before the psychiatrist, tapping a nervous foot against the floor in a steady beat, eyes fixed on the mottled sea-foam carpet patterns. A shadow of her former self. A smile hadn't lit up her wan face for some time, her dim eyes were soulless, and when she spoke, quivering words slipped out from pursed lips as barely heard whispers. Ever since that day. When the intruder came. And her mother – panicked, fearful, gasping for breath – had thrust Ilse into the dusty wardrobe just minutes before that terrifying woman broke through the locked door and grabbed her...

Those images were seared into the girl's mind as she watched through the crack of the wardrobe door, eyes round with terror.

The glint of a knife.

Purposeful strides.

The rank smell of sweat.

Sprays of red against white.

Gurgles bubbling up in her mother's throat.

Memories that engulfed young Ilse, every minute of every day.

The ghosts of those memories floated in the air around her now, as the psychiatrist gently asked her how her day had been. But Ilse never answered that question. Never answered the other one either: can you tell me what happened that day?

Instead, the girl sat quietly in the spartan office, scratching an itch on the back of her hand, and then clamping fingers between her legs. Avoiding Dr Chu's pitying smile. The dead space of silence hung between them for what seemed like an eternity. Until Ilse at last broke it. 'I... I feel like someone's in my head,' she said, her voice small and uncertain.

Dr Chu sat up, surprised at her unelicited words. 'How do you mean?'

'I hear voices.'

'And... how long have you been experiencing this?'

Ilse shrugged slim shoulders. 'Dunno. Maybe... months, years.'

Chu frowned, puzzled. 'Years? That's a long time.'

Ilse's sneakered feet stilled as she thought about it, then resumed tapping. 'I remember now. The first time I heard it was on 22nd April. Two years ago. I was in bed, reading.'

'My, you've got a good memory!'

'She always said that too...' started Ilse. 'Mama...' She trailed off, lowering her head.

'And how do they make you feel, these voices?'

Ilse shrugged again. 'Not sure. At first, I just listened. They were like... like someone thinking out loud. But then they got louder and louder. So loud, I couldn't sleep.'

'So it's mostly at night?'

'Mostly. But sometimes I hear them in the daytime too.'

Chu scribbled notes on her tablet.

Ilse dared to look briefly at the shine of the screen nestled on the psychiatrist's lap. It whispered to her, of secrets – so many secrets belonging to others, belonging to her.

Still writing, Chu asked, 'And what are these voices saying?'

'Like I said, they're like… thoughts, of everyday things.' She paused before adding, her voice lowering to a rumble, 'I don't like it.'

'It must be very frightening.'

The girl nodded only lightly, as if she didn't care. But she did. 'There were so many voices. Confusing me. I kept telling her–'

'So it's a "she"?'

'Well, one of them is a girl, a teenager. I kept telling her to get out of my head,' Ilse whispered. The word 'telling' was an understatement. She had shouted it. Screamed it. Begged. 'The last time I told her: "I want you to leave me alone! Get out of my head!"'

'When was that?'

'Two weeks ago.'

Chu waited. '…And?'

'But I still hear her.'

Silence, save for squeaky scribbling.

Ilse whimpered, 'A-am I going mad?' She glared at her pale hands wedged between denim. Pursed lips quivering.

Chu put her pencil down, and looked at the girl squarely. 'Ilse, you are not going mad. You… you've been through a *terrible* ordeal that happened only weeks ago. And it's going to take some time to recover. But I'm here to help you, and I'll do everything I can to support you. Do you understand?'

Ilse looked up momentarily and nodded, before her eyes drifted down again.

'I'm concerned about these voices though,' said Chu. 'They've been going on for quite a while. Ilse, I'm going to ask you to be really, really brave, okay? Next time you hear the voices, I want you to talk back. I know you can do it. I want you to talk to the voices and ask them what they want with you. Do you… do you think you can do that?'

Ilse stopped. Her gut instinct, a knee-jerk reaction, was to say no. No, she didn't like it. But eventually, reluctantly, she gave in. 'O-okay.' Silence again. Until Ilse said, 'But… one of them has gone completely quiet. My brother's voice.'

Chu frowned and looked down at her notes. 'I'm sorry, I didn't know you had a brother. I thought you were an only child.'

'No. Well, yes. My parents had a baby a long time ago, before they had me. But they didn't want him. Never talked about him. Ever.'

'So you hear his voice too?'

'I used to, until just after my parents were... k-killed.' Ilse gulped, it was the first time she had said the 'k' word out loud, and it stabbed her like a dagger. She grappled to overcome the wave of emotions, eventually saying, 'I-I think he's dead too, my brother... If he is, I'm glad!'

Chu stared at her. 'Glad?'

'Yes. His name was Karl. Karl König. And I *really, really* hate him!!'

Taken aback by the outburst, the doctor said, '"Hate" is a very strong emotion, Ilse–'

'No, it's not strong enough. I can't stand him! I wanted him dead!!'

Dr Chu stiffened, alarmed.

'He was messed up. Really messed up. So, in my head, I told him to... to... to kill himself!!'

'Ilse!' gasped Chu. 'Why would you want that? Why do you hate him so much?'

At last Ilse looked up at the psychiatrist. Fire in her grey eyes. 'Because he murdered my parents!'

Chu blinked, taken aback. 'I'm sorry, I was told it was a woman who killed them. She got away. The police haven't been able to find her.'

Ilse shook her head. 'My brother gave that woman the order.'

Chu sat back, flummoxed. 'A-are you sure? Our minds can sometimes make us think strange things. It can make us think things that aren't really–'

'I'm sure!!'

'I know you *believe* what you're saying but–'

'I'm not making it up! Karl killed my parents because they didn't want him. And then...' Ilse tensed, '...when he found out about me, that he had a sister, he sent someone to kill me too.'

Chu no longer knew what to think. It sounded too incredible. She took a deep breath. 'I'm sorry, Ilse. I'm sure you can understand that all of this... it's very unusual. And even if it were true, I can't figure out how you would know. Of course, after the death of your parents, you're bound to feel... confused... vulnerable.'

'V-vulnable? What's that?' she asked innocently, perplexed.

'Vulnerable means… to feel nervous or worried that you might be hurt too. Either physically, or emotionally.'

'I'm not worried,' stated Ilse plainly. 'I'm not worried about someone trying to kill me.'

'No? Why not?' asked Chu, intrigued.

'Because…' she thought for a moment. 'Because I have another father. And… and he won't let anything bad happen to me.'

Chu stared at her for several minutes, then picked up her pencil and wrote on the tablet: 'Imaginary other father', 'Death', 'Paracosm?' She circled the last word purposefully. Paracosm was the unusual phenomenon where a lonely, traumatised child retreated into a fantasy world – though it was usually a happy one. Ilse's paracosm, however, was disturbing, menacing. The doctor was worried, very worried. But she looked up at Ilse and masked it with a kind smile. 'Well! That's a lot to take in.'

'I know you don't believe me,' Ilse murmured. 'But… when they come, when they try to kill me, you'll believe me then!' She laced her fingers together, pressing them firmly between her legs, as she said quietly to the carpet, 'And they *are* coming.'

PART 1

'On that day, the LORD will whistle for the flies
from the remotest streams of Egypt
and for the bees that are in the land of Assyria.'

Isaiah 7:18
Common English Bible

1   STINKING LONDON

Present day.

The breakfast TV programme droned on in the background.

'...who would've thought that a country without flies would be so awful?' grimaced the middle-aged presenter to his partner, who sat next to him on the couch. 'As you know, dogs and their walkers going around parks, fields, and forests, were discovering alarming numbers of macabre animal and bird carcasses scattered everywhere. They also had to wade through piles and piles of leaves, vegetation, and wood – all taking much longer than usual to decay without the catalyst of flies to aid decomposition. Certain plant species have also been dwindling, as they can't be pollinated without flies. And the numbers of birds, lizards, and frogs are reaching dangerously low levels because flies are their main food source.'

'That's right,' said the pretty co-presenter, Peta, tucking a strand of black hair behind an ear. 'Since the sudden and unexpected fly depopulation 18 months ago, the gap in the ecosystem has been drastic. No wonder we've been dubbed "Stinking London"!' Frowning, she turned to her companion. 'Clive, could this be the beginning of the end? Is there any hope for us?'

Clive, with his greying hair and perfect teeth, said, 'It's still too early to say, Peta. But we're trying everything possible to replenish the gap, to stop an ecological cascade effect, which could be quite disastrous...' He turned smoothly toward the camera. 'Since the flies' sudden disappearance, scientists and farmers have been working round the clock to breed more flies. Yes, you heard right, Peta. They're breeding flies on their farms, and using food waste banks to feed them. Now, neighbouring countries have had to come to our aid by providing fly pupae in the billions. And did you know, there were about 7,000 different fly species in the UK alone, such as the common house fly, the bluebottle, the cluster fly, and the horse fly, to name just a few. So again, we've had to import the different species as well. There's been some trial and error trying to find the optimal temperature for each species, and getting the pupated flies to breed for example. In fact, one farmer resorted to playing rousing music to encourage the flies to mate! But once those hurdles were overcome, in just a matter of weeks, the larvae were able to grow about one million percent of their weight.'

Peta gasped. 'That's crazy, Clive! One million percent? And good to know that music was so instrumental in the mating process, pardon the pun!'

Clive groaned, smiling. 'I'm not pardoning that at all! But yes, that must've been very rousing music! So now that the fly population in the UK is getting back on track, we're hoping that our ecosystem will gradually return to the way it was. Which will be a great relief! No more piles of animal carcasses taking ages to decompose. And another benefit is that flies eat absolutely any kind of waste – like coffee grinds, decaying fruit, vegetables, plants. In fact, farmers believe that, once we return to normality, breeding flies for their larvae, which is about 40% protein and 40% fat – effectively turning mountains of rotten food into useable nutrients – will be a revolutionary way of providing a sustainable food source for pets, poultry, fish, and birds. They even believe that, one day, insects and their grubs might serve as food for humans.'

'Yum! Grub stir-fry,' grimaced Peta. 'I can't wait!'

'You might be pleasantly surprised. I'm told the freeze-dried grubs have a mildly nutty, slightly oily flavour.'

'Interesting. Actually, there're lots of countries, aren't there, where people eat insects as part of their everyday diet,' added Peta. 'Come to think of it, didn't John the Baptist in the Bible eat locusts?'

'I think he did!' said Clive. 'On a serious note, do we know what happened to wipe out the flies in the first place?'

Peta turned to the camera. 'Not really. We only know of the strange phenomenon of a mysterious "fly tornado" at a location somewhere in West London. You've probably seen on the internet several shaky videos taken by passers-by on their mobile phones. The flies appeared to have been pulled into a freak twister. But we still don't know what might have caused it, or where all those dead flies are. Drones have hovered over the general area of the twister, private land in London, but there's just a small lake, and several trees – nothing untoward, except for the burnt remains of one particular tree. So it's been theorised that a lightning strike decimated both the tree and tornado of flies. Though of course that doesn't explain the country-wide depopulation.' She shrugged. 'To be honest, it's still a complete mystery.'

'Hmmm... But the question is: could it happen again?'

Peta shook her head. 'The experts don't think so, no. There have been no known recordings of such an event happening before – so the likelihood is that it's a one-off.'

'That's good to know. Very good to know,' said Clive.

Brian walked into his daughter's open-doored bedroom, where she was sitting on her bed with a book – glancing infrequently at the presenters on the wall-hung TV screen. At the side was a large, packed suitcase, and boxes brimming with books. He grabbed the remote and muted the volume. Turning to his daughter, he asked, 'You okay, Midge?'

Milly snapped her book closed and sat back in her bed, bored. She huffed. 'I'm okay. But... I've been isolating for ages! I want to get out. Do things!'

Brian perched on the edge of the bed. 'And you will. When we move. As you know, this is the very last round of your treatments. And Dr Vassiliev just told me that after they've monitored you for another couple of days, you'll be free to go out and do what you want.' He hesitated. 'Within reason of course.'

'Th-that's great!' said Milly, hardly believing it.

Brian looked her over, noticing the hint of pink on her cheeks, the brightness in her eyes. Slightly plumper too, she was no longer the waif she'd been 18 months ago. 'You're looking much better! How do you feel?'

Milly beamed. 'Like a new person. In fact, even better than before! I've learnt five more languages, taken some online courses, and so far so good. My memory's holding up really well. I can remember almost everything!

Even what we ate for breakfast, lunch, and dinner every day for the past year. Including all the times you burnt the toast… 36, to be precise!'

Brian's smile turned into a frown. 'They weren't burnt! Just well done. Anyway, I thought you liked crispy toast?'

'I do, Dad. But not charcoal…'

Brian grinned. 'Well, the main thing is that Dr Vassiliev's cure worked!' he said, triumphant. He took her hand and kissed it. 'It worked!!'

Just then, a fully-grown cat, Missy Mop, her fur darkened to a deeper ginger, jumped up onto Milly's bed, followed by her striped brother, Treacle. Milly swept Treacle into her arms and hugged him, breathing into his fur, 'Baby!' She kissed the top of his head profusely. After the scare of Treacle going missing during Fitzsimmons' moments of madness at Avernus, they eventually found the cat trapped underneath some furniture, behind a box, much to everyone's relief. Treacle started squirming in Milly's arms – and so she let him jump down just as she sneezed from the fur. Meanwhile, Missy Mop was batting playfully at the remote control, and accidentally unmuted the volume.

The presenter couple had been replaced by a single newsreader, who was saying, '…documented information about the mysterious scientific project, code-named Project Ingenious.'

Brian and Milly glanced at each other with surprise before turning to the screen.

'A nurse who claimed to be working on the top-secret project where children were genetically engineered for super-intelligence, has now come forward, and has agreed to be interviewed by James Gillespie, ITV's top investigative journalist. The interview, as well as his findings, will be outlined in a special "Gillespie Files" documentary to be aired next Tuesday at 3.30 pm. Gillespie will investigate the experimental science, the rather dubious methods involved, as well as the high loss of life, all as claimed by the nurse. So, be sure to tune into the exposé of the secret government experiments. Now, on to local news near you…'

Milly pressed the 'off' button on the remote, and the TV went blank. Brian looked worriedly from the screen to his daughter. 'Oh dear,' he said. 'This is really, really bad.'

Tai Jones was lying on his back, in a daze, blinking up at the ceiling. Floating. Moving shadows cast across his form. The water around him seemed to melt right through him, so that he was all at once embryonic in a vast pool of amniotic fluid. Soft waves slapped against his ears, merging with muffled echoes, his own sibilant breaths, and the loud thud of his heart.

'Tai!' shouted his mother. She was sitting up on one of the loungers at the side of the pool.

He blinked, once, twice. Then stared again at the glimmering shoals of koi fish that were swooping and diving and nibbling all around in the lake above him, on the other side of the transparent ceiling.

Tyaishia had been reading under her breath from the large Bible on her lap – but she stopped to check her watch and look at her son again. He'd been floating in the same spot in the middle of the swimming pool for quite some time. Just staring up. 'Tai!!' she yelled even louder. 'Yuh ain't moved an inch fer ages! Yuh okay?!'

He sighed and glanced at her. Not really, he thought. But he shouted back at her, 'I'm good!'

'If yer ain't gonna swim then–'

'I'm coming out!' he told her, groaning. Since his recovery began 15 months ago, his mother had treated him like a baby. But he got it. He had died, twice. And for several nerve-wracking weeks, it was touch-and-go – until he at last came around, and slowly recovered to full health. Tyaishia had been jumpy and over-protective ever since.

Tai climbed the pool ladder, walked to the lounger next to hers, and sat down. She immediately jumped up and smothered him with a large towel. 'What's got into yuh?' asked Tyaishia, noticing the troubled look on his face.

Tai's eyes couldn't help magnetising back to the koi. He sighed again. 'I told you, Ma. It's the fish. They ain't following me around no more...'

'Tai,' she said, giving him that look, as she sat back down. 'Yuh alive!' she breathed, her Jamaican accent softening. 'Mi watch yuh slowly turn from an old man to yuh normal self. Took months an' months. But seein' you get betta… it… it like watchin' a miracle! Right before mi eyes.' She looked over her son with pride. His skin was no longer wrinkled and dotted with liver-spots – but just as fresh and smooth as any 16-year-old. His back too had straightened, and his eyes shone bright. Even his hair had darkened to its natural black, neatly cut now with faded sides and an angular top. 'Yuh alive…' she repeated, tears welling.

Tai melted, and knew by now to change the subject whenever his mother got emotional, which was often. 'What you been reading today, Ma?' he asked, nodding toward the Bible at her side.

She turned and fingered the pages. 'Beautiful things…' she said wistfully. 'There suh much wisdom inna dem yah pages, though I don't understand it all… I just know God's trying to tell us something. Something really important. But I ain't figured out what it is… I been reading to the others too, reading t'all o' them. Especially Milly… she really listen when I read t'her.' Tyaishia suddenly remembered something and checked her watch again. 'Oh! It time now, Tai. Wi haffi guh.'

Tai nodded and stood, pulling the towel around him. He looked up at the fish in the ceiling for the very last time, before he and his mother walked out of the room.

•••————————————————————•••

Miles away, in a remote building in the middle of nowhere, just outside London, Jeremy Fitzsimmons sat at a wide table made of brushed steel. He had been there for almost two years, but he seemed to have aged a lifetime. His head had been shaved so that there was just an umber shadow of hair, though his beard was still long and streaked with grey, covering most of his lumpy, misshapen face. Tired, glazed eyes glinted dully in the light. His every movement – even when he blinked – was slow and deliberate, as if he were barely conscious. As if he hardly knew who he was, where he was. Not even acknowledging the figures that came now and then, gliding around him, wraith-like, bringing him food and feeding him, changing his clothes, washing him, putting him to bed. Injecting him. He was unable to resist.

Mesmerised, he stared at the projected pictures scattered over the surface of the table. Fast-moving images, colours, musicians, and twirling, leaping figures. He watched in a haze, taking everything in, yet hardly understanding what to make of it all.

Behind him was a bed. And in the corner, a shower cubicle, and a toilet. No other furniture in the room. No personal effects. Just four steel walls, two mesh-covered air vents, and a bolted door.

Fitzsimmons swayed to the rhythm of the music that was wafting through the air, as he gazed at the images of ballet dancers twirling, gliding, leaping. Entranced.

It was surreal. A psychopathic murderer, drugged to his eyeballs. Watching Swan Lake.

2   CHATROOM

Three months earlier. 15-year-old Shamira Mahmoud sat expectantly on the bed, in the shadowy dark of her room – secretively huddling the iPad on her lap. Its glow bathed her face in milky white, lighting up the thrill of anticipation.

The browser was in incognito mode so that her internet history, search records, and cookies remained private and untraceable.

At last, there was an airy pinging sound, and words appeared onscreen in a white speech bubble against a flowery-pink background. 'Hey, beautiful. You ok?' It was Nadir.

Shamira's lips broadened into a grin that spread across a square face. Her eyes lingered on the word 'beautiful' and then on his profile picture. It was a small image that couldn't be enlarged, but it was clear the teenage boy was handsome, with heavy eyebrows and broody features that hinted of inner angst. The slight curve of his smile did nothing to lighten his intense expression.

The girl's fingers flew across the keyboard. 'I'm good. You?'

'Bad,' typed Nadir straight away.

'Hard day?'

'Just had news that my cousin's dying of Covid...'

'Oh no!!! I'm so sorry!' Shamira typed back.

'We were really close. Used to play football together when we were kids. I'm gutted!!!'

'I'm really sorry! I wish...' She wanted to say that she wished she could hug him, make him feel better, kiss away his pain. But that was haram, forbidden. Their faith was strict. She deleted the last word, and typed instead: 'I feel so sad for you. And for your cousin. Really sad.'

There was no reply.

A picture suddenly popped up onscreen. The tired face of a young man in a hospital bed, his eyes wet domes of misery. 'They told us his oxygen levels are really low. They don't think he'll make it past the weekend… We can't even go see him,' wrote Nadir. 'I can't stop crying. I've been crying all day.'

Shamira melted, imagining Nadir on his bed, face down, weeping inconsolably into his pillow. 'I'm crying too,' she replied. 'I feel so sad for you. For your cousin.'

In time, he wrote, 'Thanks.'

'For what?'

'For understanding. For letting me pour it all out. I feel like I can tell you anything.'

A pause.

'I really care about you, Shamira.'

The words glowed between them, mesmeric.

'I wish you were here,' he wrote. 'With me.'

Shamira's chest burst with emotion. She had known for a while now that she was falling for Nadir. Felt an instant connection with him, as soon as they friended each other on Facebook and he'd reached out on Messenger. He'd told her that she had beautiful eyes. And she'd laughed, and said that his profile picture wasn't bad-looking either. They hit it off immediately. And ever since, she rushed home from school every day to 'chat' with him. She daren't believe that someone like him could fall for someone like her. But just maybe…

Shamira typed back, trembling, 'I wish I could be with you too.' Then she watched as he replied. Stared at each letter as they appeared onscreen – slow, deliberate, words:

'I think I'm falling for you,' he wrote.

Her mind exploded into a thousand fizzing pieces. Heart thudding. Pulse racing. How was it possible that she was so upset for Nadir's dying cousin, yet buzzing with excitement, and desperately in love. All at the same time. Quivering hands covered her mouth. His gentle confession was everything she had hoped for and dreamed of for weeks.

She stared at those words for so long that she lost track of time.

'Shamira?' typed Nadir. 'Are you there?'

She got a hold of herself, and quickly wrote back, 'Yes. Sorry. I'm here. And…' She gasped as she typed, dizzy-headed. 'I'm falling for you too.'

Shamira stared earnestly at the glass screen. She ached for him, with every fibre of her being.

But he was five whole hours away, by train. She had already Googled his location in the north of England. Yet there was an invisible thread, a line, between them – stronger than anything. Pulling her inexorably to him. She felt the tug of it now.

Nadir continued typing. 'I wish I could hold you… Touch you…'

Shamira felt like she would burst with longing for him. Suddenly she wrote in a frenzy, 'I'm going to come to you, Nadir. I'm going to come to Rochdale, so we can be together!'

He did not answer.

She typed, 'I can come next weekend.'

At last he wrote, 'That would be amazing! But are you sure?'

'Yes!'

'What about your parents?'

'They won't have to know. I could say I'm going on a school trip. I could even do a fake school letter, to stop them asking questions.'

There was a pause, until he typed, 'Shamira.' Another pause. 'I've been meaning to tell you… I think about you all the time. I feel weak at the knees when we chat. And now I know you're coming here, I want to jump up and down, and shout with joy! Do you promise? Promise you'll come?'

She laughed out loud, delirious with happiness. Laughed at the thought of him jumping and shouting, imagining him punching the air – but she suddenly remembered herself, quietened, and listened for any sounds from the corridor. Her parents were in their bedroom, and had expressly forbidden her to communicate with anyone online. Not even with her friends. Especially not boys. Shamira listened hard, but thankfully there was only silence. She sighed with relief. 'Yes, I promise,' she typed, heart racing.

'I can't wait to see you,' he replied.

Shamira suddenly thought of something. 'We can put our cameras on. Do a video chat.'

'My phone camera's broken, remember?'

She slumped back in her bed. 'Oh yeah, I forgot.'

'I can't afford to fix it at the moment. It's harder to find work up here, outside of school hours. It's a miracle I have this second-hand mobile – a cast-off from my ammuh. But I wish I could see you, and your beautiful eyes.'

'I can put *my* camera on if you want. But...' She suddenly felt nervous. 'I'm not really beautiful, like you keep saying.'

'You are!' he declared. 'I know from talking to you that you're a beautiful, kind person. Anyway, looks don't matter to me. *You* matter to me.'

Shamira glanced across the room, catching her reflection in the wall mirror. The shadowy image of a chubby 15-year-old with braces and dark circles under her eyes, grinned back at her. She frantically finger-combed her hair into place, tucking frizzy curls behind her ears. She knew she wasn't exactly pretty – but his love for her made her feel beautiful. Made her feel like Miss World. She took a deep breath, balanced the iPad on her bed against the duvet, and, with trepidation, turned on her camera. 'Hi!' she whispered, waving nervously.

He typed, 'Shamira, you're just like I imagined. You're gorgeous!!'

She smiled, eyes bobbing skittishly from his speech bubble to the image of herself tucked in the top-right corner of the screen. 'If you say so! I'm sorry, I have to whisper because my parents are sleeping.'

'I get it,' he wrote. 'But, I can't stop staring at you. And... you have a beautiful body.'

Shamira looked down, feeling suddenly self-conscious. She fingered the top button of her pyjama shirt nervously. 'Can you... can you send some photos of you?'

'Yeah, of course.' A few seconds later, some pictures appeared. 'I took these before my camera broke, about five months ago. Just after I turned 18.'

Shamira went quiet as she flicked through several grainy images. He was every bit as handsome as his tiny profile picture suggested. A man-boy, with a wide forehead, intense deep-set eyes, a hint of a grin above a delicate jawline – and glossy-black hair. 'Wow,' she smiled. 'You're cute!'

'LOL!!' he typed. 'If you say so!' Nadir sent an embarrassed monkey emoji. After several seconds he wrote, 'Oh no, ammuh's calling me. I have to go, my sweet. We'll speak again tomorrow about you coming. I'll be thinking about you, every second, every minute, every hour.'

Shamira's heart burst. 'Goodnight, Nadir,' she said, and sent a string of pink heart emojis.

And then he was gone.

With shaky hands, she ended the chat, but went straight back to look at the photos he'd sent. He was everything she ever wanted in a boyfriend. And he was hers. All hers. She lay back in her bed – hugging the tablet to her chest, as if she were hugging him. She stared again at the image of him, and then, ever so gently, kissed it. The glass was warm, like she imagined his lips would be.

Smooth, and warm, and solid.

Abdul Hassan was fat, and wrinkly, and haggard.

He yawned as he glared at the screen and logged out of the chatroom. He leant to one side and farted. The whiff was noxious. He shouldn't have eaten that street food, he realised. And he made a mental note to never go back to that disgusting old cripple and his decrepit food cart at the end of the Riverside market. Yet still, the man's home-made kibbeh were delicious – stuffed with lamb, and seasoned with red Halaby pepper that gave the meat that characteristic smoky heat. Well, maybe he could give it just one last visit...

Hassan logged into the next chatroom, and sat back in his chair while he waited to be let in, smiling quietly to himself – smug with his natural flirting ability. Playing with emotions. Capturing hearts. He snorted as he thought about how the girl had already fallen head over heels for him, after just a few weeks of chatting. *What a triumph!* he thought to himself, before hurling a glob of spit into the bin at his feet.

The thought of Shamira made him laugh! She was young and foolish and drab, yet somehow... desirable. He thought of the story he'd spun – impressing even himself at his inventiveness. Making up all those lies. About a cousin dying of Covid, so that she would feel sorry for him. Finding those Facebook photos of a teenage boy that would do the trick in being his catfish face. And he'd come up with so many spontaneous terms of endearment! 'Looks don't matter, *you* matter,' he mumbled sarcastically under his breath – oh, his brilliance! And Shamira had fallen for it all.

She was definitely going to have the shock of her life when she came to Rochdale. They would have to make up some story, telling Shamira that Nadir's family had found out about his online liaisons with her, and so they had sent him away. Something like that. But by that time, they would have their hands on her...

Yes, Hassan felt smug with his particular art of deception. It was all too easy. Like taking candy from a baby.

The screen lit up, and Hassan found himself in the next chatroom. He threaded chunky fingers together, and stretched his arms – then peered at the screen as he busied himself messaging the next person. A young woman calling herself Jools2k – and through their near-daily dialogue, Hassan had once again flirted with her, 'seeding' her with the promise of love...

Suddenly a sound outside caught Hassan's attention, and he tore his eyes away from the screen and sat up, rigid, all ears.

He lived on the top floor of a small, derelict carpet factory that was completely empty except for his flat, and the only sounds in the building were the odd scavenging pigeon or stray cat meowing for food. He quickly switched screens and checked the cameras that he'd set up at the building entrance and exit – the pictures were dark and grainy, and he had to peer closer, squinting, but he couldn't see anything untoward. Another sound, and he turned. Someone outside on the stairs.

Quick as a flash, Hassan turned back to the computer, opened a Terminal window, and typed 'sudo ./erase-all'. Sweat-shine on his forehead. He glanced nervously toward the door, before grabbing his mobile, extracting the sim, and then putting the phone on the floor and crunching it underfoot – just as the door was kicked in with a loud thwack! Hassan turned away, slipped the sim in his mouth, and swallowed – but it caught in the back of his throat, and he doubled over and started choking.

Men in black combat uniform piled in, shouting repeatedly, 'DON'T MOVE!! PUT YOUR HANDS UP!!!' as they pointed their guns and surrounded him. There seemed to be a swarm of them. But Hassan was so intent on swallowing the sim that he barely registered. Finally, it went down. Someone thrusted Hassan's hands up into the air and pointed their gun at his temple. 'HANDS UP!! DON'T MOVE!!!' the man shouted again.

One of the men started typing frantically on his keyboard, and Hassan looked up to see that the progress bar had just completed 100%, with great relief. 'STAY DOWN!! DON'T LOOK UP!!' screamed someone else, and Hassan did as he was told.

He held his hands behind his neck and crouched on the floor, shaking. Felt a gun barrel press, hard and cold, against the back of his head – and in his gullet, the rough edges of the sim slipping slowly down.

23

'I do not associate with deceitful men,
and I avoid those who hide what they are.'

Psalm 26:4

New World Translation of the Holy Scriptures

3   THE FEAR OF KEATS

Professor Harald Wolff despised disorder.

Being blind, he needed the world and everything in it to be neat and static. Nothing, not one single thing, could be put out of place. Because if anything was moved without his knowledge, it might as well have vanished entirely.

18 months ago, when five teenagers crowded into Avernus, together with two of their parents, and yet another animal, the initial thrill of having most of the Ingenious children with him, safe and sound, was soon ruptured by hairline cracks of disorder. More and more the Professor found himself clenching teeth as he tapped and felt his way around, wondering whether he was going to bump into yet another chair, or a bag dumped on the floor, or someone's discarded shoes. Or he would discover that the milk was not on its shelf in the fridge, or the cutlery was out of order.

The Professor found himself retreating often to his bedroom – one of the few places of solitude, calm, and order. Knowing exactly where everything was in his room, gave him respite.

The other thing that kept the Professor anchored to sanity was routine. A schedule that ordered his time in neat, convenient slots. Up at 6 in the morning, breakfast at 7, lunch at 12, and dinner at 6 in the evening. The first Saturday of the month was a quiet day out – perhaps a gentle walk in the park with the Chauffeur, or a lake-side stroll with Gaia. The second Saturday was a regular medical visit to either the doctor, dentist, or osteopath. And every third Saturday, the Professor made sure to go and visit V3.

She was still in coma, but that did not stop the Professor from tapping his way quietly through the corridors of the private hospital, until he reached her room. He counted eight paces from the door to the bed, two paces to the left, until his feet bumped against the bedside table – where he would flick closed his stick, and rest it on the edge.

When he turned to her, his fingers sometimes rested on the crisp cotton bedsheet, and other times he dared to feel for the pillow, and brush timidly through her soft hair. He even plucked up the courage to smooth the back of his hand over her forehead, and a cheekbone, which seemed to sink into ever-deepening cheeks. At least the scars had completely healed, and her skin was no longer rough with scabs.

He would then lower himself into the chair next to the bed, and lift his face to the warmth of the sun that streamed through the large window on his right, quietly listening to the steady beeping and whirring of hospital equipment, the faint whoosh of the ventilator – soaking in that particular hospital smell of bleach and disinfectant.

Even comatose, V3 had become his rock, he realised. She was always there; never out of place. Lying straight and still.

The Professor often read to her.

He closed his eyes, and listened to Jasmine's narration through his earbud, then repeated the words out loud to her sleeping form. He sometimes felt for V3's hand as he read. But there was never any reaction from her, not even a muscle-twitch, or a spasm.

The Professor read his way through her favourite book of poetry, speaking with as much feeling as he could muster for someone who was unused to expressing emotion. But when he came to John Keats' 'To Sleep', he could only slow his pace and read with dispassion, his voice wooden – for, though it was a beautiful poem, and apt, he trembled at the very last lines:

> *O soft embalmer of the still midnight,*
> *Shutting, with careful fingers and benign*
> *Our gloom-pleas'd eyes, embower'd from the light,*
> *Enshaded in forgetfulness divine;*
> *O soothest Sleep! if so it please thee, close,*
> *In midst of this thine hymn, my willing eyes,*
> *Or wait the 'Amen,' ere thy poppy throws*

Around my bed its lulling charities.
Then save me, or the passed day will shine
Upon my pillow, breeding many woes;
Save me from curious Conscience, that still lords
Its strength for darkness, burrowing like a mole;
Turn the key deftly in the oiled wards,
And seal the hushed Casket of my Soul.

To the Professor, the thought of a key locking and sealing the Casket, was like bolting-in an eternal sleep... death. His hollowed soul hushed to silence once more. It made the old man shiver. Lowering his head after those last starkly uttered words, he pleaded with Death itself, always. 'Please. Don't take her as well...'

••• ———————————————————————— •••

The Professor hadn't seen the PM for well over a year, which was why he was surprised when Jasmine announced a telephone call from him, in his room in Avernus, while he and the Chauffeur were packing the last of his things into crates. The PM gave a rather brief but loaded request to meet urgently at Downing Street – not giving away much else, except that it was 'a matter of importance'. And so the Professor and the Chauffeur stopped everything and left immediately.

The Chauffeur led him into the grey police-guarded building, where they were taken directly to the PM's office.

'Ah, Professor! Very good to see you!' said the PM, getting up from his large mahogany desk and walking over to greet them.

The Chauffeur did not like his strong, vigorous handshake, and he shook out his hand afterward, rather disdainfully.

The Professor was taken to an ornate antique chair, and the Chauffeur sat him down before touch-signing to him that he would wait outside.

The PM returned to his desk, sat down, and looked over the old man who stared blankly at the wall, trying to figure something out. 'There's something different about you, Professor.'

The Professor smiled only briefly. 'The Chauffeur keeps telling me with his usual candour that my hair is almost completely grey now, and that I have more worry lines. So I expect it's that, Prime Minister. It's been… a difficult few years. Milly and Tai – thankfully – are back to normal, but it was a long and arduous process. Well over a year. And I'm afraid it's rather taken its toll.'

'I'm sorry to hear that, Professor. But at the same time, very glad that this cure of yours has been so effective on the children. I wonder, could it be utilised for others? People with Alzheimer's for instance–'

'Believe me, we've already looked into that, but I'm afraid the cure is only applicable to the very particular genetic mutation that they have.'

'I see. And Tai… is he really all right?'

'Tai has recovered well, physically and mentally, which is nothing short of a miracle! The aging is completely reversed, and he's returned to his normal youthfulness, thank goodness – though again, the regeneration took months. What Fitzsimmons did for him is a marvel! Now, if that man's powers could be harnessed…'

'I agree,' said the PM. 'But as you can imagine, it's not something we feel comfortable exploring, given what Fitzsimmons did, not to mention his mental instability.'

'Mmm…' The Professor was in two minds about this. He had never quite shaken off the disquietude of knowing the part Fitzsimmons played in the deaths of his wife and son – yet, the man had saved Tai. Was he really the monster that he appeared to be? But he couldn't ignore the fact that he'd killed one of his agents, tried to wipe out the animals, and decimated the entire UK fly population in the process. The PM was right, exploring how Fitzsimmons had helped Tai would be like playing with fire – in a firework factory. The Professor shifted awkwardly in his chair. 'Prime Minister, you mentioned on the phone about something urgent…'

'Yes, yes,' he said gruffly, and reached for a button on the desk telephone. 'Nat,' he said to his secretary, 'tell Sanderson the Professor's here.'

Several minutes later, they heard the door open and Rory Sanderson, head of security, stepped inside. He was smart in a pale-blue shirt, tie, and navy suit. He took a seat at the side of the PM's desk, so that the three formed a triangle. 'Good to see you, Professor,' said Sanderson.

The Professor nodded toward him. 'Likewise.'

The PM leaned forward, clasping his hands on the desk. 'Rory, you have permission to brief the Professor on recent events, and our... special request.'

'Yes, Sir,' said Sanderson, frowning slightly, and turning toward the old man. 'I'm sure you're aware of the increased internet activity over lockdown, Professor. Particularly that of young people. After two years, our intelligence has picked up a disturbing increase in reports of very sinister and very real online threats, targeted especially at our children. Trolling, online-bullying, cyber-stalking, exposure to websites that promote self-harm and suicide, porn, violence, online grooming, scams, fraud. Not to mention sextortion and blackmailing...'

'Sextortion?' asked the Professor. He had never heard of this term before.

'Yes, it's when a person claims to have sensitive or private material of their victim, and they threaten to distribute it online if the person doesn't give them x amount of money, or provide sexual favours, or images of a sexual nature.'

'My goodness! Does that really happen?'

'I'm afraid it does. The prevalence has been substantial for years, but recently, the NCA – the National Crime Agency – has picked up on escalated activity during lockdown. In particular, we've seen a worrying increase in online grooming. We therefore increased our own intelligence operations, and have uncovered a ring of persons who are grooming, trafficking, and sexually abusing mostly working-class local girls, but also girls they've contacted online. Recently, a breakthrough was made when they captured a man in Rochdale, who they believe is part of the ring. After months of work, one of our operatives, going by the alias of Jools2k, discovered someone calling himself "Nadir" who for months tried to "groom" her. His real name is Abdul Hassan.'

The Professor fell quiet with the gravity of this news, eventually saying, 'Your people are doing good work, Mr Sanderson. *Very* good work. May I ask, how large is this ring?'

'We don't know for sure,' said Sanderson. 'Our investigations are still in progress, but we're finding more and more members' IP addresses on a daily basis. My latest estimate is that the ring numbers into the hundreds, all over the country. That is a conservative estimate, I might add. It could well be thousands... However, we don't know *who* these individuals are, and *where* exactly they live. Unlike the media's portrayal of the government's abilities, we can't penetrate every single server, read every device. We're not all-seeing...'

The Professor was beginning to understand. 'You need Calista and Jake's help to hack through server security? Find out who these individuals are.'

'Well, yes – that would help,' said Sanderson. 'But in tandem with that, we also need the Ingenious children...'

The Professor raised an eyebrow. 'The children?' he repeated.

Sanderson continued. 'The man that was captured, Hassan, we believe he has information on many of the others involved. Both members and victims. We've interrogated him, but he's giving nothing away. In fact, he keeps protesting his innocence.'

'Oh? remarked the Professor. 'Surely examining his computer will reveal all the information you need?'

Sanderson shook his head. 'He wiped the hard drive before capture. Apparently, according to him, he just happened to be reinstalling the operating system... So we've nothing concrete to go on. He also managed to destroy his mobile, and the sim was nowhere to be found. We soon realised he must've swallowed it. So one of our men had the unpleasant job of sifting through his toilet bucket ...'

'And?' asked the Professor, curious.

'The sim was recovered. Again, Hassan told us he swallowed it because he didn't want his family and friends to be interrogated... Anyway, the sim was almost completely eroded by gastric acid. Either that, or he ate a lot of spicy food! I say the sim was *almost* completely eroded, because – amazingly – after cleaning it and examining its contents, we managed to find a few telephone numbers. One in particular was the most damning... He had been making and receiving calls from a 15-year-old girl, called Shamira Mahmoud, who we know for sure had been trafficked. It was the work of our digital scientists that uncovered her internet history, and her links to this ring. Yet Hassan keeps protesting his innocence, and insists that no grooming was involved. He says the girl came to him and had a "relationship" with him, voluntarily. We can't confirm this with her because, sadly, she committed suicide three weeks ago… We managed to retrieve her body, and a forensic examination found the DNA of *six* different men on her, though amazingly not Hassan's. They also found multiple tears, scratches, and bruising all over her body. She certainly put up a fight.'

The Professor closed his eyes briefly. 'That poor child. Her innocence ripped away by those monsters…' He suddenly thought of something. 'I see why you need the Ingenious children,' he said, his eyes fluttering downward. 'You would like to know whether this man, Hassan, is telling the truth.'

The PM shifted forward in his chair. 'Well, we're pretty certain he's lying.'

'What we really need,' jumped in Sanderson, 'is to find out from this man the details of the other gang members. Their identities, locations, etc. As soon as possible. We don't know how many other children they're taking advantage of as we speak…' His voice was grim, serious. A sharp memory suddenly came to him – as if it were yesterday – of how the lightest touch of Jemima Jenkins' hand, in the Amazon jungle, as they sat beside the fire's embers, had revealed to him whether he was dying from the same illness that had killed his father and older brother. Jemima's heartening smile afterward, tacit affirmation that he was okay, gave him the courage to get tested when he got back to London. And she had been right. The doctor had given him a completely clean bill of health. Sanderson stared at the Professor now. 'If the children can probe into Hassan's mind, and find any information at all about the other ring members, that would be invaluable…' said Sanderson in earnest.

The Professor turned slightly toward him, a flicker of frustration on his face. 'I understand,' he said. 'I wish it were that simple, Mr Sanderson. Tai is the one person who has the ability to go deeply into people's memories, but unfortunately his… particular skills diminished as his physical health returned to normal. We're still trying to understand how, and why. It's obviously some kind of side effect of the cure. We've already started working with him to try and get his powers back, but it's early days.

Saffron and Mei Hui have already returned to their home countries – but anyway, their skillsets are entirely unsuited to this kind of memory probing. Saffron has the ability to sense peoples' abstract thoughts and feelings, as they occur in real time, from a distance. And Mei Hui, by touch, can determine the veracity, or otherwise, of someone's character – whether or not they are genuine. Milly's ability is to implant memories and images, not access them. And Jemima, rather uniquely, can detect the lifespan and health of living things. So Tai really is... or *was*... the only person who would have been suited to this.'

'I'm sorry to hear about Tai,' said the PM, disappointed. 'I hope, for his sake, he's able to recover soon. But are you absolutely sure the other children are unable to help, Professor? I can't stress enough the urgency of this. We're talking about a coordinated network of child trafficking. Missing boys and girls. This child-grooming gang is a very dangerous beast.'

The Professor sighed. 'Saffie is unable to penetrate people's minds by herself – she can only sense abstract thoughts and feelings. Nothing specific. And while Mei Hui can read people's recent memories – at the most, a day or two old – it's nothing like what Tai could do.' He paused, fingering the top of his cane. 'But I will talk to the children about this, if I may...'

'Yes, please do,' affirmed the PM.

'...It's urgent, I know,' continued the Professor. 'So I'll come back to you as soon as I can.' He got up slowly, wincing from the aching creak in his hips – and then nodded farewell to them both. 'Prime Minister. Mr Sanderson.'

The PM got up, walked around the desk, and shook the Professor's hand in his usual bone-crunching way. 'Thank you, Professor. We'll wait for your call.'

Meanwhile, Sanderson, on hearing sounds of laughter outside, opened the door to find the Chauffeur sitting there, watching Charlie Chaplin videos on his mobile – clueless as to how loud he was being.

The Chauffeur looked up, glanced at them all, and wondered why on earth everyone was looking so serious.

'A man's gift opens the way for him;

it gives him access to great people.'

Proverbs 18:16

New World Translation of the Holy Scriptures

4 THE GIFT

As the Professor tapped his way quietly through Avernus' corridors, he listened thoughtfully to the echo of reverberations. Now that everything had been packed into moving crates to be sent to their new home, he noticed how hollow the empty Avernus was sounding. Hollow, like his own feelings toward the underground cavern. Avernus had once meant to him security, safety, protection – but slowly, over the course of two years, it had gradually turned into a prison. He realised that what had changed was *his* mindset, *his* view, and circumstance, because of course the place had remained exactly the same.

The sharp tap-tap-tap of his cane prodded his conscience as he walked, and he wondered what was the thing that had made him so cold toward his home of many years.

He entered the den, where Milly, Tai, and Jemima were sitting on floor cushions, talking quietly amongst themselves, as they waited for him. Dog and Acuzio were lying next to each other by the fire, half asleep, while the cats were scattered around in various states of semi-consciousness and playfulness.

Jemima – the sun having bronzed her skin and bleached her hair to a paler strawberry blonde – jumped up as soon as he entered the room. 'Prof!' she breathed. 'Can you believe it?! Our last evening in Avernus...' She took his hand and led him to the armchair, navigating between the animals.

The Professor patted Jemima's hand in gratitude, and sat down. Felt and heard the crackle of the fire next to him. The heat warmed him, gave him a measure of comfort.

He took a moment to compose himself as he took a deep breath, and then began explaining to them the situation that Sanderson had described. The capture of the ring member, Abdul Hassan. The nationwide network of groomers, traffickers, abusers – hundreds, if not thousands, of them. And as the children listened with rapt silence, it was as if sound had been sucked into a vacuum, even the fire seemed to have hushed. Finally the Professor's words petered out, and he waited for their response.

Milly piped up, 'Mei would be able to tell if this Abdul Hassan is lying. If he's really a ring member. But to be honest, he does sound guilty! I mean, he immediately wiped his computer, destroyed his phone, and swallowed the sim. So he's definitely hiding something.'

Jemima nodded enthusiastically. 'That's what I thought too!'

Tai was sitting next to Dog, hugging his knees to his chest, shoulders slumped. 'I wish I could help!' he said with more than a little disappointment. He lowered his head.

Milly squeezed his arm, deep in thought. 'I know who could help,' she said quietly. They all turned to her, just as she muttered, 'Jeremy Fitzsimmons.'

There was a gasp, and they turned to find Jemima apoplectic. 'But he's evil!' she breathed. 'He killed his girlfriend, and put her in the painting! And he killed V8!!'

They all thought about this for several seconds, imagining Fitzsimmons grinding ashes, and mixing them into paint... At the same time, the Professor thought about the small pile of dust by the great oak – all that was left of his agent, V8 – slowly disappearing in the wind. Then they heard the rustle of crumpled paper, bringing them back to the here and now. Milly shifted on her cushion as she extracted something from her trouser pocket. Two pieces of white art paper carefully folded into a neat square. 'I've been meaning to tell you...' she unfolded the pages, to show them. 'He gave me something, Fitzsimmons. A gift.' With her right hand she fanned out the papers, and both Jemima and Tai took one each, while with her left, she grasped the Professor's hand.

The old man blinked suddenly – a flurry of grey eyelashes. 'I see them,' he mumbled thoughtfully. In his mind he saw the small paintings that Milly had handed to the others. They were both signed with the initials 'MB' – and one was dated 17 August two years ago, while the other was dated 6 September of the same year. Paintings of blue cornflowers. Jake's cornflowers.

'I think you know, Professor...' started Milly, gulping. Guilt seeping into her voice, her expression. '...I was the one who let Fitzsimmons out of his prison cell, that day, two years ago. The day he escaped.'

The Professor nodded softly. 'Yes, I knew. But... you were so helpless in your own mind at the time, Milly. So confused. You couldn't be held responsible for your actions. And then you went through the traumatic upheaval of course after course of the cure... I didn't have the heart to bring it up.'

Jemima turned from the Professor to Milly, flabbergasted. '*You* let him out?! Why? Why would you do that?'

It was Tai who answered. 'To save me.'

Tears slipped down Milly's cheeks. 'Somehow I knew he wanted to help Tai. Don't ask me how. I think it was something to do with when we entered his mind. When he allowed us to see glimpses of his past. While we were so preoccupied finding out about him, at the same time, he must've put the thought into me that he wanted to save Tai, but he needed my help... You see, the guards outside could only open the outer door, but he needed someone to open the inner one. That's where I came in.'

'So you did it because he made you,' said Jemima.

Milly thought about it, eventually shaking her head. 'It was me too. I *let* him influence me, because... because I couldn't bear the thought of Tai dying!'

Tai shuffled closer to Milly and put an arm around her, their heads touching lightly.

Jemima melted at last, and stared sympathetically at them. 'I'm sorry, Mills,' she said, eyebrows slanting, just as Milly and Tai parted. 'I think... if it had been me, I might've done the same. None of us wanted Tai to die.'

'What doesn't add up...' started the Professor, 'is that, before, Fitzsimmons couldn't control people. Otherwise we would never have been able to capture him. So somehow, while he was locked in his cell in Avernus, in isolation, he learnt that this was something he could do. But how? And how did he know he could save Tai using the old oak, and the flies?'

Milly looked just as baffled, and shrugged. 'I don't know.'

Jemima was sitting on the floor next to the Professor, leaning back against his legs, the artwork in her hand. She stared at it for a long time, when something occurred to her. Tilting her head, she looked over the piece Tai was holding. 'These paintings... there's a huge difference between them. This one,' she held up her page, 'sorry, Mills, but this one looks almost child-like. But the one Tai's holding was painted really, really well... even though they both have your initials, and the dates are just a few weeks apart.'

Milly wiped her eyes dry. 'That's what I wanted to show you. Fitzsimmons' gift. An unbelievable, awesome, incredible gift! Before, I wasn't good at art – at all. I could just copy stuff, but I couldn't produce my own artwork. Even though I tried and tried. But when we entered his mind, he must've given me the ability. Because the next time I started sketching, my hand just sort of... went by itself. And then I painted, and the same thing happened. I couldn't believe it! I knew it was him. And I knew that, despite the way he behaved, there's something good in him... inside. Something beautiful. The way he paints, that heartfelt thing that he puts into his work – artistic brilliance, sensitivity – all that. He gave it to me too. And that was when I knew he wasn't the monster he appears to be. That's why I let him out of his prison cell.'

Tai bumped her shoulder with his. 'If you hadn't, I don't think I'd be here today.'

Milly smiled at him, happy that he was actually sitting there, next to her, alive.

Jemima suddenly lunged forward and gripped Milly's arm, pleading, 'Will you paint me, Mills?' Her eyes turned into two irresistible saucers. 'Please!! I'd love to be painted.' She looked around, trying to think of something to persuade her. 'I'll... I'll be your slave for a whole week.' She hesitated. 'Or maybe... three days?'

Milly rolled her eyes, 'Make up your mind, Jem!'

'A week then!' said Jemima trying hard to look decisive, and extending her hand.

Milly shook it. 'Deal! And your first job is to make us all a hot chocolate. The way I showed you – with whipped cream on top, okay? I really fancy one before bed.' Jemima was a genius, but there was much she was still learning.

Jemima jumped up, bursting with excitement – she pushed the picture into the Professor's hands, and ran out of the room.

Milly listened to her footsteps disappear down the corridor, and turned back to the Professor and Tai, looking suddenly serious. She spoke to them in a hushed whisper, 'I want to connect with Fitzsimmons,' she told them, a determined look on her face. 'I want to find out what he did with Georgina Whyte – how she came to be in the painting.'

It took the Professor by surprise, and he thought about this – raised eyebrows collapsing into a frown. 'I get how you feel about him, Milly,' he said. 'But what you know about him is obviously not the whole picture. He's not what he seems. He hides things, like he tried to hide Georgina Whyte's death.'

'I know!' Milly retorted. 'But while there's this grey area about him, we'll never know whether he's really good, or bad. If I can connect with him, I can find out what he really is, for sure.'

'And what would be your reason for doing this?' asked the Professor. 'Because of some romantic notion that he gave you the gift of artistry?' He folded the artwork into its creases as he spoke, and held it out to Milly.

Milly shook her head as she took the paper. 'It's not that. While Tai's powers are down, Fitzsimmons is the *only one* who can look into this Abdul Hassan's mind and find out what the PM needs to know. It might save hundreds of lives.'

'And what if he takes over your mind, and controls you?'

Milly looked flabbergasted. 'If... if that happens, you have my full permission to shoot me with a tranquilliser dart, lock me up, and throw away the key!' She looked at Tai, and back at the Professor, her eyes pleading. 'I just know I have to try, Prof. I... I need to know.'

Tai said quietly, 'I'm with you, Milly. He almost killed himself to save me. So I'm pretty sure he wouldn't harm you, or me.'

Milly smiled at him gratefully, and turned back to the Professor.

'You've always been so impulsive, Melody Bythaway!' sighed the Professor. 'Even when you were a little toddler, you were so headstrong, doing the most daring things without a second thought. You haven't changed one bit. I have a feeling that even if I say no, you'd find a way to do it anyway...'

Tai had to agree. 'It's true,' he told Milly. 'You would go ahead, wouldn't you?'

Milly's only reply was a wry grin.

The Professor sighed yet again. He seemed to be doing that a lot these days... Suddenly he realised why he felt so cold toward Avernus. It was because so many bad things had happened since its existence. V1's death, Karl König's suicide, his dear friend Axel Kendra dying, and V8 gone – four deaths, and at their heart was Avernus it seemed.

The underground safehouse had changed, transmogrified into a burial pit. And that was why he couldn't bear to stay there any longer.

He wanted to get out before it brought about another death – even though, rationally, he knew that Avernus itself had nothing to do with what had happened.

Still, the Professor mollified himself with the thought that they were soon moving out – so that at least when Milly connected with Fitzsimmons, she might somehow stand a chance of surviving...

5   HIDDEN IN PLAIN SIGHT

'This really couldn't be more different from Avernus!' said Milly's father, Brian, as he strained his neck to look up at the tall hotel. It glistened in the crisp winter sunlight. An organic cylindrical design, with grey lacquered detailing that spiralled up and around the building – like tendrils of a vine, winding their way upward, and fanning out into an ellipse of wood at the very top, like a giant leaf.

The sweeping glass sides of the building reflected the sky in a richer blue, with platinum clouds scudding gracefully overhead.

Tyaishia, Tai's mother, whistled as they walked along the pavement around the building, following the Professor, who himself was being led by a harnessed Acuzio. 'London's first hybrid wood tower, sustainably-built, with zero emissions,' explained the Professor, his chest swelling with pride. 'Twenty floors in total, with every fifth floor having open, interconnected gardens. We wanted a biophilic design, incorporating nature wherever possible, to increase a sense of health and well-being. Of course all the wood is treated to be fire-safe, and the entire building is stabilised by reinforced concrete cores for the foundation, and spine-like elevator shafts, and staircases.' He waved his hand skyward. 'You can't see it, but at the top there's a landscaped roof garden, a helipad, and an orangery.'

They stopped at a walled section at the back, with a tall silver double gate. On the post was what looked like an intercom with a glass panel. 'This is *our* special entrance,' said the Professor, turning toward the intercom. The gates immediately sprang open, sliding sideways. 'It has facial recognition, and is programmed with each of your facial biometrics – so you all have automatic access. However, if it detects tension in your face, it will refuse to open. Just in case!' he remarked as lightly as possible, trying not to worry both Brian and Tyaishia who, to be fair, as parents, worried about almost everything. It didn't work.

'What do you mean, Prof?' asked Brian, frowning. 'In case we're being held up, and used by some nefarious criminal to get inside?'

'Well not quite…' mumbled the Professor dismissively.

Tyaishia and Brian looked at each other. But they were too excited about their new home to take it up further. For once, Tyaishia was speechless, as she stared up at the beauty and magnificence of the building.

The Professor led them to the building entrance, where again another glass panel scanned the Professor's face, and the heavy door automatically opened to let them in. The lobby was disappointingly bare and white, and they walked through it to the central elevator. As they waited, the Professor stroked Acuzio's head absentmindedly. 'This entrance, and this elevator, is just for us,' he explained. 'The public elevators in the hotel don't have a button for the very top floor.' The doors finally slid open and they stepped in.

'Hello,' came Jasmine's beautiful voice. 'Welcome to Vivra Tower.'

When they heard her, they all smiled like Cheshire cats. 'Happy to be here!' exclaimed Brian, 'and lovely to hear your voice, Jasmine.'

'Thank you, Brian.'

As the elevator sped upward, so their anticipation mounted, until finally the lift stopped, doors opened, and they stepped out into what looked like another world. A wide lobby with pristine white walls and a brown carpet, was filled with a plethora of potted plants and ornamental trees – the delicate weeping fig, spiky foliage of the yucca, and the braided trunk of the Guiana chestnut amongst others.

Acuzio led them down a central corridor, resisting the urge to sniff the plants. 'We each have our own apartments,' explained the Professor, 'with three bedrooms, lounge, kitchen, bathroom, utility room – and all the mod cons.' They got to a point where the corridor split into two further corridors, like spokes from a wheel, with them standing at the centre. The Professor waved to the left. 'Along there's the swimming pool, spa, and fitness room…' He waved to the right. 'And down here are the entrances to our apartments. Back there, behind us, we just walked past the communal rooms – a separate kitchen and dining room, a library, and a cinema-cum-music room, which has particularly comfy armchairs I might add. There's also a computer room; that's where Jasmine is housed now. She actually controls the whole building – smart girl!'

'Thank you, Professor,' came Jasmine's cheery voice.

They heard a door open and someone rushing toward them – and they turned to find Tai running out in bare feet to greet his mother. 'Ma! Our apartment's amazing! Come see.' He took the carrier bag she was holding, grabbed her hand, and pulled her away.

The Professor smiled. The building was the diametric opposite of Avernus. While the underground safehouse was dark, hidden in the ground, with a name that hinted of the land of the dead, Vivra Tower was bright, airy, reaching for the sky, its name linked to living. And he could sense the effect it was already having on the children. One that he too enjoyed. He breathed deeply. The air was tinged with the refreshing scent of greenery and flowers. Closing his eyes, he felt none of the morbidity of Avernus. Only a cool, breezy, lightness.

Brian interrupted his thoughts. 'It's beautiful, Prof! Can't believe this is your hotel!'

The Professor opened his eyes. 'Yes, my uncle started building it several years before he died – and then I took it over and tweaked the design somewhat. Being cautious as I am, I created this hidden top floor. Again, just in case!'

'Cool! We're hidden in plain sight!' exclaimed Brian.

Nodding, the Professor said, 'Yes, I suppose we are.'

There was a pause. 'Can't wait to see my apartment,' Brian hinted.

'Ah yes. Down there, the Delta suite,' he said, waving to the right. 'Milly's already there.'

The Professor listened as Brian made his way further along, stopped, and opened a door. He heard Milly's faint voice, 'Dad, you're not going to believe this place!' And again, the Professor smiled.

At his feet, Acuzio stood in anticipation for the next command.

The Professor told him, 'Home,' as he jostled on the harness – and the dog walked obediently, at just the right pace, to one of the doors. When the Professor pushed it open and went inside, though he could not see, he sensed a flood of light – all at once warm, luminous, soothing. He sighed at the pleasing thought of his own private space. Of everything being laid out, or put away, in perfect order. Home, thought the Professor, is most definitely where the heart is.

He bent down and took the harness off Acuzio, who licked his master's hand and then his cheek affectionately. But as soon as he was released, the dog immediately turned and bounded through the flap in the wall next to the door. *His* home was where Dog and the cats were, and so he made his way to seek them out.

The Professor loosened his bow tie as he shuffled through to the bedroom – ten paces forward, four paces to the left. He sat on the bed, closing his eyes to breathe in the heady scent of the flowers that were in planters scattered around. The soothing fragrances of lavender and lemon balm were sure to give him a good night's sleep – even with tomorrow's ominous event overshadowing his thoughts. When Milly was to connect with Fitzsimmons.

They might finally find out if the man had killed his fiancée, and why he'd mixed her ashes into his painting. Too, they would be able to discover whether Fitzsimmons could be trusted to help them uncover the identities of the hundreds of ring members – a deadly menace slow-brewing in cyberspace, just beneath the surface.

43

'Anxiety in a man's heart weighs it down'

Proverbs 12:25

New World Translation of the Holy Scriptures

6 SNAPSHOTS

In the 18 months since Tai Jones had been brought back to life by the unstable Jeremy Fitzsimmons, the teenagers were themselves slowly recovering from a state of bewildered, befuddled confusion. Trying to make sense of what they had witnessed: the old oak completely razed to the ground, the destruction of a whirlwind of flies, and V8 disappearing in a puff of grey, as Fitzsimmons sucked them in, absorbing a firebolt of dark energy. His own feeble frame a conduit, juddering with pain, as he channelled the tremendous power into Tai's limp body.

Both had survived. A miracle.

And in the course of time, slowly, slowly, Tai's body changed from the crippled feeble old man that he had become – to the vibrant 16-year-old boy that he should always have been.

The teenagers – Jemima, Mei Hui, Jake and Calista, Milly and Tai, and Saffie – dealt with the after-effects in their own way. Trying hard to continue with normal life, and everyday trivialities, even though they were constantly struggling with a bedlam of emotions and mood-swings. To their credit, they coped valiantly – the hidden super power that so many have, of somehow being able to return to some semblance of normality, despite their entire world being ripped apart.

Though it wasn't as smooth a journey as one would have liked, littered with stutters, stops, and starts – they nevertheless continued on their course, bruised and scarred, but still hobbling their way along.

Their lives were not unlike others. The dance of everyday matters no different from the people around them. But here and there, wounds and scars cracked open.

And so, winding back time, here are glimpses of their lives unfolding in the aftermath of the day of the flies. Snapshots of how each of them coped after the harrowing ordeal…

•••————————————————•••

Jemima Jenkins was a girl who very much wore her heart on her sleeve.

She was what she was. Unapologetic for her childish candour and joie de vivre. No matter what life threw at her.

And so, when she returned to her large Edwardian home in London, jumping into her mother and father's arms with screeches of delight, she chattered to them no end about her journey to China to find Mei Hui, and then to the Amazon to bring back Saffie. Adventures of a lifetime, which only fed her desire to explore even more the wonders that the world had to offer. Earth, a planetary jewel in a secret universe.

Her father, Benjamin Jenkins – who worked as a much sought-after consultant actuary for insurance companies, using maths and statistics to model and predict financial risk and cost – was overwhelmed at having his only daughter returned at last, alive and well. And now – realising how very precious family, and life, were – he quickly became inspired by Jemima's passion for travel, wanting to experience what the world had to offer. There and then he decided to take off a year to spend time with his family, much to their excitement. It also had something to do with the fact that the company he'd been working for went spectacularly bust, reneging on his last months' invoices of many thousands of pounds. The company was a casualty of yet another year of global natural disasters reaching a record high. Hurricanes, wildfires, thunderstorms, floods, droughts, and extreme temperatures – all increasing by a factor of five in the past 50 years. The root cause was undeniable. Climate change. The last year alone brought about insured losses of over £60 billion worldwide.

The family, however, focused on the thrill and excitement of their dream holidays – and as soon as lockdown eased and travel was at last allowed, the family spent days and hours poring over the Oxford Atlas of the World, scouring the internet, and raced around on Google Earth, to make a list of the places they had always dreamt of going. Money was no object, though Jemima was adamant that they live like the locals, staying in modest hotels or B&Bs – not enveloped in the luxurious hotels her parents were accustomed to.

'When in Rome!' insisted Jemima, pouting.

But, for her parents, giving up their five-star, air-conditioned, swimming-pooled accommodations was going to prove difficult.

'I don't really want to rough it for every trip, sweetheart!' protested Benjamin to his daughter. He did enjoy his gourmet food, and her mother, Chloé, had a penchant for indulging in beauty and spa treatments.

After a drawn-out heated debate between father and daughter, Chloé eventually pitched in, in a kindly but firm 'this sounds like a tactful suggestion but it's very much the end of the matter' voice. 'Perhaps we can take turns in choosing the hotel?' she said. 'I think that's only fair, Jemima. You can decide on the first accommodation, while Daddy and I choose the next. Agreed?'

Jemima folded her arms. 'Fine,' she breathed, rolling her eyes. Then she started jumping up and down. 'For our first trip, I want to go camping in Yosemite, and see Vernal Falls, and hike to the giant sequoias, and sleep under the stars!!' Each word getting higher in pitch, her sentence ending in a squeak.

Chloé groaned. Sleeping inside a tent, on dirt, wasn't exactly her idea of a holiday. 'Technically, a tent is not really accommodation...' she grumbled, trying to squirm out of it.

'Mummy! You said!' Jemima exclaimed. And then she pleaded with irresistible eyes that no human could resist. 'Please!! It's one of the things on my bucket list, since... since forever.'

'Bucket list?' her father said, surprised. 'Sweetheart, you've got your whole life ahead of you.'

Jemima blinked at him. 'I-I mean, it's just something I've always wanted to do.'

Three weeks later they were sitting in Yosemite Park around a campfire, toasting marshmallows, as night fell slowly. The family chatted happily, and ate s'mores, told scary stories, and sung Phantom of the Opera songs with great gusto. Eventually they lay back on their blankets staring up. Above them, murmuring fireflies floated in a dreamlike display. And around them, the sky slowly darkened, as if a celestial artist were building layer after layer of cobalt paint on a domed canvas, deftly scattering handfuls of glittering stars across the still-wet oil.

When the family retreated to their sleeping bags, exhausted but jovial, they soon dozed off after a long day of trekking. But several hours into the night, Jemima began crying out in her sleep – tossing and turning, in the throes of yet another nightmare. Calling out to V8, screaming with fright, sobbing uncontrollably. Kicking into the seams of her sleeping bag as if it were the enemy. In time, she eventually quietened. Mewling softly as she dreamt with tear-streaked cheeks. 'No, no, it can't be,' she murmured, gasping with disbelief. 'Please, no. S-so little time...' It seemed like an age before she at last quietened. Her mind, sinking. Drowning in dreams.

Her mother and father, now wide awake, lay on the other side of the tent divider, listening. They clutched onto each other's hand and stared up at the green nylon, wondering if Jemima would come to them, distraught, as she so often did. Though there were no lanterns lit, their tent was shrouded in a glow of flickering light – outside, sparkles of fireflies, in their thousands, had settled on their tent roof. The cold light of bioluminescence softly sketching the outlines of their faces in silver. Faces that revealed a blend of expressions: concern for their daughter, fatigue, and wondrous awe at the profusion of fireflies above them. Thankfully, Jemima stayed put that night. The long, bracing walks and fresh air seemed to be good for her anxiety.

•••────────────────────•••

Unlike Jemima, Tai Jones kept everything bottled in.

He had always done so, right from when he was a toddler.

Most of the time during his childhood, little Tai was silenced as he watched colours of emotion ascend from his mother, and his father, on the rare occasions when he was around – colours that either prickled or detonated with anger or discontent, or billowed in a slow-rising smoke of calm, or flooded out in dense waves of depression.

After the Jeremy Fitzsimmons debacle, Tai had remained comatose for just over three weeks. During that quiet, gloomy period, Dog, Acuzio, and the cats took to sleeping in his room, and had learnt soon enough not to interfere with the mass of tubing and cabling that hooked Tai's sickly, emaciated form to the ECMO machine that was keeping him alive. The cats managed to find a way to jump up on the bed, and now and then they licked his cheek, or his hand, as if the balm of their saliva might somehow revive him. When they slept on him, curled into neat furry balls, their tails thumped lightly against his body. The vibration of their purrs thrumming right through him. They, like Tyaishia and the others, refused to give up on him.

What finally stirred the boy awake was not the constant, extended prayers uttered sotto-voce by his mother, watered by her tears, or Dog's whining cries when she stood up on her hind legs and scratched at his bed, or the children's visits when they told him about their day, held his hand, or read to him – it was the rousing movements of Mozart's Piano Concerto No. 20, rumbling from the speakers overhead, punctuated now and then by the snores of a dozing Professor, slumped in the chair, bedside. Bursts of orchestral music flowing and interweaving with an introspective piano. As if emotion and love had been poured into sound. As if feelings were being decanted into the air. It was a piece that Tai had been learning to play, though he had struggled with the rippling in the rondo of the final movement. But as the music whirled through the air, the pianist played it beautifully, accompanied by an exuberant orchestra. Their rendition was perfection itself. And somehow the piano sparked something deep within Tai's mind, and his sleeping form stirred. At last.

The lively crescendo of the musical finale was the perfect backdrop to the frenzied activity that ensued: an alarm ringing shrilly from the machinery; Dr Fargo and the nurse running into the room to attend to Tai; Tyaishia appearing and screaming with joy and disbelief; the Professor rousing to the commotion; thunderous applause from the recording. And finally silence… just as Tai opened his eyes.

It still took months of rehabilitation before the boy returned to his former strength. But with each day there were small improvements. His hands stopped shaking. His skin slowly cleared of wrinkles. 20-20 vision returned. And bones gradually stopped aching.

His mind, however, remained confused and disoriented in the weeks that followed. So Dr Vassiliev made the decision to start him on the same course of treatment – the cure – that they were giving to Milly. A course that both of them took for many months. Though in a deep mental fog, the teenagers focused on the pin-prick light at the end of the tunnel... eventually emerging from the darkness, blinking – and feeling brighter, stronger, and maybe even better than before.

Tai found himself returning to some semblance of normality, though nothing would ever be the same again. He often stopped to look at his mother, realising that he loved her more than words could say, more than he knew how to express. He felt gratitude for everything. Appreciated more keenly the others, the animals, the Professor, though the old man looked much frailer than before.

The first time Tai went for a walk since his recovery, he insisted that he go alone, much to everyone's protestations.

Solitude became him. He had always been a quiet child. Growing up, his only companions were time and loneliness – sauntering, inchmeal and heavy-footed, on either side of him.

As Tai walked across the fields, only the dogs and cats trailed behind. A silent procession. The cat, Pasha, who had become so fat she was almost spherical, was lagging behind, and so Tai waited for her, then bent down to pick her up. He stared at the cat's chubby face, searching once more for signs of colour around her. Signs of her thoughts, her feelings. But there was nothing. And Tai felt his heart cracking with pain – it was as though his world had changed from three dimensions, to only two. And he hardly knew how he could cope with the flatness of life without colour. He had to face the cutting truth of it, that his uncanny sixth sense was no more. And like so many things, it had been taken for granted until it was gone. He missed the colours terribly.

Hugging the cat to his chest, Tai walked slowly into the fields. Morning enveloped him with a downy warmth. Bare feet sank into grass still damp with early morning dew. He breathed deeply – the refreshing tang of air filling his lungs. Closed his eyes. Listened to the whisper of the wind, the dawn chorus. Inhaled scents of a new day, so fresh that it was like the first day ever.

As Tai walked, he came to the place where the great oak had once been. Nothing left but a gaping, charred hole. And emptiness. And that was when the full enormity hit him. He put down Pasha and dropped to his knees, breaking down there and then. Fingers burrowing into the soil where the oak should have been. In his head, a cyclone of thoughts, feelings, voices. The fragility of life. Death. His mother calling his name. Love, and abject fear. Dogs howling, cats meowing. Misery. Vague memories of people screaming. Fitzsimmons clenching him in twitching arms as he writhed in agony. Lightning strikes of pain.

As Tai's hands clenched clumps of soil and charred wood, splinters pierced his skin and he sucked in air sharply. When he looked down at his fingers he saw blood trickling, like vermilion teardrops, disappearing into the black soil. And he stopped. Stared. Saw that, from the earth, there were tiny blades of grass sprouting – new growth – delicate shafts of hope and optimism, struggling to break through.

But that was not the only thing he discovered.

He crouched down, and picked it up.

An acorn.

Quickly he dusted off the dirt, and held it up, inspecting it, his damp face lighting up with fascination. It was still whole. The shiny dome of a brown nut, topped by a bulging cup, like a knitted hat – pattern-perfect with rows of tiny scales.

Tai sniffed, and wiped his eyes and nose on the back of his sleeve. Dog came up, and licked off the residue of his tears, a light whining sound in her throat. Tai put an arm around her, patting her. 'I'm okay, Dog,' he murmured.

He turned, looking around. 'Acuzio!' he called. The beautiful husky came bounding over immediately; he had been wandering all over the place as usual, marking his territory and sniffing everything. Tai kneeled down and held out the acorn to both Acuzio and Dog. 'Find, fetch,' he told them softly, and then carefully put the acorn in his pocket, as if it were made of delicate glass. Immediately the dogs began sniffing the ground around them, and when they came across an acorn, they pawed the earth and barked until Tai came over and picked it up. They did this for some time.

After an hour or so, Tai told the dogs to stop – his trouser pockets were stuffed full with precious acorns.

Brian was quite the worrier – though he never let on, not even to himself. When his wife was dying with cancer, he worried himself sick about her imminent death, the pain she was suffering, and how their little daughter would cope when she was gone. How he could even go on living without her. When they had the house, he worried about keeping up the mortgage and paying the bills. And when Milly's mind was deteriorating, he worried that she might never recover... But recover she did. Even though it was slow and drawn out – like waiting for water to boil, not much seemed to be happening from day to day, for such a long, long time.

The tell for his worry was burnt food. It was practically a certainty that when he quietly agonised, time took on a different pace, and there were more and more cooking disasters. Even the toast – somehow he always managed to burn the toast.

But then, months into Milly's courses of treatment administered by Dr Vassiliev, Brian was in the kitchen in Avernus scraping off the black bits from that morning's toast – when he stopped, and hunched over the sink, overwhelmed. He looked at the burnt edges, and realised that, even though they had plenty more bread, he couldn't just throw it away. He had to salvage what he could. He just had to! And then Milly came from behind, resting her chin on his shoulder as she often did. 'Burnt toast again, Dad!' she moaned, rolling her eyes, and swiping the slices from his hand. She put them on a plate and began buttering them, then slathered peanut butter on one, and Marmite on the other. She couldn't throw them away either.

Brian struggled to compose himself before turning round to face her. 'Silly me!' he said, half-smiling. 'Mind you, there's definitely something wrong with that toaster.'

Milly poured herself some grapefruit juice, and crunched on the toast – little black flakes on hungry lips. 'Funny that,' she said, cheeks bulging. 'There was something wrong with the toaster at our house too...'

'Cheeky monkey!'

Milly grinned. 'I've only got five minutes before I see Dr Fargo, Dad. Never-ending treatments!' she huffed, then sat down at the dining table and patted the chair next to her. 'Join me?'

Brian brought his mug over. 'Okey-doke. I need a mo to let the coffee wake me up anyway.'

Milly glanced at the coffee jar on the counter, frowning. 'It's decaf, Dad. You always drink decaf.'

'Yeah, I suppose on a subconscious level, the *illusion* of coffee is waking me up. I think it's like that effect... psych-something-or-other...'

'Psychosomatic?'

'That's it! It has a psychosomamptic effect on me.'

'Interesting,' said Milly thoughtfully. 'Mind over matter...' She grinned at her father, and pecked him on the cheek, before resuming munching on the toast.

Brian took a sip of the coffee in question. It was still hot. 'Did you sleep well?' he asked after blowing on it.

Milly shook her head vehemently. 'I had an awful nightmare! I keep dreaming about the same thing, over and over. It was horrible. Mum was in it, so were you. Seemed to go on forever.'

'What happened in the dream?'

Milly stopped, and put her glass down. 'You really want to know? It's literally apocalyptic!'

Brian nodded uncertainly, '...I think,' he said with some hesitation.

'Too late,' said Milly, wiping hands together to dust off crumbs. She turned to face her father, and then took his hands in hers.

They both closed their eyes.

What Brian next saw in his head was an explosion of images – an out-of-control slideshow of the worst nightmare. He saw the three of them, in monochrome, sitting eating dinner quietly together – when suddenly black bags were pulled over their heads by faceless figures emerging from the shadows. The three were terrified. Struggling. Panicking. Gasping for breath. But when they eventually passed out, instead of blackness, the world opened up in their minds in glorious, crystal-clear colour. A world of disaster after disaster. Icebergs melting. Tidal waves crashing and wiping out whole towns. Animals dying of hunger. Volcanoes spewing molten lava. Earthquakes. People screaming. Heatwaves. Drought. Then Avernus, being swallowed whole as the earth split open. Plunging them –

hurtling, limbs flailing – into unknown depths. And in the fullness of time, entire civilisations were wiped out. Country after country. Person by person. Until there was nothing left. A barren, broken, wasteland – devoid of life. Instead of a blue jewel, the earth was an empty grey rock, billowing with black smoke as it orbited the sun.

When Milly let go of his hands, Brian crashed back against his chair. 'Woah!!' he breathed, numb from the overload. After several long seconds he eventually said, 'So… you're worried about the planet… and climate change?'

Milly almost gagged on her juice. She swallowed, wiped her mouth, and nodded. 'Yes, in a nutshell!' Her head felt tight thinking about the dream-like premonition. Like the future was pressing down on her. Endless, awful prospects, stamping themselves into her mind.

Brian sighed. 'You're going through your own personal existential crisis, yet you're worried about a much, much bigger one beside. One that everyone on the planet is facing.'

'We've messed up, Dad. Royally.' Her 'we' referred to the whole of humankind. 'We're all just carrying on, burying our heads in the sand, while the world's dying.'

'Well, I wouldn't exactly say we're doing nothing. Leaders of loads of countries are getting together and–'

'What they're doing is sticking a finger in the crack of a dam. A *massive* dam that's about to burst! Mum kept going on about global warming, even back then. That's why she stopped using aerosols, grew her own veggies, bought stuff from charity shops, recycled everything. Because she knew what was going to happen.' Milly paused, and really looked at her father. 'Dad… I'm sorry, I didn't mean to upset you.'

He sniffed and turned away briefly to wipe his eyes. 'No, you're right, Midge, as usual.'

Milly took his hand again in both of hers. They were damp with tears. 'You're sad about Mum…'

Brian smiled. 'Silly, isn't it? The world in crisis, and I fall to pieces seeing Mum in your dream. It's just that, what you showed me was so… real. L-like she was right there, sitting right next to me. I even felt her body warmth…' He fell silent, but then suddenly looked determined. 'I want to see more of mum,' he said. 'Your favourite memories of her.'

Milly raised an eyebrow. 'You sure?'

Brian blinked, looked at his mug as if for confirmation, and nodded. 'Yeah.'

They were still holding hands, and Milly gripped him even firmer. Dr Fargo would have to wait.

They leaned into each other, touched heads, and closed their eyes.

•••———————————————————•••

The Chauffeur was still deeply affected by Axel Kendra's death, his adoptive father. Though he had died months ago, the shock of it could still be felt in the pit of his stomach. A nausea, an ache, that seemed always to be there. But the memory of their last hug, and Axel's impromptu signing of the words – *You. My son. Love* – the last sign clutching crossed arms firmly against his chest, softened somewhat the sting of his death.

And when things got too much for the Chauffeur, with Avernus full to brimming with yet another teenager staying and a little black jaguar cub roaming the corridors, he was drawn to the one place where he could find peace and solitude. The cemetery.

As the Chauffeur lumbered between the graves, vaguely conscious of headstone after headstone, he half read the names. So many dead people, but they at least had names. He instead was very much alive, yet nameless.

The Chauffeur had been nameless ever since he could remember. Having never known his natural mother, she was nothing more than a figment deep in the recesses of his mind. But he thought about her, the hazy shadow of her, often. Who she was. Why she abandoned him and his twin sister as newborn babies. What kind of life she lived... or lives, if she was even alive. Whether she had even thought of names for her babies. Or had she just dumped them without a second thought? All these questions tumbled through his head, like notes of a recurring melody lingering persistently in the mind.

It was true, he had refused to be given a name, even by Gaia and Axel, because he had always thought that only his real mother could tell him his name. Stupid, he knew. But that was just how he felt – and he couldn't help his feelings, couldn't help being stubborn about it.

When he got to the grave, he thought about this as he fussed over the soil around the white marble slab, pulled out clumps of weeds, and brushed away the leaves. As he wiped the headstone, and prised out the moss from the hewn crevices. He stopped to rub the sweat from his face, and stared at the marble. The perfectly chiselled letters: 'Dr Axel Johan Kendra – beloved husband, father, doctor.'

And he realised that what defined Axel, was not just the man himself, but also the ones around him, his loved ones. Who they were to him, who he was to them. Husband, father, doctor.

Yet he, the Chauffeur, had refused to be defined by his adoptive parents. Refused the names they offered...

He thought about all this with a heavy heart – until the unexpected scent of flowers, wafting from somewhere, pulled him back to the present.

And he turned.

Saw Gaia standing there.

She was holding a bunch of blue roses, clearly just as surprised to find him there as he was to see her.

The Chauffeur signed to her: *I... I've never seen roses that colour before.*

Gaia squeezed his arm as she walked past him and placed the flowers in the fluted stone urn on the memorial slab. She turned to sign back to him. *Me too. I asked the florist how it was possible to get such a colour. And guess what? They were genetically modified. So I just had to get them, for Xeli.*

They both turned to stare at the flowers for some time. They were so beautiful, so lovely – a delicate blush of blue bordering on mauve.

The Chauffeur motioned toward the headstone. *I had forgotten his middle name. Johan.*

Yes, Gaia signed back. *It was taken from one of Xeli's relatives – a grandfather, or a great uncle, I think...* She threaded her arm around him, and in turn the Chauffeur draped an arm over her shoulders.

Mother and son, he thought to himself.

That was what defined him.

Yet somehow, it was still not quite enough.

•••————————————————•••

Saffron Morales, after spending a month in Avernus getting to know the other Ingenious children and the Professor, eventually decided to return to the Amazon, much to her parents' joy. They were a close-knit family, and anyway, the jungle – an explosion of flora and fauna, the incessant cries of wildlife and insects, stifling heat, and the dream-like white mists – all of it was in Saffie's blood.

Saffie was also eager to learn more about the golden flowers she and her father had taken from the wizened old dwarf trees on the table-top mountain. The curandero had been willing to risk his life to obtain them, and so she was curious about their healing properties. By the time she returned home, her parents had already fertilised several flowers by rubbing the male anthers from one onto the female stigma of another. Saffie then set up a time-lapse camera to document the gradual withering of the petals, stamens, and upper portion of the pistils. Over the following months, the camera captured the hardening of the flowers' ovaries and the ensuing bulbous swelling which, in the fullness of time, developed into luminous egg-shaped fruit, hanging from the coiling, woody vines. Each yellow fruit bore the seeds of a new generation of the plant, which in turn would grow more of the mysterious gold flowers with their healing nectar...

Another important reason why Saffie wanted to fly back to the Amazon was to return little Sabu, the last known black jaguar, to his natural habitat as soon as possible. She wanted to give him a fighting chance of survival in the wild. Even though all the black jaguars had been killed by poachers and farmers, or died from habitat loss due to deforestation (more than 50% of the jaguars' range in the Americas had been burnt), there were still a few spotted jaguars left in the wild. As apex predators, ecologically they were essential.

Saffie was very excited to read that the Wildlife Conservation Society were planning on rewilding to the jungle two captive spotted jaguars – a mother and her cub. She immediately thought of Sabu. If he could become socialised with the jaguars, and be accepted by them, then Sabu would have a mother-figure to teach him how to hunt, fish, swim, and find safe hiding places to sleep, being nocturnal. Her hope was that, by the time

Sabu left to go his own way after about two years – for adult jaguars lived alone – then he would have learnt everything he needed to survive.

Saffie exchanged several emails with the rewilding scientist of the centre, Lucas Mendes, who was greatly surprised to hear about the existence of a black jaguar – and they immediately arranged for her to come to the centre.

'Wonderful to finally meet you both!' beamed Mendes, a wiry middle-aged man with a full head of mousy hair. Saffie had just walked into the rather ramshackle building in Manaus, with Sabu on a lead – the little cub looked small as he paced the stone floor with cautious interest, sniffing the air. When Saffie stopped to shake hands with the scientist, Sabu took shelter between her legs, eventually sitting on one of her feet.

'What a beautiful little cub,' smiled Mendes. 'You can't imagine how happy we were to hear of the existence of a black jaguar!'

Saffie stooped to pick up the subject in question – and Sabu was relieved to be taken into her protective arms. 'He's had all his vaccinations,' she told Mendes, 'so you can stroke him if you like.'

Mendes held out his fist to the cub, who sniffed it delicately, before he stroked the little jaguar's thick, coarse fur. From outside, there came a sequence of loud hoarse grunts, and Sabu immediately pricked up his ears.

'That is our mother jaguar, Keira. She's very vocal!'

Saffie raised an eyebrow.

'Don't worry, they're not stress calls,' Mendes assured her. 'She's probably telling off her rather lively daughter, who is very playful, very active. Keira has turned out to be a wonderful mother. She keeps Riva, her cub, very clean, well-fed, never letting her out of her sight. Which is why we believe she is a good candidate for adopting Sabu. I'm sure you're dying to meet them. Shall we?' Mendes stretched an arm to indicate the way they should go, and then led them through several rooms until they reached an external door, holding it open for the visitors. Fresh air-conditioning gave way to humid balmy heat, and they walked along a path until they reached a huge fenced enclosure surrounded by heavy-duty mesh, where there was a large pond, boulders, shrubs, trees, and a wooden nesting box in the far corner.

The mother jaguar was lounging on a platform of decking by the water, shaded by a sturdy old willow – its cascading branches softly stirring in the breeze. Tumbling by her side was a spirited little cub, who began swiping at her mother's ears playfully – while the mother's tail swished loosely over her daughter's back, as if keeping track of her proximity. They were stunningly beautiful cats with rich golden fur, and striking rosettes of black markings.

Saffie watched them, enchanted. 'Look, Sabu – see? That's going to be your new mother!'

Sabu hadn't spotted them yet as they were quite far away, and he simply looked up at Saffie – wary both of the new surroundings and a nearby stranger.

Saffie's eyes wandered around the enclosure. 'Where's the father?' she asked.

'When we found them, there were just the two of them. Females go off alone after mating, and take care of their offspring as a single parent. It's not uncommon for males to kill and eat their young, you see. We took them in because the mother had wounded her leg and couldn't hunt – so they would have died. But thankfully they're doing very well now!' He pointed out a smaller, adjacent enclosure. 'When we found out Sabu was coming we immediately built this specially, right next to them. Sabu will stay there for a few days, so that they get used to each other's scent, and seeing each other, albeit on the other side of the mesh. And we've filled Sabu's den with soiled hay taken from Keira and Riva's nesting box – to mask any unfamiliar scents Sabu will have on him.'

'Good thinking,' said Saffie.

'Rest assured we'll be monitoring their interactions and observing their body language closely, to see if there's any threatening behaviour from the mother. I hope not! And then, if everything goes well, we'll open the divider between their enclosures, so they can finally interact. But we will only do so if we feel 100% confident there is no animosity, no danger.'

Saffie sighed and hugged Sabu. She felt divided, hoping upon hope that the jaguar's mothering instincts would make her take in Sabu – but at the same time, if it was successful, she might never see the cub again. 'If… if everything goes well, and the jaguars take to each other, when will you be releasing them?' she asked.

'Actually, we had planned on releasing our jaguars last week, but after you got in contact, we put it back by several weeks. We'll play it by ear. Scouts have located an excellent strip of land in the Pantanal Mato Grosso, a protected nature reserve, where they will be safe from poachers and have plenty of forest and wetland to fish and hunt. There'll be an abundance of trees and shrubs to take shelter in. It's ideal. So their chance of surviving there is excellent. We've been studying the wild jaguars in the Pantanal wetlands for many years, as well as their corridors and ranges – and, well, with about 150k square kilometres, we're sure our little family will thrive, with plenty of room to make a home for themselves. We would have liked them to be closer to us, but as you know, the jungle around here is turning out to be a lost cause. Only last year, land the size of Fiji was completely burnt away...'

'Yes, I heard,' said Saffie, withered concern edging her voice. The rage she had harboured for many years for the blatant destruction of the jungle was petering out to dejected resignation. 'Do you think there is any hope, Lucas? That the government might realise the effects of destroying the jungle? The effect on global warming...'

Mendes stared at her with an expression that mirrored her own. 'We try to keep optimistic, but... the problem is a worldwide one, Saffie, not just here in Brazil.'

She looked at him, puzzled.

Mendes continued. 'You see, local farmers are only responding to the worldwide increase in meat consumption – particularly in Europe and China. Supply and demand. So farmers are burning more and more Amazonian jungle to make way for land to rear cattle, as well as growing soybean crops which are used to feed livestock, both locally and internationally...

'There's an interconnectedness, and in a way, many, many countries are responsible. In fact, we're all responsible – you and I included. The huge quantities of meat we eat, the palm oil and soya products we consume. The petrol in our cars and river boats. The plastic wrapping and water bottles we throw away. Our reliance on industry in general. Factories that spew out pollution. Non-biodegradable waste in landfill sites leaking toxic gases. All of this increases carbon emissions and waste, which pollutes the environment. Even the emails that you and I send to each other, and cloud storage – data stored on servers – consume massive amounts of electricity. So there's a worldwide chain, or mesh, of many, many things that contribute to global warming. The results: a warmer arctic, warmer seas, and extreme localised cold snaps, which in turn creates more so-called "natural" disasters like flooding and forest fires. The ecological imbalance creates insect and animal invasions. Fracturing the ecosystem.' Mendes paused for a moment. 'It's funny… all these things are called "acts of God", but really, *we* are the cause. Humans. And if we don't curb this catalogue of errors, well, ultimately…' he stopped to glance at little Sabu, 'it will lead to much greater species extinction.'

Saffie took a deep breath. 'Not just for animals…'

'The extinction of humans too,' finished Mendes.

They both stared at the cub for some time, until Mendes broke the silence. 'But like I said, we mustn't give up. Both for Sabu's sake, and for ours. If our plan for the jaguars is successful, Keira will have plenty more cubs, and in time, Riva as well. As I'm sure you know, spotted jaguars usually only give birth to spotted offspring. But with Sabu being introduced into the jaguar gene pool, the dominant melanistic mutation that gave him his black coat will bring about black offspring. Wouldn't that be wonderful! Jaguars are polygamous, and can live up to 15 years, so there's a good chance that, thanks to Sabu, the black jaguar might thrive once again. But… one step at a time.'

Saffie felt suddenly tearful, her head swimming with everything Mendes had said. She buried her nose into Sabu's neck, locking in his scent, his warmth, his thick fur.

When the wet drops of Saffie's tears fell onto his head, little Sabu shrunk into himself with each drip. He growled in protest.

Over the course of the following weeks, the animal keepers did exactly what Lucas Mendes had said. They kept Sabu in the connected enclosure, and both Keira and Riva watched their new little neighbour with curiosity, just as the staff watched the three animals' behaviour intently. Mother and daughter jaguar, being more comfortable, and filled with curiosity, ventured closer to the little cub – whereas Sabu was much more cautious, and kept away from the mesh that divided them. The energetic Riva even attempted to climb the fence to reach him, only to keep falling back into the dirt, then suddenly becoming distracted by chasing her tail.

After a period of observation, the staff were pleased to see that there was no animosity on either side, and in time, felt confident to open the divide between them. Riva soon came bounding over to see what was happening, though Keira immediately let out grunting vocalisations in warning, and ran with great speed to overtake the little cub, stopping protectively in front of her. Mother and daughter looked at each other, then turned to stare at the gaping hole in the mesh, their keen eyes spotting Sabu peeking out from behind his nesting box. Little Riva let her mother lead the way, and the two cautiously crossed over into Sabu's enclosure, step by step. When they reached the quivering black cub, Keira stared at him with almost amused regard. There was certainly nothing dangerous in this terrified little runt, crouching low on the ground before her, his ears twisted flat against his head. Keira gently batted him with a paw, as if challenging him – yet he daren't react, daren't move. Eventually, Keira stooped down to sniff Sabu's fur. Sabu allowed her, remaining stock still, before working up the courage to sniff her back.

At last, Keira sat down on the ground and started licking Sabu all over, for he wasn't as clean as he ought to be.

When the staff saw this, they let out sighs of relief after holding their breath for goodness knows how long. With beaming smiles they congratulated themselves, patting each other on the back.

Over the following weeks, they watched Keira take to the cub as if he were her own. Her maternal instincts kicked in, and the trio soon became accustomed to each other, with the cubs play-fighting and tumbling in the grass together, exploring here and there, and swimming side by side. And when Keira caught the live prey that their keepers released into their enclosure, piercing her teeth into the back of the skull at its weakest point so that it became instantly immobile, she allowed the two cubs to rip off their own little portions first, before tearing into the flesh herself – ravenous after the chase. At the end of the day, they all retreated into the same nesting box, and she licked both cubs clean as they settled down to sleep. Soft warm bodies huddling against her fur.

In time, a convoy of trucks containing Saffie, Mendes, and other workers from the conservation centre, transported a large container filled with precious cargo. When they arrived at the edge of the jungle of the Pantanal wetlands in Mato Grosso, it took eight men to set it down as gently as possible on the soil. They stood back as the doors were opened, watching and waiting in silence – Saffie's heart filling with anticipation, yet cracking with pain.

Keira stuck out her head from the open box first, sniffing the air, her large paws testing the ground with caution. Eventually she dared to venture out, one paw at a time, and the cubs, Riva and Sabu, followed behind. The three of them were on high alert as they took in their new surroundings. A dense swathe of trees was just metres away. Tall palms with long stems and a spiralling crown of feathery fronds. Keira looked back at her cubs – *follow me!* – and then, in the blink of an eye, she bounded into the shadowy cover of the trees. Riva and Sabu disappeared after her without one look back, little hearts thudding nervously in their chests.

And just like that, they were gone.

Saffie cried as they drove the bumpy ride back to civilisation, knowing that she might never see her Sabu again. They were tears of both joy and sadness...

•••————————————————————————•••

Nestled away in a remote village in China, little An could not believe it when he was told that Mei Hui would be returning. He kept asking his older sister, Jiao-jie, whether it was really true – on an almost daily basis. After a week of constant questioning, Jiao-jie just folded her arms with a huff. 'Believe it, dummy!' she told him, and turned back to the books on her lap. She was in a bad mood because, try as she might, she just couldn't work out her maths homework – and while they had come to love their new guardian as a kind and patient mother-figure, Yin didn't know the first thing about algebra.

As Mei Hui walked through the fields to her home, early in the morning, she breathed in the fresh country air scented with rice flowers, grassy tea plants, and the rich earthiness of fertile soil. She soaked in too, the beautiful singing of the hwamei thrush – birds popular as caged pets, though their song was never quite as melodic as when they were free. Listening to their flute-like singing as she walked, Mei Hui tried to assess her own feelings as she returned to the farm; life there, working the land, had once been like a cage to her. She remembered the depression that often descended on her, a depression that stemmed from the utter futility of a meagre, laborious existence. Work, eat, sleep. Repeat. But now, now that she had seen a little of what the world had to offer, and tasted some of its fruits, it brought about a sea change in her thinking – as if she had pulled back the curtains to a window in her mind, letting in the light.

The understanding too of where she came from, and why she was the way she was, also made her feel liberated. The door to the hwamei thrush's cage had at last been opened.

When Mei Hui crested the hill that edged her land, she looked over at the old Longan tree, with its outstretched branches that were like arteries to the air. A connector between earth and sky. An exchanger of gases. A sustainer of life. Mei Hui's heart soared when she discovered that the wild beehive was still hanging from its branch, long and bulbous, with a faint cloud of bees swarming around it, toing and froing in their daily forage for nectar. She owed her life to those bees...

Turning to look down at her house and its jade-green roof tiles, she was pleased to see that it had been well maintained, though her head was already filling with plenty more plans to improve it.

She realised that there was someone walking up the path toward her. A boy. And by the gait of his walk, and the way he swung his arms, Mei Hui immediately recognised who it was – and she waved at An with barely-suppressed excitement as he bounded up to greet her. But he slowed as he drew closer, suddenly sheepish. 'Little An!' breathed Mei Hui, beaming, and held out her arms to him. The boy overcame his initial shyness, and ran to her.

'I'm not so little anymore!' he protested, his voice a tiny bit huskier than she remembered.

Mei Hui kissed him several times on the cheek, the sensation light as butterfly wings.

An wiped his face with a sleeve, grimacing. And then he remembered. '11!' he told her, looking down at his fingers, a digit short.

Mei Hui frowned, puzzled.

'You told me to count the number of times I felt something light against my cheek. Though I didn't include the time I tripped and fell in the mud, because that doesn't count. Or when I got bitten by mosquitoes. But all the other times add up to 11. 11 promises that you would return.'

Mei Hui couldn't resist ruffling his thick head of hair. 'And they all came true didn't they?'

'Yes... but it took *forever!*'

Mei Hui smiled. Forever, to An, was anything longer than ten minutes. She looked him over; he had lost his childish plumpness. 'You've grown!' she told him, then turned him around. 'Come on,' she said, draping an arm around his shoulders as they walked toward the house. 'Tell me everything that has happened while I was away.' She knew that if she asked the same question of the older children, they would filter out anything bad and just relate what they thought she should hear. But with An's youthful candour, he would tell it exactly as it was.

'Well,' started An, and he took a deep breath before launching into a rather frenetic monologue at 100 miles an hour, of anything that popped into his head, in no particular order. He started with how annoying his big sister was, waffled on about new chicks from the hens, the middle was filled with moaning about chores, their boring new teacher at school, and he concluded by telling her about recent flooding from the river bursting its banks, and finally complaining about the man that kept coming to visit Yin.

Mei Hui stopped momentarily, surprised. 'A man? Do you... do you think they like each other?'

An stuck out his tongue in disgust. 'Eurgh, no!! Not unless Yin's blind.'

Mei Hui raised an eyebrow. 'Do I know him?'

'I... don't think so. He only started coming recently.'

'What's his name?'

An thought for a moment. 'Don't remember.'

Mei Hui sighed just as they reached the house.

From inside there came a sudden muffled shouting, 'It's Mei Hui!!' Followed by several screams of delight, and then a stampede of feet as the children rushed out, with Yin trailing behind, wiping hands on her apron.

Mei Hui was already crying so much that she could hardly see the children's faces as they hugged each other. Yin too embraced her, apologising for her appearance, for she had just finished making jianbing – folded crepes filled with egg, spring onions, and sweet soy-bean paste. 'It smells delicious. Oh it's *so* good to see you – all of you!' cried Mei Hui. They dragged her inside where they sat down to eat and drink, gushing with conversation and a thousand questions.

'Children!' scolded Yin. 'Mei must be very, very tired after travelling – you must stop bombarding her.'

Mei Hui sat back. After hours of travelling, and now with a full stomach of food and warm soy-milk, she had to agree. 'Yes, I do feel quite tired. I might need to rest for a bit.'

Jiao-jie piped up, 'But, before you go, we need to know... Did you bring us any presents?!' Eyes wide with expectation.

'Jiao-jie!' exclaimed Yin.

Mei Hui smiled, 'Of course I did! And very heavy they were too. She tugged open her rucksack, and pulled out five shiny new iPads. 'These are for you to share. I've downloaded lots and lots of books, films, and videos for you. Not just educational things, but fun stuff too, like puzzles and games. And there are loads of apps, for drawing, writing, learning. Enough to keep you going for a while, I reckon. And whenever satellite internet eventually happens around here – which I heard looks like being next year – then you'll be able to connect too. But...' she lifted a finger to her lips, 'you mustn't tell a soul, or take them out of the house, okay? Otherwise they'll be stolen for sure.'

Some of the children went very quiet with wonder, while others gasped with delight.

'Don't worry, Mei,' said Jiao-jie. A little older now, she was turning into quite a beauty. 'We have a good hiding place that uncle Aiguo made for us in the kang room.' She was referring to the kindly building company manager whom Mei Hui had entrusted with her substantial savings.

Yin got up to stack the dirty plates, explaining, 'We needed somewhere to hide the allowance money. So he built a safe for us, refusing to accept any payment. There is plenty of room inside it to hide the… computer screen thingies.'

Mei Hui melted with affection for the man. 'And how is dear uncle Aiguo?'

'Very well,' said Yin, taking the plates to the sink. 'He comes often with his wife, aunty Ting, who–'

'Who makes the best egg tarts in the world!' interrupted An, smacking his lips.

'I was going to say,' said Yin, glancing at An with a withered smile, 'that she's always so kind as to help out with the children from time to time. She used to be a teacher, you see, and has a natural way with youngsters. And An, why are always going on about food?' she asked frowning.

'He's a growing boy,' said Mei Hui.

'Too right,' agreed Yin. 'He eats non-stop, everyone's leftovers too, and yet look at him – skinny as a pencil!'

By now, the children had taken the tablets, and were huddling around each other. They had already worked out where the 'on' button was – and were cooing as they explored the apps.

Mei Hui got up, feeling quite tired. 'I'm off to nap for a little while,' she announced. 'And then I will show you how to use the iPads.' Though they were already finding their way around, intuitively working things out for themselves.

Yin threw Mei Hui a smile. 'Your room is already prepared, and the bed made up with fresh linen.'

'Thank you, Yin,' Mei Hui told her. 'You have looked after the children well, and the house too. I'm indebted to you…'

Yin shook her head vigorously. 'No. It is I that must thank you. You have given me purpose. I am happy now, very happy, and…' She led Mei Hui into the corridor, away from the children. 'And I've been meaning to tell you. I have met a man, who I like very much. We have been seeing each other.'

Mei Hui blinked at her, surprised.

Yin continued. 'Please do not worry… He is a government official who was sent to talk to the villagers about a road being constructed nearby, linking us with the nearest town. He was particularly taken by your house, and the water pipework connected to the river.' She looked down at her apron bashfully. 'He is not very good-looking, but he is a kind man, with a good heart…'

Mei Hui raised an eyebrow. Most government officials were corrupt, looking for any way they could to extort money. Even they had to eke out a living, though most of them were just plain greedy.

'He will be visiting later today, for dinner,' said Yin. 'I would like you to meet him.'

'Yes, I would like to meet him too,' said Mei Hui, and quickly turned to leave, hiding a pang of worry. She wondered about this new development with an official who may not be what he seemed… Though she would soon find out.

Mei Hui stopped and stared when she entered the bedroom. The room was much prettier than before, with white bedding embroidered neatly with lotus flowers, and the walls had obviously been attacked by the children armed with potato stamps and a pot of blue paint – simple silhouettes of plants and flowers. The window framed a pretty little dove tree outside, with white leaves dangling like pairs of handkerchiefs from its branches, wafting on the breeze.

Drugged by tiredness and jetlag, Mei Hui lay down on the bed and closed her eyes.

She immediately remembered the dream she'd had in Avernus.

That dream.

It had seemed so real.

Vision-like images edged their way into her mind.

Walking down Avernus' corridors to the store room.

Standing in front of the Dragonfly Girl painting.

Reaching a hand to touch the paint, fingers rippling lightly along its ridges as she swallowed down the nausea that came from the knowledge she was touching the ashes of a dead person.

To her amazement the girl in the painting shimmered and shifted.

A down-cast face looked up from the babbling brook at her feet.

Jade-green eyes turned to stare directly into hers.

A breathy whisper, 'Mei Hui...'

Mei Hui found herself waking. Found herself, not in Avernus, but somewhere else. Was she still dreaming? Several seconds passed before it dawned on her where she was, before she realised this was real. Relieved, she waited until her racing heart subsided, then rolled over to pull out the iPad from the rucksack on the floor, touching the screen to check the time. She had slept for nearly two hours – and, physically, felt much better from it. Though mentally, Georgina Whyte lingered uneasily in her mind...

Mei Hui stretched, toes curling into the cotton bedding, before pulling the iPad toward her and opening the Photos app. She had taken pictures of every single one of F. Jaffrey's works, the original 19th century artist – the paintings displayed at the National Portrait Gallery, as well as those found in the house of his descendant, Jeremy Fitzsimmons. Mei Hui examined the pictures closely now, zooming into the details. Especially the eyes. Out of hundreds of pictures, she had discovered a further five in which micro paintings of figures were hidden in the eye-shine – similar to the rather macabre one Milly found, capturing a man stabbing his wife. Those six tiny paintings underlined the fact that there was a secret story behind every subject's smile, every frown, every face. The pictures also hinted of a developing story of the life that Fitzsimmons the 1st had lived. Mei Hui had become instantly intrigued – wanting to find out all she could about the sitters, and their stories.

Over time, she gradually pieced things together, and was at last beginning to understand more and more about, not just Fitzsimmons, but their own abilities. Hers, and the other children's. She pondered too what they had seen when Jeremy Fitzsimmons destroyed the old oak to save Tai, and even before that, when Tai had somehow caused the sharks to save them all – and at last Mei Hui's understanding of their powers was starting to crystallise. Every time she thought about it, the full realisation made her catch her breath.

Calista threw her head back and howled and screamed and cried at the top of her lungs. Her beautiful face distorting into a picture of agony.

A red-faced Jake stood next to her, squeezing her hand so hard it hurt – though the discomfort was nothing compared to his wife's labour pains.

A masked midwife popped her head up from between Calista's legs. 'You're doing grand, Calista, just grand! 10 centimetres dilated now, so when the next contraction comes, you can push, okay? Push with *everything* you've got!'

Calista lay back in the maternity bed, panting, the waves of pain at last dispersing. 'The contractions!' she gasped. 'They hurt *so* much! C-can't you give me something for the pain?!'

The midwife shuffled uncomfortably on her seat. 'It's too late, dear, you're too far gone. But you can do this! Just a few good strong pushes, and you'll soon see your little wean.'

Jake squeezed Calista's hand. 'You got this, babe,' he said, dabbing at her sweaty forehead with a damp cloth.

Calista blubbered, 'I can't do it! It's agony!'

Jake's blue eyes darted here and there, looking for something to distract her. 'Just… just… think about that program you've been working on. The one that's been driving you insane.'

Calista blinked, eyes glazed with pain. 'Yes, yes. Okay.'

A mobile phone began ringing, startling her. 'Gaah, again!!' she huffed, bad-tempered. 'Will you turn that thing off?! It's in my bag.'

Jake scrambled through her holdall, flustered, mumbling to himself. 'Nightdress, socks, hairbrush, baby-grows, nappies… Ah! Here it is.' He switched the phone to silent just as Calista starting puffing from the pangs of another contraction. Distracted, he quickly threw the phone back inside the bag.

'Here it comes!' she said, panicking.

Jake gripped her hand in both of his. 'Remind me of the error code, Cal.'

Pain gunned through her torso in waves. The worst pain of her life, and she cried out, 'I-I can't do it!!'

'The error code. What is it?' asked Jake urgently.

Through a foggy brain, she suddenly remembered the hateful code that had been driving her mad. 'It… it's a PCI express device error. Severity NN.

U-uncorrected, non-fatal, PCI bus error…'

'Push, Calista, push!' urged the midwife.

With a mixture of intense anger for the coding error, and the desperate need to get this thing out of her, she heaved and heaved with all her might.

'The head's crowning!' said the midwife encouragingly. 'Keep pushing!!'

Calista squealed and cried and groaned, hanging onto Jake's hand for dear life. At last, the contractions subsided.

Jake kissed her messy tangle of hair. 'You're doing amazingly,' he told her.

Calista burst into tears, 'It's horrible, Jake. Horrible.'

'Look at me,' he said as he perched on the side of the bed, staring at her squarely. 'You can do this. Just like you're going to crack that code. That error message you mentioned. It's probably something to do with the motherboard.'

She wiped her tears and returned Jake's gaze. 'N-no. I… already swapped it out with a brand new one.'

Jake kissed her trembling hand. 'Good, that's good. Did you flash a new BIOS to fix the boot problem?'

Calista nodded emphatically. 'I did that too,' she said, eyes dewy. She lay back again, then thought of something. 'But… I think I can change the way the kernel addresses the hardware…'

'…And insert a number of parameters that can be passed at boot time!' finished Jake.

'Yes, yes… Oh no! No! It's coming again!' she wailed, terrified.

'Push!!' urged the midwife.

Calista hunkered down, puffing frantically, and heaving with everything she had.

In this way, the young couple went through the tremendous upheaval of childbirth – the frenzied distraction of overcoming a coding problem, in between pushing through the agonising contractions, until, at last, a little baby slithered out into the midwife's hands. Expertly, she swept it up into a soft towel and wiped off the greasy white vernix from its skin. Then she clamped the umbilical cord, cut it, gave the infant a quick examination, and delivered it straight into Calista's arms.

The new mother hugged the little bundle to her chest, all at once exhausted, wary, and ecstatic. But the skin-to-skin contact instantly soothed both mother and child.

'It's a girl!' declared the midwife, beaming as she went about cleaning up around Calista. 'A beautiful baby girl! And she's got your full head of dark curly hair, Dad,' she told Jake.

He drew closer, awed by his little daughter. 'I'm a dad!' he beamed, smitten.

'She... she's perfect,' murmured Calista, before kissing the infant's chubby cheeks. But baby's head began stretching sideways, searching for something. 'W-what's she doing?' she asked, baffled.

The midwife smiled as she mopped up the bed with towels. 'She wants to feed, that's all.'

'She's hungry already?' she asked.

'Not necessarily. Babies suckle for comfort, not just milk. The little thing's been through quite an ordeal.'

Calista winced and whispered to the baby, 'You and me both.'

'All worth it in the end!' exclaimed Jake, beaming.

'Absolutely,' said Calista, raising an eyebrow. 'Though it's easy for you to say!' she told him. Then to the midwife: 'Men have it *so* easy, don't they!'

'That they do,' smiled the midwife wryly. 'But just imagine if men had to go through childbirth, dear! The human race would've died out long ago!' she giggled. 'Anyway, joking aside, it's a beautiful thing, despite the pain. So congratulations, Mum, Dad, on your gorgeous baby girl.'

'Thanks,' said Jake, overcome.

Calista stroked baby's little tufts of hair, and looked up at Jake, tearful. 'I couldn't be happier!' she told him.

Just then, muffled vibrating came from Calista's holdall.

'You'd better get it, babe,' said Jake, stooping down to pull out her phone. 'This is the third time. Might be important.'

'I'll take the baby, if you don't mind,' said the midwife. 'I need to do some tests. I'll be quick as I can, promise.' Gently she took the infant, swaddled it in a light cotton cloth, and went to the other side of the room.

Meanwhile, Calista took her phone and answered it. 'Hello?' She listened for a few seconds, before saying, 'Hey, Dr Lambros. Okay, sure. You've got the results?' She shot Jake a warning glance, and he sat down in the chair next to her, all ears. Calista continued talking. 'Appointment? Next week? No, no. Can't you tell me now? I need to know. Jake's here. I can handle it.'

She listened for some time, and Jake watched her face intently. Watched it contort into an expression he couldn't understand. Saw it drain of colour. And his heart skipped a beat when her eyes filled with tears. Finally, Calista ended the call, then looked at Jake – numb with disbelief.

'What did he say, Cal?' asked Jake, though he already half knew, a sickening dread brewing in the pit of his stomach.

Calista could only blink in a daze.

'Babe?'

The phone dropped on her lap, and at last she glanced across the room toward her baby as the midwife put her on the weighing scales. Then she turned back to her husband. Her sweet, adoring husband. The father of her child. The love of her life. 'I'm... dying,' she told him, her voice ice-cold and detached – as if they were someone else's words. Words that didn't belong to her. Not here, not now. Not ever.

Jake froze.

The midwife stopped, and looked over.

'That was the oncologist,' she told the midwife, dazed. Calista glanced down at the phone, the innocent bearer of awful news; mirrored in its black screen was her own face warped with devastation. She stared at her newborn baby for such a long time, until at last she told Jake: 'They got back the biopsy and scan results... The cancer's spread,' her voice cracking with disbelief and despair. 'F-five months,' she stammered. 'That's how long they think I have.'

PART 2

7 THE TRUTH

As Milly entered the large cage-like prison, alone, she looked around apprehensively. The bars shut quickly behind her, followed by the second outer security door – both controlled mechanically. Locks clanged and clicked into place. The sound echoing both within the bare room and inside her head. She looked so small, so fragile, as she walked slowly up to the man that was the architect of her genetic make-up. Her seemingly calm exterior gave little hint of the heaving mass of nerves within.

Jeremy Fitzsimmons sat there at the interactive table – pale, burly, and slumped awkwardly as he blinked into the near distance, only turning toward his visitor when she was a metre away. Within touching distance.

For the second time in her life Milly saw the full, jarring vulgarity of his face. Like swearwords and profanities to the ears of the pious, the hideous sight of him made her recoil, catch her breath. She stalled.

But at last, with great effort, she forced herself to move forward. Her small steps were preceded by nothing more than faith. Faith that this man, now that the reduced drugs had restored his full mental faculties, would not instantly obliterate her into a pile of a dust. Like he'd done to V8, and the great oak, and a cascading blizzard of flies – all razed to the ground with just his mind.

There were no words.

What use were words – clunky, blundering vocalisations.

Instead, she sat down on the chair at the side of the table, and spread trembling hands out on its surface, palms upward.

He instantly grasped them, and Milly flinched from the suddenness.

His hands were cold and clammy, yet steady. They gripped hers tightly, stopping them from shaking.

And where others had only words between them, they instead had the pureness of thought. Unadulterated, clear, unambiguous.

Don't be afraid of me, he told her with his mind, bulging eyes searing into hers. They were hideous yet beautiful, like grey crystals shining from craggy black rock.

Milly mustered the strength to hold his gaze. *I can't help it,* she thought, tears – hot as burning wax – scalding her cheeks.

He grunted, paused. *I am your father. Your true father. I made you what you are. I would never harm you.*

She did not respond.

They listened to her thundering heart for some time. The rush of blood coursing through her arteries and veins. Her staccato breaths.

I... he started, hesitant. *I could make you feel... better.*

Milly stiffened. *Don't do anything to me. Don't control me.*

He blinked at her. *I would never... I just...* He stopped. *Never mind.*

Milly surged with unexpected anger, glaring at him. *Y-you killed V8! He was innocent, he was just trying to protect us!*

Fitzsimmons grinded his teeth. *He was... collateral damage. I did what I had to, to save Tai.*

B-but you can't kill! Killing someone, no matter what the reason, it... it's just wrong!

He told her slowly, firmly, *Tai would not be alive now, if it weren't for me.*

They both knew that was true. They lapsed into a fug of silence.

Fitzsimmons closed his eyes momentarily. Absorbing her feelings. *You want to know about Georgina Whyte,* he stated, cold, calculating.

Milly knew she need not reply.

He shifted slightly in his seat. *You want to know whether you can trust me.*

Again, no response.

In their minds' eye, they both saw the Dragonfly Girl painting.

Georgina Whyte captured in oil.

Her long, ash-coloured hair tumbling in beguiling curls around slim shoulders   wispy tendrils rising on a breeze. Near her head was the flash of an azure dragonfly suspended in the air. The girl was standing on a mossed boulder at the edge of a stream, dipping a foot into the shimmering water, ivory toes creating swirls and ripples. Her clothes, long diaphanous layers of white, were so sheer that the hazy form of her slim body could be seen against the light. Her face was downcast, with jade eyes caught in the gleam of a setting sun, burnished against silk-smooth skin. She was truly beautiful. Almost too exquisite to be true. Set in double-thick layers of scumbled brush-strokes, her image seemed to extrude, like she was stepping out of the canvas, into real life.

The painting itself was evidence of the painter's adoration.

Venerating her.

Immortalising her.

Both he and Milly knew: her ashes had been mixed into the colours. The oil painting was a burial place. A tomb.

His shrine to her.

Fitzsimmons stiffened as he watched Milly inspect the painting in her mind. Her hand relaxing as she lost herself in its beauty, but then tensing again as she thought of the corpse buried within.

He said nothing to ease her tension.

Instead, his body loosened, and he adjusted his hold. Each finger unfurling and then re-gripping her small wrists.

He closed his eyes.

Milly did the same.

And just like that, they entered another time, another world.

•••————————————————————————•••

Georgina Whyte was the picture of beauty, as she sat on the couch next to the young, handsome Jeremy Fitzsimmons, waiting to meet his father for the first time.

Yet as Maxwell Fitzsimmons' footsteps reverberated within the room, and she turned and absorbed the full horror of his face, that very beauty warped into an ugly, twisted grimace. Her hand, clutching firmly onto Jeremy's, began shaking uncontrollably, and she started to hyperventilate.

Jeremy immediately swung round and kneeled in front of her on the floor. "Look at me, Georgie,' he said firmly, urgently. 'Breathe!"

A wave of panic rose in her chest as she tore unbelieving eyes from his father's grotesque face, and instead stared at Jeremy. Roamed over every part of his face, over the pitted patina of surgical scars that had almost obliterated the entire left side.

Jeremy held his breath. It felt as though she was inspecting his soul, inch by inch. Felt like the weight of it had been put on a scale, and judged.

The verdict: she wrenched her hand from his, and turned from him, turned from his parents – as if they were vermin. And she backed away, holding her hands in front of her, fingers bent and twisted. *Don't. Don't come near me.* And she turned and fled.

Jeremy started to run after her, but someone held him back. Through a dizzying whirlwind of emotions, he turned, wild eyes finding his father gripping his forearm.

'I'm sorry, son,' said Max, pale with concern.

But all Jeremy could think about was Georgina, and he wrenched himself free and ran after her.

By the time he had stumbled outside, he heard the chug of her old Ford Escort. He turned toward it and saw it accelerating down the road – its exhaust wheezing a trail of smoke.

His gut instinct was to jump into his car and chase her. But his mother had just stepped out behind him, softly panting.

'Jeremy,' she said, breathy.

He paused, and turned his head slightly to his right.

'You have to let her go,' he heard her say. 'If it's meant to be, she'll come back to you.' Her voice was tremulous – from exertion, or from emotion, neither could tell.

Something juddered through Jeremy's body; a scream. A frustrated, angry scream, fighting to get out. But it never came.

He looked down at his feet. Immobile. As though they'd been glued to the ground, both by his mother's words and his own reluctant realisation. He knew, deep down, that it was no use. He'd always known. Somehow.

And it killed him. Ripped his heart into a thousand painful pieces.

Her love for him was only skin deep.

Several months later, 23-year-old Jeremy Fitzsimmons went about everyday life as though he were in a daze.

This wasn't the real life.

Real life was in his head, with Georgina, living out a fantasy, a Utopian dream. Where everything was perfect and glossy. And they were together.

Most people, after a period of mourning, or depression, have the ability to move on – in time. Eventually realising that there are many more things to live for, instead of tethering themselves eternally to the millstone of trauma. But not Jeremy.

He couldn't let go. Helpless to his superior, overpowering mind, it was just a matter of time before inaction gave way to desperation. And he caved and phoned her, several times. But she never picked up.

He called on her grandmother too, but the house went suddenly quiet when he arrived, and the door remained tightly shut.

When his father, Maxwell, saw Jeremy heartbroken, it broke his heart too. He tried his best to make things better by getting Jeremy more involved in the family business – keeping him busy, his thoughts occupied. They owned 20 art galleries worldwide, several being in various UK towns including Oxford and London, where they worked closely with Sotheby's and other auction houses. Maxwell and his chief gallerist, as sleeper-hunters, were constantly scouring the country, searching for lost masterpieces that had either been miscatalogued or over-painted. But though Jeremy tried to go along with his father and help him with work, for he knew he meant well, the boy's efforts were only half-hearted. He was an artist after all, not a businessman. Or at least, he had been.

It broke his mother's heart to see Jeremy's brushes, oils, canvases, and frame woodwork, all coated in layers of thick dust gathering like hoar frost. Eventually she began packing up his painting things, sighing as she pulled out a crate to store everything away. She stared for some time at that last, unfinished painting – roughly-sketched outlines of a boulder, the stream, a nymph-like girl with tresses of zephyr-tossed hair – before carefully rolling it up, and wrapping it in brown paper tied with string.

But what broke Anne Fitzsimmons' heart even more was, over the following months, seeing her handsome son's face bulge and whisker and deform, until he was hardly recognisable. She tried so hard to keep a brave face, tried to stay upbeat – for his sake. But cracks in her emotions soon gave way to a breakdown, and she would find herself blind with tears, half stumbling half running to the remote drawing room in the guest wing of the mansion – kicking the furniture, screaming into the cushions, and sobbing hysterically for her son. There was nothing worse than seeing someone you'd give your life for, go through an ordeal that you can do nothing about. Watching helplessly as their life crumbled before you.

Jeremy on the other hand remained quiet during the transformation.

He had no strength to fight it.

All he could do was to avoid his reflection like the plague.

And what did it matter anyway, now that the love of his life was gone.

And so, as the nightmare became real, and the sadness and deformity gradually swallowed him whole, Jeremy Fitzsimmons did nothing, said nothing, as his face silently mutated.

•••————————————————•••

Jeremy couldn't help spying on Georgina's grandmother, Viola.

Her little cottage was in a quiet, residential road not far from the stream where he had met Georgina for the first time, and so it was easy for him to park his car further along the road under a shadowy tree, and watch as the old woman came and went.

Once, after she had driven away in her car, he even got out when he was sure no-one was around, his head covered by a hood. Looking this way and that, he jumped over the hedge of her back-garden and circled the house, looking through all the windows. Hoping for a glimpse of his painting. Even though he had a photographic memory, he still felt the urge to see it in real life. It made it more real. But either it wasn't visible from the windows, or the old woman hadn't hung it up, because he couldn't see it anywhere. He was more disappointed than he imagined.

He felt a sudden urge to break in and take a proper look around, but he would have to go away and figure out how to do that without causing suspicion.

When Jeremy came back several days later and parked as close as he dared to Viola's house, he was surprised to find three or four people leaving the cottage. He could just about see that, when Viola let them out, she was wearing black and holding a white handkerchief to her nose.

Jeremy took it for granted that one of her elderly friends had passed away, so he thought nothing of it. Until he watched Georgina's silver Ford Escort pull up in the driveway, and his heart skipped a beat. But instead of Georgina climbing out of the car, a young man appeared, also in black. He was clearly Georgina's brother. There was an unmistakeable similarity – the delicate jawline, the tilt of his head, the way he walked – though he wasn't the image of Georgina, and his hair was much darker. When Viola came out to greet him, they hugged for a long time – and on parting, they could not look each other in the eye. Instead, they squeezed each other's hand, and turned away to wipe their tears – a silent, knowing exchange that only the bereaved could share. Viola went back into the house and eventually returned with her handbag. She bolted the door, and the two climbed into the car – and drove away.

Jeremy's heart was gripped.

He knew he had to follow.

And he immediately started his car, and sped after them.

Hours later, Jeremy found himself pulling up next to a cemetery in West London. It was unremarkable, a forgotten space of depressed green, next to a grey B-road. Quickly he put on his cap and flipped the hoodie over his head, before checking himself in the mirror to satisfy himself that his face was adequately concealed. Getting out, he discovered that the intense rain that just minutes before had pummelled his car was lessening to a light patter. He followed Viola and the young man as they walked through the cemetery, staying well behind. The two joined a gloomy group of people standing, shivering and wet, under the boughs of a young elm that provided only scant shelter.

Jeremy's heart was beating thunderously, for he was sure that he would see Georgina there. But there were so many umbrellas huddled together that it was impossible to make anyone out. At last, after about half an hour, the group began to disperse, and he kept himself well-hidden behind a tree next to a particularly run-down grave, while he furtively watched each passing person. He counted them, including Georgina's mother and father – and when the last two mourners passed, Viola and her companion, he stepped back, out of sight, hugely disappointed that Georgina was not there. Even after so long, every fibre in his body still ached for her.

He was puzzled, wondering why she would not be at a family funeral that so many of her relatives attended...

He stopped to listen to the gentle rhythm of the rain, smell the must of damp soil, the rising sap of vegetation. He was alone in that part of the cemetery. In the distance were a trio of gravediggers, matchstick men, busy digging and throwing hasty sprays of topsoil behind them. No doubt they would soon make their way over to this grave to backfill the hole.

Jeremy waited several minutes, wondering what he should do.

His initial thought was to leave, carrying the heavy weight of his wounded heart back to Oakley Hall. But the dead body in the ground, just there, somehow drew him. And before he knew it, he found that his feet were taking him, hesitantly, to the hole in the ground.

The hard path gave way to clumps of clay-like soil which should have been covered with grass, but for some reason wasn't. A roll of astroturf had been laid out for the bereaved, and he stepped on that, walking silently, eyes fixed on the pit before him. It yawned open as he drew closer, and he was surprised to see that it was circular, not rectangular – the edges stark and rounded, like the rim of a black hole. For some reason that he could not understand, he trembled as he drew closer. Perhaps fearful that he too might be sucked in. Into oblivion. Maybe even into hell.

The tips of his feet stopped just inches from the edge, and he peered over.

There was an urn inside.

It seemed left haphazardly, for it was not upright, but leaning slightly backward as if about to fall.

Made of wood, it was a simple cylinder etched with a delicate rose pattern – clad in glistening orbs of raindrops.

Behind it, he spied a muddied piece of fabric of a colour and design that was oddly familiar. And Jeremy froze.

With his photographic memory, he remembered. Georgina's favourite silk scarf. The diaphanous yellow chiffon she wore when there was a chill in the air. The same scarf she wore for the painting with her grandmother. And his heart burst, just as the soil gave way under his feet, and, with shock, he found himself slipping into the grave!

It took several seconds before he realised where he was, on his knees.

The urn, tumbling over before him.

Ashes spilling everywhere.

Bewildered, he found himself covered in grey dust.

He closed his eyes.

Absorbed the specks of death on his skin.

Thick clumps of dirt wedged under his nails.

The wet of fresh-cold rain on his face.

His heart turning to ice, he suddenly realised why Georgina had not been there at the funeral – and he groaned deeply.

Felt himself dying inside.

Every cell exploding; nucleic fission.

He forced himself to look up.

Forced himself to read the name on the headstone.

The neat lines of gold lettering coming into focus through his tear-streaked vision.

The words 'Georgina Whyte' blazed out from the inscription. Chiselled in perfect italics.

He doubled over, collapsed.

And howled with grief.

•••————————————————————•••

As Jeremy Fitzsimmons relived his past, Milly Bythaway lived it together with him. She felt everything he felt, becoming overwhelmed with sorrow and horror and regret.

Both their eyes were squeezed firmly shut, yet tears still flowed.

They shared his pain until they were numb. Felt dry as husks.

And, at last, when he was able, he simply told the girl, *That's the truth of it.* Deadpan. Somehow he looked directly into her mind's eye when he said this.

Milly hiccoughed with sobs, and nodded. *I see it,* she told him feebly, eyes still shut. *I see it.*

She had been scared of what she would find. But now that she knew what had happened, her heart broke for him. For she felt every iota of the pure, agonising, sting of grief that he had carried in his heart for decades. A heart so fragile, so delicate, it was as if it were made of thin glass – yet she had smashed it, just to peer inside, to satiate her curiosity. She had ripped apart his wound. Picked through the bloodied shards searching for clues. And she despised herself for it. 'I-I'm sorry,' she whimpered, again and again.

But they were only words.

Small, weak words, barely audible in that hollow cage.

'For we see as yet through a dim window obscurely,

but then face to face;

as yet I gain knowledge in part,

but then shall I fully know

even as I was also fully known.'

1 Corinthians 13:12

New Living Translation

8 THE OTHER TRUTH

Innocence is a beautiful thing. It is light, and whole. And as pure and delicate as fresh-fallen snow.

Yet snow can easily be muddied. And there are those with dark, shattered hearts – who perhaps once, a long time ago, were also innocent, who had terrible things happen to them, who no longer remain the victim. But they alchemise, gradually, almost indiscernibly, into the same evil that was perpetrated against them. Desensitised now, they in turn find themselves grappling with evil thoughts, and evil ways... cached into shrouded pockets of their mind.

And so, as Milly Bythaway connected – innocently – with Jeremy Fitzsimmons, and saw what she thought was his past, he, with his superior intellect, kept the *other* truth, the *real* happenings, hidden from her. Unseeable. Untold.

Little did Milly know, as she felt the cold, bristly grip of Fitzsimmons' fingers around her wrists, that this altered past was being projected into her mind, just as she herself, and the others, had projected an alternative past into Karl König's memories. Karma, some might say.

And so, here now is that *other* truth, the ugly reality, the true sequence of events that happened between Georgina Whyte and Jeremy Fitzsimmons. The version that he had carefully kept hidden from Milly.

Happenings, one might add, that are not for the fainthearted...

•••———————————————————•••

Georgina Whyte was the picture of torment as she fled Oakley Hall, the home of her fiancé, Jeremy Fitzsimmons.

She had seen his father for the first time – her heart struck cold by the horror of his appearance, as well as the sudden understanding of that terrible truth: that Jeremy too was changing into a hideous monster. She had seen that monstrosity with her own eyes. And quaked with fear from the sight of it.

She shivered even now as she drove, flustered hands changing jerky gears. It was a two-and-a-half-hour drive from Oxford to her home, but her mind was in such turmoil that the next thing she knew she was pulling up into the driveway of her Edwardian detached family home, sign-posted by a bright blue 'For Sale' board.

She flew into the house, and when she saw her mother sitting at the table, she couldn't help crying out to her. 'Mum... it's over!'

Agnes Whyte looked up from the laptop on the dining table, and immediately rushed to her daughter. She didn't need to ask what exactly was over, it was obvious from the state of her.

'Oh no! Poor Georgie!' Agnes exclaimed as they embraced.

Georgina buried herself in her mother's arms, sobbing. Eventually they pulled apart, and Agnes led her to the sofa. 'Come. Sit down, baby,' she urged. 'Come and tell me what happened.'

They heard a door opening, and Georgina's father, Tom, emerged from his home office – dressed in slacks, a Pringle jumper, and herringbone slippers. He came into the sitting room, curiosity aroused from the commotion. 'What's going on?' he asked.

A shaky Georgina got up to pour herself some barley water from the jug on the table, gulping it down – and so her mother explained to him: 'All I know is that it's off.'

'The engagement?!' he asked, taken aback. He lowered himself onto the sofa next to his wife, the colour draining from him.

She nodded. 'That's all I know,' she repeated.

Georgina returned blowing her nose into a tissue, eyes rimmed red. 'Dad, it was horrible. Really horrible!' she said.

Agnes blinked at her husband, nervous, then turned to Georgina. 'Oh dear, that's most unfortunate. Yes, break-ups are awful... Before I met your father–'

Georgina shook her head emphatically as she sat down next to her mother. 'No, no. I'm talking about his father. Jem's father.' She found herself quaking again, and she wedged her hands under her thighs, trying to stop the trembling. 'It was horrible!'

Tom looked at her, puzzled. 'It?'

'I-it's not human…'

He struggled to understand. 'Jeremy's father? What on earth do you mean?'

Georgina's expression creased with anxiety as she remembered. 'His face, it's like… like a monster. And my Jem! The same thing's happening to him!' She was beginning to sound hysterical.

Tom grabbed her arm firmly, trying to calm her. 'Georgie. You're not making any sense.'

'It's true, I tell you!' Wild eyes lurched from one parent to the other.

Tom said, 'So, you and Jeremy are over? The engagement's off?'

Georgina nodded.

'Did you end it, or Jeremy?' he asked.

'No, I-I just took one look at… it, and I had to get out of there. I couldn't stay a minute longer! I heard Jem calling out to me, to come back. But I had to get out!'

It took her father several seconds to absorb this. 'So… neither of you actually ended the engagement. You just didn't like his father?'

Georgina paused, then nodded uncertainly.

Tom shifted awkwardly, the thread-veins on his cheeks blooming red. His features rearranged themselves into a nondescript expression. Agnes threw him a warning glance, but he didn't notice – she instead touched his knee. 'Tom,' she said as firmly as she could, though her voice cracked.

He stiffened from her touch, but turned toward his daughter. 'Tell me it's not over, Georgie,' he said, jaw clenching, his entire body stiff.

'I-I can't marry him, Dad!' She shrank back and shook her head with fear. 'Not if he's going to turn out like that…'

For quite some time, they just sat there. Father quietly fuming, mother tense, and Georgina still in shock. The silence between them was an unwanted stranger unwilling to leave; Tom glared right into that stranger, his eyes getting harder and harder, until he exploded. 'You have to go back there!' he told his daughter. 'You have to make up!'

Georgina shook her head with disbelief. 'D-dad, please,' she repeated, her voice quivering. 'Don't make me.' She turned to her mother with pleading eyes. 'I won't. I can't.'

Mother darted a nervous glance toward her husband, then got up and sat on Georgina's other side. She put a protective arm around her shoulders, drawing her daughter closer, away from him. 'You look tired, Georgie. I think you should go to your room now, and get some rest. We can talk about it later.'

Dad got up slowly. 'You. Will. Not,' he seethed through clenched teeth. 'You will not break off this marriage because of some nonsense about the way his father looks!!'

Georgina found herself shouting back at him, 'You can't make me! You never listen to me. Ever! You're selfish. Selfish!!'

In a fit of rage, Tom's hand whipped through the air and slapped Georgina across the face. She fell back against her mother, winded, stunned. Her cheek hot-red from the strike.

Agnes enveloped her with both her arms. 'Tom!' she begged, her heart racing. 'Please! I'll talk to her. Please!!' There was something feral in her eyes, like an animal finding itself face to face with a predator. But she wouldn't go down without a fight. 'Don't do this!'

Tom stepped closer, his hand flicked upward – and both mother and daughter tensed. They smelled the alcohol on his breath, the sweat from his body. The wildness in Georgina's eyes transferred into his. 'Dad, no!!' shrieked Georgina, her voice cracking with fear.

And he froze. His hand raised high, stopped mid-air. He looked up at it, as if it were a thing possessed, as if he didn't recognise who it belonged to. At last, it dropped slowly down. He turned and walked out of the room, swiping an aggressive hand behind him – done with their stupid pettiness.

Agnes heaved a deep breath, and pulled her daughter into her. They sobbed with both relief and despair.

•••————————————————————————•••

Two weeks later, mother, father, and daughter looked like the perfect family when they arrived at a private club, Home House, dressed for lunch. None of them though were in the frame of mind to go out, let alone dine in public. But they had already booked a table a month ago, in honour of Georgie's cousin, Maisy, who had recently graduated from Warwick University. They met her at the Central London Georgian townhouse, and went straight through to the drawing rooms, where they enjoyed the plush 18th century décor interlaced with touches of modernity. They sat down stiffly, and settled in – and before long they were regaled with delicate pastries, finger sandwiches, and a rainbow of macarons that were as light as air. Georgina and her mother had the social wherewithal to elicit a light stream of polite conversation with Maisy, as tea was poured into bone china cups, and the delicacies shared – whereas Tom, on the other hand, could not, and indeed did not, hide his obvious disquietude.

'A-are you all right, Uncle Tom?' asked young Maisy rather nervously, daring to look upon the man's stern face.

He harrumphed and nodded dismissively. 'I'm fine, girl. Don't bother about me,' he said, and went back to filling his plate with more of those ridiculously tiny sandwiches.

'Moving doesn't agree with us,' said Agnes, smiling at Maisy. 'It's jolly hard work, you know, liaising with the moving people! We also had to put a lot of our things into storage because the new house is a little smaller – so that in itself was an ordeal. Though I have to say that things are much more manageable now! It was such hard work looking after that big old place before. House-keeping was a nightmare I can tell you. Never-ending work for the cleaner.' She glanced across at her daughter. 'Don't you agree, Georgie?'

Distracted, she blinked at her mother, saying 'Yes,' rather half-heartedly, before realising she needed to put in more effort. She turned to her cousin. 'You must come and visit, Maise,' she breathed. 'It's in such a quiet location. The old place was far too noisy in the centre of town. And my little bedroom has much, much more light. It's so lovely to be woken by birdsong, rather than noisy traffic.'

Agnes smiled, proud of her daughter, before noticing a passing waiter and taking the opportunity to hale him.

Tom glared at his wife. 'What now, woman?'

'I-I just thought we could do with some more tea and sparkling water,' she said, faltering slightly.

The waiter arrived and heard her. 'More drinks? Certainly, Ma'am!' he said with a smile, before turning on his heels.

'Hang on a minute,' said Tom, and the waiter stopped and turned back to them. 'Cancel that,' Tom told him. 'We've had more than enough. While you're here, you can put all this on the tab because we'll be leaving soon.'

The waiter hesitated, looking from Agnes to Tom, before nodding and walking off.

'Well, I'm stuffed,' said Georgina brightly, hoping to diffuse the tension. 'The pastries were to die for, and I've eaten far too many.'

'It was lovely!' smiled Maisy. 'Thank you, Uncle Tom, Aunt Nessie.'

Agnes squeezed the girl's arm affectionately. 'Oh you're more than welcome. And again, congratulations on your graduation. John and Bel must be so proud.'

The waiter returned, looking embarrassed. 'Erm, Mr Whyte, I'm so sorry but it seems you haven't settled your account for several months, and the Visa card details we have on file for you aren't working.'

Tom turned bright red. 'Must be an old card,' he mumbled as he got up. 'I'll go over and sort it out,' he said, not wanting their guest to hear any more than she need to.

When he went off with the waiter, Agnes smiled nervously. 'The bank sent him a replacement card recently. That must be it! I suspect, with all the moving business, he forgot to inform the club.' She rolled her eyes.

After several minutes they noticed a commotion, and they looked over to find Tom going through his wallet, taking out card after card, getting more vocal as they tried each one on the card-reader – but they all failed. 'There must be something wrong with your machine-thingy!' they heard Tom say gruffly from the other side of the room.

The manager frowned. 'It's been working all morning, Mr Whyte. This is the first time it's failed today. Perhaps you should phone your bank?'

Tom glared at him, 'What are you suggesting, man! There's nothing wrong with my bank accounts!'

'I'm not suggesting anything. It could be a simple banking error – one that a phone call might easily remedy.'

A flustered Agnes scraped back her chair, grabbed her handbag, and quickly went over. She spoke discreetly with the manager, nodded, then took out her purse and pulled out some cash. When she returned, she looked quite pale. But as always, she smiled bravely at her daughter and Maisy, smoothing back loose strands of hair behind an ear. 'Well, looks like we might have to change our bank! They're getting more and more unreliable recently. Dreadful service. Oh is that the time?' she said, glancing at the old grandfather clock ticking quietly in the corner. 'I'm afraid we need to dash off, Maisy. Tom's got boring old business stuff to deal with.'

'Yes, yes, of course,' said Maisy, looking at her watch. 'Actually, it's perfect timing, because I'm meeting a friend to go to shopping in half an hour. Might as well make use of being in town and all the lovely shops! I've been meaning to go to Fenwicks for ages,' she said with obvious delight. Turning to Georgina, she asked, 'Do you want to join us, Georgie? You remember Alice, from school? Alice Bailey. I'm sure she wouldn't mind if we made it a threesome.'

Agnes gave her daughter a warning glance, but Georgina already knew what to say. 'Thanks, Maise. But I've got some boring old application forms to complete. For internships. I've been putting them off for too long.' She held her arms out to her cousin and they embraced. 'So lovely to see you again!'

'Likewise,' smiled Maisy, and they parted.

They looked around for Tom, but he had already left the room, so they went to the cloakroom to fetch their jackets. They found him at reception using one of the desk phones, deep in a rather intense conversation.

Maisy waved farewell before going off, and Georgina and Agnes walked a few metres away, out of earshot.

'That was horrendous,' muttered Georgina, glaring with shame at the neat bows on her leather slip-ons. 'I didn't think it would come to this!'

'Business has been bad for quite some time,' said her mother feebly. Now that there was no-one around, she didn't need to put on a front. 'Dad doesn't talk about it much, but the company's been in trouble for years. And now that we're in recession, it's just made everything worse.'

Georgina looked up and stared at her. 'Is that why...' she stopped, hesitated. 'Is that why Dad was so desperate for me to marry Jeremy, and why he got so mad when I broke off the engagement?'

Agnes turned away to put on her jacket.

That was all the answer Georgina needed. 'It was to get at Jeremy's money, wasn't it?' Again her mother avoided her gaze. Georgina shook her head, 'I knew it. I knew it was something to do with the business. And now that we're broke, we're down-sizing, moving to some... some rubbish house in the middle of nowhere!'

Her mother didn't answer for a long time. Eventually she heaved a laboured sigh. 'This rubbish house you're talking about,' she said quietly, 'enjoy it while it lasts, because even that...' she paused, unsure if she should tell her, but decided to anyway. 'Even that's uncertain.'

Georgina blinked at her, dumbfounded. She shook her head. 'I... I don't believe you.'

Her mother glanced at her briefly before swiping away a slither of a tear. 'Believe it,' was all she said, her voice low.

••——————————————————————••

Almost a year had passed, and the Whytes were still in their new house. But only just.

Tom's crippled business had been bleeding money, with an accrued debt of millions, which meant that they needed to spend hundreds on putting the company into voluntary liquidation. The family then had to gather everything possible to survive, eventually exhausting all their liquid assets. But their sizeable mortgage of just over £90 a month, plus all the usual outgoings, still had to be paid for – so they began to sell anything and everything they could. After storing their furniture, they ended up having to take it all out again, to be sold to raise funds. The Prime Minister Edward Heath's three-day week to conserve electricity had ended in March – but the Whyte household continued with electricity-saving, as well as conserving gas, food, and water. Hard times called for hard measures.

It came to the point when Agnes had no choice but to – reluctantly – ask her mother, Viola, for help. Though very soon, even Viola's savings were in danger of being wiped out. Viola knew that to keep her daughter and granddaughter with a roof over their heads she would have to start selling the antiques her husband had collected over the years… and maybe one more thing.

She had hung Jeremy Fitzsimmons' painting in the lounge, giving it pride of place. It took up an entire wall, but she didn't mind, because it brought her such pleasure. She often stopped to stare at it for countless moments. Breathing in its beauty, and silenced with awe and wonder that not only did she own such a unique painting, painted (she had convinced herself) by the progeny of the great F. Jaffrey no less – but also that it perfectly depicted the relationship she had with her dear granddaughter. Each daubed brush-stroke blending, interweaving, and criss-crossing into a sublime whole. A true work of art.

It broke her when she realised she had to sell it.

It was either that, or the cottage. And Viola could not bear to leave her home, for it had been in her family for generations.

Finding a buyer for the painting was easy enough. The purchaser used a specialist arts removal firm, who sent round three men in pristine overalls – they carefully took down the painting, protected the edges with foam tubing, bound it in special anti-scratch blankets, and lastly, placed it in a custom-built wooden crate.

All that was left was a faint rectangle on the wall, and a hole of pain in Viola's heart.

Had Georgina come to visit her as often as she used to, Viola imagined that she too would be upset that the painting was gone forever, because she loved it so. But the truthful reality was that, almost a year after her break-up with Jeremy, Georgina was still ambivalent about her feelings toward him – she at times imagined she still loved him, but at others, the very thought of being with him in that… hideous state, made her want to retch. Which is why she stopped visiting her grandmother, because to be in such close proximity to Oakley Hall where Jeremy lived just a few miles upstream, would have been torturous. It was hard enough floundering through the unpredictable waves of conflicting emotions, let alone moving home, and coping with the stress of starting a new job working as an intern in a major pharmaceutical company.

One thing was certain after everything, she would never be the same.

The carefree, happy-go-lucky girl that met Jeremy by the river, that chased after the Polaroid tumbling downstream, laughing and shrieking, and, when they sat down to catch their breath, that picked grass from his hair – such an innocent yet intimate gesture – *that* Georgina was gone, never to return. She was a memory from aeons ago, visiting her only in her dreams.

And in those same dreams, she saw Jeremy's perfect, handsome face. She cupped his cheeks with golden hands, and looked deep into those crystal-grey eyes. Eyes that were raw with love for her. Eyes that told her he would live and die for her. And when he murmured those words out loud, 'I love you,' in every dream, almost every night, Georgina found that she could only stare at him, unable to answer, despite wanting so badly to return his words. Instead, she was rendered mute – as if someone had bound her mouth with a rag so tight she could hardly breathe.

•••————————————————————•••

Tom Whyte, Georgina's father, also would never be the same.

He could not express himself: the powerlessness of being unable to provide for his family, the feeling of abject failure as a businessman, a husband, and father – the only alternative was to retreat into silence and slowly drink himself into oblivion. And in between sleeping off hangovers, rare occasions of being sober, and drinking some more, he ripped into his family with anger and criticism. Because then the focus would no longer be on *him* and *his* shortcomings.

Agnes returned to work as a chartered accountant, because they needed every penny they could get – though she soon discovered that working actually made her happier than she had been for a long time, because now she had a purpose, and a job that she was good at. And in this way, with both Agnes and Georgina bringing in money, together with Viola's sizeable gift of money, they began to claw and scrape back at the mountain of debt under which they were buried.

Things were beginning to look up, at last... until Georgina befriended someone at work.

His name was Robert Chambers – an amiable chap, and a neat freak, having agreeable features though with a slightly crooked nose. He was one of those charming, endearing people that everyone warmed to instantly, working as a physician in the pharmaceutical company's R&D department, where they were developing new and effective antibiotics. Georgina was asked to assist his team due to staff shortage, and the two soon became friends.

When he asked her to join him for lunch, Georgina agreed quite breezily, barely giving it a second thought.

They sat opposite each other in the staff cafeteria – Georgina with her usual salad, this time chicken, and Robert with a plate of steak and chips – he looked her over as she quietly crunched a carrot.

'You seem distracted,' he told her, unabashed. 'In fact, now I think about it, you're distracted quite a lot.'

Georgina looked up at him, brought back to reality. 'Do I?' she asked, surprised. She was remembering how, whenever she ate with Jeremy, they always helped themselves to each other's food, as though nothing between them was exclusive. It was always shared.

Robert watched her. 'You're doing it again – that faraway look. You look like this all the time in the lab. I thought it was because you were concentrating on your petri dishes and pipettes, but even here, having lunch, it seems like you're here physically but your mind is somewhere else.'

She blinked up at him. 'I'm sorry, Robert. I didn't realise. It's just that… there've been… family problems, sort of. And, well, I can't seem to get them out of my mind.' She swallowed. 'Has that… has that ever happened to you?'

'Me? Usually, any kind of family problem and I run a mile!' he smirked.

Georgina sighed wistfully. 'That's exactly what I did. Run away. But after almost a year now, nothing's changed.' She shrugged, smiling sadly. 'Not surprisingly, sticking my head in the sand hasn't made the problem go away!'

Robert thought about it. 'You need a distraction. You need to get away and have a change of scenery, clear the cobwebs, don't you think?'

'If only it were that simple.'

He put down his fork and looked at her head on. 'D'you want to tell me about it? A problem shared, as they say.'

'You... you really want to know?'

'I do!' he said encouragingly. 'You're my friend, I care about you.'

She thought for a while. 'You probably wouldn't believe me if I told you. It... it's quite fantastical. I can hardly believe it myself.'

'Try me!' he said, daring her.

She seemed just on the verge of telling him – but then quickly shook the thought from her head. 'I-I can't. Sorry! It won't help, telling you, I don't think...' She was paralysed by indecision.

He stared at her, narrowing his eyes. 'Can I make another suggestion? You said you ran away. What about facing it. What about going right up to that big ol' hunk of a problem, and telling it what for! Just let rip. Let it all out, and get it off your chest. Don't you think that'd help?'

Georgina slanted her eyebrows, intrigued by this novel idea. 'Let rip...' she repeated thoughtfully, before suddenly doubting herself. 'I don't know if I can.'

'You might at least get some resolution... possibly,' he shrugged.

Georgina paused to absorb the flutter of nerves exploding in her chest – it was waking up something deep within her. Fear? Anticipation? She wasn't sure. But she suddenly realised, she had to try. Strangely, the thought of it both excited her, and terrified her.

•••———————————————————•••

Georgina stared at the page in her little white address book for some time. His cursive handwriting was neat and deliberate, that sequence of letters and digits so familiar. The page was worn from the many times she'd thumbed her way there, the edges yellowing. She remembered well that time he wrote in it with his fountain pen. He became oddly quiet as he carefully lettered his address and telephone number, the colour draining from his face – while she, instead, watched with mounting excitement as she leant eagerly over his shoulder, so happy to at last be making the appointment to meet his family. She understood now why he was nervous, though he had tried to cover it with a weak smile.

Remembering all this, she ran her fingers along the lines of faded ink.

Finally, Georgina took a biro and a leaf of vellum writing paper, and scribbled: '*I need to see you. Will you meet me by the stream where we first met?*' She wrote the date and time, and finished it off with: '*I just want to say a proper goodbye. G.*' She didn't want him to get his hopes up.

Compared to his writing, hers was scruffy, the lines uneven – perhaps a reflection of the state of her mind. But she refrained from rewriting it to make it perfect, because it didn't seem right – nothing is perfect, not really. Though in the beginning, to Georgina, Jeremy was perfect in every way. He was handsome, kind, loving, considerate, generous. And that was her downfall right there. Thinking he was perfect for her, when no-one is faultless, no-one is without defect. No-one is good all the time.

She stared at the note, eventually folding the paper into an envelope and licking the edge of the flap to stick it down. Copying out his address was even more painful than writing to him – it was to be the last time she would have anything to do with Oakley Hall. The last time she would see him. Her hand began to shake, and she paused, waited several seconds until she was calm again, before finishing it off. She stuck on a first-class stamp, then put it in her bag for taking to the post-box later.

There, it was done. And she heaved a sigh.

•••———————————————————•••

Of course, it did have to rain that evening.

Thankfully it was only a light patter, a spring shower, so at least it wasn't going to soak them through. The air was ripe with the heady perfume of jasmine – the scent, as she walked along the stream, seemed to bewitch her, making her feel lightheaded, dizzy, intoxicated.

Beside her, like an old friend, the dark stream gurgled and trickled as if in melody. Above, a thousand leaves rustling on the wind's breath was its accompaniment.

She felt a ray of warmth on her neck, and she stopped, turned, and looked up through a parting between the trees. The light from a setting sun dazzled her, and she lifted a hand to her eyes, mesmerised by the gold that seeped between her fingers. As she continued along the path, she glanced sideways at the sky – and her mouth dropped open. A rainbow appeared, as if by magic. A spectrum of hues in a flawless arc – like iridescent arms wrapping around the sky.

A voice came from behind her, 'Impossibly beautiful, isn't it…?' The tone of his voice was so heavy with sadness that it was unrecognisable. Yet it could only be Jeremy.

Georgina's heart leapt, and she turned round to find him in the shade of a weeping willow – above him, pendulous, twisting spirals swaying softly.

'Jem!' she breathed, eyebrows slanting. Though she was pale, with dark circles under her eyes and hair scraped back in a messy ponytail, she was still incredibly beautiful.

She stared for a long time, but was only able to discern the form of him – those long, slender legs, arms hanging loosely by his side. His upper chest and head were swathed in shadow, making his voice seem disconnected, detached, when he said, 'It… it's good to see you.'

Georgina blinked at him. 'Is it? I treated you so badly…' Pausing, she wiped a furtive tear, willing herself to go on. To bare her soul. 'I-I wanted…no, *needed* to tell you… my head, it's been all over the place since that day. Since I ran away. And I haven't been able to forgive myself for the way I behaved. For not answering your calls. For not explaining.' She stopped to see if there might be some reaction, a sneer, or hurt words, anything. But he said nothing. She asked warily, 'Do you… do you hate me?'

He took a deep breath. 'Not anymore.'

'You should,' she said, gulping. 'I deserve to be hated.'

Jeremy shifted awkwardly, foliage rustling around his feet. 'It's not all your fault,' he admitted. 'I wasn't exactly honest with you… about the surgeries I was having. I told you it was because I had skin cancer, but that was a lie. It was hard for me to tell you the truth because… I couldn't bear the truth myself. I convinced myself that it wasn't going to happen, that I could fight it. You see, in my family, on my father's side, there's some kind of inherited defect… a physical defect.'

'Your father,' murmured Georgina, remembering the image of his face as if she'd seen it only yesterday.

'You worked it out, didn't you? That day, when you saw my Dad. You worked out that the same… defect was happening to me.'

Georgina looked down. 'Yes, I did. It was a shock. But I should never have left you like that,' she said, ashamed of herself. 'So suddenly.'

'It doesn't really matter anymore. This *is* the final goodbye, after all...'

Georgina wondered whether he was trying to end the conversation, whether their meeting was too painful. But then she remembered the note she had written: *'I just want to say a proper goodbye. G.'* She paused, trying to analyse her feelings. Was this the resolution she so desperately needed? Did she still love him? Or was it really over? She breathed in, and out, trying to work out what her heart was telling her. After several minutes, she began to feel something. That was it. She ached. Her chest ached for him. As if her torso was being rent asunder. And she suddenly felt an intense desire to run to him, and embrace him, and tell him that everything was going to be all right. She closed her eyes, willing herself to do it, but her feet remained unmoving. Tears fell down her cheeks – small, unseen drops of water, seemingly insignificant, yet they carried with them a flood of despair and regret. She at last managed to say, 'I came here because... I thought... I thought I wanted to make a clean break.'

Jeremy wasn't intending to respond, being so overwhelmed with sadness, but he found himself saying, 'I think after almost a year, it's granted that we're broken.'

Broken. He didn't say that they had broken up, he said they were broken. *He* was broken. And the thought of it made her feel awful. 'I'm so sorry!!' she cried. She hated herself for doing this to him. Hated her ambivalence. One minute she yearned for him, and the next, she wanted to run. *What's wrong with me?!* she thought, again and again. In the end, she was so miserable, that she just decided to tell him – her voice lowering to a rumble. 'I meant to come here to end it with you, Jeremy, but... but I feel so conflicted. I don't know! I just don't know what to do, how to feel, what to think! I-I'm sorry I'm such a mess...'

She heard him breathe deeply several times, as if readying himself, bracing himself to break through a wall of reluctance.

At last he said softly, slowly, 'I never stopped loving you.' He paused momentarily. 'You hurt me, a lot. But... seeing you here, now, I know that I still love you. And somehow I know I will always love you. When you leave this place, when you've forgotten me. Through every twist and turn of the dark stream of my life, through every moment – I will be quietly loving you. Even when I'm old and grey and senile. Even when I'm gone. In the end, my love, for you, is all that will be left.'

Those words. Those sweet, tender words! So overwhelmed was Georgina, so filled with emotion, that she didn't know whether to cry with happiness or despair. Her head was in turmoil, her heart was breaking. Every fibre of her body throbbed with that aching pain.

Jeremy took one step forward, dappled shadows moving over his form.

A short, brass-blond beard came into view.

He said, 'There's only one way for you to find out how you really feel.'

As he stepped out into the light, Georgina braced herself, gasped, raised a nervous hand to her mouth. She blinked, as if blinking away cobwebs from her vision. And she at last saw his face.

Her expression changed from surprise, to shock, to horror… and then to deep sorrow. 'Oh Jeremy!' she cried, and found herself going to him, magnetised, stopping so close she could feel his body warmth and the silk of his breath on her forehead. Her eyes roamed over every detail of his face – and before she knew it, her hands reached up to cup, so tenderly, his misshapen, bristly cheeks. Hot tears dripped between her fingers.

Her expression was carved with grief. Grief for the death of his natural, beautiful appearance, swallowed up and buried deep underneath a grave of hideosity. And her heart broke again and again – for him. Before she realised what she was doing, she leant in and kissed him. Their trembling lips melting into each other. And they kissed as though this was the only kiss, in the whole world, throughout all of time. The sweetest kiss of their lives. So sweet, that when they parted, Georgina touched her mouth as if it was honeyed.

Jeremy opened his eyes, unable to stop the tears. He knew now what he'd been wondering ever since she left him. 'You do love me,' he murmured, choked. He had sensed it in her when they touched. Where she had been blinded by a blizzard of confusing emotions, his powers were able to pierce right through to the heart of her and discern what she herself could not.

Like an epiphany.

Standing here, alone with him, Georgina at last realised it too – after the kiss. 'Yes,' she said, smiling with wonder. She beamed when the full realisation hit her. 'I do! I love you!' And she threw her arms around him and laughed. Smelled that familiar musky warmth of him. The weight of his body against hers. It was like coming home after being abroad in a strange land.

Jeremy picked her up in his strong arms, and twirled around and around with her – becoming dizzy with vertigo and sheer happiness.

The perfume of jasmine. The golden hues of a setting sun. The patter of light rain underneath a perfect rainbow. The discovery of their love for each other. All conspired to make this evenfall as wondrous and as enchanting as a fairy-tale.

They tumbled onto the damp ground, laughing.

Falling into each other's arms, they kissed again. Eventually lying back to watch the rainbow for those few hours that it existed, whispering to each other, until the sun disappeared and the colours were gone.

●●●————————————————————————————————●●●

Two days later, when Georgina returned to work after the weekend, Robert Chambers was amazed to find her a different person. There was a glimmer in her eyes that he'd never seen before. It made her even more irresistible to him.

After Georgina greeted him, she turned to put on a white lab coat over her bell-bottoms and wide-collared shirt, habitually pushing up the sleeves.

Robert lingered as he looked her up and down admiringly. 'You're different!' he said with a wry smile. 'I take it you took my advice?'

'I did!' she said, turning back to him and raising an eyebrow – a tantalising expression on her face. 'And it was very good advice, Robert. Thank you!'

'I need to know more!' he said, intrigued. 'Coffee?'

Georgina looked at her watch. 'It's late… We should work.'

Robert peered over her shoulder to glance at her watch. 'Is that the time!' They turned and started walking to the laboratories. 'How about lunch instead?' he asked.

She thought about it. 'No can do. All of us interns have to meet Suggs for assessment.' Suggs was their R&D department manager.

'Sounds daunting! Though I should tell you that the old guy isn't half as bad as he looks – I'm sure he'll give you a glowing report. What about a drink after work then?' He put on a mock arch-villain German accent, saying, 'I must find out all your secrets!'

Georgina laughed. 'Okay, okay! A drink after work it is. Though I can't stay long, I'm meeting someone later.' They turned into the laboratory, and she went over to her workstation.

Robert stopped to watch her, a strange look on his face – until a work colleague came along the corridor and greeted him, distracting him, chatting with him for several minutes. When at last the colleague left, Robert turned to look for Georgina again, but she was not there. Remembering that he too was late, he quickly walked down the corridor to his laboratory.

•••————————————————————•••

The Black Lion pub was, predictably for a Monday night, rather quiet.

The lighting was subdued, the ambience relaxed, and the earthy patina of oak tables, stools, and bar gave the place a rustic, homey feel. Georgina and Robert sat on the soft brown leather of a Chesterfield sofa, their drinks – two glasses of wine, white for Georgina, red for Robert – were set on the coffee table before them with a complimentary bowl of pork scratchings. They chatted animatedly about Georgina's assessment, which had gone well, before Robert took a gulp of his wine and asked her how her weekend had been, raising eyebrows expectantly.

'Firstly,' she said, smiling, 'we've had good news in that Dad's just been given work by the Dorchester Hotel. They head-hunted him, and offered him a senior marketing role. They think his years of experience can add value to their team – which is great news! Things have been pretty tight recently, but they're looking up at last.'

Robert beamed. 'I'm really happy for you, Georgie. That's great news! Is that why you've been on cloud nine all day?'

Georgina blinked, her expression dissolving into wonderment. 'No.

Well, yes, that's part of it. But it's mostly to do with the fact that I took your advice, Robert. That thing I was telling you about the other day, when I ran away, well... I contacted him, like you suggested, to talk–'

'Him?' asked Robert, a nondescript expression on his face.

'Yes, an old flame. Actually, we were engaged. But... but something happened. I found out something about his family last year, and I just couldn't go through with it. That's when I left him, without a word of explanation. I... I'm not proud of myself. It was quite a shock, a knee-jerk reaction I suppose. But like I said, I took your advice, and contacted him – and we met on Saturday.' She sighed. Even recounting it was dredging up so many feelings.

'I thought... I thought you said it was something to do with family!' said Robert, looking miffed.

Georgina raised an eyebrow, surprised by his reaction. 'Did I?' she thought about it. 'Maybe I did. My Dad didn't want me to break off the engagement, and things kind of blew up. So yeah, it caused a big rift in my family. He...' she stiffened, remembering the sharp sting of her father's slap '...Dad didn't speak to me for ages.'

Robert shifted awkwardly. 'Georgie! If I'd known it was an ex you were talking about, I would never have suggested going to him. You should have told me!'

Puzzled, she wondered why he was taking everything so personally. 'I- I'm sorry, Robert. I didn't think. Anyway, I didn't want to go into detail. It's still quite... raw. Even after all this time.'

He shook his head, a withered look on his face. 'Never mind. Anyway, you said you were shocked by something about his family... What could have been so shocking?'

Georgina hesitated, but eventually caved. 'Well... there's a kind of hereditary disease in his family. I-it changes their appearance for the worst. His Dad has it, and I discovered that he has it too. I feel terrible for them!'

'Really?!' exclaimed Robert, both intrigued and inwardly glad. 'Is it really that bad?'

She nodded slowly, seriously. 'Yes. I saw the full effects of it in Jeremy for the first time when we met on Saturday. That's his name, Jeremy. H-he was completely different! It broke my heart.'

'So, I guess you ended it, once and for all?' asked Robert, matter-of-fact.

Georgina was brought back from her thoughts. 'That's the thing. I thought it was over, but... but it turned out that I fell in love with him all over again!' She beamed, her expression a mix of both amazement and happiness. 'I can hardly believe it myself. You see, even though he isn't the same person physically, essentially he's still my Jeremy. Inside. He's still the same man I fell in love with.'

Robert looked suddenly out of sorts, and glared at his glass of wine for some time. He eventually grabbed it and gulped it all down – his face slowly turning red.

Caught in her own little bubble of happiness, Georgina only just noticed his frown. 'Robert? You look... funny.'

'Funny?' he repeated drily, slumping back and folding his arms. 'I'm guessing you mean odd funny, rather than ha-ha funny,' he smirked. He couldn't look at her.

They lapsed into silence, until it suddenly dawned on her. 'Robert, do you... do you like me...?' It was half question, half dread.

He finally managed to look up at her briefly, sparks of anger in his eyes. But he said nothing.

Disarmed by the change in him, Georgina found herself floundering. 'Robert, I... didn't know. You're always so charming and nice – to everyone. I-I didn't think you thought of me any differently to anyone else. I thought we were just friends. You yourself kept saying we were friends...' she trailed off, at a loss.

'Just friends?' he repeated.

'I'm sorry! If I knew you liked me, I would never have chatted so much with you. And of course I wouldn't have told you about Jeremy like that.'

'I suppose you wouldn't have come to my house the other day to "discuss work", either? Or have lunch with me, or come here for a drink?'

Georgina's eyes zigzagged, looking for words. '*You* asked me to your home to go over a work plan for the next day. You said it was important. And I lunch with other work colleagues too, though not all that often...'

Robert glowered at her, incredulous. 'So, I'm just a work colleague to you!' he said through gritted teeth. When she didn't answer, he turned to grab his jacket, draped across the arm of the sofa. Taking out his wallet, he extracted a £1 note, and threw it on the table, grumbling, 'I find it hard to believe what you say, Georgina. We've been working together for months now, and I'm pretty sure you knew how I felt. I don't buy that you had no idea...' He got up and made to leave – but then stopped, turned his head slightly, and growled, 'I never thought you'd be such a tease...' – before marching out.

'Robert!' called out Georgina, not caring about the strange looks from the others in the pub.

But he had already left – and she stared after him, flustered, cheeks flushed, as the pub door swung closed. Her eyes gravitated downward, and she noticed her watch, realised the time. A shaky hand grabbed her handbag and cardigan, and she too left the pub with her head down.

•••———————————————————•••

The Whyte household got a phone call just after 9 o'clock at night, and Georgina's mother, Agnes, padded down to the hallway in her nightgown and slippers, with sponge rollers in her hair, sure that it would be her daughter telling her she was on her way home.

But it was a voice from the past, and it threw her. 'Jeremy?' she breathed, stunned to hear from him after so long. Out of the blue.

'Agnes,' he said. 'I-it's nice to speak to you after... after so long. I'm sorry to be calling late, but is Georgie there?' His voice was more subdued now, his confidence gone.

'No...' she said, trailing off. 'She went out for a drink with a colleague after work. They probably went to get a bite to eat as well. Actually, I'm expecting her home anytime now.'

'A colleague?' repeated Jeremy, confused. 'She was supposed to meet me. At seven.'

'You were meeting together?' asked Agnes in disbelief. 'She never mentioned. She only told me she was going to the Black Lion straight after work. That's all.'

Jeremy's momentary silence was filled with disappointment. 'Well, when she gets back, will you ask her to call me?'

'Yes, yes, of course. Where are you staying?'

'I'll give you the number of the B&B. I'm in room 104.'

'Hang on a mo.' Agnes opened the drawer of the phone stand, took out a pad and a pencil, and scribbled down the telephone number he gave her, followed by the room number. Finally she said, 'It's good to hear from you, Jeremy. Really good.'

'Thank you.' His voice was tinged with sadness.

'Take care, Jeremy.' They hung up.

Agnes stared at her scribble of the '01' telephone number for some time, amazed that Georgina hadn't told her anything about Jeremy, and meeting him in London. But it explained why her daughter had been so much happier since Sunday. He was back in her life. Agnes heaved a deep sigh, left the pad and pencil next to the telephone and turned to leave – when the phone rang again. She went back to answer it, quite sure it was her daughter – she wanted to quiz her about Jeremy. But it was a stranger's voice.

'Agnes Whyte?' said a woman, apprehensively.

Puzzled, Agnes said, 'This is she.'

'You're listed as Georgina Whyte's emergency contact... I'm the head nurse at the Wellington Hospital, and I found your details in her purse.'

Agnes' heart stopped, and she held her breath.

The woman continued. 'I'm afraid your daughter's been badly injured... You need to come to the hospital immediately.'

'W-what happened?!' asked Agnes urgently, trembling with fear.

The woman paused. 'It's best that you come straight to the hospital, right now.'

'Yes, o-okay.'

'If you're driving, please be careful,' warned the nurse. 'We'll be expecting you.'

'Th-thank you.' Agnes' hands shook as she pressed and released the phone prongs and redialled a number from memory. 'Hello? Can I speak with my husband please, Tom Whyte.' She listened to the other person for several seconds. 'Yes, I know they're having a dinner meeting, but it's urgent. Okay, yes, you need to find him immediately – and tell him that his daughter's in the Wellington Hospital. Tell him I'll meet him there. ICU. Yes, the Wellington. Thank you. Please hurry!'

She put the phone down and was about to rush off to get ready, when she stopped. She turned back, picked up the handset once more, and dialled Jeremy's number. But this time she was unable to hold herself together. 'Jeremy!' she sobbed. 'I-I just got a call from the Wellington hospital. Georgina's there, in the ICU ward. They wouldn't tell me what happened, just that I had to go there straight away...' She paused to get a hold of herself, and heard his phone being dropped – a sharp thud against a hard floor. 'Hello? Jeremy?' But he was already gone.

•••————————————————————————————•••

The Wellington Hospital Accident and Emergency department was impossibly busy that evening, with the sick and the wounded filling every corner, looking miserable or staring into space, waiting to be called – the staff stressed, running around, and over-worked. No-one noticed the tall, hooded stranger weave silently between them. Head down, he made his way along the bright white corridors to the North wing, and up to the Intensive Care Unit, where the nurses at the desk had their eyes glued to computer screens, or were filling in patient allocations and assigning staff on the white-board. Somehow he knew which room and which bed to go to.

Quietly he closed the curtain around the bed, and fell upon the scarred patient lying there, barely recognisable with matted hair, her face scratched and bruised, one eye swollen and puffy.

'Georgina!' breathed Jeremy, pushing his hood back slightly so that he could see her.

She lay so still that for a moment he wondered whether he was too late, but then she stirred, and opened her one eye – it was completely bloodshot. 'J-Jem,' she managed to whisper, her voice hoarse. A single tear dripped down. Feebly, she reached for his hand.

He gripped it immediately, and kissed it. 'I'm *so so* sorry!' he groaned, unable to reconcile the husk of a person lying before him with the bright, beautiful girl he had met just two days earlier.

She opened her mouth to speak, but started coughing instead – a weak, wheezing cough.

He really needed to find out what had happened. Who did this! Where? Why?! But he instinctively knew she could not talk – the dark wheals around her throat evidence that she had been throttled, her voice-box damaged.

It killed him to see his Georgina like this, like a knife was being plunged into his chest with every breath.

He found himself leaning in, kissing her.

Their lips fusing together.

Needing each other.

And suddenly – with a bolt of energy striking through his heart – inky black images materialised in Jeremy's mind, out of nowhere.

A dark alley.

Hurried footsteps.

A tormented soul.

Someone jumping her from behind.

Hot breath, a crooked nose.

A hand clamped over her mouth.

The taste of salty skin, and the reek of alcohol.

Unable to breathe.

Fighting.

Gasping.

Crying.

The man pulled her down, to the side.

His strength almost inhuman.

Grit on the ground scraping bare flesh.

A fist punching into bone.

Bursts of searing pain.

And though it killed him, Jeremy watched on, eyes wide with mortification.

Screaming inside, raging within.

Silently he forced himself to keep watching, himself a victim to the awful, painful, degrading attack.

Blood staining vision.

The tang of blood in the mouth.
Blood spattering everywhere.
Powerless.
Humiliated.
Violated.
Left for dead.
And – at last! – unconscious.

Jeremy slumped back, gasping. Trying to absorb the explosion of sordid images in his head.

There came movement from the hospital corridor – the patter of footsteps running – the sound of Agnes Whyte's distressed voice, asking frantically for her daughter. Jeremy squeezed Georgina's trembling hand – stooped down – whispered something in her ear. And then flew out of the room like a raven. The staff and Agnes Whyte turned to find someone running down the corridor – already at the swing doors – disappearing through them. Gone.

Jeremy Fitzsimmons ran through the night.

Grunting with exertion, puffing and panting, and a thin whining emitting from his throat – as if anguish itself had become sound.

He ran and ran.

Nearly 30 minutes later, he found himself in a residential road, in front of a house – standing, staring, gasping for breath.

A moment of hesitation rose up before him – but he thumped it right down, punched it to the ground, and kicked it senseless. With dark eyes, he marched up to the front door, and whacked it with his fist.

Bang bang! Bang!! Bang!!!

After several seconds, a bedroom light turned on.

Bang! Bang!!

Jeremy followed the sound of someone descending, cursing, eventually coming to the door. Bolts unlocking.

Robert Chambers appeared behind the door. Fresh scratches on his cheek, dressed in pyjamas, and wrapped in a feminine-looking nightgown.

'What on earth–!!' he started.

With all his might, Jeremy pushed him inside the house, and stepped in, closing the door behind him.

Chambers fell to the ground, trying to scramble back, away from the intruder. 'Please, don't hurt me,' he whined, spineless.

The small hallway was dim, but Jeremy groped for the light switch and flicked it on. He pulled back his hood, and stepped forward.

Robert's eyes widened at the sight of him, and he froze with fear. Jeremy swooped down next to him, pushing one knee hard against his ribcage, pinning him to the ground. He grabbed the man's wrists, and held them firmly.

Then he closed his eyes.

And in the space of minutes, he saw everything that had happened. Saw it through this heinous man's eyes.

How he had hidden in the shadows, waiting for Georgina to leave the pub. Tormented by her beauty, humiliated by her rejection. Craving her.

He followed her until she reached an alleyway, a shortcut – where she stopped, undecided if she should go down it. She looked at her watch, and finally walked into the alleyway. Robert slipped behind her, a silent shadow. Halfway along, he ran up behind her, clamped a hand over her mouth, and pulled her into him. Their cheeks touched momentarily, and he breathed in her heady perfume – that was all it took for him to cave in to his animalistic desires. He pulled her down and dragged her to the side of the alleyway...

When Jeremy at last jumped out of those awful memories, he seethed with anger, horror, disgust. Glaring at the man whimpering before him, he eventually said, 'Close your eyes.' Each word hard with menace.

Chambers shook his head in desperation, fear distorting his face.

'Close. Your. Eyes!' hissed Jeremy through gritted teeth.

The man at last did as he was told, and Jeremy leant forward and told him slowly, deliberately, 'This is what I will do to you...' Chambers flinching at every dark word.

When Jeremy himself closed his eyes, with his mind, he showed Robert Chambers a montage of images. Of prolonged torture. Horrific pain. And a plethora of agonising deaths.

It was hell made real. Black images soaked in blood-red.

The minutiae of the worst imaginable revenge, in slow, gut-churning detail. Hours and days of torment condensed into mere seconds. Chambers' body becoming nothing but a brutalised, lacerated, mangled mess – and he screamed and screamed and screamed. But the screams were all in his mind. The torture planted in his imagination. Lies made real; the real turned into lies.

Eventually Chambers' shock and terror overcame him to the point that he was, quite literally, dying of fright.

The last breath wheezed from his throat.

He gazed up at Jeremy, the last thing he would ever see.

The soft whisper in his ear, the last sound he'd hear:

'This is for Georgina,' Jeremy breathed into him, words like flint.

Finally, Chambers' body twisted with rigidity, and then collapsed, limp. And he expired.

Jeremy Fitzsimmons let go of the corpse's wrists – heavy arms dropping down with a thud. He stood up, tugged his shirt straight, and stared blankly at the body before him.

Without even inflicting one blow, he had killed the man.

He examined his feelings, but there were none. Just the acknowledgement that life was fleeting, and he had made sure that Chambers' was particularly short-lived. He didn't deserve one second more. And Jeremy felt vindicated that the world was better off without scum like him.

He stopped to really look at him. The cadaver had once been good-looking, yet was the ugliest and the worst of men. When he was alive, he had it all, outwardly – but inside he was nothing. And now, he would eventually become what he deserved to be, a stinking mound of rotten flesh.

When Jeremy left the house, he calmly closed the door behind him and slipped the hood over his head. Walking quietly down the road, into the blank darkness of night, he kept his head down and tucked hands into empty pockets.

Yes, the world was a much better place now, he thought. And Georgina would be glad of it.

But she never got to find out. For that very night, Georgina Whyte died in the arms of her inconsolable mother.

•••——•••

Jeremy lingered behind a tree at the cemetery, beside himself with grief. Watching the funeral procession from afar.

When everyone had left, he waited several minutes, and then went over to the grave. Felt the cold pitter-patter of rain on his skin. His mind was so dazed that the next thing he knew he was standing right on the swollen edges of the black hole in the ground, staring at the wooden urn left inside – it was slightly askew, leaning backward as if it were just about to fall.

He thought of the thing he had whispered in her ear, in hospital, before leaving. 'I love you, Georgina.' Nothing more than that. And he felt some solace that they had been his last words to her.

Suddenly the clouds parted, and the sun appeared.

Something felt oddly familiar about that moment, and he looked up at the sky. Through the blur of tears, he discovered a rainbow. It appeared momentarily, until the clouds gathered together again – and then it was gone. It came and went so quickly that Jeremy blinked with uncertainty, wondering whether he had really seen it, whether it was real. That moment. A moment when beauty graced his eyes, just as Georgina's love had blessed his life. Yet it was so ephemeral – both the rainbow, and Georgina. And he doubled over and sobbed.

But the soil gave way, and he found himself falling into the grave – sliding downwards until he landed on his knees. He clenched his teeth, smarting from the pain. And the next thing he knew, he saw that he was covered in grey ash. Heart beating wildly. He stared at his chalky hands for some time, unable to move. Not quite believing that a fine veil of her was covering him.

The dust was all that was left of his Georgina.

Her beauty, wit, and intelligence, her charm and grace and kindness – none of it was left. Just dust. It wasn't right. It didn't do her justice.

It wasn't her.

Then a thought came to him.

It started out as the tiniest of sensations, an itch – and the more he dwelled on it, the stronger it became. He needed to re-capture who she really was. Wanted to re-create her beauty. Enshrine her, immortalise her, paint her.

Hesitantly he reached out for the urn, hardly believing what he was about to do. His tremulous hand dipped into the container, and cupped a handful of the ashes. Slowly, gently – not wanting to drop even a speck – he pulled it in and poured it carefully into his jacket pocket.

'I'll do you justice, Georgie,' he muttered, as he put the lid back on top of the urn and straightened it.

He got up slowly and climbed out of the grave, acutely aware of his precious cargo.

As he walked back to his car, and all the while he drove back to Oakley Hall, he talked to her, as if she were right there. Right next to him.

'Just wait, my love,' he kept telling her. 'Just wait…'

'Dear friends, never take revenge.

Leave that to the righteous anger of God.

For the Scriptures say,

"I will take revenge; I will pay them back," says the LORD.'

Romans 12:19

New World Translation of the Holy Scriptures

9 STRENGTH IN NUMBERS

By the time Milly Bythaway had returned to Vivra Tower, she was no longer the quivering, pale person that had entered Jeremy Fitzsimmon's cell and connected with him. She was different.

After she was seen by Dr Fargo, who had given her a thorough medical examination, and after she hugged her father, Brian, for such a long time, the Professor sat her down in the dayroom to discuss Jeremy Fitzsimmons. But not before Jemima gave her a glass of freshly-made lemonade. 'Drink this, Mills,' she told her. 'I made it myself.'

Milly gulped nearly all of it down, and wiped her mouth. 'Thanks. I needed that.'

They all drew closer – including Tai, Tyaishia, and Brian. Missy Mop, the young ginger cat that followed Milly around, immediately jumped up on her lap, and pawed her trousers, before settling down for a nap. Milly gathered her up, hugged her, and planted several kisses on her head, before letting her curl up into a ball. 'It's good to be back home!' breathed Milly, beaming. Her eyes looked brighter and more alert, and her cheeks were rosy pink. Even her father, Brian, had to remark, 'You look really great, Midge! Better than I've seen you in a long time.'

The Professor sat on one of the lounge chairs – the colour, and the décor in general, was much lighter and more modern than the dark depressing colour of Avernus. He rested both hands on top of his cane. 'So, you survived...' he said, a look of both worry and relief on his face.

'Yes,' said Milly, fully realising how concerned he had been. She was eager to reassure him. 'I talked with Jeremy a lot when we connected – he means no harm, Prof. Really. He would never hurt me. I sensed that straight away. He just wanted to show me the truth of what really happened. The simple truth,' she said. Those words, his last to her, seemed to echo in her mind. She smiled at him, and somehow the Professor heard the smile in her voice. 'I'm fine,' she said, extending her arms as if to prove it. 'And Dr Fargo's given me the all-clear!'

'That he did,' the Professor agreed. But it wasn't her *physical* health he was worried about.

Jemima drew closer and sat on the sofa next to Milly, linking arms with her. 'Tell us everything!' she said. 'I'm dying to know more.'

Milly herself was eager to tell them, and her eyes lit up with anticipation. She thought about the emotional upheaval Jeremy Fitzsimmons had gone through with the transformation – that, to her, was just as startling as his powers. 'As you know,' she said, looking around the room at each of them, 'he didn't always look the way he does now. He changed when he was 23 – and up until then, he was normal. In fact, he was really handsome! And his romance with Georgina Whyte... it was so touching, like something out of a movie. They loved each other so much. But when she left him after the shock of discovering their family secret – it completely broke him, and he never really recovered from that. Connecting with him, I felt everything he went through. His love, his loss. I cried – a lot! I felt so sorry for him...' A hint of pain flickered across Milly's expression. 'He's never been the same since. Then later, he found out by accident that she had died, and it was a real shock. He went to the cemetery, and broke down, and found himself falling into her grave – horrified to find himself covered in her ashes. That was when the thought came to him to use them in the painting. It was like his shrine to her, his way of immortalising the essence of her... her beauty. So, I'm not going to lie – he is damaged! Very damaged. A lost love, his transformation, her death. It was just one terrible thing after another – and each time, it broke him even more.' She thought about it for a moment. 'When we connected, he opened himself to me. Nothing was hidden. I saw his inner self, plain and clear. And I'm a hundred-percent sure that, at the heart of him, he's a good man, and he can be trusted. You know, I don't think he even meant to kill V8. He went through so much pain and desperation trying to save Tai, he didn't even realise what he was doing, what effect he was having on others around him. Really, he wouldn't hurt a fly...' Milly stopped. 'Bad choice of words. Sorry!'

'He told you this?' asked the Professor. 'About V8?'

Milly shook her head. 'Not in so many words. I sensed it. It's hard to explain, but... I just know.'

'So,' said Brian, 'do you think he's willing to do the mind-meld thingy with that Hassan bloke then?'

Milly looked a little embarrassed. 'I was so upset after seeing his life, and so caught up in the moment, that I never got round to mentioning that. I think he knew I needed to see if he could be trusted – though I didn't tell him why. He just accepted that I had my reasons.' She thought about it. 'Saying that... I think he would help with Hassan anyway.'

Milly remembered the glass in her hand, and finished off the last of the lemonade. 'Delicious!'

Jemima immediately jumped up, like any good slave, and took the empty glass. 'More?' she asked eagerly, her bright blues eyes widening.

Tyaishia had a soft spot for Jemima, and remarked to her, 'She got feet, girl, and they be workin' fine as far as I can tell. Why you waitin' on her hand and foot?'

Jemima quickly remarked, 'Because I want her to paint me!' – at the same time as Milly said, 'She offered to be my slave.'

Tyaishia lifted an eyebrow at Milly. 'I didn't know you could paint!'

'I can't... I couldn't,' said Milly. 'Jeremy gifted me the ability.' The thought of it still amazed her.

Tyaishia took some time to absorb this.

Quite out of the blue, Tai said, 'I wish I could help you, Milly. With Fitzsimmons...'

'Woah, hang on a minute!' frowned Tyaishia, glaring first at Milly and then her son. 'Yuh thinkin' what I think yuh thinkin'?'

Tai sighed. 'That's just it, Ma, I don't know what you're thinking. I can't see no colours. I can't *feel* nothing.' The cracks of his frustration were appearing. 'I might as well be blind!' he exclaimed. He suddenly turned to the Professor in afterthought. 'Sorry, Prof.'

Tyaishia faltered, surprised by her son's outburst. 'I-I didn't realise it was affectin' you suh much, son,' she said meekly.

'It is... I just wish I was back to before, so I could help, is all.'

Thinking about it, Tyaishia asked, 'I don't understand how you got to lose the colours in the first place?'

The Professor jumped in. 'I'm almost certain it was a side-effect of the cure Dr Vassiliev administered. While Fitzsimmons somehow managed to reverse the aging, Tai's mind was still… not quite right. So Vassiliev started Tai on the same cure he gave Milly, which helped immensely to bring back his mind back to normal. But unfortunately, in healing his mind, it seems to have affected his powers…'

Milly nodded thoughtfully. The cure had worked incredibly well on her, bringing her out of her confused depression – but in the process, she had lost something very precious to her as well. Her mother's voice. And she was still struggling to come to terms with it. She missed her terribly. Missed the warm whispers in her ear. And now, bereft, it felt like a part of her was broken. A part of her had disappeared. She had lost her mother's voice. Lost the connection. Lost herself.

'Yes, I agree,' she said quietly, swallowing down a choke. 'It's definitely linked to Vassiliev's treatment…' She remained wordless for some time, until she remembered something. 'We know that when the others and I connect with each other, it's kind of like a drug, we feel good together. In fact, my headaches have almost completely gone since we started doing it. Then, when I connected with Jeremy Fitzsimmons, it made me feel even stronger, more clear-thinking, like I was sort of… energised. So I think… I think the more we connect with each other, and especially with him, the better it is for all of us. It might even be helping him too, I mean, Fitzsimmons.' She shrugged. 'I hope so anyway.'

The Professor shifted awkwardly in his seat. 'It's an unknown science, Milly. We should be careful, vigilant.' Years of experience had made him doubt, made him warier than ever. Surely things couldn't be as smooth and positive as Milly thought. Life was never that simple. He had already seen how Project Ingenious had turned out – and at that time, their scientific knowledge, their hubris, made them think they could do anything, even play with the very stuff of life, without consequence. Yet it had backfired on them badly. Like a Faustian bargain – there was always a hefty price to pay. A pact with the Devil never came without a price. And up to now, the Professor still didn't entirely trust Fitzsimmons, despite Milly's convictions. His own dear wife, Chiara, and his son, Christian, were no longer here because of the man. Even if the fire in their house was an accident, Fitzsimmons had been right at the centre of it. 'We should proceed with extreme caution,' he said gently but firmly. He sighed. He knew from Sanderson and the PM that the urgency of the task at hand, with young people's lives being brutally ruined, was critical. 'Saying that, Sanderson keeps badgering me about what progress we've made. He and the PM are eager for Fitzsimmons to connect with Hassan asap.'

Milly said, 'I'll need to tell Fitzsimmons first, about Hassan, and the ring, and the information he needs to extract from him.'

The Professor frowned. 'I'm in two minds about your exposure to him, Milly...'

'I can join her,' said Tai, 'support her. Even though I don't have my abilities.'

'Well!' jumped up Jemima, eager as ever. 'If Tai connects with him, I want to be there as well. There's strength in numbers, isn't there?' she said, quite used to getting her own way.

Tyaishia wasn't convinced. 'Isn't anyone else worried about all this?! It feels like we be playin' wi' fire!' She turned to Brian for support, raising her eyebrows.

Brian scratched his head and looked from Tyaishia to his daughter. 'I don't know! I kind of agree with Milly, and I trust her judgement.'

Jemima was bursting with excitement. 'You're outnumbered – we win!' she told the Professor. She sat back down and gripped Milly's arm even tighter, beaming up at her, 'It's going to work out just fine, I can feel it!'

On Milly's lap, Missy Mop, disturbed by all the commotion, looked up and meowed emphatically. 'And there you go!' smiled Jemima. 'Missy Mop agrees!'

The Professor blinked in resignation. It was no use fighting them. At the end of the day, there was one thing that he was absolutely certain of. Fitzsimmons would never harm the children. 'All right,' he said, wondering if he might one day regret this moment. 'Since you're all so determined, I suggest that, tomorrow at 0900 hours, we leave Vivra Towers to go to the cage.' The cage was the name they had given to the high-security prison cell where Fitzsimmons was being held. 'I'll tell Sanderson to get Hassan ready...'

10 ABDUL HASSAN

Jemima held firmly onto Tai's hand when they entered the cage.

She had glimpsed Fitzsimmons only once, through a tornado of flies, but nothing prepared her for being in such close proximity. When she saw his deformed face, in all its grisly detail, she gripped Tai's hand so hard that her fingernails dug into his palm – but Tai didn't even flinch as they quietly walked in, behind Milly.

Fitzsimmons was leaning back in his chair in front of the table, arms hanging awkwardly, shoulders slumped – his beady grey eyes staring at each of them. They seared right through them, like lasers, and eventually settled on Jemima. He seemed to pick her out as the one that feared him most; he knew exactly who she was. One of his progeny.

The more Jemima dared to look at him, the more she was losing her resolve – Tai instinctively squeezed her arm, pried her hand from his, and pulled her to the chair furthest away from the man. Tai then sat between her and Fitzsimmons, with Milly sitting on Fitzsimmons' other side.

Greedy for communication, Fitzsimmons quickly extended his hands, whiskery fingers unfurling. Hesitantly, Tai and Milly held out theirs – and his sinewy hands swooped so suddenly, first onto Milly's wrist, and then Tai's, that it made Jemima jump. Slowly, fearfully, Jemima reached for the others' hands, and the circuit was closed.

They all shut their eyes.

They stared into the blackness for some time, getting used to the 'feel' of each other – not quite inhabiting anyone's mind, they teetered just on the fringes, it seemed, of a vast chasm. Fitzsimmons broke the silence. *I know about the prisoner,* he told them.

Thrown, Milly could only stutter, *H-Hassan? You know about him?*

Yes.

She suddenly realised that they were dealing with someone far more powerful than she had realised. *Is there… is there anything you don't know?* asked Milly as casually as she could muster, trying to hide a sudden bout of alarm – sweat-shine on her forehead.

No. But did you really think that you could examine my own history, without me examining yours?

Of course. I… I think I always knew you would do that, Milly told him. *I just didn't realise how… subtly it could be done.* She thought of something. *That's how you found out what was happening before, in Avernus, wasn't it? When we first connected, that was when you discovered Tai was dying. And what Saffie could do.*

Yes, he said, already wearying. He heaved a deep breath, deciding that, instead of talking, he would show them. And with a single invisible push, the teenagers found themselves falling, falling into Fitzsimmons' endless well of memories. As they fell they were battered by those recollections that rose up and whizzed past them, all skewed and warped: looking from the inside out, upside down, back to front. Memories that he himself had gleaned from the minds of Milly, Tai, and Mei Hui, when they connected for the very first time. They had supplied him with a wealth of information. Through them, he had discovered Karl König's duplicity – and saw through their eyes Karl's entire life course, and their attempt at mind-editing to bring about a change of the boy's heart. But it only led to Karl's mental instability, and eventual suicide… Fitzsimmons grieved for him then, as deeply as someone grieves the loss of their own son.

Fitzsimmons had also learnt about Tai's amazing abilities – the precision with which he was able to manipulate minds and, deep undersea, control hundreds of sharks. To save them. So clear and real were the teenagers' memories, that it was like Fitzsimmons was right there, with them, paddling freezing cold water – engulfed by bursts of bubbles and surrounded by hundreds and hundreds of gleaming, gliding sharks. And even when the children were lying on the back of the whale, semi-conscious, Fitzsimmons too was lying next to them.

Mining their memories had taught Fitzsimmons about the teenagers' abilities – so that he eventually came to the realisation that he must have the same powers; he was, after all, the provider of their genes. And so, while he was locked in the cell in Avernus, he began to experiment with the one thing he had at his disposal – flies. And he eventually mastered full control of them as he sent them out in droves to roam every inch of Avernus, silently sentient, tasting, waiting, hovering, watching. The little creatures becoming a swarm of tiny black ears and eyes for him.

Lastly, Fitzsimmons showed Milly, Tai, and Jemima how he had discovered what Saffron Morales had done to save her cub in the jungle – a revelation! With the gradual comprehension dawning on him that, in him, in the force that flowed through him, as surely as the ruby-red blood coursing through his veins, was the very thing that could save Tai.

Hence, Fitzsimmons escaped from Avernus, running straight to the old oak next to the lake – for he knew in advance that Tai would be there.

The three teenagers absorbed all of this, watching his memories, of their memories, sweep right through them until they were sick with vertigo. They eventually thudded to a halt, landing miraculously on their feet – and the three instantly huddled together, silent and stunned. It was humbling, revealing, sobering. But there was yet one more realisation that settled in the pits of their stomach – this man, their father, like any devoted father, would give his life for them, just as he had been willing to sacrifice himself to save Tai.

Fitzsimmons' thoughts reverberated through the blackness. *In Avernus, I learnt a lot from you, all of you. The things you were able to do with your minds was... quite astonishing. I had given you my genes, so ultimately, your powers had come from me. Only, you were able to harness them and use them in a way that I never could. You were extraordinary, and brilliant. And from you I learnt how to utilise my own powers. Thanks to you, I have become what I am now.*

I suppose, said Milly, *we are what we are because of you...*

They all thought about this for some time, until Fitzsimmons told them, *I will help you with this prisoner. But on the proviso that you do something for me, in return.*

Surprised, Milly said cautiously, *It depends what it is...*

I have discovered a girl... an eighth Ingenious child.

Milly's jaw dropped, and she struggled to comprehend this. Jemima and Tai too were shocked. Milly said, *No, no. You must be mistaken. There were only seven of us. Both the Prof and Dr Kendra told us. We still haven't discovered the last one, though Saffie can 'feel' him, sense his emotions. So she knows he's a boy, and we think he's somewhere in the East.*

I know all this, Fitzsimmons told them simply. *Believe me, I was just as surprised when I heard the girl's voice in my head and–*

A girl? repeated Milly dumbfounded.

Irritated by her interruption, Fitzsimmons continued. *She was in trouble, and I did my best to help her fight back... But then I was captured, drugged, imprisoned – and lost contact. So you need to find her.*

Trouble? Milly repeated again, still dazed by the thought of another Ingenious child. *What kind of trouble? And how could you hear her when you were locked in solitary confinement?!*

Flaring with anger, Fitzsimmons blurted, *You ask too many questions!*

Milly paused for some time, eventually saying, *I'm like this because of you...*

Fitzsimmons breathed deeply, tamping down his frustration. *You need to find her, this girl. She has the power to communicate inside my head over distance – something that none of us can do, though I have tried. She can help you find the last Ingenious child.* There was a pause, and then, for the first time he addressed the others, his voice softening. *Tai. I am glad you are well. And Jemima, you do not need to fear me.*

Jemima could only gulp. For once, she had nothing to say.

Tai said quietly, *Thank you... for saving my life.* The lightness of his voice belied the depth of emotion.

Fitzsimmons became silent, eventually grunting acknowledgement. Finally he said, *Where is this prisoner?*

Milly let go of Fitzsimmons and opened her eyes, blinking in the light. She looked up, around the ceiling, for a camera – there was one in the far corner opposite her, and she motioned to it.

After several minutes, they heard the automatic bolts being unlocked and the cage door swinging open. An overweight, middle-aged man was pushed inside, dressed in plain grey joggers, a matching top, and squeaky white sneakers. With glazed eyes he looked around as he staggered uncertainly toward them, drugged up to his eyeballs. Milly jumped up and took his hand, though he flinched at every movement. She looked at his face only briefly, his crepe-paper skin, tired eyes underlined by bulging bags, the look of confusion and fear – and led him to her seat. He slowly sat and she pulled up another chair next to his.

Fitzsimmons immediately grasped his wrist, as was his usual way, and the others held hands.

When Fitzsimmons closed his eyes, his eyeballs moved manically behind his eyelids as he read the man's mind. Seconds churned into minutes, and Fitzsimmons' face gradually contorted from deep concentration into anger. The anger mounted and mounted, until he was fuming. He suddenly opened his eyes – the whites bloodshot and filled with disdain – and with a burst of rage and an animal-like growl, he twisted and wrenched Hassan's wrist with tremendous force! There was a sickening crunch of breaking bone – and the man screamed with pain. The teenagers snapped their eyes open just in time to see Hassan detonate outward into an explosion of dust, cascading into the air with a puff. There came a sizzling sound. The stench of burning.

Chairs scraped back.

Jemima started screaming hysterically.

Tai exhaled and slumped onto the table, unconscious.

Milly found herself a white spectre, covered in dust, cowering and staring in utter shock at the empty chair next to her, where Hassan had been.

Small grey-white particles rained down on them like macabre snowfall. In a moment of eerie silence, it was almost beautiful.

But the horror of it tore right through them, even as blaring sirens burst their eardrums.

The cage door sprang open, a ninja appeared, crouching low – he shot at Fitzsimmons with a gun.

There was a spray of blood, and the old man fell back onto the floor clutching his shoulder, the feathers of a tranquilliser dart protruding between his fingers.

He descended into unconsciousness, exhaling breath.

Ashes still falling, Jemima's screams, the ensuing chaos, and the deafening screech of the sirens whipped them into a dizzying frenzy.

More ninjas appeared out nowhere, grabbing each of the teenagers, and silently tugging them out of the cell to safety.

11 A WIFE, A MOTHER, A CODER

Calista Matheson gazed dolefully at the strange, paradoxically young yet old woman before her, who, in turn, stared right back.

They regarded each other with a quiet weariness, poring over the landscape of each other's face. The hills, the valleys, the smooth, glassy ponds. Lovely ponds that shimmered with light, yet below, hinted of deep, deep wells of bitter water.

Calista sighed. The polished glass of her vanity mirror reflected only the outside, but it was impossible to see beyond that. To see the hidden things. The things we try to hide, or that are hidden even from ourselves; not even a cracked mirror with a hundred-thousand shards, reflecting a hundred-thousand images, can show us what we really are. Yet in some unfathomable way, those who love us most can see those hidden things far easier, far better, than we can.

A young man appeared behind the uncanny reflection – all at once a mess of black hair and sleepy eyes and an expression of tenderness. He wrapped his arms around her, hugging her softly, and said, 'You're beautiful, Cal. Don't ever forget that.'

She sniffed and kissed his arm. 'I was...' she mumbled.

'You *are,*' Jake told her firmly. He squeezed her once more, before going back to finish tucking in the bedsheets.

She blinked at the reflection in the mirror, hardly recognising herself – sallow, sickly skin, dark shadows under her eyes, and the puffiness that came from chemotherapy.

Tearing eyes away, she looked over the dusty relics littering the dressing table. Bottles of perfume, creams, eyeliners, powders, lipsticks – searching for something in particular. Her hairbrush lay stiffly on the side – strands of gold hair interwoven through the bristles. The sight of it made her sigh. Her usual morning routine was to reach for it and brush through a thick head of hair – luscious locks that, in the sun, bleached to a pearly white. Taking her time, she would relish the stimulating feel of the bristles against her scalp, the soft tumble of hair on her shoulders – admiring the sight of it, her pride and joy. But instead, this morning, she quickly opened a drawer and shoved the brush deep inside. Laying it to rest.

Ah, there it was, the cream blusher she had been looking for. Though she had tried, no amount of make-up could make her look any better – but at least a dab of blusher gave her cheeks colour.

Jake soon came back to her after his messy attempt at making the bed; he had never been great at housework – but they both knew now that in the grand scheme of things, it didn't really matter. He kissed the top of her smooth head, and asked, 'Which one today?'

Calista turned to regard the spectrum of square fabrics hanging from hooks on the wall. She usually liked to choose a different colour each morning, but today she didn't have the energy to even think about it. She shrugged. 'You decide.'

Jake reached for the yellow, but Calista said, 'Not that one, it makes me look like an egg.'

He paused, put it back, and picked out the lilac silk instead. She didn't object, so he tied it around her bald head, careful not to make the knot too tight. 'That okay?' he asked her reflection.

She adjusted the scarf a little, and turned her head this way and that. 'Mmm, thanks.'

There was a loud clattering noise from downstairs and they looked at each other with alarm. Jake helped her up, and she leant on his arm as he carefully led her out, down the stairs, and into the open-plan sitting room.

Gaia Kendra and the Chauffeur were staying with them – both to help with the baby, as well as to take care of Calista. The couple walked in to find Gaia sitting on the sofa with the baby lying beside her, while the Chauffeur was busy in the kitchen making breakfast. The unmistakeable smell of freshly made cinnamon waffles and bacon with maple syrup was delicious.

Jake brought Calista to the sofa to sit down next to their daughter, after which he continued into the kitchen to see what had happened. The

Chauffeur was in his element, cooking – and even in the comfort of their home, he couldn't break the habit of wearing his cook's hat and apron. Jake tapped his shoulder, and the Chauffeur glanced round and beamed a friendly smile. With a wooden spoon he motioned toward the sink where a pot lay, its handle completely broken. 'You okay?' asked Jake.

The Chauffeur read his lips, and called out to Gaia in a gurgling vocalisation. Gaia turned round, whereupon he signed to her. 'He's fine,' Gaia told Jake. 'The pot was filled with hot milk when the handle broke, but fortunately he was standing over the sink at the time, so he didn't burn himself – thankfully!'

The Chauffeur signed once more to Gaia – and she watched for a few seconds, and then told them, 'He said he's going to get you some really good pots. He doesn't like these cheap ones.'

Jake raised an eyebrow. 'Cheap? They were a wedding gift, quite a good set from John Lewis I was told.'

'Oops, sorry!' said Gaia on the Chauffeur's behalf. She turned back to finish taping baby's nappy down, and then buttoned up the peach-coloured baby-grow. She lifted baby into the air, kissed her cheek, and then carefully put her into Calista's lap.

'Good morning, Evie!' breathed Calista, beaming. 'Did you sleep well?' she murmured.

Delighted to see her mother, baby instantly reached for her, needing physical contact. Calista grasped her chubby little hands, and kissed them several times. She smelled of soap and talcum powder.

'She's had her bath,' Gaia told her as she got up, 'so you're just in time to give her her feed.' She got up to get the bottle from the kitchen which had been warming in a container, as well as a tall glass of something from the kitchen counter. She gave Calista the bottle, and placed the glass on the coffee table, next to a plastic pill-tray filled with tablets. 'Milk for Evie, and a smoothie and drug cocktail for mum!' Gaia told the baby animatedly. Calista never had much of an appetite after chemotherapy treatments, so the Chauffeur always made her a nutritious smoothie in the morning, which she sipped only half-heartedly. Evie's eyes lit up as soon as she saw her bottle, and she began fussing for it immediately. 'Okay, okay, it's coming,' Calista told her. 'Greedy dumpling!'

Jake came over and sat perched on the arm of the sofa. He never tired of staring at his baby daughter, never tired of contemplating the miracle of life – though a knot twisted in his stomach. Evie reminded him so much of his sister, Kara. She had those same blue eyes, and porcelain-smooth skin against a tangle of hair. Evie's eyes, though, were slightly crossed as she focused hungrily on the bottle she was drinking from, little fingers gripping firmly onto it. Every now and then she gasped for breath. 'Wow! There's nothing wrong with *her* appetite!' Jake remarked. 'She's practically inhaling it.' He gently tickled the soft tufts of baby's hair. 'Slow down there, Evie, you're going to choke!' But baby firmly ignored father, and continued gulping down the milk like there was no tomorrow.

The doorbell chimed suddenly, and Jake turned round to look at the front door. 'Who on earth could that be?' he wondered.

Gaia came back with a mug of coffee for Jake, and handed it to him. 'Oh, I forgot to mention. Harry said he was coming round to talk to me about something or other. Do you mind?' she asked, looking from Jake to Calista, as she made her way to the door.

'Course not,' said Calista. She loved the Professor like a grandfather. 'In fact, I've been wondering why he hasn't been round…' She looked over her shoulder to find Gaia opening the door. They hugged each other and then she explained to him who was in the room, and where.

'Hello!' said the Professor, as he slipped off his shoes. Acuzio was standing faithfully by his side, sniffing the air.

Calista called out to him, 'I was just saying, Prof, that I've been wondering why you haven't been round recently!'

Acuzio led him over, and Jake jumped up to make space for him on the sofa next to Calista. The Professor said, 'I'm sorry, Cal. I've wanted to come, believe me, but things have been quite… full-on!' he remarked with his usual degree of understatement. He sat down, while a released Acuzio wandered over to Evie.

The dog regarded the baby with keen interest, and started whining and licking the side of her face. Giggling, Evie stopped drinking, and struggled to sit up to see the magnificent beast accosting her – Calista put down the bottle and propped her up. Instinctively, baby reached for Acuzio, opening and closing an eager hand, toes pointing with excitement. When she delved exploratory fingers into the husky's soft grey fur, she let out a squeal of delight. Calista laughed.

After all the goings-on with Jeremy Fitzsimmons, it was refreshing for the Professor to hear happy, unrestrained laughter, and the sounds of a normal family life. It made him smile briefly. 'How old is Evie now?' he asked.

'Nearly six months,' Calista replied, and reached an arm for the Professor – they shared a long hug. 'I missed you!' she breathed.

The Professor realised how much he needed that hug. 'I missed you too,' he said – though the joy of 'seeing' her was tempered with the sadness of her situation. 'How have you been?' he asked, concerned.

Calista squeezed his hand. 'Not great,' she said. 'The chemo's been tough, really tough. But... Jake's been the best. Mrs G and the Chauffeur too.'

'And we're here for as long as you need us!' said Gaia, bringing the Professor a little cup of strong Greek coffee, just the way he liked it. 'I made you a vary-glykos, Harry. It's hot, so wait a few minutes, okay?' She placed it on the coffee table.

Calista suddenly remembered. 'Did you two want to talk in private? If you want, you can go into the conservatory.'

Gaia turned to the Professor, curious. 'Is it private?'

The Professor blinked. 'Well... it's about Fitzsimmons.'

Calista became all ears. 'Fitzsimmons?!' she remarked, fascinated. 'Did something happen?'

Jake came in, chewing a waffle. He sat in the chair opposite them, immediately filled with curiosity. 'Did you say Fitzsimmons?' he asked, cheeks bulging. Even the baby tore her eyes from Acuzio, glanced from her father to her mother, and then stared at the Professor.

Gaia shrugged and sat in the chair next to Jake. 'Well, so much for private...'

Somehow the Professor sensed that all eyes were on him, and he became suddenly serious. 'They connected with him...' he said, subdued.

Calista shrieked, 'What!! Are they out of their minds? The man's stark raving bonkers!'

Startled by her mother's outburst, Evie's arms jerked outwards, at the same time letting out an almighty unexpected burp – the bottle next to Calista spilled over, squirting a stream of milk onto the sofa. Baby started crying.

'Oh no!' said Calista. She put the baby in the Professor's lap, got up, and tried to rub off the milk stain. Jake jumped up to help her. 'It's okay, Cal. Let me,' he said, grabbing a cotton towel from the table and rubbing at the stain. 'There, all gone.'

The Professor sat awkwardly, finding himself quite unexpectedly with a chunky little baby on his lap. Evie, facing outwards, strained her neck to see who was holding her. The Professor reassured her, 'It's okay, Evie. It's only me,' he said warmly, kissing the top of her head. Amazingly, the sound of his voice calmed her, and she relaxed, and sat back against him – yawning.

Calista sat down again, away from the wet patch – catching her breath from the exertion, yet still overcome with curiosity. With her usual lack of inhibition, she urged, 'Right, tell us *everything*, Prof!'

Feeling baby's body go limp, the Professor quietly began telling them the events of the past week – on his lap, a drowsy little Evie was being lulled into sleep by his voice. He started by recounting his visit to Downing Street, and Sanderson's disclosure of the captive ring member, Hassan – a man who adamantly maintained his innocence, though no-one believed him for a second. The Professor told them about their need to discover whether Fitzsimmons was trustworthy or not, in order to be able to use him to read Hassan's mind for intel on other ring members and maybe even the victims. Finally he told them of Milly, Tai, and Jemima connecting with Fitzsimmons – with Hassan between them – only to watch, with horror, as the prisoner exploded into a cloud of ashes right before their eyes.

Everybody in the room was stunned into silence, except for the Chauffeur, who was still in the kitchen blithely banging and clattering as he put things away.

At last Jake said, 'What. On. Earth! Fitzsimmons killed him?!'

'The children,' said Gaia, concerned, 'please tell me they're okay?'

'Yes, they are,' the Professor assured them. 'They're fine. Obviously in a state of shock, but fine.'

'Why did Fitzsimmons kill the man?!' asked Calista.

The Professor shook his head. 'I can only imagine the awful things he saw as he sifted through Hassan's memories. The man had groomed and abused young girls and boys, trafficking them for sex. Their last victim – a 15-year-old girl by the name of Shamira Mahmoud – had suffered terribly. She'd been drugged, brutally battered, and doctors found the DNA of six different men on her...'

Calista's eyes gravitated toward her daughter, who was by now fast asleep in the Professor's arms, snuffling lightly. The thought of someone harming people's daughters hit home.

The Chauffeur came over. Glad to see the Professor, he patted him lightly on the back – and then wondered why everyone was looking so grim. But he wasn't so bothered; baby was his main concern. He signed to Gaia, who translated: 'He's saying it's time for Evie's nap – he's going to put her in the cot upstairs, is that okay?'

Jake gave him the thumbs-up, then lightly tapped fingers on his chin and extended his hand toward the Chauffeur. *Thank you,* he signed.

The Chauffeur returned his thumbs-up, picked up the sleeping baby very carefully, and then took her upstairs. They listened to his footsteps fade.

The Professor continued recounting. 'Because the children were connected to Hassan and Fitzsimmons at the time, they were able to get all the information as well. There's a lot. Years and years' worth of intel. They're transcribing his memories as we speak...'

Gaia found this amazing. 'They're transcribing memories?!' she repeated.

The Professor nodded. 'Yes, they're inputting all the details into Jasmine – dates, times, profile names, even some IP addresses. Everyone Hassan had dealings with.'

'He's guilty as hell then!' said Calista slapping her thigh. She immediately grimaced. 'Ow that hurt,' she winced, 'shouldn't have done that...' Jake jumped up, but she told him, 'I'm okay, don't worry.'

He still went over, sat on the edge of the sofa next to her, and rubbed the top of her arm. She leaned into him, biting her lip from the pain. 'I'm such an idiot!' she mumbled.

'You're okay, babe,' said Jake. He turned to the Professor. 'Tell us what happened, Prof.'

The Professor cottoned on to Jake's distraction strategy. 'Of course. Well... where was I? Ah yes, the reason why I wanted to speak to you, Gaia, was because Fitzsimmons told the children something rather... startling.'

'Oh?' said Gaia, curious.

'He mentioned that there was an eighth Ingenious child...'

Everybody stopped, dumbfounded.

Quickly the Professor said, 'Now I can tell you for sure that I was there during the entire project, and only seven children were produced. So...' he turned toward Gaia, 'since Axel was the only person with the technical know-how, as well as the DNA, to produce an eighth...'

Gaia was flummoxed. 'Believe me, Harry, I'm just as shocked as you are.' She shook her head, trying hard to remember. 'When we left Project Ingenious, Xeli eventually took up working on his father's scientific research. He really wanted to continue and complete what he had started. The genetic cure for dementia as you know. It took him over, consumed him in every way – and we hardly saw him. Plus we were moving house quite often, so we were in a constant state of upheaval. Then, in time, the Alzheimer's began to set in...' She sighed, suddenly feeling tired. She reached for the coffee she'd left on the table and gulped it all down. 'Sorry, Harry. I needed that...' she said, already lost in her thoughts. Remembering something, she frowned. 'There was one time when he had to go away quite suddenly for a week. What was it for now...?' she mumbled to herself, wracking her brains. 'It was connected somehow to Project Ingenious... Oh that's it! He told me that one of the parents, one of the mothers that had given birth in the project, needed Xeli to help her conceive again. I remember feeling quite incensed about it, telling Xeli that he wasn't a fertility clinic! They'd already had one child through the project, surely that should be enough! But apparently that first child had been rejected by the mother.'

The Professor nodded. 'That must have been the Alpha. His parents, the Schäfers, were the only ones who refused to take their baby when we escaped from the project.'

Gaia lifted a hand to her mouth. 'Yes of course! I didn't connect it before, but it makes sense now! We – me and Xeli – were going to take one of the children with us, but the night we were supposed to get him, Xeli had a heart attack! I-I thought he was going to die. It was horrible.'

'A most unfortunate turn of events,' remarked the Professor. 'But how on earth did the Schäfers contact you when you changed your name and moved away?' asked the Professor.

'They were family friends,' said Gaia. 'I mean, on Xeli's side of the family – I hardly knew them. So Xeli kept in touch with them now and then. He told me that they had tried many times but failed to conceive a second child, so they contacted Xeli out of desperation.'

'The problem is,' said the Professor, 'if he was simply helping them have another baby, why would he introduce Ingenious DNA? *Fitzsimmons'* DNA. It doesn't make sense. That would have needed to be done in a very specific way, involving embryonic stem cells being knocked in with the DNA modification, and then implanted into a viable blastocyst.' The Professor paused. 'Axel definitely had access to the knocked-in DNA material, that is, the frozen modified stem cells.'

Gaia thought about it. 'He must've taken it when we left then.'

'But why would he use Ingenious DNA on the Schäfers' embryo?' asked the Professor.

'It's baffling,' admitted Gaia. 'The only explanation I can think of is that... well, Xeli's mind wasn't quite right. He started doing strange things, getting muddled, quite early on. He'd talk about things from decades ago, as if they had just happened. He'd mention having recent discussions with people that I knew had died years ago. He even talked about things from Project Ingenious as if he was still working on it... At first, I put it down to him being over-worked and exhausted. But in time, it soon became evident that something was very wrong. And then they diagnosed that he had Alzheimer's. So yes, I can quite easily see him thinking he was still working in Project Ingenious and using DNA samples...'

'Wow,' said Calista, flabbergasted. 'Karl König has a sister! And she's Ingenious!'

'I wonder what she's like,' said Jake.

The Professor got up, and Acuzio – who was sitting at the bottom of the stairs, looking up – immediately returned to his master and nudged his hand with his head. The Professor bent down to grab his harness, patting him with affection as he always did. 'Well, we'll soon find out,' he said. 'Now we know who this eighth child is, I'll send an agent over to bring her in. Thank you, Gaia – you were very helpful!' He made to leave.

Gaia got up too. 'But why do you need to bring her in?' she asked.

The Professor stopped. 'Fitzsimmons seemed to think she was in danger. And he also discerned that she has a… unique gift. She was able to get into Fitzsimmons' head, from wherever she is – so she has a special ability to communicate. We're hoping that she might be able to help us find the last missing Ingenious child.' He paused. 'With Axel gone, we had no way of finding him. Only Saffie was able to discern that he was somewhere in the east, possibly Asia. But that's all we know.'

He turned back round to Calista, 'I'm sorry I can't stay, my dear, there's a lot to do. I'm sure you understand. Quite apart from the urgent need to deal with this girl, we've years and years of information yet to assimilate – after which we'll be cracking into computers to find the people Hassan was colluding with. So it's all hands on deck!'

Jake looked from Calista to the old man. 'I… ordinarily, I'd be happy to help, but…'

Quickly, the Professor said, 'No, I didn't mean you, Jake. I don't want to take you away from–'

'I want to help!' said Calista suddenly.

Jake glared at her with disbelief. 'Cal, you need to rest! You need to conserve your energy, to… to…'

'To what? Get better?' she said, raising a weary eyebrow. 'I think we all know that I'm *never* going to get better. I was given five months, that was nearly six months ago. So I'm living on borrowed time…' She looked at the stairs. Thought of her daughter. Thought of the entire lifetime that Evie was going to have without her, going to school, making friends, graduating from university, maybe getting married, having children of her own. She was being snatched away from her daughter's future. And she felt cheated. Life was cruel, horribly cruel.

Calista closed her eyes, mustering the strength to hold it together. Every second of every minute of every day, she was trying to hold it together. But while she was cherishing being with Jake, and Evie, and her extended family, the more she thought about it the more she wanted to do this. 'I *need* to do this,' she told them quietly. 'It will be the last thing I do, I know, but I need it.'

Gaia dared to speak up. 'But Evie...'

Jake added softly, 'Evie needs you, Cal.'

'I'll be here,' she told them. 'A little distracted, but still here. Anyway, she has to get used to being without me, sooner or later...'

'But why...?' asked Gaia, confused. 'Why do you need to do this?'

Calista thought about it. 'Pretty soon, all that's going to be left of me, is a name on a slab of rock.' She caught her breath. Saying it made it more real. Gut-wrenchingly real. 'So I guess.... I guess I just want to make a difference. I want what little life I have left to have purpose, and meaning. I don't want to just die... I want to do something that I'll be remembered by. I know. I know I'm a wife, a mother, a coder, and I've built a super computer. But if I can save a life – just one life – then it'll all be worthwhile. Even all this suffering... it'll be worth it.' She rubbed her temple, feebly trying to rub away the constant ebb and flow of pain. 'This never-ending cycle of agony – I want it to go away, so bad. But dying is the only way to get out of this...' She leaned into Jake again, exhausted, and he put his arm around her. 'I'm sorry,' she mumbled to him, closing her eyes briefly. 'But if I can save one person, and that person goes on to live a full life, a life that I never will, then I'll die happy...' She stopped, grimacing from the pain. 'Death and happiness,' she said, gritting her teeth, 'they shouldn't be in the same sentence should they?'

Jake groaned inside, pulling her into him. *No*, he thought, and he wished that that sentence never had to be uttered by his wife.

12 BEAUTIFUL COLOURS

Tai Jones swam and swam, releasing what seemed like an age of pent-up frustration.

He sped through the water, arms alternating up and round like a windmill, propelling him forward – legs kicking in a flutter, trailing a spray of white behind him. His slender body stretched thin, muscles tight, spearing the water. Now and again he turned his head to the side to gulp air, before tucking it back in the water to streamline himself.

Vivra Towers' pool was different from the one in Avernus. This was in the shape of a perfect circle, just as the building was spherical. The walls of the pool room were embedded with an aquarium – giving a 360-degree view of the orange, gold, and white koi. They glittered in the sunlight that streamed through a metre-high window rim between the tank and the ceiling. The water swayed with long slithers of eelgrass, and on the surface floated water lilies and hyacinth – their long roots trailing down.

Tai had been swimming for almost half an hour, and when he came up for breath again, this time he noticed something with a gasp. The fish. They were glowing with a dream-like aura of orange. It billowed about them in clouds. And as Tai rolled onto his back and gazed open-mouthed at the aquarium wall, he realised that the koi had gathered into a single shoal, and were following him around the pool. When he reached the ladder, he flipped round and climbed up – a shower of drops falling from him like liquid diamonds.

Tai went over to the wall, as if sleep-walking. His mouth tugging up into a huge grin.

He planted his hands, slippery wet, onto the thick glass of the aquarium. The koi gathered around him, hundreds of bustling, wriggling bodies. Their whisker-like barbels twitching with curiosity.

Tears of joy came to Tai's eyes as he watched their colours – lovely, wondrous colours – turn from orange, to peach, to rosy pink.

PART 3

13 THE BLACK FOREST

17-and-a-half months earlier.

Ilse Schäfer was living with foster parents until a permanent home could be found for her. They were a sweet couple in their 50s who'd had no children of their own, but devoted their lives, out of kindness and charity, to help others. Their four-bedroom semi therefore was able to home three foster children: 15-year-old Ethan Frank, Laila Abrams who was 17, and Ilse Schäfer, the youngest, who had just turned 10. A disparate set of children – their troubled pasts hung about them like an indelible stain, and mistrust soured their expressions and hunched their shoulders, eyes darting around at sudden movement or noise. But sometimes, just sometimes, they forgot about their inner wounds and scars. And they smiled, or laughed, or chatted together like normal children (though those moments were far too rare and fleeting), until they retreated once more into their shells.

That fateful Saturday was just such an occasion.

The children had reluctantly climbed into the old blue Volvo estate with a tatty picnic hamper packed to bursting, thrust into the boot – ready to drive south to the Black Forest, an hour away. 'It's not the Black Forest in Germany,' smiled Susan Wilkinson, one of their foster carers, glancing over her shoulder as she buckled herself in. 'It's the one here in England, north of Brighton,' she said, for Ilse's benefit, who knew only of its German namesake, the Schwarzwald. For most of the journey, Ethan moaned because he had been taken away from his beloved PlayStation, and Laila pitched in with outbursts of 'It's not fair!' for being told that phones had to be switched off on their special day out. Ilse on the other hand simmered with quiet intensity, arms crossed, as she stared blankly out of the window – her brass-blonde hair scraped back into a messy ponytail, and a nervous foot tapping incessantly against the seat.

But when they got to the forest, the tall beech trees, the carpet of green interspersed with wild bluebells, and the play of sunlight that broke through the canopy in dazzling shafts, all seemed to have an enchanting effect on them. Above, birds sang gaily – the strident tchik-tchik of the woodpecker, and the airy warblers' song, among others, drenched the air with music. 'Woah, this is sick!' gasped Ethan as he slipped out of the car and looked up and around at the scenery, wandering off to explore.

'Don't go too far!' called out Susan after him.

Laila pretended she wasn't excited at all, swanning around picking bunches of bluebells – and when she came across wild strawberries, she quietly ate them, evaluating their taste with a curious expression on her face like a connoisseur of fine wine, sometimes shivering from the odd sour one. Ilse, meanwhile, helped their foster carers, Susan and Tom, lay the picnic blanket and set out the food and drink: homemade rose lemonade, gala pies filled with herbed pork, pickled eggs, sandwiches, a large bowl of trifle, and cupcakes piled high with swirls of buttercream, already melting in the balmy warmth.

Tom called out to Ethan and Laila, telling them to come back to eat.

Meanwhile, Ilse sat down cross-legged on one corner of the picnic blanket, and bowed her head low. She was accustomed to praying before she ate. Her mother had taught her, for though they had not been staunch Lutherans, mother's own parents had drummed into her the need for grace before meals. It was usually a short prayer – *Come, Lord Jesus, be our guest, and let thy gifts to us be blessed. Amen* – and the Wilkinsons were always kind enough to wait for Ilse to finish before they started. But Ilse's prayer was taking much, much longer than usual. The couple waited patiently in their squeaky picnic chairs – when they realised, with alarm, that the girl was shaking. Ilse's head suddenly bolted upright, and she looked frantically roundabout with panic in her eyes. 'Ethan!!' she called out loud, as she stood up. 'Laila!! Where are you?!'

The girl's panic was infectious, and Susan looked at her, looked at Tom, then jumped up and ran into the woods where she had last seen them, shouting for them too.

Tom put a comforting hand on Ilse's trembling shoulder. 'What's wrong?' he asked, worry in his eyes.

Ilse blinked up at him. 'They're here!' she blurted out, her face bright red. She walked backward, away from him, looking around with alarm. 'I-I'm sorry! They came for me, not you. Stay away from me, for your own sake!' Fear brought out her German accent. Strong, clipped vowels. And she turned and ran into the woods before he could stop her.

'Ilse!!' called out Tom, running after her. 'Come back!' But he stopped at the edge of the woods, combing a hand through his mousy brown hair, not knowing what to do.

Her voice came out from the dark of the woods. 'Stay. Away. From me!!' Each word emphatic, and getting fainter as she ran.

'Ilse!!' called Tom. But it was no use. He looked over to the place where he had last seen his wife disappear, and then turned to where Ilse had gone – trying to keep calm. 'Don't panic, don't panic, don't panic...' he muttered to himself. But it wasn't working. And that's when he heard a blood-curdling scream. He jumped, and spun round, prickling with fear. Quickly he ran to the picnic hamper, took out the sharp steak knife, and bolted into the forest where he'd heard the scream.

After running for several minutes, the first thing he found was a bunch of picked bluebells, cast on the ground, trodden with dirt and stained red. His stomach churned and he gripped the knife firmly in his fist, holding it in front of him.

He ran deeper and deeper into the woods, the canopy above him becoming thicker, the forest turning darker. He gulped. 'Susan?! Ethan! Laila!' he kept calling out, but to no avail.

And then he saw movement from afar.

Heard Ethan's voice shout out, and a girl screaming.

Between the trees, he caught glimpses of something in the distance.

What looked like a tall, burly man tackling Ethan. But the skinny teenager was no match, and he was soon knocked down, crumpling to the ground.

Another figure, his wife Susan, grabbed a stick, and ran in front of the children. 'Get away from us!' she shouted, anger in her voice. A terrified Laila appeared, trying to help Ethan get up. But as Tom drew closer, his heart sank, for he saw that there was not just one stranger, but several –

surrounding the two children and his wife, advancing toward them.

Adrenalin and panic pushed Tom closer, even though he was outnumbered. He stepped out and revealed himself. 'Stay away from them!!' he growled at the six men. He ran at one of them, shrieking, and raising the hand with the knife. But the man he was aiming for deftly stepped aside and knocked the knife from his hand – in one smooth motion. The others screamed, and Tom cried out in pain, gripping his wrist. The burly man picked up the knife, stretched forward, and grabbed Tom from behind. He held the knife against Tom's throat, the serrated edge nicking his skin. Tom's eyes widened with fear, each scattered breath making his neck bulge against the blade.

Susan screamed. 'No, please!' holding a hand out to her husband.

The man glanced at her, menace in his eyes. 'Where did the girl go?' he growled, and looked at Laila. 'The little German girl.'

'Please, don't hurt him,' whimpered Susan. *Please...*'

Impatient, the man with the knife shouted out. 'Just tell me where she is! Now!! Or I will cut it out of him, chunk by chunk...'

In nervous panic, Laila inadvertently glanced back to where they had come from. Seeing this, the man pushed Tom toward them – where he stumbled against a tree next to his wife, clutching his throat with hands stained red by his own blood. The burly man motioned for one of his companions to come with him, and told the other men, 'Kill them all,' nodding irreverently toward their four captives. Laila screamed as the men advanced upon them, while the first man walked off with his companion.

Tom hurled a puny punch at his attacker, but the man stopped it with one hand, and with the other, punched Tom's jaw. He floundered backward, and the man leapt forward and gripped Tom's throat. Large hands and thick fingers, strangling the life out of him.

Several metres away, Ilse stepped quietly out of the shadows.

Such a little girl.

Her form waifish, insignificant, in comparison with the tall stocky men advancing toward her.

Laila noticed her from the side of her eye, just as one of the assailants grabbed her neck and began throttling her. Laila beat him and scratched him, trying to make him stop, as she gasped for breath.

Ilse was terrified of the approaching men.

But she stood firm, lifting her face heavenward as if in prayer – eyes clenched firmly shut. 'F-father, wh-what should I do?!' she said, her small voice quivering.

Susan and Ethan too were being strangled, practically on their knees, bent backward. Soundless, except for their choking and gurgling. Faces red. Eyes popping.

Still facing skyward, Ilse listened intently, brows furrowed.

She nodded as she listened – uncertain, hasty nods. And then she opened her eyes.

They were black, filled with rage.

She reached a hand toward the two men advancing toward her. They were nearly upon her, just a few steps away, when they stopped dead in their tracks. The knife dropping into the undergrowth.

Ilse concentrated with all her might, her face scrunching up from the effort. 'Like this?' she asked the sky, tearing her eyes away from them.

With Ilse's hand static, the men suddenly found that they could not move, feet cemented firmly on the ground. Unable to budge even an inch.

And then, when Ilse swept her hand around, the burly man turned slowly toward his companion, against his will, like a puppet on strings.

The men's panicked eyes locked onto each other – round orbs crisscrossed with thread-veins. Though they could not speak, their eyes said it all: the burly man's, filled with disbelief as he watched his own hands clench into tight fists, and the second man's, widening with fear as those fists swung against his head, again and again and again. He wasn't even able to scream.

And then Ilse brought her arms together, one crossing over the other, crooked fingers still pointing at them.

Suddenly, the two companions began attacking each other.

Ilse looked away, fully sobbing now, unable to watch as the two men tore into each other in a silent but deadly fight to the end.

She ran around them, keeping a good distance away – to find, with alarm, that one of the attackers was standing over Tom's body which lay motionless on the ground, another was still throttling Susan, and the other two were grappling with both Ethan and Laila.

Ilse reached out her hands toward them all, shrieking, 'Stop!!!' That one word spat out with fury.

Amazingly, the four men let go and slowly stood upright, arms falling feebly to their sides. Leaving their victims writhing on the ground clutching their throats, and coughing and gasping for air.

Then the men turned toward their companions, and began tearing into each other like wild animals. Punching and smashing and throttling and beating and bashing and pounding. Until, after what seemed like an age, they fell to the ground one by one, either lifeless, or twitching into unconsciousness.

Little Ilse hid behind a tree, crying her heart out – every now and then she dared to peep out, glassy-eyed.

And at last, when all was still and quiet, she found the courage to call out to the others. 'A-are you okay?!' Her thin voice quivering with worry. 'Please, *please* be okay!' she sobbed. But there was no reply. She dared to look out, and when she was sure that all the men were lying still on the ground, she came out and picked her way across the undergrowth. To her relief, she found that Laila was alive, but dazed. Tom too was getting up and helping his wife to her feet. Ethan was already sitting up and looking around in disbelief – staring at the men lying scattered around. 'Wh-what happened?!' he croaked, gulping. 'Who are they?' The boy had many, many more questions. But he somehow knew that no-one had any answers.

Ilse got up and ran into Susan's arms, sobbing. 'I'm so sorry!!' she cried, again and again, her little body trembling violently.

14   THE PIANIST

Tai Jones sat in the fourth row of the stalls, and listened with rapture to the lone Korean pianist, Ha-Ru Kim, on the stage of Cadogan Hall. The internationally acclaimed artist's story was well known: as a 12-year-old child, he had fallen in love with Rachmaninov's Piano Concerto No. 2, vowing that one day he would learn to play that monumental piece. And he did. In time, he became one of South Korea's most famous classical musicians.

Tai listened quietly to Kim's rehearsal, sometimes with his eyes closed, sometimes opening them to soak in the subdued ambience of the auditorium – the ceiling arches, the low galleries, the steeply raked stalls, and the stained windows with their clean lines and Celtic knot motifs. Sometimes his eyes lingered on Kim's nimble fingers trickling along the black and white keyboard with almost effortless ease, absorbing his art. He played, not Rachmaninov, but Beethoven's Piano Sonata No. 14. A piece that Tai knew well. And at last he came to the part that Tai had been waiting for – the 3rd movement – and the boy sucked in air and held his breath.

That was the piece Tai had been learning in Avernus, when he first had the grand piano moved to the BC. The 3rd movement was, technically, undeniably hard. And he remembered his own playing like it was yesterday – releasing the music onto the keyboard, presto agitato, ravaging the keys as his hands flew up and down with dynamic energy. But Tai had found himself floundering, and with the first error came doubt, and then loss of confidence, until mistake followed mistake. In the end it became unbearable, and he wrenched his hands away from the piano, gritting his teeth with frustration, and scraping the stool back with a harsh noise.

But as Tai watched Kim play the ferocious and extreme movement with fire and beauty, dynamism and poise, he lapped up the perfection of his artistry. *How was it possible*? Tai asked himself with quiet admiration, to play not one wrong note, with the phrasing, the spacing, the softs and hards, flawlessly executed.

As he listened, in the back of his mind he also thought about the last few days. How connecting with Fitzsimmons had somehow not only given him his powers back, but had dialled up the intensity, so that he, Milly, and Jemima's abilities had become much more. Much stronger than they were before. And now that he could see all his glorious colours, he felt whole again and fully restored, energised, dynamic, the colours more vibrant. It was nothing short of a miracle. Yet Tai's joy was tempered with a sickening feeling as he thought about what the return of his powers had actually cost. Remembering what Fitzsimmons had done to Hassan. That image fixed indelibly in his mind, in slow motion: the man exploding right before their eyes, even as Kim's music erupted through the air.

In time, after about 15 minutes, Kim's sonata came to an end – and as the last note disappeared, as if wafting through the stained glass into the blue sky outside, the pianist allowed his hands to rest on his lap.

Tai immediately stood up and clapped loudly, cheering and whistling with admiration. He was the only person in the 950-seat hall, and Kim turned to him and waved. 'Did it meet your approval?' the pianist asked, grinning.

'Yes, absolutely. It was wonderful!!' raved Tai. 'Bravissimo!'

Kim lowered his head with gratitude and lightly touched his chest. He got up and called out, 'You will come tonight?'

'Of course,' said Tai enthusiastically. 'I wouldn't miss the concert for the world. We're all coming.'

'That makes me very happy,' smiled Kim as he walked across the stage. 'I will make sure you all have back-stage passes, and I look forward to seeing you and the Professor after the concert.' He stopped, sneezed, and quickly wiped his nose with a handkerchief. 'Sorry,' he sniffed. 'I must rest now. See you tonight.' He waved a final goodbye.

'Yes, all right! Thank you for letting me watch your rehearsal. Goodbye!'

Tai slumped back into his seat, adrenalin coursing through his veins. He listened to the racing rhythm of his heart – thunderous beats, cloistered in a room filled with silence. The music had given him life, energy. And as he watched Kim slip out of the stage door, billows of grey smoke trailing behind him, streaked with fine lines of brown, Tai realised that the man's confidence was mired with worry. But as he revelled in the aftermath of such beautiful music, he was far too emotional to wonder why.

Jemima had made two jugs of lemonade in expectation of their visitor coming to Vivra Tower. It was a simple water and sugar syrup with freshly-squeezed lemon juice – then piled with ice cubes, and topped with a sprig of mint. Continual taste-testing as she made the drink, adding more water, then a squeeze of lemon, meant that her stomach was already swimming with the stuff. They had also bought from Harrods' food hall some cheese straws, as well as six scones, laid out with little bowls of jam and cream – arranged on the coffee table in the dayroom.

Milly and Tai sat waiting on the sofa, when they heard the tap-tap of the Professor's cane coming down the hall. The old man walked in with a 12-year-old girl holding his hand, two messy plaits of hair dangling just above her shoulders.

Milly gasped when she saw her; she was clearly Karl König's sister. Her heart skipped a beat as she remembered the last encounter she'd had with him. The fright of waking up in the middle of the night to find a shadowy figure standing over her in the dark, the automatic light switching on, his red-rimmed eyes, a glazed look of confusion – as she grappled with the sickening thought that he had come to kill her...

Milly felt Tai's hand take hold of hers.

It's okay, Tai told her with his mind.

Milly smiled briefly at him. *Thanks.*

Why... why are you afraid? came a third voice inside their heads. It was a little girl's voice. And both Milly and Tai stiffened as their eyes locked onto Ilse's.

Tai raised an eyebrow. *We can hear you...* he remarked with surprise.

She stopped right in front of them, a mixture of shyness and innocence in her expression. 'I know,' she said out loud.

The Professor let go of her hand, and cocked his head. 'I'm sorry?' he asked.

Ilse looked up at the Professor. 'I am talking to Milly and Tai,' she explained. 'I am telling them that I know they can hear me in their heads. Just as I can hear them in mine.'

The Professor blinked, blank eyes staring into nothing. 'How... did you know their names?'

Ilse turned again to Milly and Tai. 'Father told me.'

'Father?' asked Tai.

Milly elbowed him. 'She means Fitzsimmons.'

Ilse nodded. 'He told me about all of you. Including Jemima, Saffron, Mei Hui. And I also know about my brother, Karl, and what happened to him.'

Milly and Tai glanced at each other.

Ilse's eyes dulled as she thought of the past. *Karl killed my parents. Which made me hate him so, so much. That is why I told him... I told him to kill himself.* She said this dead-pan, without emotion, as though everything that had happened to her, the death of her parents, the attempted murder by those awful men in the Black Forest, had squeezed every last drop of feeling out of her.

Milly's jaw dropped. *You told Karl to kill himself?!*

Ilse nodded, grey eyes darting from Milly to Tai and the Professor. *He did it, didn't he? Kill himself,* she asked, already half knowing the answer.

Yes, said Tai.

A curious expression appeared on Ilse's face, a mix of shame and disbelief. *I-I didn't think he would actually do it. I didn't know what my mind could do...*

They all paused for some time to think about this.

You had no way of knowing, Ilse, said Milly. *None of us really understood what we could do at your age. But it wasn't just you. We'd messed with his mind – all of us. We're as much to blame.*

Eventually Tai said to Ilse, *You... you can talk to us without touch?*

You need to touch? asked Ilse in return.

The Professor, who had discerned that something unusual was happening between the three children shuffled sideways to sit next to Tai on the sofa, remaining silent. Without being asked, Tai rested his hand on the Professor's, and the Professor blinked with wonder as he absorbed the miracle of sight, the assault of colours – everything that Tai was seeing. He took it all in with a frisson of disbelief and wonder – saw the room for the first time. The pastel décor. Milly and Tai, who both looked older since he had last seen them. The blonde girl standing before them, wearing a pale-yellow jumper with a pattern of bees.

Oblivious, Milly turned back to Ilse. 'We should speak out loud, for the Prof.'

'Okay,' said Ilse. She looked around, and went to sit on one of the chairs at the side. She swung her feet in and out, opposing pendulums, and eventually reached forward to grab a cheese straw from the coffee table and began nibbling on it. Little crumbs fell on her lap, merging into the fabric of her tan jeans. 'I like cheese. You knew I liked cheese, didn't you?'

Tai and Milly couldn't help looking at each other again.

'No,' said Milly. 'We didn't know anything about you. Our abilities are... different to yours. Unless we touch, *physically* touch, we can't get into each other's minds. You're the only one who can communicate without it. And... you seem to be able to connect us all.'

Ilse thought about this as she finished eating her cheese straw. 'These are very good.'

Tai smiled. 'You can have as many as you want, Ilse.'

They watched her take another straw. She seemed a little self-conscious as she quietly munched the pastry and looked around the room. 'Is Father here too?' she asked.

The Professor stiffened. 'You call him "Father"? How well do you know him?' he asked cautiously. They all knew she was referring to Fitzsimmons.

'I heard his voice inside my head. And Dr Chu, the psy- psychia–' she huffed with exasperation.

'Psychiatrist?' offered Milly.

Ilse nodded, 'Yes. She told me that I had to be brave, and face the voices, and ask them what they wanted with me. There were so many voices. So I had to be very brave,' she said hesitantly, not looking brave at all. 'And the first one I asked was Father's...' She wiped the crumbs from her mouth with her hand, then cleaned her hand on her trousers. 'I'm glad I did, because he helped me. He helped me understand what I could do with my mind.' She noticed the jug of lemonade, her eyes lingering on it.

Milly reached forward and poured her a glass. 'Jemima made this specially for you. It's very good,' she smiled, handing her the glass.

'Thanks!' Ilse took it and sipped some warily. 'I like it,' she said, licking her lips. She looked around the room. 'I like it here too. It's pretty.'

The Professor couldn't help smiling. 'That's good, because we were rather hoping you might stay here with us, in Vivra Tower. It's all been approved by social services, so it's up to you, Ilse... By the way, I heard from the Wilkinsons what happened to you two years ago. I'm sorry, very sorry. But it's safe here. It's a very secure building.'

Milly and Tai had heard about the Black Forest too, and already knew who had given the order to kill her – having delved into Karl's mind, they had seen for themselves the memory where he had ordered a hitman to do away with her. It was chilling. But he was gone now. Tai told her, 'You won't have to worry about anyone coming for you again, Ilse.'

Ilse nodded. 'I know.'

'It's almost time. We should get ready,' said Tai, looking at his watch.

Ilse glanced from one to the other. 'Can I come too? I'll be good, I promise. I like music.'

The Professor stared at her. 'You know about the concert?' he asked, realising that she must have read his mind because he definitely hadn't told her about it.

She nodded enthusiastically. 'My father, my *real* father, Hanno, liked such music too. He used to listen to it all the time. Please can I come?' She looked at the Professor with wide eyes. And then out of the blue, she said, 'You don't need to be scared of me. I'm not crazy...'

The Professor blinked at her, hardly knowing what to say.

Tai jumped in. 'It's just that we don't think you'd enjoy it. It's classical music. Beethoven. You might get bored.'

The girl slumped her shoulders, visibly disappointed. 'Oh...'

Milly sat up. 'I don't mind looking after her, if she really wants to come...' she told the Professor. 'We can get to know each other.'

The Professor was rather relieved to hear this; the prospect of baby-sitting a rather incisive young mind-reader was quite daunting. 'Yes, okay,' he said.

A big smile erupted on Ilse's pale face – and she stopped, suddenly realising that she hadn't smiled in a very long time.

They all sat in the same fourth row stalls that Tai had sat in when he'd listened to the rehearsal earlier that day. But this time, Milly, Jemima, Ilse, and the Professor were with him – all dressed in smart casual. The place was bustling with crowds for the concert had almost completely sold out.

The Professor sat at the end of the row in an aisle seat, with Tai on his right, because he wanted to relish the joy of not only listening to the concert, but also seeing it. He had every intention of soaking in this wonder – the miracle of sight – that he had already decided to be thoroughly unsociable, and keep to himself. On Tai's other side sat Milly, with Ilse sandwiched between her and Jemima, who sat towards the centre of the row. The two girls had already hit it off, and were whispering incessantly to each other, and looking around excitedly, and admiring each other's shoes, or clothes, or hairstyle.

For some reason that Milly couldn't understand, she turned round to look back several rows behind them, remembering how she had spotted Agent V3 for the first time when they had visited the Royal Opera House. A pang of guilt erupted in her chest, knowing that the agent was still in a coma and unlikely to wake up... Milly caught her breath and battled to control her emotions as she turned back round to face the stage.

She suddenly remembered to remind the girls not to make any noise at all during the concert, because the artist needed the utmost concentration – and also not to applaud at the end until the last note had faded to silence. The girls listened thoughtfully and nodded, then quickly went back to whispering to each other and giggling. 'Oh, and Ilse,' said Milly, looking at her quite pointedly. She touched her arm. *You can't read people's minds without their consent, okay? It's an invasion of privacy.*

Ilse looked upset.

Don't worry, Milly added. *You didn't know before. That's why I'm telling you now.*

Nodding uncertainly, she asked, *Am I in trouble?* Her grey eyes tearing up. *I'm sorry!*

No, no, you're not in trouble. It's just that… I think you spooked the Professor a bit when you told him you knew about the concert and stuff. So just remember not to listen to people's thoughts unless… unless it's absolutely necessary. At that moment, the lights dimmed and the audience began to hush. 'Let's enjoy the concert!' Milly told her out loud with a smile. 'Tai's been looking forward to this for ages.' Milly pressed her index finger against her lips as a reminder, and Ilse nodded.

I'll be very quiet, Ilse told her silently, and sat forward with anticipation, craning her neck to see.

Ha-Ru Kim walked across the stage to rapturous applause, dressed in a black tuxedo and burgundy bow-tie. He had a commanding stature despite being a diminutive figure, with a full head of thick hair, and fine cheekbones. He waved to the audience, looking up and around the galleries, and then the stalls. Tai waved to him, but Kim was unable to see them because of the blinding spotlights. He sat down on the stool, took a moment to gather his thoughts, and then began to play.

To anyone else, the man played exquisitely. But Tai immediately knew something was wrong. The Professor felt the boy's hand stiffen in the crook of his arm, as they watched and listened to the first movement unfurl in lyrical waves. But after several minutes, Kim stopped playing right in the middle of the 54th bar – he bowed his head, his chest rising and falling frantically. He suddenly gripped his neck, unable to breathe, and he fell forward onto the keyboard – a jarring clanging clash of musical notes marked his fall to the floor, and the audience gasped collectively. There was a hurried squeak of shoes as people from back-stage burst out and gathered around the pianist, obscuring him from view. Unlike other concert halls, there were no curtains, and so the audience watched on as events unfolded before their eyes.

Eventually a couple of men wearing medical vests arrived, bearing a stretcher between them, and they rushed over to the fallen pianist. Flipping him unceremoniously onto the stretcher, they picked it up and rushed away, disappearing just as quickly as they had arrived.

Before long, the stage was empty again – save for the grand piano standing resolute in the centre, and a piano stool fallen on its side.

The audience gave in to ripples of hushed whispers, and they looked around, wondering what they should do. Would Kim be revived and return to the stage? Was he seriously ill? Should they leave?

Nobody knew anything. Least of all Tai.

But the boy found himself standing up, like he was in a dream.

Found himself shuffling past the Professor and walking down the aisle toward the stage, fingering the back-stage pass in his pocket.

He climbed up the side stairs, and with long strides pushed his way through the stage door, into the back. He showed his pass to the security guard, a middle-aged man with long side-burns, wearing a shirt tucked into jeans, and holding a clipboard. The man looked at the pass, checked his list, and finally stepped back with a nod to let Tai through.

'Where is he?' Tai asked, looking around.

'They took him away already,' said the man. 'To the hospital. The Royal Marsden.'

'What was wrong with him?'

'They weren't sure, but they were saying something about Covid. His last concert was in Hong Kong you see, and he'd flown directly from there to London just last week. Strange, because he was supposed to've quarantined...'

Tai looked worried. 'Do you know if he's going to be all right?'

The man shrugged, 'No idea, mate. But I'm pretty sure he's in for a long stay at the hospital. He looked really bad. Could hardly breathe.'

Tai remembered Kim's colours in rehearsal – grey streaked with brown; confidence broken by waves of doubt. He had sneezed, and it all suddenly began to make sense to Tai. Kim must have felt the beginnings of it even then, and wasn't sure if he could make it through the concert...

The guard shook his head. 'Such a shame. It was a full house too!'

'He didn't have a standby?'

'Kim? No!'

Lost in thought, Tai thanked him distractedly, turned back and walked through the doors. From the side of the stage, he glanced across at the piano and stool, and found himself walking over to it. Bending down, he picked up the stool and placed it at exactly the right distance away from the grand, central to the piano's width. He turned, and was just about to walk away, when he suddenly realised that the audience chatter had silenced. He looked out into the auditorium, blinking in the dazzling light, unable to see a soul beyond the light. But out of the blinding whiteness came a lone voice. A girl's.

You can do it, Tai!

It was Ilse.

Tai, in his grey jumper and trousers, and white sneakers, faltered. He stared at the piano stool for some time. Closing his eyes momentarily, the music from the rehearsal instantly filled his head. It was all at once achingly beautiful, poignant, and dynamic – and now, indelibly printed into his mind. Tai's heart leapt just thinking about it.

Before he realised what he was doing, Tai found himself walking quietly around, and sitting down on the stool, just as he remembered Kim had done earlier. He stared at the dazzling array of polished keys – resplendent white and black – remembering the grand in the BC in Avernus. He hadn't played since his mother had come out of the coma. Hadn't played for years. And the more he stared at those contrasting keys, the more they seemed to draw him in. Kim's music echoing in his mind. The memory of the man's fingers rippling effortlessly up and down.

Tai positioned his feet on the pedals.

Planted his hands over the keys.

Lowered his head.

And with the lightest exhalation, his fingers began to play.

The music poured out of him like liquid.

All at once smooth and fluid.

Sonorous, and beautiful.

He played breezily, effortlessly, working his way through the first two movements, until, seven minutes later, he came to the breath-stopping moment of truth. He paused for just a second, hands wafting up above the keyboard, before launching the third movement onto the piano. It was an eruption of fire and beauty and passion, as his hands ravaged the keyboard, making even Tai gasp – as if his fingers had a life of their own, as if they had played the piece a thousand times. The mistakes that he had made when he last played seemed like they belonged not to him, but to someone else – a forgotten acquaintance from a distant past.

Tai's heart thundered in his ears, beating a perfect tempo, like a metronome. His shoulders swaying, his head lowering and rising with the music – he was unable to discern where his body ended and where the music started, both resonating in perfect synchrony. But he did not play exactly as Kim did. Tai varied the hardness and softness of notes, changed the accents, tempered the fortissimo section, bringing his own unique personality to the piece. A modern teenager's take on two-hundred-year-old music. When Tai came at last to the coda, his fingers ran up and down the keyboard in a flurry, until he played the last notes with grace, poise, finality – hands bouncing up high, as if the keys burned red hot, scorching him. And he at last sat back, spent. A glow of sweat on his forehead.

For several seconds there was just the sound of his rapid breaths.

Until he heard hundreds of chairs creaking, and a sudden burst of uproarious applause – so many people jumping to their feet in standing ovation. Cheering and whistling. The applause seemed to go on for ages, until several voices called out, 'Encore! Encore! Encore!!'

Tai stood and turned to the audience, allowing himself a flicker of a smile, and bowing his head briefly. In time, he turned back to the piano. The immediacy of their hush to silence was flattering, respectful – and as Tai sat down, so did the audience. Tai gathered his thoughts, recalling the music. He drew the piano stool closer, the scrape of wood on wood reverberating along the arches of the auditorium. Positioning his hands and feet again, he paused for several seconds, then began playing the first movement of Rachmaninov's 2nd Piano Concerto. Kim's inspiration.

The first notes were intense, clanging ominously – like harbingers of doom...

Outside the hall, the faint sound of piano music leaked out of the building – tinkling delicately in the air. Several passers-by stopped to listen for a few seconds, before carrying on walking.

A homeless man, wearing over-sized, too-short trousers tied around his waist with cord, bustled along the back entrance of the hall, carrying plastic shopping bags packed to brimming. When he spotted the deep, broad threshold of the stage door, his eyes lit up, and he put down his bags on the step, one on each side, then took out a scratchy wool blanket. He snapped it into the air to get rid of the dust, and then folded it, matching up the corners into a perfect quarter. He laid it out carefully next to the stage door, and then lay down, resting his head on one bag, and putting up his feet, with mismatched shoes, on the other. It was a good spot – and, after scratching his head from the lice, and scratching his ankle from the flea bites, he stretched his arms back and tucked both hands behind his head, looking up into the indigo of a dusk sky.

He recognised the melody of the piano music echoing through the door, and began humming along – pleasure creeping across his face.

A black mass swooped across the sky, and the man stopped, sat up, and blinked, trying to work out what he'd just seen. The mass curved round and swooped again – and he at last realised that it was a murmuration of starlings, high in the sky, twisting and gliding and fanning out.

His body loosened again as he lay back, and he watched the spectacle above, while at the same time listening to the music being played in a way that he'd never heard it before. It was turning out to be a delightful end of the day, until he suddenly realised something, and his jaw dropped.

The starlings. They were moving in rhythm to the music. Soundwaves made visible. Getting closer and closer. The birds began swooping low into the alleyway en masse, a rush of air current gusting up the tramp's long, straggly hair. All around him, the starlings prattled noisily and dived and glided in such perfect time with the music, that the man wondered if he was dreaming. But a sudden barrage of droppings began raining down on him, splattering him, the building, and the alley. And he realised that this was most definitely real.

Quickly he took out a newspaper, unfolded it, and covered his head and shoulders. Crouching low under its flimsy protection.

15 BOY WONDER

Tai Jones was an overnight success, albeit an anonymous one, for no-one knew the name of the mysterious boy who had quite inadvertently stepped onstage out of nowhere.

Music critics, who had originally come to hear Ha-Ru Kim, commented on the fact that when they first saw the boy walking meekly across the stage, they thought he was a cleaner, or a stagehand. But to their amazement he sat down at the piano, and quite unexpectedly began playing the piece in a way they had never heard it before. It was rapturous, unique, magnificent, sublime, extolled one of the critics. Another wrote that the boy wonder was a musical genius. And yet another said that this single young man was certain to inspire not just a whole new generation, but also an entire cultural group, to appreciate the virtues of classical music. There were shaky, indistinct photos of Tai playing, surreptitiously taken by members of the audience, despite the fact that cameras and recording devices were prohibited during concerts. His young, skinny form was clear in the pictures, but his facial features as he moved to the rhythm were, thankfully, blurred.

Though Ha-Ru Kim was no longer in the limelight, he had not been forgotten. Several newspaper articles mentioned that he must have caught Covid during his visit to Hong Kong, where he performed in the City Hall just five days ago – with his manager saying that, due to a heavy tour schedule, and reduced flight services, it was impossible to quarantine for the required amount of time. But Kim's was just one of hundreds of new Covid cases in the UK, and the media was drowning under the weight of the news and the burgeoning death toll.

After Tai's musical performance at Cadogan Hall, the boy immediately ran to wash his hands thoroughly – and after emerging from the toilets, the Professor and everyone else crowded round to hug him, or pat him vigorously on the back, or shake hands. The front of house was swarming with people, so the teenagers exited through the backstage door – surprised to find a homeless man fast asleep on the threshold, and the place covered in birds' droppings. They carefully stepped over the vagrant, and the Chauffeur immediately whisked them away in the FX4. He drove them back to Vivra Towers – where the car disappeared smoothly behind the tall rolling gate.

The next day, they found to their surprise that Calista, Jake, Evie, the Chauffeur, and Gaia had all moved into Vivra Towers as well – and were starting work on searching for all the people that Hassan had contacted, as well as pinpointing possible ring members – along with a 20-strong team of computer programmers based in Downing Street. Calista was weak physically, but undeniably driven to 'catch them nasty criminals' as she so eloquently put it. Jake sat close-by, their computers set on a wide bench desk in one corner of the dayroom. As he worked, he often stopped to sneak a glance at his wife.

Calista's form, in front of the computer, was like an alabaster statue carved into the space beside him. So poignant, so still. A statue that he had always thought would be eternal...

Her skin was sallow, the baggy t-shirt she was wearing, one of his, clung to a disturbingly skinny form. Calista absentmindedly scratched beneath the edge of her headscarf in between tapping determinedly at the keyboard. Every now and again she paused to look around for Evie, or ask Jasmine where she was, or wink reassuringly at Jake, before returning to her work.

Time often stopped for Jake. He struggled to catch his breath and gulp down the panic that swelled like a wave inside him. He hated that every passing moment was one less second with her. Hated that her days were numbered.

When he brought her tea, he'd set down the cup and gently kiss the top of her head. Or when she struggled to get up, puffing and panting, he forced himself not to jump up to help her, because she'd have none of that.

For him, being with Calista was like standing on the edge of an ocean. She was so near, so close, her waves lapping constantly at his feet – yet at the same time, she was impossibly distant. Vast. Unreachable. Even when they hugged, when she huddled herself inside his tightly-wrapping arms, there was a farawayness about her. She couldn't help it, he knew. The disconnect was a protection, against the fear. The silence, a cocoon of sadness.

Evie of course was blissfully unaware of the tempest that was in store.

She hardly ever cried. She was such a happy baby, having the loving – if somewhat distracted – attention of both her parents, as well as Gaia, the Chauffeur, and Acuzio too, who had taken quite a shine to the baby, and was constantly at the infant's side. The dog jumped up and whined and licked her for attention, or nudged her chubby little hand to be stroked, or, when she was asleep, he settled down on the floor at the foot of her crib, or the sofa, himself dozing off as he guarded her.

Dog meandered over from time to time, wondering what had caught his attention. She would sniff Acuzio, sniff the baby and lick her cheek, in the same way she often did with the cats, before wandering off to find somewhere to nap; she was getting lazier these days, eating more, and was putting on quite a lot of weight around her middle.

•••————————————————————•••

Jake, Calista, and the team of programmers had made good progress, coming up with 10 names and addresses in a relatively short space of time. Sanderson immediately arranged to pass the information to the police. However, one of the names was already on their radar: Yazan Ekren who was known to live in North London.

The Prime Minister and Rory Sanderson took a special interest in the man, because they believed he was the leader of the ring. They had already arrested him several times, and charged him, but he always managed to elude conviction due to some loophole or other. They knew he was guilty, but just lacked the evidence.

'This is one person we cannot let slip through our hands!' said the PM emphatically to both Rory Sanderson and the head of the National Crime Agency, General Peter Arnold.

The tall, silver-haired General agreed, though he looked sceptical. 'I'm not going to question your source, Prime Minister. But if I've understood you correctly, that you've somehow retrieved intelligence from a rather... dubious informant, we're still going to need hard evidence to be able to lock this man away for good. *Hard* evidence.'

The PM harrumphed. He hadn't told the General the whole truth, that a deranged mutant, Jeremy Fitzsimmons, had read the mind of a gang member in order to glean years of incriminating information, right before killing him in a puff of ash. He most certainly would not have been believed. The PM looked at the General thoughtfully. 'We'll cross that bridge when we come to it. But for now, the important thing is bringing him in...'

'By coincidence,' said Sanderson, 'Ekren lives not far from the house where Vassiliev was abducted, on the other side of the forest. So we know the area quite well after our investigation a few years ago. Definitely an advantage for us.'

'Right, send me the coordinates for our special ops team to bring him in,' said the General. 'They're on standby as we speak, and rest assured, they'll get the job done!'

Sanderson, looking slightly awkward, told him, 'Actually, I've been instructed to use our own team, headed by David O'Connor, because he knows the area well.'

The General glanced from him to the PM. 'I don't think you understand. Our men have trained for years for this sort of thing. *Specialised* training. Believe me, Prime Minister, their skills are far above that of your... security detail.'

The PM suppressed a smile. 'And believe me when I tell you that our team are more than just bodyguards. I have the utmost faith in their rather, quite frankly, unique expertise. In fact, some members have been taken from various other elite corps, and certain others have quite particular... abilities. So please have your team stand down on this occasion. Sanderson and O'Connor have everything under control, and they'll be briefing our men fully. They will be deployed first thing tomorrow at 0600.'

Sanderson nodded respectfully at the PM, though he was far from convinced himself. Even though he knew that there was something rather unique about the newcomer, Ilse, and her amazing ability to reach through space to communicate and control minds, not needing touch like the others. Tai's connection with animals too, and Milly with her ability to implant images into people's minds. And even though he had seen with his own eyes Saffron Morales' and Jemima Jenkins' quite incredible powers on their trip to the Amazon jungle, Sanderson was still dubious about using teenagers, children effectively, in an operation that involved very dangerous criminals. It felt like throwing kittens into a den of lions.

But the PM was adamant. He was going to use the Ingenious children to bring in the gang leader, Yazan Ekren.

16 ANIMALS

The little red squirrel scampered through the forest undergrowth, racing against the dark that was fast descending.

Though the creature had excellent visual and spatial memory, the bright orange orb floating low in the sky was already half hidden behind the horizon, making the light fade, the terrain more difficult to see. The squirrel relied now on its sense of smell and touch – its vibrissae, highly sensitive whiskers located all over its body, discerned every vibration and every breath of the wind. Stopping to look this way and that, it divined the direction of its nest – and it turned to go back home before night came.

Stomach growling, it ran and ran. But it couldn't help stopping when its keen sense of smell detected a cache, buried underground. It was not a nut that the squirrel had hidden, yet it dug it out nevertheless, ran further along for several minutes, and buried it in another location, making sure to rub its cheek gland against the spot to mark it with scent. The nut was his now. The squirrel made sure to hide the fresh mound of soil with a layer of leaf litter, before turning to run home.

It jumped up onto a pine trunk, its sharp claws digging into the bark as it scurried vertically, higher and higher. It then ran to the end of a branch, and launched itself off – flying through the air almost two metres to the branch of another tree. Scampering further along, it jumped again onto the next tree, until it finally reached one of its four dreys – a bulbous collection of twigs, leaves, bark, and moss, nestled in the v of a branch, 30 feet above the ground.

But it did not go inside straight away. It scuttled across to a hanging pine cone, nibbled it off, and sat back on its haunches, exposing fluffy white belly fur. Now that summer was coming to an end, its fur was getting thicker, the stripes on its back disappearing into the rich red that was deepening even more – perfect camouflage against the mottled red of the pine bark. The squirrel rolled the cone in its paws, this way and that, then busied itself with gnawing through each cone scale until it reached the inner seeds. As it munched on the delicious nuts, the peach-gold glow of the bright sky orb melted behind the horizon.

When the squirrel finished eating, the light was fading rapidly, but there was just enough time for a quick grooming: it pulled its tail forward, nibbled methodically from the base to the tip, then crouched down to clean the thick mound of its thigh, then its belly, then its feet. Lastly, licking its paws, it drew them over its head and face several times until it felt satisfactorily clean. A spontaneous, wide yawn could not be suppressed – a tiny pink tongue slipping out and back over two sharp incisors – before it turned to scamper to its drey.

Suddenly it stopped midway along the branch and twisted round – facing north-westward. It sniffed the air and cocked its head, bright eyes looking far into the distance, divining something unusual, something out of the ordinary. It did not understand exactly what this thing was, all it knew was that it was definitely coming.

Though not quite yet...

•••———————————————————•••

The male robin made sure to sit perched as high as it could in the crown of a tree.

Though its song was sweetly melodic, it was in fact a threatening war cry against other robins. Its breast swelling out prominently, serving as a bright red warning to others: stay well away! It had no qualms about swooping down on birds that flew over its territory, no qualms about fighting to the death; the tiny 13-gramme bird was viciously territorial.

When it spotted the squirrel digging below, it swooped down, hopped nearby, and waited. At last the squirrel ran off, and the robin quickly jumped over and picked out a wriggling worm that had been dug up with the soil – fortunately for the bird, the squirrel had missed it. Grabbing the writhing worm with a sharp beak, the robin flicked it several times against the ground, until a morsel broke off – which it swallowed down hungrily.

It repeated flicking and eating, until the worm was consumed, and its belly full. The robin launched itself forward and flew into a thick bush at the base of a tree, tunnelling through to a neat cup of moss, dried grass, and leaves, lined with fine strands of hair. Breast throbbing delicately from exertion, its head tilted this way and that as it sensed something new and different. It hopped around, turning north-westward, beady eyes scanning through the bush, past the waning light of the great orb that had almost disappeared beyond the horizon. It leaned an earhole – nestled underneath feathers just beyond its eye – toward the faraway thing, to try and hear. It stayed still for some time, listening, discerning. Then it stretched out wings, brown feathers fanning and fluttering, as though preparing itself for flight.

•••————————————————————•••

The colony of feral cats lived in a secluded area deep in the heart of the forest. They had multiplied, and were now 29-strong, taking shelter in several stacks of large flat overlapping boulders, covered in blooms of yellow-green lichen, and dotting a broad, leafy clearing. The cats' lair was well hidden, surrounded by dense thickets and closely-packed trees of ash, beech, lime, oak, and yew – ancient columns that sprung from rich soil, creating a protective canopy.

Four of the cats had separated from the main group, and were prowling the area. They were a mother and her surviving kittens of seven months, searching for food. They sniffed as they went, air ripe with humus, wild garlic, and other delicious scents, their tails swishing leisurely this way and that as they walked. They were not fussy eaters, but were entirely opportunistic, pouncing on anything that crossed their path – spiders, grasshoppers, small lizards, and even snakes. Other delicacies were mice, rats, squirrels, shrews, and moles. But most of all, they loved eating birds, though hunting them required much more skill.

It was already getting dark by the time they had eaten their fill, when one of them spotted the flash of red – a robin, eating amongst the leaves. The young cat stopped, then crouched flat on its haunches. Springing up suddenly, it dashed after the bird – but the robin had already whizzed away through the air, disappearing between the trees. The cat listlessly pawed the ground where the bird had been, and sniffed the leaves. He had missed his chance, and he meowed to the others that were only just catching up with him, telling them so. The other cats meowed in reply, before turning round to go back the way they came. Night was fast descending, and they needed to return to the safety of the lair.

As they approached the clearing where their home was, they were surprised to hear the caterwauling of the entire feral colony, meowing and howling shrilly, pacing nervously around the rocks. The group of four walked over and felt compelled to join in with the yowling. When darkness engulfed them, the mother at last jumped into one of the rock crevices, followed by her kittens – huddling together and settling down for the night. The mother lifted her face north-westward, blinking sleepily, knowing that at the crack of dawn they would be called. And they must be ready.

••—————————————————————••

Though his window blazed with magnificent oranges and golds from the setting sun, Yazan Ekren paid no heed as he sat at his desk in the semi-dark of his bedroom, hunched furtively over a computer monitor. He tugged at his wiry grey beard, eyes lit up by the onscreen images – a strange look on his face: thrill, mixed with a hint of something... primeval.

He didn't notice his eight-year-old son standing hesitantly in the doorway behind him, rubbing his eyes.

Sleepy yet unable to sleep – the child had tumbled out of bed, pattering barefoot to his parents' bedroom in search of his mother, hoping that she would read him a story, or let him watch an episode of Teenage Mutant Ninja Turtles on the tablet. But only father was there, sitting at his desk, his back turned to him – watching the monitor. The boy noticed a flash of orange onscreen, and he suddenly wondered if it was a video of the Turtles, for his favourite character, Michelangelo, wore a bright orange eye mask. Being small for his age, the child tiptoed and craned his neck to see past his father's slouched shoulders. It didn't help that the room was dark and shadowy, with the light of a lamp weakly filtering through the black.

Instead of the Turtles, the screen showed a girl wearing a crumpled, grubby night-dress lying on an old orange bedcover. To the side of the screen, standing over her, was a man. The girl had dark skin, her hair looked dirty and straggly – and she seemed to be fighting sleep, her head bobbing up and down, eyes half closed. 'Please stop. Please!' she whimpered.

The boy watched on for several minutes, filled with childish curiosity, with his mouth hanging open. And then he saw what the man did to the girl – and he gasped and froze.

Ekren turned to see who was there, only to find his son standing in the doorway, in shock. Crying.

Quickly he switched off the monitor, scraped back the chair, and turned to him. 'Why are you out of bed!' he growled, his face darkening with rage. He was just about to jump up and deliver a swift blow, when footsteps came from behind.

The boy's mother appeared, and she grabbed the child's hand, thrust him back, and stood in front of him – trying not to show her fear. 'I-I'll take care of the boy,' she said, catching her breath. 'H-he won't do it again.'

'Control your child, woman!' snarled Ekren. 'Can't you see I have important business?! What kind of a mother are you, indulging such unruly behaviour.' He turned away, disgusted. 'Leave. Now!!'

She turned on her heels and pushed the child hastily down the corridor, opening the bedroom door and steering him to his rumpled bed. For the first time she noticed her son's tears, the look of shock on his face.

He sat down, white as a sheet, eyes wide with images that he wished he could erase. Images that he desperately wanted to un-see. But they were locked in his mind now. Forever.

His mother's voice, lowering to gentle but pressing concern, brought him out of himself. 'Tahir. What's wrong?' Her brown eyes flicked over his face, and, pulling a sleeve over her fingers, she wiped his tears. 'Tell me…'

He shook his head stiffly. He couldn't vocalise it. Words would have been like the long stretched-out shadow of something just out of sight; the hint, the shape, of those awful images. Again he shook his head, mute.

Mother closed her eyes briefly, trying to gather strength. She glanced over her shoulder, toward the door and listened for signs of movement, before turning back to Tahir. He looked so fragile, like a puff of wind might shatter him to pieces.

She watched as he absentmindedly pulled his pyjamas tight around his chest, and she caught her breath, suddenly realising what he had seen. Her mind raced. 'You... you saw one of his videos... didn't you?' she asked, wondering what you could possibly say to a child who had witnessed those awful things. She stroked down a wayward tuft of Tahir's hair, though it only sprang stubbornly back up. She murmured, 'We cannot judge people for what they choose to watch, or choose to do, if we don't want to be judged ourselves.'

Tahir sniffled and wiped his nose on the back of his sleeve. 'B-but in the video... that man was doing bad things to that girl. Hurting people is bad, isn't it?'

Mother glanced sideways. 'It depends. If they're bad children, maybe they deserve it.'

'No!' cried Tahir unexpectedly.

'Shhh!' hissed his mother angrily, pressing her hand firmly over the boy's mouth. But he wriggled out of her grasp.

'I don't believe you!!' he shouted even louder. 'I don't like what that man did. I HATE him. I HATE father too!!'

Mother gasped and began struggling with the boy, but he squirmed and whined so much, that before she realised what she was doing, she slapped him hard across his face.

Tahir fell sideways onto the bed, clutching his cheek. The searing sting made his skin glow bright red.

Mother stared down at him, eyes narrowing into cruel slits, nostrils flaring. 'Don't *ever* say those words again!' she breathed through clenched teeth. Each word made the boy flinch. 'It is haram to disrespect your father. Continue in this way, and you will end up in hellfire. For the hereafter. For eternity!'

But the boy had stopped listening. Instead, he pressed his face into the soft bed – hot tears soaking into the duvet. Wishing that he was anywhere but here.

He squeezed his eyes shut. Trying to smother the surge of hate that was firing up inside him, burning him.

He hated his parents, hated his life.

Hated himself.

17   RAID!

Just north-west of the vast, ancient forest was a sleepy old town that was characterised by a tangle of unremarkable residential roads, filled with unremarkable rows of houses.

One particular four-bed house was typical of local architecture that may well have originated in the Stuart era: rectangular, with a gabled roof and dormer window, clad in faded brown brick, and creeping with thick trails of ivy. Look closer though, and one could see the cracks. The dormer window's single glazing had lain broken for years, landslip crazed the external walls with fissures welded together by metal plates that were like giant sticking plasters, and the wooden window casements had bulged and splintered from decades of damp.

Dawn was just breaking, the air fresh with dew, and a bush at the edge of the forest suddenly trembled and swayed.

A little red squirrel stuck its head out, and then flattened itself against the ground to creep underneath the fence skirting the forest. It sat up for a second, its fur somewhat dishevelled, a shiny-moist nose twitching, as it took in the beige-brown shapes of the town, stark contrast to the organic verdancy of the forest. Eventually, it scurried onto the road and followed its course – a tiny figure swallowed up in a river of tarmac – until it reached the run-down four-bed house. The squirrel paused to stare up at the building for several moments – scratching its cheek, as if trying to figure something out. Quickly it scampered up to the side fascia and leapt onto the thick woody stem of the vine – jagged-edged leaves wobbled under the movement, their glossy leaf-shine glowing dimly in the first light of dawn.

Silently the little creature climbed, nimble and dexterous, sometimes leaping from one twisted branch to another, until it reached the roof and scrambled into the guttering. It jumped up onto the sloped tiles, but several loosened and fell off – cascading and smashing onto the ground. The squirrel stopped, twitching nervously as it listened for signs of life. But there was nothing. It turned and resumed its journey, this time proceeding more cautiously on the slippery tiles.

When it reached the jutting-out dormer window, it jumped onto the narrow ledge and eyed the teeth-like shards of broken window. The glass seemed beguiling and enticing, twinkling in the morning light, but the squirrel knew better. Carefully it picked itself over the jagged edges, and then jumped inside into the attic, landing lightly on the dusty floorboards.

It ran straight across to the descending stairs and scuttled down them, its protruding eyes – with sharp, peripheral vision – looking around as it went. Silently, the little squirrel crept from top to bottom of the entire house, reconnoitring every inch with its keen eyesight.

Not far away, behind a clump of bushes, Ilse Schäfer and Milly Bythaway stood quietly together.

Both had their eyes closed – Ilse, with one hand reached out to her upper right, like an antenna toward the sky, the other stretched toward the ninjas metres away. They were hidden in the shadows outside Yazan Ekren's house, pressed, poised, still as statues against the wall. In her mind's eye, Ilse saw everything the little squirrel saw as it moved through the building, and at the same time, through Milly standing next to her, her arm wrapped around Ilse's shoulders, the two teenagers transmitted the images to each of the ninjas.

By the time the squirrel had finished casing the joint, they all knew that there were three adults and four children in the house, fast asleep – two younger children sharing a bedroom, one older boy in his own room, and the youngest, a toddler, sharing a bedroom with an elderly woman, possibly its grandmother, who was snoring loudly. A middle-aged male and female, likely the children's parents, were in the last bedroom, sleeping separately in two single beds.

•••———————————————•••

The ninjas were pools of black shadow, clinging to the faded brown brick of the house.

Each closed their eyes, sensing everything the squirrel sensed, every image, every scent, every vibration. In their minds, they watched as the small mammal cautiously entered the dark of Yazan Ekren's bedroom, the air stale with must. Stealthily, it jumped up onto a chair, then a chest of drawers, then flung itself onto the top of a wardrobe with ease. It settled down, bright eyes glancing from one bed to the other, and then remained glued to the mound in one of the beds, its whiskers twitching with tension.

Two of the ninjas in the backyard stepped out of nowhere, next to the door, both grasping each side of a 25 kg enforcer that they jointly swung and smashed against the lock with a loud thwack. Quickly they stepped back, allowing three ninjas to run inside, then discarded the battering ram and followed after them.

On the other side of the house, two other ninjas did the same to the front door, with the exact same timing, bashing it open. They swarmed silently into the house, and now that they knew the exact layout, and every occupant's location, each ninja made their way to an allocated room and the inhabitant they must detain.

As they bounded up the stairs, they heard muffled noises from one of the bedrooms.

The squirrel watched as a rather hirsute Yazan Ekren, startled by the noise, jumped out of bed dressed in an old shirt and shorts. He pulled open a bedside drawer, and withdrew a military grade combat knife which he clipped onto his elasticated belt. Next he took out a 9 mm semi-automatic Glock, and with shaky hands he pushed the slide back, eyed the loaded magazine in the chamber, and made sure the gun was cocked.

Ilse gasped. 'He's armed!' she told the ninjas with her mind.

But they already knew, already saw, thanks to Milly transmitting the images in real time.

Ekren pointed the gun nervously at the door, then glanced at his wife who was sitting up with alarm, holding the bedcover tight against her chest, as if it afforded her any kind of protection. She looked tired, with a pale, puffy face. Ekren caught her attention and held a finger to his mouth, then went over to the sash window and pulled it up. When the bedroom door suddenly swung open, he panicked and shot at it before he could even see who was there. Bang, bang! Bang, bang! Bang, bang, bang!!

His wife squealed with fright at every shot – wondering with a sickening feeling if it was just one of the children...

But nobody fell to the ground, nobody appeared.

The door continued swinging back, hitting the wall, and the noise caused the jittery Ekren to shoot reflexively again, several times.

Then, just at the edge of his vision, he saw movement at the top of the wardrobe – and he shot at that too. Splinters of wood and lumps of plaster flew in all directions. He looked back at the bedroom door, straining to see through the murky blackness of the hallway.

The tension was palpable.

The silence deafening.

Holding onto the gun with both hands, he tried hard to calm his nerves. Sweat poured into his eyes, stinging them. He blinked them dry as best he could, then motioned with a nod to his wife to get up – and she scrambled out of bed.

When Ekren took his eyes off the doorway, a flurry of black spectres poured into the room. He tried to shoot at them, but the gun only clicked, emptied of its round. Quickly he dropped it, whipped out the knife, and – wrenching his wife's arm toward him – he gripped her against himself, and held the blade to her throat.

She jolted with shock. Knew what he was capable of. Knew that, after nine years of marriage, living every day with his mercurial temper and tyrannical ways, such treachery from the man she called husband was very real. And though she was the mother of his children, he would show her not one iota of mercy. She whimpered as the cold edge pressed into her flesh. 'Yazan, no!' she gasped, catching her breath – her bloodshot eyes rolling sideways, pleading with him.

But he ignored her, as he always did, and shouted instead to the two black-clad men in front of them. 'Move away, now, or I'll kill her!!' the words pithy with middle-eastern accent.

The shadows stepped slowly backward.

Ekren thrust his wife toward them, and she stumbled and fell to the ground with a thud and a weak cry.

Quick as a shot, Ekren jumped out of the window, landed on the shed roof, and then jumped over the garden fence into the shrubbery-filled edge of the forest. Running for his life, he disappeared between the trees.

Meanwhile, the ninjas tried to circumnavigate the woman, but she grabbed hold of their legs, first one, then the other, clinging on with such might that she was dragged across the floor.

The ninjas stopped and looked down at her with stunned surprise, unable to comprehend why she would return her husband's traitorous ways with such loyalty. They dealt a light but firm blow to her inner elbows, making her release her grip – and they flew out of the window. The light flap of their cloth ties was the only sound as they disappeared. A third ninja immediately appeared at the door, grabbed the wife's arms and twisted them back, so that she was incapacitated.

By the time the two chasing ninjas reached the densely-packed forest, there was no sign of the man. No sound either. And they scanned the woods with narrowed eyes to try to home in on any movement. But it was no use. He was gone.

The little red robin flitted noisily between the trees.

It was making long thin tweets that signified a warning alarm – and in response, the morning song from other birds immediately quietened. The robin's tiny black eyes watched the human keenly as he ran and stumbled and crashed clumsily through the woods.

When the man stepped behind a tree and tried to catch his breath, the little bird rested casually on a branch just above him. But before long, the human started running again, deeper and deeper into the forest.

Quickly the robin flitted high up amongst the top branches – which made the giant human diminish more and more until he was much smaller. In this way, the bird never lost sight of the fleeing man even for a minute, as the haze of dawn turned gradually to the bright light of day. The man ran and ran, and the tiny bird flew and flew for some time, until the two were deep into the forest.

When at last the human reached a steep bank topped with a wall of bushes, he made a concerted effort to run up the slope, then scrambled through a gap and hid inside the foliage. The man wiped his brow on the back of his sleeve and sat back – his body loosening in the knowledge that he had lost the ninjas. Relieved that he was almost safe.

The little bird fluttered down to the bushes and dived in, stopping on a branch just a metre-and-a-half away from the man's sweat-drenched head. It tilted its head, and eyed the human.

The man, in turn, looked up and regarded the red-breasted robin curiously.

The bird hopped closer along the branch, puffed out its chest so that it became round like a ball, and began singing a mesmerising song – one that resounded far and wide.

Yazan Ekren watched the little robin and listened with admiration, sure that this was a good omen. What else could bring such a bird close-by, making it sing so beautifully?

Even though he was on the run, Ekren indulged himself for a few seconds, closed his eyes, and listened quietly, respectfully, to the melodious music. The firm line of his mouth gradually loosening into a wry smile – a moment of serenity, in a storm of emotion – as the little robin sang sweetly to him.

•••——————————————————•••

The wild forest cats left the safety of their shelter, but this time it was not to search for food. One and all, the 29 felines jumped down from the rocks and trees, and slunk soundlessly through the forest, moving as a single entity. A riot of fur, and colour, and markings.

Where normally the dawn chorus consisted of a smattering of birds perched here and there, the cats heard only the singing of a single bird. The robin.

The felines' slow walking turned to a light trot, which soon sped up to a bounding run, as they got closer and closer to the singing. At last the cats found themselves surrounding a thicket of bushes atop a steep, leafy bank. Somehow they knew that within the dense foliage was a man, hiding, and that they must keep him there. He must not be allowed to escape.

But the cats, with their own special powers, sensed before the man even moved that he was going to get up and attempt to leave – and so the cats stopped, hackles raised, as they listened to the rustling within the bushes. Then something caught their attention, and they turned. They glanced southward, realising that their master was coming. It would not be long before he arrived.

When the man suddenly burst out of the bushes looking strangely calm and serene, he stopped suddenly when he set eyes on the wild cats surrounding him. 'Shoo! Shoo!' he called out, trying to wave them away. He scrunched his nose and muttered something about disgusting filthy animals, before attempting to walk around them. But the cats shuffled and reconvened in a circle, surrounding him again. The man tried to kick at the cats, though his clumsy ways were far too crude for their vastly superior reactions; they jumped easily out of harm's way. Some of the cats arched their spines and hissed back at him. Ekren picked up a fist-sized stone and threw it at them, whereupon the animals immediately divided as they leapt aside.

Ekren launched himself through the gap, and ran as fast as his stubby legs would take him. The cats instantly followed, bounding after him effortlessly.

As usual, the cats' heightened senses discerned that their master had nearly reached them, and so they began to slow, in time turning to wait for further instructions.

When Ekren himself heard the running patter of human footsteps not far away, he dived behind the wide trunk of a nearby tree for cover – surprised and panicked as to how they managed to find him in such a vast forest.

•••————————————————————•••

The ninjas sped through the forest, following the images in their head of the robin as it fluttered and flew after Ekren.

They came to a sharp slope where the ground seemed to step up a level into denser woodland, where even daylight could barely penetrate through the thick crown of trees. Racing up the incline, and going around the bushes, they at last caught sight of Ekren as he burst out from behind a tree and ran for his life. They were just about to chase him, when someone came from behind and stopped them.

Tai Jones, unrecognisable in a grey outfit and mask, at last caught up with the exceptionally fast ninjas, panting. The ninjas were eager to follow, but Tai told them, 'Leave him.'

Tai slowed to a walk, eyes trained on glimpses of the running Ekren between the trees – he motioned to the cats with a flick of his finger.

The colony immediately turned and sped after the man. Bounding with agility, the creatures caught up with him in just a few seconds. When they were within jumping distance, they leapt upon him – yowling, claws extended – and latched on with all their might. Ekren screamed in agony! At the same time, hundreds of tiny black dots emerged from the cats' fur and jumped onto Ekren's exposed skin. Fleas! They covered his face, neck, arms, legs – their tiny claws at the end of their six tarsi gripping his flesh firmly. Each flea opened its mouthparts to reveal maxillary lacinia, tiny sword-like blades, that slashed into his flesh before needling in an epipharynx and feasting on his blood.

Ekren screamed as he fell to the ground, and rolled this way and that – desperately trying to fling the cats off, trying to scrape at the dust-like fleas. But it seemed that as soon as they were thrown off, something else would jump in its place. Wave after wave of cats and fleas, fleas and cats. Ekren howled and screamed and rolled and scratched at his bloody skin.

And then suddenly, everything stopped.

The cats jumped off, and backed away.

The fleas disappeared.

The man lay there in shock.

Eyes wild, looking around in fear.

The cats – some sitting, some standing poised – still surrounded him.

Tai stepped out of cover and drew nearer. He looked down at the pitiful man. 'Give yourself up,' Tai said. His voice as always was soft and lilting.

Ekren made to scramble up, but the cats hissed, and he immediately shrank back. He finally capitulated – nodding weakly.

As the ninjas moved toward the fugitive, the cats parted to give them access.

While Ekren was being handcuffed, he watched with wide eyes as the cats instead swarmed around Tai, but this time with affection. They purred loudly, rubbing against his legs, and meowing like kittens. 'Good cats,' Tai told them, a tender expression on his face as he bent down to stroke them. 'Good cats.'

The little robin watched all this from a nearby branch, and when Tai straightened, it flittered over to the boy and landed on his shoulder. Tai stretched out his index finger and the bird jumped onto it, light as a feather. It cocked its head and took in Tai's face – it had never been this close to a human before, but it was not afraid. Tai stroked its feathers; they were soft as down. 'You did well too, little robin. Thank you!' The bird swelled its red breast with pride, satisfied that it had done a good job. In time, it flitted off and disappeared into the forest, chirping noisily as it went.

By the time Ekren's house was evacuated and Sanderson took the family into custody, when all was still and quiet, the red squirrel at last emerged from behind a bullet-hole riddled suitcase on top of the wardrobe. It scuttled down, and made its way straight to the kitchen. It had a field day raiding the cupboards, and when it found a bag of nuts it greedily stuffed them, one by one, inside its cheek pouches until they were bulging. Reconnoitring was hard work, and the bounty of food was a welcome and well-deserved reward.

18   THE GOOD, THE UGLY, AND THE BAD

Capturing Yazan Ekren was just the first of many crackdowns and sting operations that were made throughout the UK.

The children were instrumental in many of the raids in England, working in tandem with the ninjas as well as Sanderson's team, to bring into custody what turned out to be hundreds of gang members who were either involved in or were aiding activities. The special ops team – their identities and unique methods – were kept secret from the public as they wore black outfits and masks and operated mostly under cover of night. The children were able to connect with and utilise whatever animals and insects were in the immediate area: tawny owls and pine martens in Scotland, red stags in the Yorkshire Dales, hornets in Manchester, wood mice in Nottingham, bronze shield bugs and hares in Wales – and in London, which seemed to be the epicentre of activity, a Peregrine falcon, stag beetles, foxes, rats, and even cockroaches in one particularly run-down housing estate.

With every raid, it became startlingly clear to them that the children's unique abilities had become much, much stronger through that last unfortunate connection with Jeremy Fitzsimmons, at the expense of Abdul Hassan – and with each crackdown, the children became more adept, more agile at controlling and using their powers. It seemed they were unstoppable.

•••———————————•••

Meanwhile, a parcel had arrived for Dr Fargo from Brazil. Angry red lettering stamped in all-capitals growled, 'URGENT. PRIORITY. HANDLE WITH CARE.'

It was from Saffie Morales.

Dr Fargo immediately took the parcel to the medical room.

Calista lay on the bed, ashen grey. Her droopy eyelids bobbing up and down – half awake, half asleep. Near death.

Next to her was Jake, one hand clenching hers, and the back of the other pressed against his mouth, as if trying to stop the swell of emotion from bursting out of him. When he saw Dr Fargo arrive with the package, he sat up and watched with keen interest.

The doctor unboxed the precious contents very carefully – lifting out a rectangular block of black foam, embedded with eight glass ampoules. A nurse stepped forward, but he motioned for her to stay back. He wanted to administer the medication himself. Taking one of the ampoules, he held it up to the light to satisfy himself that there were no cracks – it glittered pretty as amber. Folding some gauze, he wrapped it around the head of the ampoule and broke it off with a clean snap. Then he took a syringe and drew up all the liquid, flicking the barrel to disperse any bubbles. He went over to Calista and took a deep breath, before pinching the flesh of her upper arm, sliding the needle in, and plunging down the barrel. He looked at Jake, who glanced up at him, a glimmer of hope in his eyes. 'It's done,' said Fargo.

Jake only managed to nod, overcome. He watched Calista's eyelids slide gently closed as she fell into a deep sleep.

Two days later, in the evening, Calista was still deep in sleep, nobody else in the room, when Tyaishia came in, hugging a large book to her chest. She set it down on the bed, and took Calista's hand, kissing it gently.

Then she bowed her head. Closed her eyes. 'Please, Lord,' she murmured softly. 'Please, just... just make her better. She so beautiful, inside and out. Got a baby. A sweet baby girl, who needs her mother. She got a husband who really, really loves her. She got her whole life in front of her.' She trembled, tears dripping from creased eyes. 'It ain't fair!' she breathed, voice quivering. 'It ain't right! Why would you let this happen? Why?!' She paused, as if waiting for him to answer. 'Please...' she begged. 'Please!'

Not knowing what else to say, not having any more words, she swiped away the tears and then reached to open the Bible. The dry pages crackled as she searched through for a prayer that would convey what she wasn't able to. Somehow the pages parted by themselves, opening at the Psalms, and she read the text slowly, respectfully, in an undertone:

'The LORD is my shepherd; I shall not want.

He maketh me to lie down in green pastures: he leadeth me beside the still waters.

He restoreth my soul: he leadeth me in the paths of righteousness for his name's sake.

Yea, though I walk through the valley of the shadow of death, I will fear no evil: for thou art with me; thy rod and thy staff they comfort me.

Thou preparest a table before me in the presence of mine enemies: thou anointest my head with oil; my cup runneth over.

Surely goodness and mercy shall follow me all the days of my life: and I will dwell in the house of the LORD for ever.'

Someone said, 'Amen,' and Tyaishia looked up to find her son standing there. He went over and hugged her.

She clung on to him for some time, so grateful that he was there, firm and solid in her arms. 'Son,' she breathed, painfully aware of the fragility of life. 'I almost lost you too. Them... them Bible words is so true. "The valley of the shadow of death." You were there, before. Trapped in that valley. Is it... is it too much to ask God to do it again, to save Calista?'

They parted, and Tai looked into her pleading eyes. 'No, Ma. It ain't too much.'

He drew a chair next to hers, sat down, and put an arm around her. He stared at the open pages of the Bible, and asked, 'D'you think that... God gave us these powers, Ma? D'you think he's using us?'

Surprised, she said, 'Maybe.' But then thought about it some more. 'I don't know, son. I don't think so. I... I just know that he, I mean God, he's trying to tell us something through them there pages of the Bible, though I ain't figured out what it is yet. To be honest, I need someone to help me understand.' She sighed, absentmindedly stroking the gilt page edges, as though the leaves were alive, as though she could coax answers out of them – and then she thought of something. 'You know, I read accounts of some people making miracles in the Bible. Not just Jesus. And it must've been for a reason they did them miracles. So there must be a reason for *your* powers too, Tai, though I don't know what that reason could be. I... I'm sorry, I wish I had the answers, but I don't.' She lapsed into silence for a while. 'Actually, no. I don't think your powers are from God. They're from whatever experiments the Professor did. It were an accident maybe. A good accident.' She felt suddenly tired, and rested her head on his shoulder.

The two lapsed into silence and stayed together for some time, arm in arm, watching over Calista – the words of the Psalm trickling softly through their thoughts.

The next morning the Chauffeur came into the room – Calista was still sleeping peacefully. He was holding a small pot of peonies, their petals silky-delicate in a shade of pink so pale they were almost white. He put them on the bedside table, turning them this way and that until he was satisfied they were at the perfect angle. Looking at Calista, he sat down, sighing loudly – he took her hand and kissed it ever so lightly. He noticed the Bible still left open on the other side of the bed.

Curious, he walked round, and lowered himself into the chair where Tyaishia had sat the night before. He leant forward and read it very slowly – being deaf, his reading comprehension was not as good as he would have liked. He mouthed the sentences, trying to associate each word with a BSL sign, but it was a struggle. Clearly frustrated, he eventually stood up, squeezed Calista's hand gently, and swept the Bible into his arms – making sure to keep it open on the same page. He walked out of the room to find Tyaishia.

Two days later, something woke up Jake, and he turned to look for Calista in the bed next to him – he stared at the empty space for a few seconds until he remembered why she wasn't there. Sitting up, he rubbed the sleep out of his eyes and heard Evie gurgling in the cot against the wall. She was lying awake, amusing herself by fingering a foot in each hand – her toes were like tiny pink beads.

When Jake appeared over her with his messy black hair, she jolted with surprise before letting go of her feet and squealing with happiness – stretching out her arms, she opened and closed her chunky hands, eager to be held.

'Good morning, beautiful!' beamed Jake, as he picked her up. 'You're my little morning alarm clock, aren't you?' He turned to look at the actual clock. 'Though you're late, it's almost nine! Let's go and see Mum, okay?'

On hearing the word, baby looked around for her mother.

'We'll see her soon,' he said, smothering her cheek with kisses. Jake padded out of the apartment in bare feet, still in his pyjamas – and they went down several corridors.

All the while, baby chattered gaily, 'Na-na-ma.'

Jake stopped. 'Did you say Mamma? Say Mamma, Evie!'

She looked at him. 'Na-nnn-na.'

'How about Dadda. Say Dadda,' he asked expectantly.

'Na-na-nuh!' she chattered happily.

Jake rolled his eyes. 'Oh, well! Wishful thinking.'

Evie giggled and grabbed his nose, squeezing it hard.

'Evie!' he cried, nasal. Jake pulled her hand off and kissed it. She gurgled with delight, and grabbed his nose again.

'Shhhh,' Jake told her as they entered the room.

But Evie did no such thing. 'Na-nn-nah!' she cried out, even louder.

Calista stirred, and Jake drew in breath as he sat down and put the rather heavy baby on the bed next to her. Evie stared at her mother, her feet stretched to an expectant point, ballerina-style.

'Hey,' Jake said softly to Calista.

'Hey,' she murmured back, groggy.

'How're you feeling?' he asked, stroking her cheek with the back of a finger. There was some colour in her face, a good sign.

Calista blinked sleepily as she thought about it. 'I... feel okay, I think. Feel like I've slept for days.'

Jake smiled. 'You have! You've been out for five whole days, ever since Dr Fargo gave you the first injection.'

'Saffie's jungle juice!' gasped Calista. 'It came!'

Jake nodded, smiling. 'Yes, finally. Let's hope that whatever's in those mysterious yellow flowers does the trick.'

Evie had quietened down, as if she could sense the gravity of her mother's illness – glancing from one parent to the other as they talked.

Just then, Dr Fargo walked in cradling a large tablet computer in the crook of his arm. 'Ah, I thought I heard voices. Calista! My dear! I'm so happy to see you awake!' he beamed.

Calista looked up at him. 'Jake told me I've been out for days after the first treatment. You know... I think I feel better.' She pushed herself up, and Jake stretched over to arrange the pillows behind her.

'That is good news! Good news indeed!'

He noticed that Evie had turned round and was staring intently at him, as if she were following the conversation. Dr Fargo pushed the tablet on Jake and picked up Evie. 'And look at this adorable girl!' he exclaimed. He blew a playful raspberry at her, and Evie scrunched her shoulders and squealed with laughter. Dr Fargo spoke very animatedly to the baby. 'And I have good news, Evie,' he told her with big round eyes. 'If Daddy looks at the tablet, he'll see a comparison of Mummy's tumour, won't he? He will! Yes!' Dr Fargo's voice was getting sillier with every word.

Jake did as he was told, and he swivelled round to show Calista too.

Dr Fargo continued chatting to the baby. 'It's a comparison of that very naughty, very bad tumour, Evie – an image from a week ago, next to an image taken just yesterday, while Mummy was fast asleep!'

'Na-nnn-nuh,' chatted Evie back to him.

'Oh but it's true!' the doctor told her.

Her parents stared at the two images for some time, trying to understand what they were seeing. At last Calista gasped. 'The tumour's shrinking!'

Dr Fargo kissed Evie's cheek and gently put her back down on the bed. He took out his pen as he walked round, then tapped the screen, pointing at a section of one of the images. 'Can you see this rather large nodule?' he said excitedly. 'It's reduced considerably, here. It's only by about four millimetres, but it's still a breakthrough! You see, up to now, the tumour has been steadily growing, no matter what we've thrown at it, so it's definitely reversing. And all the bloodwork confirms it too. Saffie's sent me their data, and everything correlates with her findings through the trials she's done on some animals. It's small beginnings, but definitely cause for hope!'

Calista wiped the tears from her eyes. 'I... I can't believe it,' she said, looking at her husband in a daze.

Jake squeezed her hand, but was more sceptical than his wife. He looked up at the doctor. 'So how can we be sure it's really working? What if it's just coincidence that the tumour shrank?'

'That's a valid point, Jake. Yes, it's possible that it's coincidental, but that's why I'd like to do a full course of the treatment, not only to give Calista the best chance, but also so that we can really gauge the effectiveness of the drug. So Saffie will be sending more ampoules as soon as she can.'

Jake still looked doubtful. 'Can a simple flower really be so effective?'

'You know,' said Dr Fargo, 'many cancer treatments that we've been using for years have come from natural sources. For example, the drug Paclitaxel was found in the bark of the Pacific yew tree, and has become one of the most commonly used treatments against solid tumours. Eribulin too was developed from a sea sponge and is used against breast cancer. In fact, about 70 percent of current cancer drugs are either derived from natural compounds or taken from natural products. We're on the search for new treatments, new remedies, all the time – and it's only the lack of available scientists and funds that are stopping us from finding more. Where Saffie's based, the Amazon jungle, it's perfect for such discoveries. Its rich biodiversity is a vast untapped resource, and frankly I'm not surprised that this unique compound was found there. They're still discovering new species of flora and fauna there on a daily basis.'

He suddenly thought of something. 'Case in point, I read a scientific article recently highlighting a certain bacterium found on fungus-growing ants, which has antibiotic properties – and could possibly be developed into a new antibiotic for humans! So don't be fooled by the fact that this drug comes from a rather beautiful flower – it can still have a very powerful effect against tumours. And with Calista being the first human trial patient, we will know for sure in a few months as to its effectiveness. But the fact that the tumour has already shrunk is, in my mind, solid evidence that it's working, even at this early stage. So don't despise the day of small beginnings, Jake...' He stopped to think about what he'd just said. 'Actually, I think that phrase is in the Bible. Tyaishia will be pleased,' he grinned.

Jake looked again at the images on the tablet, and dared to allow himself a glimmer of hope. He squeezed Calista's hand, a flicker of a smile lighting up his face.

Calista told him, 'It's a slim chance, Jake, but at least it's a chance.' She turned to Dr Fargo. 'Thank you *so* much doctor!'

She and Jake stopped to look thoughtfully at their daughter, nestled against Calista's arm, noisily sucking her thumb. Calista was too weak to pick her up, but she took her girl's little hand and jostled it up and down playfully. 'Things are looking good, Evie,' Calista told her, tears brimming. 'Mummy's going to get better, just you wait and see.'

•••——————————————————•••

Agent V3, or Grandma Ninja as the children affectionately called her, had remained in coma for such a long time that nobody held out much hope for her.

That is, except Milly.

She thought about V3 as she sat outside on the parapet roof of Vivra Towers, a book in her lap, gazing at an incredibly beautiful sunset: the horizon glowing pink, blue, and gold – a spectrum that reflected in the large circular pond in the park across the road. A flutter of green speckles – swirling parakeets – settled on one of the trees in the park, and even from 20 floors up, Milly could hear their noisy squawking as they rustled around for seeds and insects.

Lost in thought, she fingered one of the dried flowers that Tyaishia had used to bookmark a favourite verse in her Bible. Though Milly loved books, she realised she had not yet read the Bible in its entirety, and she therefore borrowed Tyaishia's prized possession now and then to read in her spare time. But she became aware of her fingers hurting, and she looked down to see that her nails had been chewed to the quick, the tips bulging over the nail stumps.

She'd never had the habit before, but recently, every time she visited

V3, or thought about her, she would go into a daze and just nibble and nibble at her fingernails. They were ruined now, and sore, and she had to hide them from people. Her father never usually missed a thing, which meant she had to be extra careful around him.

Milly heard the familiar tap-tap of the Professor's cane, and she turned to find him appearing at the door to the stairs – looking unusually grim. His eyes were rimmed red, as if he had been crying, the circles underneath them seemed deeper. She got up and went to him, concerned. 'What happened…?' she asked, steeling herself. A light breeze slapped her hair against her cheeks.

The Professor remained still and quiet for some time, unable to speak, until he at last forced out a single word. 'V3…' he croaked. Stumbling into a chair, he sat down, and turned his head away.

Milly shook her head, not wanting to believe. 'No, no, it can't be,' she gasped, backing away. But the pain distorting the Professor's face was too jarring for it not to be true. She found herself spinning round and running down the stairs.

Half an hour later she arrived at the hospital, huffing and puffing, stitches in her sides pinching her like a bad conscience. A doctor was just coming out of V3's room. He muttered 'I'm so sorry' as she passed. But Milly couldn't look at him, didn't want to believe, until she saw it for herself.

Pausing at the doorway, she stopped to listen for the familiar whoosh of the ventilator, the steady beeping of the machinery around her. But there was nothing.

The air seemed different. Seemed as if it were laced with acid – it made her choke, cutting through her lungs and heart with razor-sharp pain.

V3 was lying stock still as she always did.

Nothing more than a bag of bones covered by loose, waxy skin.

Her beautiful white hair was luminous and glowing despite the gloom. It was always lovely. Always flourished. Like it had a life of its own, even as her body wasted away.

Struggling to breathe, Milly came slowly nearer.

Eyes searching for the tiniest movement – the flicker of eyelids, the gentle rise and fall of her chest.

Eventually Milly reached out a hand to V3's face.

Sore fingertips rippling lightly over her skin.

The map of her life had been etched into every contour. Every moment of love, each wince of regret.

The lines at the side of her mouth.

Wrinkles around her eyes.

Creases stretched across her forehead.

Proof of her humanness. Proof that she had lived.

Milly at last inhaled a gulp of air, and fell onto V3's lifeless form.

Her sobs sprung from the depths of her heart.

As she cried and cried, as the salty tears flowed, their source was slowly depleting... and soon she felt empty, spent, a dried-out husk.

At last, Milly sat up, shoulders slumped, eyes dull – staring blankly at the lifeless body before her.

Glaring at the ugly, ugly reality – the soulless truth.

V3 was gone.

And it was all her fault.

•••—————————————————•••

After almost two full days of wrangling with Yazan Ekren (who was demanding an interpreter for him and his wife, though they could speak perfectly good English, also complaining that he was ill and needed medical attention), Sanderson was eventually able to bring Ekren's wife in for interrogation, with her lawyer by her side. But the woman refused to say anything that would incriminate her husband, remaining loyal to the man that had threatened to slit her throat. To every question Sanderson asked of her, she responded uniformly with a po-faced 'No comment.'

But they had both Ekren's computer, and his children – taken into care by social services.

And the oldest, an angry eight-year-old Tahir, was willing to talk.

The little boy sat, alone, in the sterile interview room on one side of a desk, looking around with wide eyes and more than a little apprehension. He seemed so small, sitting in the big chair.

The door opened, and he quickly looked over.

In stepped, not scary-looking policemen as he had been expecting, but a blonde girl, who seemed just a few years older than himself. She walked over, also alone, smiling sympathetically and extending a hand toward him. Tahir's parents had told him that their faith frowned upon shaking hands with members of the opposite sex, but in all the commotion the boy completely forgot, and he hesitantly extended his arm and shook hands – feeling grown-up in doing so. Tahir decided immediately that he liked this girl, not least because she reminded him of his best friend at school. 'I want to see Maman...' he told her.

The girl pulled up a chair next to his, and smiled that sweet smile that somehow made people trust her, made them want to be her friend. 'You will, I promise, Tahir. Very soon. Sorry, I know your name, but you don't know mine. I'm Jemima. Jemima Jenkins, and I'm very happy to meet you.'

The boy looked at her. Her colouring was so different from his: creamy skin, light hair, deep-blue eyes. 'Where's Maman?' he asked.

'She's here, nearby, and absolutely fine. Your father too. They're both being well looked after. In fact, they're bringing your mother some tea and biscuits as we speak. Would you like some too? You must be hungry. It's almost 11 o'clock, and I'm told you haven't had breakfast yet.'

'Yes, please,' he said, brightening a little. 'Can I have Jammie Dodgers? They're my favourite.'

Jemima grinned. 'I'll see what we can do,' she said, nodding over at the two-way mirror. She turned to face him, suddenly serious. 'We brought you here, Tahir, because there are some questions we'd like to ask you about your father.'

The boy looked afraid. 'Is it... is it about that video I saw on his computer? That girl, and the bad man? I didn't mean to see it, honest! It's just that I couldn't sleep and–'

'Tahir,' Jemima said gently. 'You're not in trouble, I promise. But... you say you saw a video. Was it...'

'It was horrible!' cried the boy, tears glistening in the corners of his eyes. 'I hated it! I hate what that man did to that girl!' He covered his face with both hands, sniffling.

Jemima put an arm around his shoulders. She closed her eyes briefly, breathing in his energy. Discerning that he was a strong, healthy boy, having his whole life ahead of him.

Absentmindedly, the boy touched her hand with his, and the prickle of static electricity made her jump. Jemima recoiled, instantly withdrawing her arm and cradling it in the other, jarred. Blinking furiously, she tried to understand the picture appearing suddenly in her mind. *A girl lying in bed, drugged and semi-conscious – standing at the side was a man, waiting in the wings.*

As the rest of the memory unfolded, Jemima froze in fear as she saw the awfulness of what was done to her.

'It's not right!' declared Tahir, glaring at his feet, oblivious to Jemima's sudden turmoil. But then he looked up, saw the wet rivulets slipping down her cheeks. 'Why are you crying?' he asked innocently, eyebrows slanting with concern.

'I... I think I saw what you saw, Tahir. I saw that man, and the girl...'

Tahir gasped. 'You saw the video from my father's computer too? It was horrible, wasn't it?!'

Jemima quickly wiped her eyes, caught her breath and, underneath the desk, balled her hands to stop them from trembling. 'Yes, I saw the video,' she said. It was easier than explaining that – somehow, inexplicably – she had just seen what was in his mind. She thought of Fitzsimmons. Remembered being in a circle connected with him, Tai, and Milly. Remembered the sizzle of energy that passed through their bodies, their minds. The feeling of euphoria and elation. The power.

Fitzsimmons had brought back Tai's abilities, making them even stronger, his connection with animals becoming much more powerful. Was it possible that – as she grasped Tai's hand for dear life, as the energy passed through her – she had absorbed some of his abilities?

Jemima at last managed to calm herself, calm her breath, though her skin was still crawling from those sickening images. She said quietly, 'Tahir... I'm so sorry you saw that horrible, *horrible* thing.'

His long eyelashes were dewy. 'I'm sorry too,' he sniffed. 'I wish I could delete it from my head! Every time I close my eyes...' he whimpered, unable to finish the sentence.

'...It's there on repeat,' said Jemima, finishing it for him. It had been passed to her mind now, and she was doomed with the same nightmarish images. But then, a thought suddenly occurred to her. She remembered Tai's ability to erase Karl's memories as easily as wiping dry marker from a whiteboard. She held out her hand again to the boy, this time her palm upward. He looked down at it, and slowly placed his little hand on top. Jemima grasped it and, instinctively, they both closed their eyes.

Locating the memory was easy.

It was hot and blistering red.

It blazed with pain, mortification, horror.

She just needed to put the fire out.

And she willed and willed for it to be extinguished.

But Tahir's hand suddenly pulled away from hers.

Jemima opened her eyes.

Saw the boy falling sideways out of the chair, his eyes rolling back into his head.

His head bumped with a muffled bang against the edge of the desk, and he crashed onto the hard floor.

Jemima gasped. Scraped back her chair.

Tahir's body suddenly went rigid, then loose, and began convulsing uncontrollably in jerking movements. Blood seeped out of the side of his mouth.

'Tahir!!' cried Jemima, falling onto her knees next to him.

The door opened, and Sanderson and another man rushed in.

They pushed her aside, and Sanderson took off his sweater, rolled it up, and placed it next to Tahir's head. They rolled the boy sideways onto it, and stood back. The other man, David O'Connor, a nondescript expression on his face, called urgently for an ambulance.

Jemima started crying – arms hugging her torso, as if consoling herself. 'I was just trying to make it go away,' she whimpered.

Sanderson stood up and looked from the boy to the distraught Jemima. He put an arm around her, and she buried herself into him and cried.

19 X + Y = ?

By the time the Professor had returned to Vivra Towers later that afternoon – still reeling from Jemima's interaction with Tahir in the morning, and having to rush him to hospital – they had missed the James Gillespie documentary. It was advertised as an exposé of a 'secret government project that, two decades ago, had produced genetically engineered child prodigies' – based on the claims of a nurse who says she worked in the laboratories.

The dour-faced Professor and Gaia were in the common room, trying but not succeeding in making themselves comfortable on a sofa. Gaia asked Jasmine to play the recorded programme, and they sat back stiffly and listened to the dramatic opening music of the show with quiet dread.

James Gillespie appeared onscreen, sitting in a beige tub chair and staring meaningfully at the camera, fingertips pressed firmly together. 'Welcome to the Gillespie Files! Today's episode will spotlight the realities of human gene modification. Many of us have seen films like Jurassic Park and Blade Runner, where fictional gene-editing makes for riveting viewing. In Jurassic Park, dinosaur DNA found in mosquitoes preserved in amber, was utilised to recreate extinct species. And in Blade Runner, genetically engineered humans, Replicants, were hunted down as lesser beings, quasi-humans if you will. In today's special episode, we will look at real-world human genetic engineering, and the moral implications of tampering with DNA, which one could say is the instruction manual, the genetic blueprint of life.'

The shot changed to a closer view of his face, eyebrows creasing with intensity. 'Human gene-editing is by-and-large forbidden by law, even in countries that permit human embryonic stem cell research. And yet we have a former nurse – we're calling her Nurse X – who claims that she worked within a science project, sanctioned by the government in the early-noughties, where they carried out such experimental gene-editing. It was a secret project, that has only just come to light.' Gillespie turned slightly, and the camera panned sideways to reveal someone sitting across from him. He greeted her, 'Nurse X, welcome! And thank you for agreeing to appear on the show.'

His guest appeared only in silhouette – a dark outline of a short, overweight woman, hair pulled back in a limp ponytail, shoulders slumped, sitting against a backdrop of what looked like an expensive hotel room. Behind her, opaque blinds had been drawn, daylight filtering in dimly. The caption 'Original voice dubbed over by actor' appeared briefly onscreen. 'Thanks for having me,' she mumbled apprehensively.

'Tell me, what has made you come forward now, after all these years, to expose this supposed secret science project?'

The interviewee thought for a moment. 'It was when the cancer outbreak in Oxford happened, and killed those seven uni students. That's what set it all off for me. See, cancer on the whole isn't contagious, you can't be infected by other people. Not generally. But the news said it'd "spread" to seven students, *only* seven students in the entire university, and they all studied genetics under the same professor, and in the same year. They said that they fell ill during the period when they were studying CRISPR genome-editing technology. As I was listening, I had this nagging feeling. And then it dawned on me. The similarity to the project that I worked on almost 20 years ago – it was unmistakeable! That science project was top-secret, sanctioned by the government, where they genetically engineered super-intelligent babies. *Seven* of them. D'you see? Child prodigies. Well, it couldn't just be coincidence. Someone must've infected those Oxford students on purpose, to make a point, and it had something to do with that same project I worked in. I'm absolutely certain of it. The project and the Oxford students were definitely connected.'

'I see,' said Gillespie thoughtfully. 'Yes, I agree that the similarities are uncanny. We'll discuss the Oxford students later, but I'd like to focus on this secret government project for the moment. You say that it was to produce child prodigies. Do you know what kind of science they used?'

The woman shook her head. 'Not really. I was just a nurse, my job was to look after the mothers who bore the babies – I took their vitals, checked their blood pressure, gave their medication. You know, routine stuff. I never saw or heard about the actual science. All I knew was that they used genetic engineering to modify the babies, and the doctors kept a close eye on the developing foetus in utero. I didn't have much to do with the science side of things.'

The interviewer nodded. 'I see. And do you know why they wanted to breed these super intelligent babies?'

'We weren't told. Military stuff I guess,' shrugged the woman. 'I mean, I think they wanted to breed super soldiers, like that Robocop film, you know – or something like that.'

'Uh-huh, that's interesting... So you think they were used for military purposes. Do you have any proof of this?'

'No, I don't have proof. But what else could it be?'

'Okay. When we talked before, you mentioned the names of some of the people who worked on the project. Do you remember?' asked Gillespie.

The nurse nodded vigorously. 'Yeah, I do! The two scientists who overlooked all the experiments were Dr Kendra and Professor Wolff. They headed up the project.'

An old photograph of a much younger Professor appeared onscreen, probably in his forties, smiling uncertainly at the camera. It was soon followed by a photo of Dr Kendra from 20 years ago, lecturing a class of students.

Gaia stiffened at the mention of their names, yet melted when she saw that familiar photograph of her husband. She tore her eyes off the screen, glanced at the Professor sitting next to her, and squeezed his hand. He looked tense.

Gillespie looked down at his notes. 'Right, well, our investigators have done some thorough research on those two names, but apart from pre-project references, which were abundant because they published many papers, our investigators weren't able to uncover any sign of their existence *after* the project. So it seems likely that they died in the fire that destroyed the laboratories, marking the tragic end of the project...'

'Yeah, it's *possible*,' said the nurse uncertainly. 'A bunch of us were sent on a training course for a few days, and while we were away, that was when the fire happened. I've often wondered what'd happened to them, but yeah, if there's no reference of their existence afterward, it's possible they died.' She paused. 'But I have another theory…'

'I'd like to hear it in due course,' said Gillespie. 'But later, if you don't mind. So were you resident at the laboratories?'

'Yeah, we were. The labs were in a remote countryside location, and us staff lived in a residential block on-site, while the children had rooms in a wing off the laboratories. It was all very hush-hush. We had to sign strict NDAs before they employed us, and we were forbidden from telling anyone where we were, what we were doing. We didn't know the location anyway, because they blindfolded us for the journey to and from the laboratories. They really wanted to make sure nothing got leaked. Absolutely nothing.'

'Interesting… Right, okay, I'd like to talk about the children themselves. Did you have much interaction with them? Were they markedly different from other children their age?'

'I saw them around. They weren't locked away or anything. They had one-to-one educators, as well as staff to look after them, kind of like nannies. Though I didn't have any direct contact with them, I'd see the kids here and there, either playing, going from one place to another, or sitting in a room with their teachers, or being tested. They had to go through loads of tests. They *looked* like ordinary toddlers, ordinary children. But the way they stared at me and watched me when I passed, their eyes boring into me, was just… creepy. Like they were trying to figure me out. And when they were old enough to speak, the way they spoke, you could sort of tell they were different. They didn't chatter like most kids their age – they talked like little adults. Prim and proper like. And the oldest – they called him the Alpha – he gave me the willies. He was just… weird. Everybody hated that one, gave him a wide berth. He used to do the strangest things. One thing that I'll never forget – we had an aquarium in one of the rooms, not just for fish, but it also had one of them small turtles…'

'You mean a terrapin?'

'Yeah, them. The kid, the Alpha, managed to climb right into the aquarium somehow, and smashed that little terrapin to smithereens – on purpose! He just stomped and stomped on it. It was horrible! Really horrible!' She looked down, shaking her head. 'Oh, and another thing, when the Alpha got anxious, which to be honest was most of the time, he used to tug at his hair and sometimes actually pulled out clumps of it. He just kept tugging and tugging, OCD like. And you should have seen when he got angry! He was terrifying. Used to throw things all over the place, and bash himself, like he wanted to punch you, but he knew he couldn't do that, so he kept bashing his leg instead. That boy was *crazy*. Right from the start.' The nurse shivered, as if trying to forget a bad memory. 'All them kids were seriously odd. There was this time when I'd accidentally cut myself trying to open the packaging of something-or-other with some scissors. Medical supplies I think. But the scissors slipped, and I gashed myself.' She absentmindedly rubbed the inside of her forearm. 'Blood dripped all over the place, and I cried 'cos it really hurt. One of the other nurses helped clean me up, put on a bandage. But then I noticed that some of the kids were watching me, laughing their heads off, like they got off on someone else's pain. I saw them whisper something together, sniggering at me. It was humiliating, and horrible. I'll never forget that...'

'My goodness!' remarked Gillespie. 'The children sound quite scary.'

'They were! Gave me the shivers.'

'So the whole experience was quite an ordeal for you?'

The nurse nodded emphatically. 'Yeah, it was. I regretted almost from the start that I signed the two-year contract...' She heaved a sigh. 'But there was nothing I could do. I was stuck between a rock and a hard place. I needed the work, needed the money. My mum was in care, y'see. She was old, and really ill, and I had to help pay for her care-home – while I lived in a grubby old studio flat to cut costs. But that job... those kids... it was too much.' She shook her head.

'You said the children did lots of tests, can you explain further?'

'Yeah, they were tested right from the start, but especially when they got a bit older. They had to do really full-on, gruelling tests – almost every day, or every other day. There were mental tests – where they had to answer pages and pages of questions, all within a set time. Like answering 100 questions within 30 minutes. Or they'd have to solve IQ puzzles. Then there were tests to monitor their physical development, reactions, skills, and so on. Again, I had nothing to do with that side of things, but us staff talked with each other, and I found all this out from the others. I was told each child was well above average for their age. In fact, they were off the charts. There was this one kid, the Delta, she could recite all the nursery rhymes off by heart, word-perfect. Another one could do the Rubik's cube in, like, three seconds! It was crazy.'

'Interesting, very interesting,' remarked Gillespie. 'Child prodigies indeed. But, you called one of them "the Delta" – didn't they have proper names?'

'No, they were just called Alpha, Beta, Delta, and so on. Like they weren't kids, just numbers, just experiments.'

'That seems rather a cold way of referring to them. Were they all of the same background?'

'No, they came from difference races, one was Chinese, one was German, another one was Indian looking. A couple had English parents. There was a black boy from Jamaica I think, and also a girl from... South America, or somewhere like that.'

'So they were from all over the world? Very interesting. The children sound quite... remarkable.'

The nurse spluttered. 'That's one way of putting it! I'd've used other words to describe the little freaks, but I don't think I'm allowed to swear here...'

'No, not really! Okay, so going back to the fire that destroyed the laboratories, you said you had another theory. What do you think happened?'

'Well, that was the one and only time me and some of the staff were sent away on a training course. Afterward, when we heard about the fire, we were absolutely devastated because we were sure our other work colleagues had died, including the kids. But they never let us go back to the site. And – thinking about it after all these years – to me, it just seemed odd that the one day we were sent away, that's when the fire happened.'

'So, let me get this straight,' said Gillespie, sitting up with keen interest. 'You're implying that the fire was a ruse to fake their deaths?'

The nurse nodded, though not so convincingly. 'I think so... I-I can't say for sure. It's just that the timing with our training course was too convenient…'

'I see, I see. Well, if you're right, that would mean that those genius kids are still alive. Professor Wolff and Dr Kendra too… So if they are, how old would the children be now?'

'Well, the oldest, the Alpha, would be around 19 years old, and if I'm remembering correctly, the others would be ranging from about 14, 15 years old, I think.'

'So they're all teenagers?'

'Yeah, teenagers.'

'And do you have any photographs of them by any chance?'

The nurse shook her head vigorously. 'No, no. We were forbidden from bringing cameras and camcorders to take videos. In those days our mobile phones weren't as sophisticated as today's. They were brick phones. We didn't use them for much except making calls and playing Tetris. We weren't allowed to tell anyone our location, or give any details. Like I said, it was top top secret. They were constantly checking our phones, searching our bags when we went in and out. I hated it, really hated it. Like Big Brother watching over you all the time.'

'I hear you. It sounds like a very strict and harsh working environment… Okay, I want to talk about the Oxford Uni students now – that really was horrific, and very tragic. Our hearts go out to those poor youngsters and their families. If you remember when it happened two years ago, the whole country was on tenterhooks, not least because it was, in the beginning, feared to be some sort of contagious disease. Thankfully it turned out not to be. But you said you were sure that there was a connection between the project you worked on and the Oxford deaths. Can you explain?'

'Well, yes, I'm pretty sure that those seven university students' deaths had something to do with the child prodigies. Though I can only speculate on what that connection might be. I mean, it could be that one of the doctors from the project, possibly Kendra or Wolff – if they're still alive – were disgruntled in some way, and *they* might've had something to do with those students dying. Or, it might even be one of those weird kids. I mean, those kids were really clever. Maybe one of them, or all of them, had a point to make. I wouldn't put it past them.'

'Really? You think the Project Ingenious children killed them?'

The nurse nodded. 'Yeah.'

'You think they turned bad, even though they're only teenagers?'

'You can be psychotic at any age, James.'

'So, let me get this straight. You think these genius children became twisted and evil? Psychotic, as you say? And you think they were behind the deaths of those Oxford students?

The nurse shrugged. 'Like I said, it's only speculation, but I think it's definitely a possibility. In the labs, they were definitely showing signs of... being that way.'

'If you're right, then that's quite worrying. If they're still around.'

'Yeah, it is worrying. I know it's weird, but, somehow, I feel it in my bones. I feel like they're still alive.'

The camera switched to Gillespie, looking quite perturbed. He turned directly towards the lens, speaking to the camera. 'That's the million-dollar question: are the secret genius children still around? Did they die in the fire? Or are they alive, and possibly living amongst us? After the break we're going to speak to someone who claims they *are* alive. He says that he first met and spoke with some of them two years ago, right here in the UK. He also claims that Professor Wolff is very much alive. And lastly, he claims that – very recently – one of the teenagers did something quite disturbing. Which he saw with his own eyes. So don't go away!'

The dramatic music marked the commercial break, and Gaia turned to the Professor. 'My goodness!!' she gasped, mortified. 'They... they're twisting everything. That nurse is making the project sound really bad, and I can't believe the way she's describing the children... as evil, psychotic.'

The Professor fell back against the sofa, dumbfounded. 'I-I suppose it's perception, Gaia. You often see what you want to see – you remember the things you want to remember.'

'Do you know this stupid nurse, Nurse X?!' she asked, outraged. 'Did she even work on the project really?'

The Professor floundered. 'I... I can't be certain. But she certainly knows things about the project which suggests she was there. I mean, she knew about the Alpha, and the way we named them. We weren't like Big

Brother by any stretch of the imagination, but we did have to monitor everyone's comings and goings, and be strict about security...'

'What about that ridiculous story of the children laughing at her when she cut herself?!' snorted Gaia. 'I suppose we can ask them about it, but would they even remember? I know they've got flawless memories, but the oldest must've been just two or three years old at the time.'

'You know them, Gaia. They've never been like that, ever. It's possible the nurse misread the situation.' He thought of something. 'I just remembered – some of the rooms had one-way mirrors, which might not have been obvious to people on the viewing side, because it looked like normal glass. So, maybe the kids didn't even see her. Maybe they were just looking at their own reflections, and laughing amongst themselves.'

'Ah yes, that could explain it,' said Gaia. 'And who on earth is this person who claims to have met them recently!'

The Professor shook his head, overwhelmed. 'The mind boggles!'

The two lapsed into silence, the jingle of commercial music tinkling in the background. Soon the adverts ended and dramatic music marked the next segment of the programme. Both Gaia and the Professor sat forward.

Gillespie appeared onscreen again, this time in a street, across the road from tall grey buildings with two policemen standing guard on either side of a familiar black door. Gaia gasped. 'He's at Downing Street!' she told the Professor.

Again, Gillespie spoke to the camera, a hand gesturing toward the door behind him. 'I can reveal that my next guest also wants to keep his identity confidential, because he works right here in Downing Street. He came forward and got in touch with me when he saw the teaser trailers for this episode – so we've had to make some very rushed last-minute edits right before airing. He too is very disturbed by these genius children, much like Nurse X. We will be calling our next guest Mr Y. Join me, now, in a private interview he gave earlier today, where he claims to have met several of these teenagers.'

The screen switched back to the original hotel room where Nurse X had been interviewed, but this time the silhouette of a thick-set man sat before Gillespie – his back rigid as a pole. Gaia got up and stood closer to the television screen, a curious expression on her face. 'I know this man...'

she murmured. 'There's something familiar about him.'

Gillespie spoke to the man: 'Thank you very much, Mr Y, for coming forward. I appreciate that this is putting your job on the line, so again, we'll be dubbing over with an actor's voice. Welcome! I was fascinated to hear your claim that you've actually met some of these teenage prodigies. Can you tell me more?'

Mr Y nodded soberly. 'Yes. During my work for the government, I came across three of these children for the first time about... two years ago. It was while I was working with a team investigating the unusual disappearance of a Russian doctor. He'd been drafted in specially – though I wasn't privy to the precise reasons why, because information was on a need-to-know basis. But it was clear that it had something to do with the health of the so-called genius teenagers. You see, when our team were sent to investigate, three of the teens were there too, and one of them was suffering a strange disease that made him look... well, really old, even though he was only about... 15 years old, or so. He was crippled and confined to a wheelchair. So it was obvious to me that this Russian doctor was brought in to help the sick kid. I was actually introduced to three of the "genius" kids at the time. Apart from the wrinkly-looking kid, there was an English girl, with short, dark hair, who was pale as a sheet and really moody. And the third one was a precocious know-it-all Chinese girl.'

'That matches up with the descriptions given by the nurse,' remarked Gillespie. 'As you're speaking about them, it's obvious from your expression and the tone of your voice that you disliked them...'

'Yes, I did! Precocious teenagers are bad enough, let alone know-it-alls who are constantly correcting you and putting you down. They made me feel like rubbish. So, yeah, I didn't care for them at all.'

'And where did you meet them?'

'It was at a certain location in the Midlands. That's all I can tell you without giving too much away...'

'Right, I see,' said Gillespie quickly. 'We'll move on then. Can you tell me what these teenagers were like? Anything that stood out to you?'

'Yes, yeah. One thing really stood out... how can I put this? They claimed to have a special... connection with animals.'

'Animals? A connection? In what way?'

'They thought they could communicate with them. You know, read their minds.'

'Uh-huh, I hear you,' said Gillespie, taken aback. 'So are you saying they have... mental problems?'

'You can say that again. They were mad! Like they thought they were that doctor from that film where he talks to animals.'

'Erm, do you mean Dr Dolittle?'

'Yes, that's it. I mean, please!' Mr Y threw up his arms in disbelief.

'So,' said Gillespie. The camera zoomed into his face, nervous creases at the side of his eyes. 'There are teenage prodigies running around – here in England – who are very disturbed, and have mental problems. This is very worrying...'

'Unfortunately, that's the least of our problems,' said Mr Y, leaning slightly forward. 'I saw something really shocking today, that *really* turned me against them. One of them, this girl, a blonde girl, deliberately hurt a completely innocent boy. She grabbed his hand, and... he just keeled over and had a seizure! I was right there. Saw it, with my own eyes. The poor boy had to be taken straight to the hospital. Thanks to *her*.'

Gillespie's eyes widened. 'That is terrible. I-is the boy okay?'

Mr Y shrugged. 'Who knows! Like I said, we're only given info on a need-to-know basis. After the incident, after he was rushed to hospital, everyone's been hush-hush about the whole thing. I don't know if the child's dead or alive. I'm sure they're going to cover it up, like they did with everything else to do with this project.'

'That's very troubling indeed. Can you tell me in more detail exactly what this girl did to the boy?'

Mr Y nodded. 'It all happened really fast. All I can remember is that the two of them held hands, the teenage girl and the young boy, and some kind of power shot out of her, like electricity – it... it... zapped him.'

'A power?'

'Yeah, she had this power that zapped right through the kid. He collapsed, and was rolling around on the floor, convulsing.'

'That sounds quite disturbing, and terrifying.'

'It was!'

'You say it was a girl who did this. Can you describe her to us?'

'Yes. She was blonde, Caucasian, and I would say about 14 or 15 years old. She was short for her age, about so high.' He held his hand out, to above his head.

'So around… one-and-a-half metres?' said Gillespie.

'Yes, around that. She looks like any teenager, ordinary really – but… she had this way of looking at you, with vacant eyes. Actually, I can do more than just describe her,' he told Gillespie meaningfully. He paused. 'I can tell you her name. She's called Jemima Jenkins.'

Gaia gasped, and the Professor immediately stood up. 'Jasmine!' he called out. 'Tell the agents to bring in Jemima straight away. As a matter of urgency!' He started pacing up and down, anxious. 'Jasmine? Did you hear me?!'

Jasmine's perfectly calm voice was a stark contrast to the Professor's. 'I'm sorry, Professor, but I was trying to locate Jemima. Her last known position was when she entered the Royal Marsden hospital earlier today, together with Sanderson, Tahir Ekren, and the ambulance men.'

'Oh dear,' gasped Gaia. 'They were probably asked to turn off their phones in the hospital.'

The Professor spoke to Jasmine, even louder. 'Tell the agents to locate her, extract her, and bring her back – immediately!' The force of his last words made Gaia jump. But she was distracted by the television again, the interview of Mr Y still ongoing.

The camera zoomed into the silhouetted head of the interviewee as he continued talking to Gillespie, '…and the names of the other teenagers that I know about are Tai Jones, he was the wrinkly one. Another was Melody Bythaway, who they call Milly. Then there was Saffie Morales, and also Mei Hui Li. She was the Chinese know-it-all.'

'That's amazing that you could reveal their names, thank you! But… the nurse told us there were seven. Together with Jemima Jenkins, that's only five.'

Mr Y shrugged. 'That's all I know about. As I said, need to know. I'm not high up on the pay-scale if you know what I mean, so that's all the info I've been privy to.'

The Professor angrily whipped out his white cane, and flicked it out to full length. He hurriedly tapped his way out of the room. Gaia could only watch him go, listening as his voice got fainter. 'Jasmine, get the agents to recall *all* the children immediately!' he told her. 'Not just Jemima. All of them!!'

'Done,' said Jasmine.

Perturbed, Gaia's eyes darted from the doorway where the Professor had just disappeared, back to the screen. The dark image of the despicable Mr Y. Her eyes widened suddenly as she at last figured out who he was. The close-cut hair. The broad shoulders. The way he sat bolt upright. She had only seen him a couple of times in the country house where Dr Vassiliev had disappeared. But it was definitely him.

The camera panned across to Gillespie, looking very serious. 'I can reveal that Mr Y has provided a video of the incident, where Jemima Jenkins deliberately injured, and perhaps killed, a young boy whose identity we have kept hidden by obscuring his face. The footage is shaky, and just a few seconds long, recorded secretly on his mobile phone – but we will slow it down so that you can see what's happening.'

Gaia gasped, wide eyes watching the screen switch to grainy blown-up footage. A camera from high up looked down on a teenage girl and a younger boy, the only occupants of the room. The older girl had curls of short blonde hair obscuring her face – she held out an open hand to the boy sitting next to her. Slowly, hesitantly, he placed his hand in hers, and they both closed their eyes. A flare of light – whether it was camera flare, or something else – spasmed between them, and the boy suddenly fell sideways. They repeated the brief video twice, slowing down playback each time so that the footage of the flare of light and the boy keeling over – banging his head on the table, tumbling to the floor, and fitting – was shown in all its alarming detail.

Gaia held a hand to her mouth, hardly believing what she was seeing.

A notification beep on her phone distracted her, then it beeped again and again. She tore incredulous eyes from the screen, and looked around for her phone. Bewildered. Trying to grapple with the footage she had just seen.

20 LITTLE TROOPER

After the seizure that Tahir Ekren suffered in the interview room, he had been taken immediately to the Royal Marsden hospital, together with a distraught Jemima who insisted that she accompany him. She sat in the waiting room, clutching Sanderson's hand in both of hers as if her life depended on it, lapsing into a dazed silence that came from the possibility that she had done irreparable brain-damage to the boy. The weight of guilt rained down on her. Stuck to her like mud that was slow-drying, crusting on her skin, clothes, hair.

They were there for hours. The hospital room was packed to brimming, and it seemed that people were staring at her – their eyes, cold and accusatory. Some even looked fearful of her, of what she might do to them. A man was on his phone – was he pointing the camera at her? Filming her? Sanderson shifted round, shielding Jemima from view, and at the same time he rippled his fingers within her grasp, trying to loosen the sharp pinch of her fingertips digging into his palm.

At last someone emerged from A&E and walked over to them. Jemima let go of Sanderson's hand, and jumped up from her seat. 'Is he... is he okay?' she breathed, tense.

The weary lady doctor looked from Sanderson to Jemima. Her hair had been tightly plaited into neat cornrows, though frizzy strands had teased out at the edges. 'He's going to be absolutely fine, dear,' the doctor smiled, touching her shoulder consolingly. 'We managed to get his records from his GP, and we discovered he has a history of epileptic fits which explains the seizure...'

'Oh thank goodness!' cried Jemima, tears welling up.

The doctor frowned slightly. 'I don't think you understand. Epilepsy is actually a *bad* thing... And the particular type of fit Tahir suffered is what we call a grand mal seizure, which is quite a serious form of it. Saying that, his records show that he's only ever suffered from two fits, the last one being about three years ago, which was much less severe. So I think the seizures are quite isolated, and he therefore doesn't need ongoing medication – especially since there don't appear to be any underlying conditions. Though...' She paused to look around the waiting room. 'Are... are the parents here?'

Sanderson pulled the doctor to the side, extracted his ID from his pocket and showed it to her, lowering his voice. 'We've taken the parents into custody for... security reasons. Meanwhile the boy is in our care. So you can tell us everything.'

The doctor sighed. 'In a way, I'm glad they're not here... There are bruises and markings on Tahir's body consistent with being physically beaten. And x-rays have shown evidence of three previously fractured ribs, none of which have healed properly – evidence that medical help definitely wasn't sought when it happened. Tahir told me that he has aches and pains, and those past fractures may well be the reason why.'

Jemima gasped. 'Poor Tahir!' She looked up at Sanderson and clutched his arm. 'That might explain why he couldn't sleep last night.' Jemima's heart was breaking for him.

Sanderson, who had a son of his own whom he loved dearly, gritted his teeth and shook his head. 'Awful, just awful,' he murmured.

'I was going to call the police and contact social services...' started the doctor.

'No need,' Sanderson assured her. 'He's with us now, so we'll handle everything. We'll apply for an emergency child protection order to remove him from his parents. And I'm personally going to make sure the boy is well looked after.'

Jemima asked the doctor, 'H-how is he now?'

She smiled. 'The seizure wasn't prolonged, so I'm pleased to say that he's recovered quickly, though he's a little sore. I've given him painkillers for a headache, and he was sitting up in bed, quite alert, when I left him. But... for some reason, he keeps talking about Jammie Dodgers?'

Jemima beamed, eyes glistening with damp. 'The little trooper!' she exclaimed with enormous relief.

'That he is,' smiled the doctor.

Just at that moment, a nurse brought the bleary-eyed boy out of the A&E into the waiting room. He had a bandage around his head, his hair was messy, his clothes rumpled.

Jemima rushed over to hug him. 'I'm *so so* sorry, Tahir!' she cried. 'I... I was just trying to help. I didn't mean for you to have a fit. That video that you saw, of the girl, I was trying to... to help you forget it, when–'

Sanderson looked around warily. 'Lower your voice, Jemima,' he warned.

Tahir blinked at Jemima, genuinely puzzled. 'What girl? What video?' He didn't have a clue what she was talking about. Instead, he huffed and folded his arms. 'But you promised to bring me tea and Jammie Dodgers, and I'm very hungry!'

Jemima took a moment to absorb what he'd just said, and then beamed with both delight and relief. She turned to her bodyguard and glared at him. 'Sanderson, that was your job!' She winked at Tahir.

Sanderson raised an eyebrow, then said, 'I'm sorry, Ma'am!' A wry smile crept across his face. 'I'll get my men on the task with the utmost urgency! They'll be ready and waiting with a tray of tea and biscuits the moment we return,' he promised.

Jemima took Tahir's hand, and they turned to leave. 'About time!' she told Sanderson, who followed behind. They made their way out. 'And you'd better pick us up a bucket of KFC on the way back, seeing as it's almost dinnertime!' she told Sanderson. 'What do you say, Tahir?'

Tahir gasped. 'Jammie Dodgers and KFC? Yes, yes please!'

As they walked past the people in the waiting room, one of them suddenly jumped up in front of them. It was the man with the phone. He was middle-aged with premature balding, wearing an old tracksuit top and bottoms, though he didn't look at all fit with a rotund belly. 'Are *you* one of them Ingenious weirdos?' he asked strangely.

Taken off-guard, Jemima was about to say something when Sanderson pushed her along, and stood between her and the man. 'We don't know what you're talking about!' he told the man. 'Move along please.'

Quickly turning away, Sanderson steered the two children out of the hospital waiting room.

21 THE FALL OF JJ

Jemima Jenkins rolled over in bed, cursing the existence of school.

The alarm clock had rudely awoken her, and she slapped her hand on the clock to stop the irritating burps of sound, groaning from the hazy realisation that today was the beginning of a new school year after the summer break. The first day back was always the worst, especially after a long holiday. She rubbed her eyes to find her uniform hanging from the top of her wardrobe, pressed to within an inch its life – her mother's tormenting reminder of where she had to be at 9 o'clock on the dot. Jemima jolted upright – it was now a race against time. She had 50 minutes to wash, dress, tame her hair, eat breakfast, and catch the 8:35 bus.

Downstairs, her mother was already dressed and in their tiny kitchen, humming and dancing to the latest Adele song playing on the radio, while she prepared breakfasts and lunchboxes. She was in a good mood because her kids were going back to school. After a long school holiday, she was completely frazzled from trying to keep them entertained, fed, and watered for six whole weeks – and though she loved her children with all her heart, she couldn't wait to see the back of them...

'Good morning JJ!' she exclaimed to her daughter far too brightly for a Monday morning.

Jemima shuffled in in her too-large uniform, her blonde hair perfectly combed, and wearing knee-high socks that were sagging mid-calf. Jemima threw her head back. 'I hate school!' she groaned loudly.

Her mother eyed her legs. 'Pull your socks up, love. I mean, literally.' She thought for a moment. 'And actually, you need to pull your socks up the other way too, like we talked about. Your grades weren't great last year, JJ.' She waved a wooden spoon at her. 'Mess this up and you'll have to retake the year, which is the last thing you want. Now, hurry up and eat, it's getting late.'

Jemima huffed obstinately as she plonked herself down on the sofa. A bowl of cereal and a carton of milk were waiting for her on the coffee table. 'I'm not hungry,' she protested.

'Jem, you *have* to eat!'

'But I'm not hungry. In fact, I feel sick.'

Her mother stopped, walked over, and pressed the back of her hand against Jemima's forehead. 'You're fine,' she said, hesitantly. 'I think. Tell me honestly. Are you *really* ill?'

'I don't want to go to school! It's making me feel sick just thinking about it!'

Mother rolled her eyes. 'Look. I don't always want to go to work, but I have to. Who else is going to pay the bills?' Tutting, she marched into the hall and hollered up the stairs. 'Brent! You're going to be late! Get a move on!!' Returning to the kitchen, she stuffed the lunchboxes with food, clicked them shut, and left them on the counter. 'I've packed your fave, Jem. Egg and cress sarnies, Dairylea dunkers, and fruit salad – I've even put a chocolate roll in there specially, for your first day back. Please *please* eat up all the fruit!'

Thunderous footsteps vibrated through the house as Jemima's rotund older brother bounded downstairs and raced into the kitchen. 'Mum! I'm so late! Why didn't you wake me up?!' he asked, vexed.

'I did,' protested mother. 'Twice!'

He thought for a second. 'Well, you weren't loud enough.' Somehow, everything was her fault.

'I'm not your flippin' alarm clock, Brent!' she remonstrated. 'You're 17. Set your own alarm!!'

Brent retorted, 'If I get detention for being late, I'm telling Mrs Martin it was because of you!'

'Mum...' winced Jemima. 'I'm not feeling good.'

'Yeah, yeah,' mother shouted back at her son. 'I'm sure your teacher's heard that excuse a thousand times.'

'Mum,' Jemima repeated.

When Brent saw the black Batman lunchbox waiting for him on the counter, he groaned, 'Not that again!' He sprung the box open, and began stuffing the contents into his rucksack. 'I can't take that to school! I'm not two years old!'

Mother stopped and raised an eyebrow. 'You sure?'

But he'd already turned and was hurrying out.

Jemima jumped up, annoyed, and stomped over – mumbling under her breath, 'Ignore me why don't you…' She swiped the lunchbox from the counter, brown eyes glaring at her mother. 'It's going to be a bad day,' she told her. 'I can feel it. And you're going to regret making me go.' She turned on her heels, swung her bag over her shoulder, and marched out.

'Jemima! Your breakfast!'

But she was answered only by the loud slam of the front door.

Her mother stared after her, blinking.

Seconds trickled by as she listened to the quiet of the house in their wake. Absorbed the tantalising taste of long-awaited freedom.

As she stood there, she was blissfully unaware that, for the rest of her life, her thoughts would return – uncountable times – to that very moment. The glimpse of her daughter's back as she disappeared, the slam of the door, and the silence left in her wake.

Little did she know that those feather-soft moments of calm before the storm would forever haunt her. That the searing pain of regret would follow everywhere she went, and everything she did, like a shadow that never went away.

Because that was to be the last time Diana Jenkins saw her daughter, alive.

•••——————————————————————————•••

By the time Jemima had marched to the number 65 bus stop, she realised that, actually, she really was ill. She tried to swallow down the nausea, and closed her eyes as she sat on the red bus-shelter seat, next to an old lady, sure that her mother would never believe her if she returned home.

Two boys, wearing the same uniform as Jemima, arrived at the stop, rudely bumping into her as she passed. 'Sorry,' one of them mumbled as he glanced back at her with a goofy grin, not sorry at all. Ordinarily she would have told them to watch where they were going, but she was feeling light-headed, and her eyes were droopy. The old lady next to her got up, staring at something in the distance, and Jemima saw that the bus had appeared further down the road. She got up too and stepped forward, deciding that very second that she was going to turn round and make her way back home, when one of the boys backtracked and stopped right in front of her. The other soon followed. 'Hey, you're Jemima Jenkins, aint-ya?' said the first boy. 'You're the girl from that documentary! The weirdo that killed that boy!'

Jemima pulled a face. 'What're you talking about?!'

'Yeah,' said the other boy, agreeing with his friend. 'You're that freak!'

But Jemima was feeling so poorly, so dizzy, that she could only step away from them, toward the curb.

The old woman overheard and turned to her, frowning. '*You're* Jemima Jenkins?! Shame on you for what you did! Hurting that poor boy!!' She bashed her with her handbag.

'Ow!' cried Jemima, stumbling back.

Just then, the bus swooped into the stop.

The boys suddenly shouted out, and one of them tried to grab her blazer to pull her in, away from the road.

But Jemima had already lost her balance. She toppled backward, and the moving bus hit her head with a sickening thwack.

She fell sideways with force.

Crashing onto the pavement.

But she was dead before she even hit the ground.

As she lay there, blank eyes frozen wide, a pool of dark liquid seeped onto the paving slab underneath her head.

22 PANDORA'S BOX

When Ilse Schäfer and Jemima Jenkins were brought into the secret top floor of Vivra Towers, the girls stepped out of the elevator chattering happily together, a guard on either side of them, and Professor Wolff following closely behind.

But the girls suddenly stopped in their tracks, and the Professor bumped right into them. 'What...?' he started, surprised.

Ilse stared straight ahead, glanced at Jemima in amazement, and then turned to the Professor. 'The wall!' she said, flabbergasted. 'It's covered in... in... lots and lots of drawings.'

The usually pristine white lobby wall opposite them was filled with a plethora of charcoal sketches. Some of them had been painted over with frenzied strokes of sepia, raw umber, burnt sienna, and touches of light ochre – murky monochromatic underpaintings. The images exploded outward from the far-left corner, and stopped around two-thirds of the way along. Crazed artwork of a deranged mind – as if a Pandora's box of images had been opened, spilling out a drove of painted curses. The expressionism style of artwork was flawless, the rendering breathtakingly immaculate; every stroke of charcoal, every lick of paint against the white, seemed of great significance. Yet the images rumbled with dread and angst. So much so that as Jemima's eyes pored over every inch, her chest heaved with emotion. 'These sketches, the style...' she said, worried. 'They're like–'

Just then, a door opened, and Brian appeared from further down the left corridor. He ran over to them, his face pale. 'Professor! Thank goodness.' He gulped, trying to swallow down his distress. 'It's Milly. Sh-she's... going back to the way she was. Maybe even worse than before. I... I don't understand. The cure. Dr Vassiliev's cure. I thought it had worked.

But... it's backfired.' He combed a distraught hand through his hair, overcome.

'Where is she?' asked the Professor. He inched forward and felt for Brian's shoulder. He was shaking.

'She's sleeping in her room. I woke up this morning to find her out here, in a... a painting frenzy.' He indicated toward the wall, though he couldn't bring himself to look at it. 'She was muttering to herself. Didn't even see me. Just kept working away.' He blinked, eyes glistening with damp. 'I had to drag her away. Had to physically pull her back to her room. It was...' He shook his head, too overwhelmed to finish.

Jemima threw herself on him, hugging him. Brian, helpless to an onslaught of emotions, closed his eyes and surrendered to her embrace.

'Jasmine,' called out the Professor. 'Call Dr Fargo! Tell him to come urgently.'

Her smooth voice responded, 'He is already on his way, Professor. I called him 13 minutes ago.'

'I asked her,' explained Brian, wiping his eyes on the back of his sleeve.

There came the sound of another door opening, and Tyaishia appeared in a nightgown, her hair wrapped in a stocking. 'What's all this commotion?' she asked as she padded over to them in bare feet, followed shortly by Tai in his pyjamas, yawning, and sleepily scratching his head.

Tyaishia stood in front of them, looking at each of their shocked expressions. She saw one of the agents staring at the wall – and she turned, gasped, wide eyes roaming over the entirety of chaotic artwork. 'What... is... this?' she mumbled.

As she spoke, a gobsmacked Tai went to the Professor and took his hand. It was cold. And the boy turned to look over the wall.

The Professor blinked furiously. Scales fell from his eyes. The dazzle of light and depth, and colours, and forms, was overwhelming, pulsating with each thunderous beat of his heart. And then his vision came into focus. And he saw it all.

He saw sketch after sketch. Lines of insects flying out in droves, intertwining frenzied drawings. He saw an upside-down drawing of Karl König in the style of Vitruvian Man, pyjamaed arms and legs outstretched, encircled by Jemima, Milly, Tai, and Mei Hui, lying on their sides, sleeping in foetal positions. From their heads wafted images of Karl's life, from conception, embryonic stages, to birth, childhood, Carey, Ambrosia, and a field filled with cornflowers, surging with fragile petals. The petals themselves came to life, carried by curls of wind, fanning outward to form images of Jeremy Fitzsimmons. His young handsome face floating softly, and then redistributing into the grotesque, bulging old man of today. And the last images, nothing more than incomplete outline sketches, seemed to be of four horses, each with a rider on its back. They were the largest images of all, galloping – as if with great speed – toward the foreground. Despite the vagueness of form, faint lines drawn with the lightest of touches, the figures were somehow imbued with a solid sense of doom.

'Them horses,' murmured Tyaishia to herself. 'I know them from somewhere...'

One of the agents turned away, touched his earpiece, and listened. 'Excuse me, Professor,' he said eventually, 'I've just been instructed to withdraw our security detail – with immediate effect.' He indicated to his colleague that they should leave.

The Professor turned to him, baffled. 'I... don't understand. The PM specifically instructed 24-hour security–'

'I'm sorry, sir,' interrupted the agent. 'But the PM is currently undergoing a vote of no confidence.'

'What!' exclaimed the Professor.

'It's something to do with that documentary,' the agent explained, ending the call on his earpiece. 'All they told me was that the Ingenious project was sanctioned without the proper parliamentary approval.'

'That's ridiculous!' said the Professor. 'That was decades ago, and the PM had nothing to do with it. He wasn't even in office at the time.'

He held up his hands. 'I'm only following orders, sir.' The two agents turned round and left by the stairwell, their footsteps reverberating and fading.

The Professor shook his head, mumbling to himself. And then he said out loud, 'Jasmine, recall agents V2 and V4, and send them to our location – immediately.'

'Done,' said Jasmine. Then several seconds later she spoke up again, 'There is a call for you, Professor, from agent D2. Would you like it through the speakers?'

'Yes,' he replied without thinking, still thrown by the news about the PM.

'Professor,' came the voice of a young woman. 'I've at last heard back from our contacts in both China and Brazil – unfortunately they haven't been able to reach Mei Hui and Saffron Morales.'

The Professor huffed with frustration. 'How could they lose them?!'

'The flash floods in China from ongoing torrential rains – it's been on the news. There've been 16 confirmed dead and 36 missing from the resulting mudslides in the Qinghai province – so far. And in Brazil, wildfires are raging through the Pantanal as we speak...'

The Professor closed his eyes, as if drawing strength. 'This can't be happening,' he mumbled to himself. His eyes shot open and he said determinedly, 'Tell them it's imperative they find the girls, pronto!! Leave no stone unturned, do you hear? I want them found!'

'Yes, Professor,' came D2's grave reply. A click signified the end of the call.

Just then, the elevator pinged, and the doors opened with a whoosh. Out stepped Dr Fargo wearing a face-mask, surprised to find everyone in the lobby looking so grim, and even more surprised to see the pandemonium of images on the wall. 'Great Scott...' was all he could say as he looked it over. He eventually tore his eyes away and asked, 'Where is she?'

Jemima motioned toward the corridor. 'She's in her room.'

'Right,' said the doctor, and was about to rush off when he paused to address them all. 'You do know we have another wave of Covid on our hands? You should all be wearing masks! Yesterday alone, there were over 18,000 new test-confirmed cases in the UK, and 923 deaths...' He shook his head as he rushed past them. Brian followed him.

Jasmine's voice resounded from the speakers yet again, making the Professor jump. 'Professor, I have Rory Sanderson on the phone for you. He says it's urgent.'

Tai let go of his hand, and the old man's vision clouded over once more. He took a few seconds before he was able to speak. 'S-Sanderson?' he said out loud. 'I heard the news. How is the PM?'

'Not good. Not good at all. All his authority and powers have been revoked until we know the outcome of the vote, and it's not looking in his favour – it's highly likely we'll be kicked out of here by this time tomorrow. But that's not why I'm calling, Professor. I have bad news. We've just received a report of mistaken identity. A young girl was attacked at a bus stop this morning, on her way to school. A girl by the name of Jemima Jenkins... It was a case of mistaken identity – they thought she was *our* Jemima. I'm sorry to say that during the tussle, she slipped, and was hit by a bus. She died instantly.'

Jemima, who was standing to the side huddled arm-in-arm with Ilse, gasped with shock. 'Oh no!' she cried. 'The poor girl!' The colour drained from her face.

A frightened Ilse looked from Jemima to the Professor. 'People are turning against us,' she said with round eyes.

Tai shuffled closer, brows furrowing. 'Everything's going bad...'

Nobody said anything for a while, until Tyaishia pointed a finger at the very last outline sketches of the horses. 'I remember! I remember where they're from, them horses, them riders. Th-they're from Revelation, the last book of the Bible. They're the four horsemen of the apocalypse! Riding to the final battle. They're a sign,' she said, slowly looking around at the others, eyes wide. 'A sign of the end of the world.'

23 THE VERDICT

The world at last knew about the existence of the Ingenious children. And it quivered from fear of them, and at the same time, mocked and laughed at them. Others even glorified them.

Thanks to social media, the blurred video of Jemima Jenkins and Tahir Ekren had been shared so many times, that it had come to the point where memes were being made of stills – blowing the whole thing up into a viral media storm. Fingers were pointed at certain teenagers by wannabe detectives, who were subsequently trolled, abused, cancelled. Their lives made a living misery, simply because they had the same names or similar sounding names to those mentioned by Mr Y from the Gillespie Files exposé. The internet allowed people to hide behind the mask of a fake profile, or an avatar, giving them free rein to be their worst, most brutal selves. Judge, jury, and executioner. Naming and shaming as many Ingenious teenagers as possible had turned into a blood sport, and they weren't taking any prisoners.

Gaia had correctly identified David O'Connor as the mysterious Mr Y from the documentary – the chief of security at the country house where Dr Vassiliev had disappeared. He had also been present when Jemima interviewed young Tahir. O'Connor was subsequently removed from office with immediate effect, just before the PM himself was given a vote of no confidence, and, ironically, thrown out of office. But a disgruntled O'Connor made sure to publicly identify one of the Ingenious children, Tai Jones, as the pianist who played at Ha-Ru Kim's concert, and who the newspapers had dubbed 'boy wonder'. It was even speculated that Tai had something to do with the maestro's falling sick – the boy's 'evil plan' to shift the spotlight onto himself and his playing, in order to steal Ha-Ru Kim's thunder. Though the newspaper photographs of Tai were fuzzy and unclear that evening in Cadogan Hall, people who knew him could easily identify him – and his old schoolmates were having a field day, coming forward, and making up incredible and mischievous stories about Tai, loosely based on true events.

At least Ilse, Milly, Tai, and Jemima were safe within Vivra Towers. Milly's mental health, though, after V3's death, was wavering, and Dr Fargo had no choice but to give her sedatives to calm her. The others were told by the Professor not to go out openly in public, and he threw them right back into their studying programme, until the media storm abated. Whenever that might be. The Professor ordered them all to keep a very low profile, especially online, which they were happy to do – that was, until they received news that the trial of Yazan Ekren was failing. It seemed that Ekren's aggressive lawyers were, once again, wrangling him out of a guilty verdict and the prison sentence he so deserved – on a technical hitch. The most damning evidence, the videos of abuse found on his computer, had been copied by a rookie forensic computer analyst in a way that failed to produce digital fingerprints to match the originals – and in so doing, the analyst had unwittingly overwritten much of the metadata for those files. Rendering the evidence inadmissible.

At last, in the court trial, after hearing both defence and prosecution for Yazan Ekren's case, and after the judge gave final directions, the jury were invited to retire to consider their verdict. The 12 deliberated for days, unable to come to a unanimous verdict, so that the judge was compelled to intervene and call for a majority verdict where at least 10 of them agreed.

On the eighth day, it was declared that they had at last come to a decision, and the court gathered for the hearing. Amongst those entering the courtroom were three inconspicuous teenagers, quietly filing into the public gallery amongst the crowds to take their seats – one wearing a hoodie, another glasses, and the third a cap.

The jury took their seats, the judge entered wearing a black robe and white wig, and finally the defendant, Yazan Ekren, returned to the dock behind a clear screen, dressed in a grey prison-issue uniform – looking despicably smug.

The sight of him sitting there brought an intense physical reaction in the children that they could barely breathe, such was the strength of his presence. They had heard many of the sordid details of his crimes as reported by the media, and the thought of the man being freed to continue his abuse on unsuspecting young girls and boys was sickening.

The most incensed was young Ilse Schäfer.

Ilse sat there in the gallery, pale and still, uncomfortable on the hard wood of the chair.

Thanks to Fitzsimmons, her powers had been fully unlocked and she was already exploring what she could really do with them. Unlike the other children, she did not need touch in order to probe someone's mind, and, in the past weeks, with her childlike curious need to learn more about her genetic father, she found herself compelled to reach out to Fitzsimmons. Though the man was constantly drugged to keep him from using his mind abilities, it was when he was fast asleep, in a REM state – eyes darting from side to side underneath crinkled eyelids, his mind let loose in dreams – that Ilse was able to connect with Fitzsimmons, to learn more about him. And she learnt so many things...

And now, as she stared at the evil man sitting so coolly before her in the courtroom, that same curiosity compelled Ilse to explore Ekren. Ignoring the scream of sensibility in her head, and the thunder of a pounding heart in her chest, she found herself staring right into the murky darkness of Ekren's mind. Found herself stepping into his head. Stepping into evil. She closed her eyes as the court proceedings reverberated in her ears.

The court clerk was calling the jury foreperson to stand.

The squeak of shoes against the floor, someone shuffling in the jury box, someone else coughed.

The clerk asked whether they had reached a majority verdict, to which the foreperson replied, 'Yes.' A slight tremor in his voice.

And at last, when they were asked for their verdict, there was a brief, unbearable pause, until the foreperson said with quiet finality, 'We find the defendant not guilty.'

The courtroom exploded with outrage.

With gritted teeth, Ilse absorbed their anger.

The indignation of the parents of the now-dead Shamira Mahmoud.

The families of so many other broken young victims.

A tsunami of fury roiling throughout the courtroom.

And the little German girl found herself jumping up with an equal and opposite force, hands clenched at her side into tight fists, screaming, 'No! No!! You're wrong!!!'

Tai tried to pull her down.

Jemima grabbed her arm. *Ilse!* she hissed.

But Ilse pulled herself from their grip. Her eyes darkened as she pointed to Ekren who looked incredibly amused, practically chuckling to himself.

She wanted to wipe that smirk right off his face.

Wanted to make him pay.

Her hand reached out to him, crooked fingers stretching to grab his mind. Teasing out his memories.

She held out her other hand across the courtroom, to every single person there, and poured out those images, sounds, sensations, right into their heads.

A deluge of Ekren's awful thoughts.

Evil desires.

Foul cravings.

Each terrible act that he had committed.

The reek of his own body odour, sour breath, the brush of hairy skin.

Every awful video that his ring members had shared.

The cries of the girls. The boys.

Their pleas to stop.

The victims' struggles to fight their drugged stupor.

Their impotence.

Helplessness.

Gasping, panicked, sick with dread.

Wanting to be anywhere else, but there.

Wanting to die.

Ilse's body heaved with sobs as she discharged everything in Ekren's head to everyone in the room. For what seemed like an age.

Inside her swirled disgust, shock, outrage. Imploding, exploding. A sickening mix of emotions.

And she knew that, with just one twist of her hand, she could end him.

Right there and then.

Someone forcibly yanked her arm.
It was Tai, grabbing and pushing her, steering her out of the gallery.
Jemima running close behind, her eyes scrunched with angst.

People around them were writhing with horror.
Their minds overwhelmed by the torrential downpour of horrific memories.
Tears streaming down their faces.
Crying out no, they couldn't bear it, please!!
Make it stop!!!

As the children disappeared, the court officials' and observers' torment at last subsided, and they collapsed in their chairs. Shattered. Breathless.

In time, everyone began to come to – except for one person.
Ekren was found collapsed on the floor.
His face, his body, contorted from incredible pain.
Still as a statue.
Dead.

24   A CLOUD OF GREEN

The wail of police sirens.
A helicopter flying overhead.
Gasps for breath.
Feet pounding against concrete.

As Jemima, Tai, and Ilse ran with blind panic, they realised how stupid they had been to slip out of safety to go the courtroom. And the full enormity of what Ilse had done was prickling their every sense. But it was already too late.

Just as they reached the back entrance of Vivra Towers, police cars screeched to a halt around them. Locking them in.

Kevlar-vested officers jumped out of the cars, surrounding them, pointing guns. Shouting at them to put their hands up.

Tai had managed to get the gate to start opening, but Jemima shoved him inside and slammed her hand on the close button, so that it reversed direction. She told him between clenched teeth, 'Get help!' The gate gracefully locked shut, with Tai inside. Jemima stepped in front of Ilse, glaring at her. *Don't do anything stupid!!*

'But–' started Ilse, her cheeks red hot. A wisp of hair fell across worried eyes, darting from Jemima to the policemen, and she lost her steam.

'Just... do as I say!' hissed Jemima. 'You've gotten us into enough trouble!!'

Ilse snapped her mouth shut, she couldn't argue with that – and hid behind her.

'We're unarmed!!' Jemima shouted out to the policemen. Actually, that wasn't quite true, she thought. Ilse's mind was turning out to be the deadliest of weapons.

The officers swarmed around them and grabbed them. And though the girls struggled and scratched and kicked against them, the men managed to wrench their arms behind their backs, and cuff them. The click of the ratchet teeth locked the handcuffs firmly into place.

One of the officers stepped forward. It was David O'Connor. 'Open the gate!' he snarled at Jemima. Seeing that there was a camera, he forcefully spun the girl round to face it, and stepped next to her. 'Open the gate!!' he repeated, and slapped her across the face.

Jemima winced, and threw a warning glance at Ilse. Fire in her eyes. Her cheek stinging. 'I can't!' Jemima shouted. 'We can't get in.'

Above them, high up in the air, the thak-thak of helicopter blades resounded, and they craned their necks to see a police helicopter hovering over the top of the building.

O'Connor sneered at the girls. 'Check mate. We'll get in from the top anyway.'

Black bags were pulled over the girls' heads, the sting of a needle sliding into an arm – and they suddenly felt dizzy, soundwaves reverberating in their ears. The world evaporated as their bodies went limp.

•••——————————————————•••

Tai ran, gasping for breath, into the elevator.

'Hello Tai,' came Jasmine's pleasant voice. 'I detect an increased heart rate. Would you like me to call Dr Fargo?'

'No!' snapped Tai, bending over and fingering the stitch that was digging into his side. 'Tell everybody we're in trouble,' he panted. 'The police... they've got Jemima and Ilse, and... they're coming for us. We... have to leave.'

'I'm sorry to hear that, Tai. I've passed on your message.'

'Where's my mum?'

'She is outside on the roof terrace, in the orangery.'

The elevator seemed to take an age to glide to the top floor; annoyingly cheerful music tinkled in the background.

At last the door slid open and Tai burst out of the elevator, running straight for the stairs that led up to the roof. As he went, a loud muffled noise from outside confused him, and when he opened the door, strong gusts of wind hammered against him. He turned to find the police helicopter settling onto the helipad at the roof's centre, its rotor blades slowing down. Tai started running across to the glass structure on the opposite side, but four men jumped out of the helicopter, and two of them immediately intercepted and grabbed him. Tai struggled against them, but it was no use.

Someone shouted out 'Tai!!' and they turned to find Tyaishia emerging from the orangery, a trowel in her hand dropping to the floor with a clang. 'Let him go!!' she screamed, face contorting with anger.

'Stay where you are!' shouted one of the men, as he pointed a gun at her. 'Put your hands up! Don't come any closer!'

Wild thoughts galloped through Tyaishia's mind as she raised her hands above her head, not sure what to do. She glanced at her son... the men... looked around the roof. She began edging toward the parapet, and suddenly leapt up onto it, grabbing hold of the low balustrade. 'Let him go!!' she shouted. 'Or... or I'll jump!'

'Ma, no!!' Tai cried out.

Even though Tyaishia had no such intention, the damp lead flashing on top of the parapet made her slip, and she lost balance – the strong gusts from the helicopter throwing her back. She toppled over the edge.

'No!!!' screamed Tai, horrified. He wrenched himself free to run to her. Looking over, he saw her plummeting – her eyes wild with panic, arms paddling.

Tai's heart burst out of his chest as he stretched a futile arm toward her. 'Ma!!!' he yelled.

There came a strange sound from far below.

A cacophony of squawking.

From the trees in the park across the road, fluttering green speckles burst out, and raced upwards.

Several flocks of parakeets merged into one.

They flew toward Tyaishia at breakneck speed, beady black eyes fixed firmly on her, wings flapping furiously, orange beaks opening and closing as they screeched with determination. They whooshed right under Tyaishia – the force of her body against theirs winded them, but wave after wave of parakeets bolstered her from underneath. The birds cushioned her as she fell, and deflected her diagonally toward the large, deep pond just 20 metres away.

Tai held his breath as he watched the cloud of green swoop lower and lower, skimming the water, with his mother rolling off them and splashing into it.

Seconds passed as he fixed his eyes on that single point.

Excruciating seconds.

The difference between life and death, held hostage by time.

In his head, Tai screamed with the thought that his life was about to fall apart and explode with pain, yet at the same time, something was telling him wait. Wait. She may still be alive...

The fluster of wings swirled around and around, obscuring his view.

Tai held his hand out, calling for the parakeets to return to him – and two of them broke away from the flock and sped upward. All the while, Tai held his breath. When the bright green birds fluttered onto his hand, their piercing squawks ceased, and scratchy talons dug into his skin. Tai closed his eyes and absorbed their memories, heart pounding.

From their perspective, he saw his mother splashing into the water.

Saw the birds circle around, their black eyes combing over the surface.

Suddenly Tyaishia bobbed up out of the pond, spluttering and gasping for air – she looked around, disoriented. But then at last swam to the edge.

Tai doubled over with relief, even as the reel of the birds' memories continued playing: a dripping Tyaishia climbed out, gasping, and she stopped to blink up at Vivra Towers – disbelief and incredulity on her face. Her quivering lips moving in silent prayer. She looked at the beautiful parakeets flying above her in dizzying circles, green feathers tumbling. And when the birds parted, she squinted to focus on the top of the tower, worried for her son.

Tai caught his breath, reassured that she was all right. Slowly he turned toward the two policemen – anger brewing deep within. They were looking over the edge of the parapet, their mouths hanging open in disbelief. When one of the birds on Tai's hand squawked, they looked up at the boy facing them, just metres away.

From behind the men, a flock of parakeets, a thick mass of feathers, suddenly swooped up and descended upon them – joined by the two birds on Tai's hand. The policemen started screaming, running this way and that, trying in vain to bat them away.

Tai quickly ran off, entered the stairwell, and ran down to the top floor, where their apartments were.

But as he went, an acrid smell itched his nose, and then a fog rose up from nowhere – engulfing everything in a dreamlike whiteness. He coughed, eyes stinging. His legs went numb and buckled underneath him. As he fell to the floor, he saw two dark figures approaching – the two other policemen from the helicopter. They became clearly visible only when they stood right over him, gas masks clamped on their faces.

Tai exhaled as he closed his eyes.

Everything turned to white.

And he lost consciousness.

25 VOICES

The police, under David O'Connor's direction, took the unconscious bodies they had captured in Vivra Towers, and – when they came to – each of them was interrogated as to the existence, and whereabouts, of the Ingenious children. But they refused to comment. Calista was inconsolable, for they had taken away Evie, and no amount of her pleading, coaxing, screaming, would impel them to let her see her baby.

O'Connor also took over the cage, where Fitzsimmons was imprisoned. They created four more rooms within the building, for Tai, Milly, Ilse, and Jemima – drugging them with the same chemical cocktail that was being given to Fitzsimmons, to stop them from using their powers. O'Connor's hatred for the children had festered to the point of obsession. And he had every intention to hunt each one down. He would not rest until he was sure that these aberrations of nature, these Frankenstein children, were locked away for good.

•••————————————————•••

In a dark, crudely-made cell, young Ilse Schäfer lay curled up on her side, fast asleep on a dirty mattress, sucking her thumb. Her hair was greasy, her cheeks streaked with scabbed-over scratches.

Eyes flitted from side to side under eyelids that were like wet silk.

Dreams filled her head.

And voices.

So many voices.

A single tear trickled down the side of her face, pausing – exquisitely – on her jaw, before dropping down, and disappearing into the folds of her.

PART 4

26 THE STORYTELLER

New Delhi, India

The 16-year-old Indian girl was inexplicably drawn to the group of young children sitting huddled at the side of the street.

Filled with curiosity, she wandered over to see, and discovered a teenage boy at their centre, cross-legged on the ground, telling his little audience a story. He recounted it in the most animated, most fascinating way, that even she became instantly entranced. The boy's expressions, the lilt of his voice, and the sparkle in his eyes were utterly mesmerising.

The air around them was heavy with the usual pollution – smelling like a thousand acrid campfires – laced both with garbage and the spicy notes of the Saptaparni trees lining the road. Saffron strokes of sun tinged the dawn, giving the grimy backstreet a hushed beauty, and deifying the slum children with golden light.

As the girl listened to the young man, whom she guessed was perhaps a year or two older than herself, she felt an unexpected emotion begin to stir within her. He was different. And she somehow knew that they would be connected in a meaningful, though as yet unknown, way. She couldn't comprehend how or why this thought suddenly struck her. It just seeped through her as imperceptibly as the fragrance of milkwood flower soaks the air. She looked him over. He was clearly a dalit – an untouchable – the lowest caste there was. Probably a toilet cleaner, or garbage collector. Yet, physically, he was squeaky clean, sitting on his sheet of newspaper, surrounded by the usual Delhi dust, scatterings of rubbish, and a cowpat just metres away buzzing with flies. It seemed he was so untouchable even the dirt daren't go near him.

And when, in turn, the young storyteller glanced up and set eyes on the girl standing there, he took in her gazing face, the bright colour of her salwar kameez, the tiny diamond in her left nostril gleaming in the last rays of sun – and he suddenly came to the heart-stopping realisation that this was the girl he was going to marry. Even though she was indisputably of a much higher caste.

He faltered, caught his breath, and stammered – then quickly flashed her the lightest of smiles, and turned back to his audience to resume the story. The children sitting around him, most of whom were no older than 10, did not notice the pause – except for little Ria. The girl glanced from the storyteller to the beautiful stranger, and giggled quietly. The other children were so hooked on his every word – some cross-legged, others cross-eyed, and others still, cupping cheeks in their hands as they listened to him with bated breath – they barely noticed the blush that reddened the young man's cheeks.

By the time the storyteller came to the end of his fantastical, exciting, gripping, funny, yet moving story, he looked up to his right, and scanned the area. But the girl was gone.

He did not despair. For he was still riding high on the awe and thrill of discovering the love of his life.

Somehow, he knew, it was just a matter of time...

After the breath-taking finale, the children burst up onto their feet and cheered the storyteller in rapturous applause! Living in slum jhuggis, shelters made from nothing more than mud and corrugated iron, they had little entertainment, but for his stories. Which was why they were so drawn to him. He transported them to different places, times, worlds. Brought a kaleidoscope of colour to their grey lives. Breathed air into the vacuum of mundanity. Better still, he was one of them, living in the same settlement.

Unfurling his body as he stood, the storyteller watched as the children left one by one, shouting out to them that they must go straight home, as it was getting late. The last, a small boy with a mop of brown hair, used a stick to shove the cow dung onto a piece of cardboard, before squeaking goodbye and running off – holding the dung-laden board in a wobbly balancing act.

The storyteller sighed as he picked up the newspaper, noticing a job advert in the corner of the page – but he was too distracted to absorb anything now. Folding the paper, he wedged it under his arm, and walked slowly home. Of course, there was only one thing on his mind. The girl. That beautiful, forbidden girl.

•••———————————————————————•••

The next morning, the storyteller awoke to find his father, Vijay, sitting on the dirt floor in one corner of their four-square-metre jhuggi, squinting fixedly at something.

The dusty blue plastic sheeting on one side had been rolled up to let bright rays of sun stream in. Vijay leaned into the light to see – his hair glistening with black onion seed oil, stray wisps zigzagging upward as if in testimony to the oil's hair regrowth properties. On his left was a sheet of plywood piled with shoes and sandals in various states of disrepair – and on his right was a wooden crate containing tools, reels of thread, battered tins of polish, and folds of leather. He was inspecting a pair of shoes with intensity, before rummaging around for a tube of leather cement. He applied just enough glue, but not too much, to the inside of the soles, and pressed them down firmly, one at a time. Taking an awl, a needle, and thread, he began stitching and looping, bonding the rubber to the leather. He worked fast, his strong hands pushing and pulling with efficiency. Hearing a yawn, he glanced across to find his teenage son awake, watching him sleepily. He smiled at the boy, took in his half-opened eyes and mussed hair. 'What time is that job interview you mentioned last night, Inder? The one in the newspaper.'

Inder sat up and stretched. '10.30,' he muttered, glancing across at the old wind-up clock.

His mother appeared outside, heaving a large plastic canister filled with sloshing water.

Quickly Inder jumped up, carefully walked around his father's legs, and helped her carry it to just outside the entrance. 'Amma! You bought water again. You could have used the handpump, it's free.'

'True, it's free, but polluted!' she frowned.

'The DJB said it was okay,' replied Inder.

'And you believe them?' she said, tutting and shaking her head. 'It's too close to the public latrines for comfort. It's bound to be contaminated.' She looked around their home. 'We don't have much, but at least we have our health – so we need to take every precaution.'

'Don't worry, Chhaya,' Vijay told his wife, 'things will change once he gets this job.'

'I wish! I really like the sound of the company,' said Inder. 'There's something about them...' He sighed. 'But I've been to four, no, *five* interviews this month, and none of them gave me work.'

Unscrewing the canister lid, Chhaya poured some water into a plastic basin. 'Wash, my son. Get neat. And think positive!'

His father finished off the first shoe, inspected his handiwork with satisfaction, then put it aside. 'You're over-qualified for this work anyway, beta,' he told his son. 'You passed out of college with flying colours – so in the interview, they will see how clever you are, what a hard worker you are, and appreciate you.'

Inder rolled up his rivergrass sleeping mat into a tight cylinder, and leaned it against a tall, perfectly-aligned stack of newspapers. 'There are hundreds of applicants for each job, baba, all with good qualifications. What chance do I have?' He stripped down to his shorts, grabbed a bar of Medimix, and crouched down outside next to the bowl of water – soaping himself all over until he was covered with a froth of suds.

Chhaya tutted. 'If those savarnas had any sense, they would change...'

'Why bother talking about it?' interjected Vijay. 'What good are words? It has been the same for centuries. They talk about change, they pass laws for change, but nothing has changed. Look how long they have been promising us brick houses, and more water pumps with *clean* water. Millions of us lacking basic needs, and jobs, while they waste billions of rupees on sending a rocket to the moon, arre yaar!'

Inder rinsed himself down, and began drying himself with a frayed towel. 'If nothing changes, then should I even bother with this interview?' he asked, raising an eyebrow.

Chhaya gave her son a withered look. 'You can at least try, beta! What harm is there in trying? You want to become a ragpicker like your cousin-brother, picking through rubbish all day?'

Stepping back into the hut, Inder sighed and began rummaging through several plastic bags suspended on hooks hanging from the top of the corrugated sheeting. 'My good clothes, amma... where are they?'

'Blue bag,' she said distractedly as she crouched down next to an aluminium pot astride glowing coals. She dished out some chole bhature and set it on the stack of newspapers – spicy chickpeas topped with a deep-fried bread. 'But eat before you dress. You don't want to stain your clothes.'

Vijay finished polishing with a flourish. 'And here's a good-as-new pair of shoes for you – your size. You will at least look like a shudra.' He set them proudly next to the wall under the bags.

'A shudra?!' his wife spluttered. 'What's the point! Do you also want him to change his name, and where he comes from? Those things alone will tell them he's dalit.'

'It's also written on one of my school certificates,' said Inder.

'Pakau!' breathed Chhaya, scolding him for being annoying. She handed him a foil container, warm with food, and a paper bag with some puffed breads. 'Here is some chole bhature for Sunil uncle. He loves my chole.' She placed it next to Inder's bowl, put the lid on the cooking pot, and swivelled round to inspect a pile of mended shoes. 'Are these the shoes for selling at the market?' she asked her husband.

'No, no, not that pile! The other one.'

Chhaya shifted round some more, and began packing the correct shoes into a large bag. She glanced sideways at her son. 'Hurry up and eat, you need to leave soon!'

Inder knew not to argue with his mother, and he quietly did as he was told. After he had eaten, brushed his teeth, and dressed, he placed the container in his rucksack and said goodbye to his parents. Stepping out of the tent, he looked clean and handsome in a simple white shirt and cotton slacks.

His mother stopped what she was doing and watched him go. The hopes and dreams she harboured for her son were palpable; they filled the hut like the spicy warmth of mogra incense, and trailed behind him as he disappeared. Chhaya sighed, but then remembered something and quickly ran after him. 'Inder! Inder!' she called out as she ran down the narrow passageway, dodging colourful lines of hanging laundry. The boy stopped and turned, curiosity in his green-flecked eyes. When she reached him, she pulled out two glossy betel leaves from the folds of her sari. 'I've already offered some leaves to our Paradevatha, our family god. But make sure to stop at the temple for morning puja and offer these to Lord Ganesha. He will certainly bless your interview.'

'Amma,' frowned Inder. 'Where did you get these from?'

'Never you mind. Now go.'

'Please tell me you didn't take them from someone's garden? If anyone saw you, you could get beaten. Or worse...'

'No, no, it's fine,' said Chhaya coyly. 'I brushed past a vine growing up the tree of a fat amira-adami, and these leaves just... fell off.'

'They fell off? So you didn't steal them?'

'Just like that,' she said evasively. 'Anyway, Brahma made the trees and the leaves for everyone, not only for fat moneybags.'

Inder tutted at his mother and put the leaves carefully into his pocket. 'Please don't do it again,' he implored as he turned. He hurried down the narrow path.

After Inder exited the slum, and made the leaf offerings at the local temple, he strolled at a leisurely pace through the streets of New Delhi; it was just over an hour's walk to the interview offices, but he had left early, and could take his time. He was grateful for his father's cobbling expertise, for the shoes were pleasantly comfortable to walk in.

The smoky pollution had not yet risen, and so he inhaled deep breaths of early morning air as he made his way. Although it was longer, he walked along the Nala Road which followed the course of the Sahibi River – the route was simpler, the road much quieter this time of day. Taking a slight detour to reach the Deelip petrol station, he craned his neck to look for his uncle. There he was, sitting on the curb at the side of the road, under the shade of a young jamun tree.

'Sunil uncle!' called Inder.

Sunil was much slimmer than his younger brother, Inder's father, but his thick head of hair was just like Vijay's. He reached for a newspaper from the stack at his side, and folded it neatly in half. 'Ah, Inder. You're early today!'

'Not out of choice, uncle. I have an interview,' Inder explained as he shrugged off his rucksack and extracted the food container and bread. He handed them to him in exchange for the newspaper, the Times of India. 'Anything outstanding today?' he asked, as he carefully folded it once more to fit inside his rucksack.

Sunil shook his head, perturbed. 'Terrible news everywhere, Inder – it seems the entire world is getting worse, *much* worse. Russia has launched another missile attack in Ukraine. Israel is pummelling Gaza also. There have been flash floods in China, with mudslides killing about 16 people. In East Africa, a plague of desert locusts has decimated crops. Then, in the Amazon jungle, they are continuing to battle massive wildfires. Worldwide, more and more people are dying from Covid. And here in New Delhi, they are predicting yet another drought... I am afraid for the world, Inder, very afraid. Yama, the god of death, must be very busy...'

'Arre yaar!' exclaimed Inder in astonishment, pausing to absorb it all.

Sunil eyed his nephew up and down. 'By the way, you are looking very smart. An interview, you say? They should give you the job.'

Inder looked down at himself. 'I think an interview will require more than smart clothes, uncle,' he smiled.

'Well, you're also clever, *super* clever! The top of your class. For that, as well as your snappy dressing, they should give you the job!'

Inder patted his uncle's shoulder. 'If they do, I can at last buy your newspapers with money.'

'Achcha, I think I prefer your mother's food as payment.'

'She will be pleased to hear that. By the way, amma made chole bhature today.'

Sunil looked slightly disappointed. 'I was hoping for saag aloo. I love her saag aloo!'

'You will enjoy the chole just as much, it is delicious. Uncle, I have to go now, I don't want to be late. Same place tomorrow?'

'Yes, business is good here, I sold all my newspapers yesterday. People here like to read depressing news. So I will stay for a while.' He motioned upward, to the plum tree. 'Also, I am getting some sweet jamuns now and then. I will save you some next time.'

'Haa, I guessed as much from the purplish stain around your mouth!'

smiled Inder as he walked away. 'See you tomorrow, uncle,' he said, as Sunil began wiping his face vigorously.

Inder back-tracked the way he came, re-joining the Sahibi along the more scenic river path. At last he reached the junction of the tributary with the wider, sprawling Yamuna river.

The Yamuna, itself an important tributary to the Ganges, was revered as sacred by many who worship it as a goddess, their 'mother'. Their deity flowed from the lower Himalayas, and just north of the city she sparkled with clear, fresh water, teemed with fish, and sprouted great swathes of water hyacinth. But when the river entered the city, she was routinely deluged with factory effluent, industrial waste, dirty laundry water, and cremation ashes, with residents throwing bag after bag of rubbish into her waters, until most banks were piled with stagnant muck. Where there were clearings, cattle were washed and watered in her. Humans sat on river steps and bathed in her. Men picked their way across her broad, swampy banks, and crouched to defecate as they chatted on their phones, or replied to texts. And further downstream, the poor drank from her, and got sick from her. In this way, as the Yamuna flowed disconsolately through Delhi, she was befouled, and violated – and part of her died. Nothing could survive in her there, no plants, no fish, no algae.

As Inder walked along the busy ring road next to the sludgy Yamuna, he shook his head in despair at the state of the river. Worryingly, and just as Inder's uncle had mentioned, the water level was much lower than usual, the flow torpid, which meant that rubbish was building up – stagnating in stinking piles on the banks. It didn't bear thinking about, the terrible impact the river's receding waters would have on the fish and vegetation, let alone for the inhabitants of New Delhi – the lack of river water, as well as ground water, did not bode well at all.

Inder quickened his pace, both to avoid the foul odour, but also so as not to be late. There was something different about this job; he had instantly been drawn to the advertisement in the Times – and he wanted to give it his best effort. He arrived at the imposing building a stone's throw from the river, and stopped to take in the gleaming sign 'i-Nation Bionics' – his jaw dropping. The wealth of the company was evident, even from the outside, which was confirmed when he stepped into the lobby.

He felt suddenly conscious of his second-hand, market-stall clothes. Rows of verdant bamboo plants lined the building's glossy interior, stretching up to the glass ceiling – and honey-coloured bamboo furniture gave a luxuriant ambience that felt airy and light, as if the building itself were alive and breathing.

As young Inder approached the receptionist girl, opening his mouth to speak, she eyed him distastefully, handed him a paper ticket, and immediately waved him toward the seating area. Her look of disdain was so striking that Inder could almost hear her think, 'Bah! A dalit, if ever I saw one!' He returned her disdain only with a humble nod, and followed her direction. Turning, Inder found a crowd of people, young and old, all sitting and waiting quietly. He looked down at the number on his ticket – 46, disconcertingly – and picked his way through them to an empty seat. Taking out his newspaper, the rustle of the broadsheet broke the silence, and some turned to eye him over.

Reading the newspaper was the highlight of Inder's day. He read every paragraph in every article, even the adverts, with keen interest – poring over the words and pictures in each section: national news, city, business, technical, sports. He often shook his head, sometimes alarmed, frequently ponderous. He had reached halfway through page 2, when a middle-aged man appeared before the interviewees, dressed in creased slacks and a pale-blue shirt, quickly finger-combing his messy hair into place. With eyes rimmed red, he looked as if he'd had many sleepless nights. Glancing over the crowd, he sighed inwardly, and said somewhat wearily under his breath, 'There are so many...' Speaking out loud to all of them, he started saying, Thank you for coming–' when he spotted Inder reading his newspaper. He stared at him for several seconds, and then called out, 'You, boy, reading the Times. What is your good name?'

Inder looked up at him. 'Me?'

'Yes, you,' said the man impatiently.

'My name is Chauhan. Inder Chauhan.'

'Follow me,' he said, before turning on his heel, and striding over to a corridor on the far side of the lobby. A surprised Inder quickly folded the newspaper, stuffed it into his rucksack, and jumped up to hurry after him.

When they arrived at an office, they went inside, and the man sat at his messy desk.

Inder pressed his hands together and dipped in a light bow. 'Namaste,' he said respectfully.

'Namaste! Sit down, sit down,' said the man. Though he sounded gruff and looked tired, he had an affable face.

Inder found himself in a room with a blue couch at the side draped with a rumpled blanket, a wastepaper basket filled with empty food containers, and a large window behind the desk – the ledge of which was lined with a chaotic array of volumes, letters, magazines, and books.

'I'm Anand Amir. I'm head development engineer here at i-Nation. Do you know what we do?'

'Yes I do, sir. You design myoelectric prostheses that use electric signals generated by muscles to control artificial limbs – ones that you are proud to make sustainably, and with extra strong materials and technology that greatly reduce the cost when compared to other prosthetic brands in the marketplace.'

Anand's eyebrows shot up. 'Impressive!' he nodded with a smile. 'You memorised our company info.'

'It is an impressive company, sir. I was very interested to read about it.'

'CV?'

Inder rifled through a folder in his rucksack, and pulled out a rather battered copy that he had printed out at school several months ago. He handed it to Anand, who promptly went quiet as he read. Eventually he said, 'I see that you too have an impressive CV...' and was about to say something more, but stopped himself. They both knew he meant to finish with 'for a dalit.' Discrimination was frowned upon, yet there was always the hint of it just below the surface.

Inder wobbled his head gently from side to side, smiling. 'I will not pretend to be what I am not, sir. Yes, I am over-qualified, but I am also hardworking, reliable, intelligent. And... if you hire me, you will not regret it, sir.'

Anand stared at this bold yet likeable young man for some time, seemingly lost in thought. He eventually said, 'In the waiting room, I noticed you reading the TOI... It is not often you find a teenager reading a broadsheet.'

Inder smiled. 'I am enjoying reading it every day. It is my window to the world.'

Anand stroked his chin thoughtfully. 'Are you adaptable?' he asked. 'Only, the job is to clean our offices, but our plantsman has not turned up for a few weeks now, and we need someone to take care of all the plants around.'

Inder blinked at him, remembering the rows and rows of bamboo in the lobby. 'But... there are a lot of plants.'

'Yes, and I will pay you for the extra work.'

'I do not know about plants.'

'And I see you don't know about cleaning either,' he said, glancing down at the CV. 'You're straight out of school with no experience, yet you applied for the job. If you are so intelligent as your CV appears to show, then you can learn. You also say you are hardworking?'

'Most definitely I am!'

'Well then, you will be able to cope with the extra work.'

'Most definitely I will!'

Inder stopped, then smiled slowly with realisation. 'So... am I hired?'

'You better not make me regret it.'

Inder wobbled his head with delight. 'Sir, I promise, you will not regret it in a million years.'

'You are hired then! You will be required to work outside office hours for the cleaning. Our last cleaner worked in the evening, but if you prefer, you can come early morning and finish by 9.30 a.m. It takes about five hours to clean everything well – four, if you're quick. You will be required to clean the six office rooms, the reception and lobby, the lounge, and the toilets. The kitchen staff already clean the kitchen and dining room. And for the workshop, fitting room, and storage rooms, you must not touch any of the equipment – do you understand?'

'Yes, sir. I understand.'

'Do you want to write this down?'

'No, sir.'

'You will need to sweep, vacuum-clean, wash and polish floors, and wipe furniture. You will also disinfect toilets and washbasins. We like everything to sparkle here at i-Nation. Now, the plants. You can care for them in business hours if you wish. It's up to you. But you must look after them well! We cannot have dead plants. We cannot have dry, sad-looking plants. They must be fresh and healthy, okay?'

'That is most definitely okay,' said Inder enthusiastically.

Anand lapsed into a long, thoughtful silence, which Inder dared not break. As he waited, he looked around the room, and then through the window behind the desk. He basked in the air-conditioning too – refreshing respite from the muggy heat outside.

At last Anand said, 'I was thinking about your wages. The cleaning salary is 2.6 lakh rupees a month – so for looking after the plants as well, I can give you another 500.'

Inder's eyes widened. '3,100 rupees every month?'

'I thought you were intelligent? Yes, of course that is 3,100 rupees.'

'I-I think that is most definitely fine.' Inder knew that the average wage for a slum worker in New Delhi was 3,000 rupees, so for two jobs the wages were not so generous, but as someone with no experience he was just grateful to be given work in a good company. He looked around the cluttered desk, a little dazed. 'Do you... do you want me to sign anything? A contract?'

Anand laughed. 'It is good that you are eager.' Looking down at the CV, he searched for an address, but there was none, and he realised that he must be living in a slum, as camps are not always registered. 'You don't have an address?'

Inder looked at him uncertainly.

'A mobile phone?'

Again, silence.

'Then wait in the lobby,' he told Inder. 'I will have the contract drawn up and printed by the receptionist immediately. You can read it, sign it, and take a copy with you today.'

Inder jumped up, grinning. 'Thank you very much!'

'Thank me by doing good work, Inder.'

'Yes, yes,' he replied eagerly. He pressed his hands together and said 'Namaste' again and again as he backed out of the door.

In the corridor, Inder turned round and practically flew through to the lobby – just as the receptionist received a telephone call. She listened for a few seconds, put down the phone, and stood up to announce to the other applicants that the position was now filled, and they had to leave. There was a wave of disappointed mutterings, someone even groaned, and one by one they got up to go.

When Inder reached the desk, he smiled cheerily at the grumpy young receptionist. 'I will wait here,' Inder announced to her. 'For the contract.'

But even her stony silence was not enough to wipe the smile from his face as he sat down. He was imagining his parents' elation when he broke the news to them. And deep down, he had somehow always known, this work at i-Nation Bionics was the one job that he absolutely had to get.

On Inder's first day at work, Anand made his way to the offices, intrigued to see how well this novel boy would perform his duties. He stepped into the building at around 9.20 a.m., and as he walked around, he found to his delight that the place was not only spotless, but sparkling. The surfaces had been dusted, wood polished, and glass wiped streak-free. Screens had not even a single smudge. Floor tiles were hoovered and mopped to perfection. The toilets and sink basins shone so brightly it was as if they were brand new. When he peered into his office, his desk had been tidied, and even the messy collection of books and magazines on his window ledge had been arranged in an orderly and neat fashion. And the room had a pleasant, airy smell.

Anand went to search for the boy, and discovered him in the utility room, filling a canister with liquid – looking fresh and bright-eyed, though he must have been up very early in the morning.

'Achcha, there you are!' said Anand, standing at the doorway.

Inder greeted him with his usual 'Namaste,' bowing respectfully.

'You have done an excellent job for someone who's never cleaned!'

Inder smiled. 'My mother's friend, Lakshmi aunty, is also working as a cleaner, though a domestic one. She has given me a lot of advice.'

'Excellent. And there is a refreshing perfume in the air that I can't quite place...'

Inder waved toward a glass spray-bottle on the counter. 'I believe the smell you are referring to may be from the spray I used to wipe the surfaces. I made it myself, from water mixed with white vinegar, baking soda, and rosewood essential oil. Rosewood is antibacterial and good for concentration and elevating the mood.'

'Rosewood, that is it!'

'The fragrance will clear your head, sir, for working.'

'Will it now?' smiled Anand as he gave him an approving nod, and turned to go back to his office.

Weeks passed and Inder worked hard at i-Nation.

He preferred to get up early in the morning to clean, and took great pride in what he did. But his greatest joy turned out to be caring for the plants. He had not realised what an affinity he would come to have with the living, breathing organisms. He felt almost fatherly toward them, as he gently sprayed them with water, checked the soil by digging fingers knuckle-deep into pots, and fertilised each one with the appropriate mix of minerals. He would often be seen leaning into each plant and whispering to it as he went around with his watering can, even stroking their leaves, or turning pots this way and that, to ensure they got the best light. He would pat each plant gently with affection before moving on to the next.

•••————————————————————————•••

Early one morning, Anand Amir woke up on the couch in his office, to find on his desk a pot of tea and a small clay cup. He knew it had been left by Inder for no-one else would be around at that time, and the fragrance of rosewood hung delicately in the air. He padded over in bare feet and poured the milky masala chai, spiced with cardamom, cinnamon, and cloves – inhaling the aroma as he drank the entire cup.

Just then, Inder walked in holding a spray bottle and a cloth. 'You are awake,' smiled Inder. 'Suprabhat!'

Anand held up his cup. 'Thank you for the tea,' he said as he poured some more. 'It is delicious! And tastes much better from clay, don't you think?' He slurped it down.

'I agree. The chaiwallah at the end of the road mixes his own blend of tea and spices, and I am becoming accustomed to buying from him every morning after work. So when I saw you sleeping here, I thought some of his good tea is just what you need.' He thought for a moment. 'By the way, it is a completely new cup,' he hastened to add, for dalits were forbidden to drink from the same tea stall cups as upper castes. He went over to one of the four potted plants – almost two metres high – and began spraying and wiping the creamy heart-shaped leaves. Anand stretched and yawned, which reminded Inder of something he'd been meaning to ask him. 'I have been wondering, sir, and I hope you don't mind me asking. But why are you so many times sleeping in the office?'

Anand swirled the pot to gauge the amount of remaining tea, but put it down, thoughtful. 'You are dusting the money plant, Inder, one of many we have here. It is a plant known for bringing good fortune and attracting wealth. For years, its effects on the company were just so. Business was good. We have been working with hospitals, helping many who lost limbs, especially unfortunate factory workers involved in terrible work accidents. But recently...' He sighed deeply. 'Recently, the money plants have not been so effective. People are finding fault with our products, they are not paying invoices, and they have given bad reviews which are affecting sales.' Anand tutted as he went back to the couch, sat down, and slipped his feet into his shoes. He looked tired. 'If things do not change soon, by the end of the year we will be bankrupt.' He shook his head. 'I am sorry to tell you this news, Inder, and you must not repeat it to anyone. But this is why I have been sleeping in the office for many months now, to trouble-shoot the problems with our products, and to cut costs – trying my best to save the company.'

Inder gulped. 'Does this... does this mean I will be out of a job?'

'You and me both,' he replied resignedly. 'Our CEO has put the onus on me for this mess, unfairly I have to say. He wants someone's head to roll. So we will all be out of a job...'

'Well then,' said Inder defiantly. 'We must not be allowing any rolling of heads, sir.'

Anand smirked. 'I appreciate your determination, but it is not so simple.' He waved toward his computer. 'I have been trying to problem-solve all night. But nothing is working.'

Noticing a streak on the computer screen, Inder walked over and rubbed at it with his cloth. A document was open onscreen, with reams of equations, figures, notes. 'It looks complicated,' he remarked, sitting down in Anand's chair.

His boss came and stood behind him. 'You will not be able to understand it, Inder… unless you have degrees in biomechanics, prosthetics, mathematics.'

'I did not go to university,' mumbled Inder as he started reading.

'Understandably. University fees are exorbitant. I know you have excellent higher secondary qualifications, but it is not enough to understand my work.'

Inder drew closer to the screen. 'As you know, I passed all my subjects with distinction, sir, including logic, chemistry, biology, physics, mathematics and statistics for science, and information technology for science, amongst others. But what I did not tell you was that my grade for every single one was cent percent.' Inder twisted round and flashed him a smile. 'So, if I may say so myself, I am having a highly analytical and logical brain. True, I do not know anything about robotics, or prosthetics, but I am a fast learner.'

Anand blinked at the boy, flabbergasted. 'You got a hundred percent in everything? *That* was not on your CV.'

'My parents are constantly telling me that I must blend in with the crowd because nobody likes a know-it-all. Especially a dalit know-it-all.' He paused – deciding not to tell him that he was just 13 years old when he first started passing his exams. He turned back to the screen. 'Your work is very interesting to me. Please, sir, I would like to read your notes.'

'Be my guest,' said Anand, opening a drawer to get a washcloth, toothbrush, and toothpaste. 'I am curious what a cent percent student will make of them. I have an appointment with one of our customers shortly, so I will get ready, go to the appointment, and be back at lunchtime.'

Inder nodded, but he had already turned back to the screen and was absorbed with reading.

When Anand returned to his office laden with boxes, he found that the room was empty, and there was no sign of the boy. He set the boxes on his desk, before going off to look for Inder. When Anand turned out of the door, just as Inder was turning into it, they almost crashed into each other. 'Aha, Inder! I was coming to look for you.'

'I am here.'

They went into the office. 'First of all, I got us lunch,' Anand announced, and opened the first boxes to reveal a large plate of deep-fried momos, and a trio of sauces – a chutney of charred tomatoes, mint, and a cucumber raita. The last box contained fragrant chunks of pineapple, watermelon, and mango, scattered with gem-like pomegranate seeds. 'I passed these stalls on the way back from my meeting, and I could not resist.'

'This is most welcome, sir,' said Inder gratefully. 'A feast!' Despite his mother's delicious cooking, food was not high on the boy's agenda, and he would often go the whole morning and afternoon forgetting to eat if he was busy. But the delicious aromas were teasing out his appetite, and he pulled up a seat while Anand sat in his chair and divided the food onto two plates. They both ate heartily. In between bites, Anand joggled the mouse to clear the screensaver and reveal the desktop. He peered at the screen. All the documents were closed away neatly into the dock; even digitally, Inder was proving to be tidy. 'Did you read through everything?' he asked, as he dipped another momo into the refreshingly cool raita. 'There was a lot.'

Inder wiped his mouth with a paper napkin. 'I did speed-read it all,' he said, swallowing the food. 'And I noticed that, from your last test subjects, the rejection rates of your prosthetic limbs were 37% in children, and 24% in adults.' He cited this from memory.

'Yes, that is correct,' said Anand.

'The test report also showed that two of the most common reasons for rejection were poor functionality and lack of sensory feedback.' Inder took a toothpick, stabbed a large chunk of mango, and held it up. 'Grasp control and grip force proved to be the most desired functionality among your participants. You therefore needed to research both invasive and non-invasive EMG sensory recognition improvements.' He popped the mango into his mouth; it was syrupy sweet.

'Yes, yes, exactly,' said Anand, sitting up. 'That is the crux of the problem!'

Inder swivelled his chair from side to side, deep in thought. 'I was thinking, that is, I was wondering if perhaps the implementation of exteroceptive sensory feedback into your prosthetic devices might enhance user experience? Equally, improvements in the prosthesis control method might be made through shorter, thinner wiring – because, as you know, if line width increases, capacitance per length increases, and characteristic impedance decreases. Thus reducing the signal time. In the same way, for your hand prosthetics, improved programming will also shave off seconds so that control can better represent real-time hand speeds. Additionally, I am thinking that we really need to compare modality matched grip force feedback in somatotopically-matched and non-matched conditions, say, during a delicate object transfer task. That surely is critical, sir.'

'Chal! That it is!' An excited Anand clapped his hands together.

The boy was still deep in thought. 'I have many more ideas, but... you said we have until the end of the year? Sir, we will need to work really hard, in order to test my ideas and complete the research and upgrades in time. Also, we will be needing test subjects to volunteer, to help with feedback. As many as possible.'

'I'm sure that can be arranged! I will look up some of our past test subjects, as well as speak to some hospital contacts. Leave it with me.' Anand's eyes were filled with sparks of excitement. 'Achcha!' he exclaimed to himself. 'I never would have believed it. A slum boy might just save the company...'

That slum boy continued eating the crispy momos with renewed hunger, along with Anand. But then he thought of something. 'Sir, I am thinking that if I am to be working with you on improving and remodelling the prostheses, then I will not have time for cleaning. I will not be able to do three jobs.'

Anand wiped his mouth and sat back in his chair. 'That is true...'

'But I have an idea. It involves friends of mine who live in the same camp as me. I would like to call upon them for help. Is that acceptable to you?'

'In principle, yes, but... we do not have any extra cash to pay them.'

Inder stared at the food on the table. 'I have a suggestion,' he told Anand. 'From your canteen, I have seen that every day there is surplus food and drink. A lot of it. I am sure my friends would be happy to have food as their payment. They require only healthy food, and clean water, that is all.'

Anand thought about this, a smile coming over his face. 'Yes, that would definitely work, and can certainly be arranged. Then I trust you to organise your replacements as soon as possible, so that we can start work on the prosthetics immediately.'

A delighted Inder agreed, and they continued eating and discussing the work together, with great enthusiasm, until finally they sat back in their chairs, their minds buzzing and their stomachs full.

•••————————————————————•••

Inder's young neighbourhood friends were disappointed to be told that he no longer had time to tell them stories in the evening, at least until the end of the year. He explained that the company he worked for required him to work late in the office on an important project that involved robot arms, legs, and hands. The children cooed with awe at the thought of a half robot man or woman, despite being disappointed not to have their daily stories.

Still, like most slum children who did not have the luxury of toys, they spent their afternoons finding plenty of ways to have fun together, including playing cricket with a flat piece of wood as their makeshift bat, and the remains of a sponge ball someone had found. They also played football with the same sorry ball until it had completely disintegrated. Or  they practised the latest <u>Bollywood dance moves</u> together. And created kites by tying a flattened carrier bag to a cross of wooden rods, decorating it with ribbon and crude bows of coloured tissue – they even organised competitions amongst themselves. The children played with anything they could find amongst the rubbish. They did not feel deprived, and thought nothing of their hand-to-mouth existence. No hint of self-pity or depression. Rather, their playing was exuberant, filled with laughter, and excited chatter. The only limit to their joy was their imagination.

One late afternoon, when Inder showed up on his way back home, the children cried out to him to come play with them – but he was far too exhausted. And though they pleaded, he kept refusing.

Six-year-old Ria was the only one who did not insist. Her eyes lit up when she saw Inder, and as always, she ran to him crying out 'bhaiya!' – referring to him affectionately as 'older brother', though they were not related. She stood before him, still as a statue, and a smiling Inder stooped down and pressed her button nose with a loud 'boop!' She immediately came to life and began twirling around and showing off her dress, strutting up and down like a catwalk model. She always wore a dress, never trousers or leggings, and though her family were poor, they saved up to indulge her penchant for pretty second-hand frocks. Her fine, curly hair was always messy though, and her shoes scuffed and worn.

'Your dress is beautiful, Ria!' exclaimed Inder when she finished her little show. She jumped next to him, grabbed his hand, and they turned to walk back to the camp together. Ria looked up at Inder sideways, a grin on her face. 'I saw her again,' she said shyly, and giggled.

'Her?' asked Inder, distracted.

'The pretty girl,' she replied, busying herself with pushing and pulling Inder's hand in wide swings as they walked. 'You know, the one that listened to your story about the lake with the white swans that danced and twirled. The girl with the salwar kameez blue as the sky.'

Inder stopped. 'She was here? Again?'

Chuckling, Ria said, 'I saw you two smiling at each other that day. Do you want her to be your *girlfriend*, bhaiya?' she chided cheekily.

Inder mock-frowned and started tickling the little girl's arms, whereupon she shrieked with laughter.

A frazzled woman shouted out from a nearby building. 'Will you be quiet!! I'm trying to get my baby to sleep!'

'Sorry, aunty,' called out Ria sweetly.

'Sorry, aunty!' repeated Inder.

They quickly walked on, until Ria jumped in front of Inder and held up her hand in his face. 'That is how many times I saw her since that day.'

'Three times?'

Ria frowned, looked at her fingers, and put one down.

'Two times...' Inder said, pleasantly surprised.

The girl nodded. 'The last time – today! – she was walking along the road, that way,' Ria explained, pointing westward. 'I think she was looking for you, because she was doing this...' The girl lifted a hand above her eyebrows and looked around exaggeratedly.

'Ria, please tell me the truth.'

She nodded vigorously. 'She was! She was looking for you.'

They walked on in silence until they eventually arrived at their camp and turned into a narrow passageway between the jhuggis. As the path was only wide enough to go single-file, she let go of Inder's hand and skipped gaily ahead, flouncing the frills in her dress.

They eventually reached Ria's home, and Inder took a box from his rucksack and pressed it into her hands.

'What is this?' she asked with bright eyes.

'Gulab jamun. I know it is your favourite.'

She jumped up and down. 'Like the ones you shared with all of us the other day?'

Inder wobbled his head with a smile. 'But these are just for you and your family,' he said, and raised an index finger to his lips.

She hugged the box to her chest, spun round, and ran excitedly through the door, calling out to her parents about the sweets.

Inder waited to hear her mother's response, before turning back to continue walking home. But before long, he heard the sound of Ria's little feet running after him, and he stopped and waited for her to catch up. 'Forgot something?'

She threw herself onto him in a hug. 'Thank you for the sweets, bhaiya!' she breathed. 'Oh! And I almost forgot...' She tiptoed and stretched up to whisper something in his ear – her breath warm and tickly against his skin. Chuckling mischievously, she finally ran off back home.

Inder watched her go, an astonished grin spreading across his face, before he continued walking in a daze. He buried his hands in his pockets and kicked the dirt as he went. He looked up at the gap between the jhuggis and the laundry lines, and saw that the sky was a spectacular golden-blue as the sun made its grand exit, sinking serenely into the earth. In the distance, a flock of pigeons rose from the mishmash of roofs, like smoky rose-petals thrown up into the air, rising on the wind this way and that, before tumbling down – softly they kissed the horizon before disappearing from view.

On the face of it, 16-year-old Alia Pujari lived a charmed life.

The day after she had seen the storyteller for the first time, she awoke early in the morning, her mahogany hair fanning across the silk of her pillows. She stretched and yawned, opened one eye, then the other, concentrating on the digital clock on her bedside table. It was 7:18, a Tuesday, and a buzz of anticipation zipped through her as she realised she had class that day. And then she remembered the storyteller. She smiled to herself as she got up and padded to the en-suite bathroom, the marble flooring refreshingly cold underfoot as she thought of that beautiful boy with a pang of guilty pleasure. His ruddy face, the glow in his eyes, his hands gesturing animatedly, the children listening to him with rapt attention. How fitting that he was recounting the story of Swan Lake, she thought, for it was one of her favourite ballets – since she was little, her dream had always been to dance as Odette.

When Alia turned on the washbasin faucet, and let the water flow as she brushed her teeth, she could not help moving her legs into the classical position – left foot behind her, pointed toes resting on the floor. She placed her free hand lightly on her hip. The tinkle of water was the music, while, in her head, she counted '5, 6, 7' and on '8' stepped into a tombé, then a demi-plié, followed by five counts of changing coupé – her legs criss-crossing as she bounced diagonally across the spacious bathroom, ending with her left leg raised behind her, toes stretched into an elegant point. She repeated the steps back to the sink, where she spat out, rinsed, and gargled with mouthwash.

There was a knock on the door, and the fantasy in her mind – a sun-kissed storyteller, sitting on his newspaper at the side of the road, watching her dance in the street – vanished. She glanced around to find the maid entering. The middle-aged woman was holding a tray of breakfast things: small bone-china plates and bowls filled with food, a teacup and saucer, and a Lucknow silver tea set etched with intricate motifs.

Alia emerged from the bathroom, wiping her face with a towel. 'Why are you bringing breakfast to my room, Saanvi?' she asked, puzzled.

The maid checked behind her to see that the door had closed, before placing the tray on the bedside table. 'Miss, your parents are in the dining room, and... they are arguing again.' She spoke in a hushed tone. 'So I thought it would be better for you to eat here.'

Alia nodded her understanding. 'Haa, I see,' she said, sighing. Her parents argued a lot. Alia sat cross-legged on the bed as the tea was poured and handed to her. 'What are they fighting about now?' she asked, before sipping on the creamy chai.

Saanvi shook her head. 'Money. Always money. Your mother bought some expensive sari material from the fabric store, and sir said it is costing too much. But it is for Ishaanji's wedding, miss! And ma'am doesn't often buy for herself such expensive fabric, but being mother of the bridegroom, of course she wants something special. Your poor mother was near tears.'

'Arre-nahin!' exclaimed Alia, indignant. 'Surely for such a special occasion, papa should indulge her! I see I will have to be careful when I shop for myself.'

Saanvi nodded. 'This wedding will be costing sir a small fortune, especially with the bride price, so...' She stopped, suddenly noticing something in the top right-hand corner of the window beside Alia's bed. Layers of gossamer threads billowed gently. 'My goodness, there is a spider's web...' – she peered closer – 'and a big spider!' Flustered, she looked around for something to wipe it away.

But Alia quickly said, 'Please, leave it alone.'

Saanvi blinked at her, incredulous. 'But... the spider. It needs to be cleaned.'

'Actually, I like the little thing,' smiled Alia, shrugging. 'It is causing no harm, and it is not poisonous. In fact, it is doing good catching flies.'

The maid raised an eyebrow, unconvinced. 'Okay, miss,' she said, backing away reluctantly. 'Whatever you say.'

'Thank you.' Satisfied the spider was safe, Alia looked over the little plates and bowls of colourful delicacies on the tray. She picked up the sabudana khichdi – translucent tapioca pearls mixed with ground roasted peanuts, spices, herbs, and coconut. 'You have prepared a lot today, Saanvi, but I cannot eat all this,' she said, motioning to the other dishes. 'I must not put on weight. My ballet master would never forgive me.'

'That's what I thought, miss, but ma'am insisted. She is worried for you. She says you are too skinny.'

Alia tasted the tapioca. 'Mmm, delicious! But please take the other dishes away.'

'Yes, miss.' Obediently, Saanvi left the teapot, cup, and saucer – and took away the surplus food.

After she had finished eating, Alia dressed, brushed and pinned back her hair into a tight bun, then slipped quietly out of her room, avoiding her parents. She ran downstairs to the large exercise room cum dance studio in the basement. One entire wall was mirrored, with, on the adjacent wall, a ballet barre fixed at waist height. After she stretched and did her warm-up exercises, she practised for just over an hour before it was time to leave for class, which was to start at 10 a.m. on the dot. The ballet master did not take kindly to late-comers, especially since they were rehearsing for Sleeping Beauty where it was whispered that, in a few weeks' time, scouts from the Rambert Dance Company in London would be in the audience, searching out talent to join next summer's ballet school. And Alia was determined to make them notice her. 

Outside in the gated driveway, their driver was already waiting in the Audi A8, its gleaming silver paintwork marred by several small dents and scratches along the sides. When Alia emerged from the house, the driver immediately turned on the engine, and the car came to life with a gentle hum. Alia climbed into the back seat.

'Suprabhat, miss!' he grinned, briefly touching his driver's cap. He was an elderly man of average build, with wisps of grey hair protruding from underneath his hat – a contrast to his dark skin.

'Suprabhat, Arjun,' she said, a little flustered. 'Please wait a moment...' She checked frantically through her designer duffle bag to see if she had packed the gauze and tape, which she at last discovered wedged inside her ballet slippers – relieved, she zipped up the bag, put it to one side, and sat back. 'Okay, we can go now,' she breathed. 'How are you today, Arjun?'

'All is well, miss. I cannot complain. I have a good job driving this magnificent car for such a respectable family, so I am happy!' he beamed, glancing at her in the rear-view mirror.

They soon joined a highway, and though the markings divided the road into five lanes, the onslaught of cars, autorickshaws, vans, trucks, buses, motorbikes – and even the odd cycle rickshaw with distressed passengers holding on for dear life – created a chaotic seven lanes, as each vehicle scrambled and beeped at each other to pass by.

Old Arjun careened through the traffic at top speed, completely oblivious to the possibility of collisions, let alone danger to life. He nattered quite happily to Alia while he weaved this way and that, though the conversation was mostly one-sided, practically a monologue, as he chatted and laughed at his own jokes. Alarmingly, he spent more time looking over his shoulder at Alia, or in the rear mirror, than looking at the road ahead.

When they reached the junction with Arya Sumit Road, the opening of which was blocked with bright yellow bollards, Arjun pulled over, stopped the car, and touched his cap again. 'Here you are, miss. We made it in good time!'

'We did!' agreed Alia, patting the old man on the shoulder. 'I will see you later.'

'No, no, please don't forget that, like yesterday, I will be taking your father to his business conference again this evening. In fact, he has several conferences to attend in the coming weeks. So you will be needing to get a taxi home today. You must remember, miss, or you will be waiting for me and I will not be coming.'

Alia paused briefly as she got out of the car. 'Oh yes, I'd forgotten. Thanks for the reminder. I will make my own way home tonight.'

Arjun grunted satisfactorily and wobbled his head. 'I am sure you will be having a very splendid day, miss!' he shouted out, just before she closed the door. He immediately put his foot down and zoomed off, eliciting angry beeps and shouting from an autorickshaw driver who had to swerve out of the way.

Since Arya Sumit Road had recently been included as part of a pedestrian-only zone, Alia walked a further 10 minutes before she reached the ballet school. She would then change into her leotard, and tape and wrap the painful sores on her feet, grateful for the scant relief they provided, before putting on her ballet slippers. That was followed by six gruelling hours of technique practice, training, and rehearsals, before school finished at 5 p.m.

Alia decided to walk home that afternoon.

Something pulled her inexorably in a certain direction.

Taking the same route as she did yesterday, she walked to the outskirts of the pedestrian-only zone, where she had seen the slum children by the camp on the western perimeter. They were there, on the other side of the road, chatting happily amongst themselves as they played. She slowed down to a stroll as she made her way along that stretch of road, looking all around. But the storyteller was nowhere to be found. A little girl in a pretty dress, with a tangle of curly hair, jumped up and down and waved in her direction. Alia looked behind her but there was no-one else, and so she waved to the girl hesitantly.

The rest of the walk home was a daze of disappointment.

Her feet hurt. The sores and ulcers rubbing against her sandals were wretched complements of the ache that was beginning to needle into her heart. She wondered at her feelings. How they could be so drastically affected by a boy she had seen and heard only briefly the day before. As if the lightest flutter of a butterfly's wings were enough to make her tumble and fall to the ground. As if the merest breeze could throw her broken body up into the air. That smile of his, that flush of red in his cheeks – why were they so devastating to her? Her heart could only answer with its pounding palpitations.

Yet at the same time, she felt sick to her stomach.

She knew without a doubt that her parents would never allow such a match. It would be as impossible as asking day and night to join together;

their co-existence was only ever separate, and opposite, light dawning as darkness waned – the two never unifying.

Alia caught her breath and fought back the tears.

Dizzy with emotion, she almost stumbled.

But she had to accept the painful truth.

Her relationship with the storyteller was doomed before it had even begun.

•••————————————————————•••

It took all of Alia's willpower not to go back to that street.

For weeks she held on to her resolve valiantly.

But the Rambert officials did not pick her out for their summer school, and she had also not been chosen as the principal dancer for Sleeping  Beauty, so she was crushed. Instead, she was to play the Lilac Fairy, the queen of the fairies who counteracts the curse from the evil Carabosse, saving the princess baby from death. And for Alia, all it took was one night of tossing and turning, and a dream that brought the storyteller's face back to her – in devastatingly gorgeous clarity – for her resolve to weaken and shatter.

She woke up the following morning, defiant.

Throwing off her bedsheet with a huff, she got up, and wrapped a silk robe around herself as she stood in front of the large bow window – angry eyes searching for the little brown spider. Quite unusually it was still out, waiting with ceaseless patience. The silk fibres of its web vibrating delicately under its eight legs. The sight of it calmed her for a moment. 'Oh, what I would give to live a quiet life like you, chotu!' she breathed, tiptoeing closer to look at it cross-eyed. The fine, fur-like hairs on its body bristled from the air movement, and it immediately scrambled deep into the corner, disappearing from view.

Alia straightened and huffed again.

Perhaps it was the lack of sleep, or perhaps it was the bitter disappointment of not getting the part she had yearned for, but she stomped down the stairs to the dining room, knowing that her parents would already be there having breakfast together. As the winding staircase brought her closer, their voices became louder – her father's usual gruff, no-nonsense tone, and her mother's silky softness.

'Good morning!' announced Alia with a cynical smile as she walked into the room. Though it was not a good morning at all.

Her parents stopped talking and turned to her, surprised by her tone of voice. Even Saanvi, who was bringing a jug of juice to the table, paused, and glanced curiously at Alia.

Alia went over to kiss the foreheads of both parents, before sitting at the dining table, and taking the napkin from the plate.

'Is it?' asked her father, Mahit.

Placing the napkin on her lap, Alia waited for Saanvi to pour her tea and leave, before responding with a glare. 'It would be, if you allowed mama to get the sari she really wants, instead of that cheap material you made her exchange it for! And it definitely would be, if I had been chosen as prima ballerina in Sleeping Beauty!'

Her parents looked at each other, nonplussed.

'Anything else…?' ventured her mother, Azarin. Though her father was tall, and her mother short, both were chubby, with salt-and-pepper hair, fair complexions, and brown eyes – yet their personalities were very different. Mahit was definitely the boss, though his loud, gruff exterior belied the soft heart he had within, and Azarin was quietly submissive but oftentimes stood up strongly for what she truly believed to be right.

Alia looked around the table filled with colourful food. 'And… and… it certainly would be if… this archaic system of arranged marriages was abolished, and you allowed Ishaan a love marriage. And, it would be even better if this out-dated caste system did not exist, and people weren't marginalised because of their family line, or where they live, or… or how much money they earn. It's just not fair!'

Mahit blinked at his daughter, trying to take it all in. 'Wait a minute. Is Ishaan interested in someone else?' he floundered. It was just a few months before the wedding, and almost everything was arranged, booked, and paid for.

Alia looked at him. 'No, no, that's not what I meant. There's no-one else. I just meant that maybe you should have let him meet someone *naturally*, and fall in love *naturally*, instead of arranging his marriage.'

Mahit sat back, relieved. 'Well, I don't entirely disagree with love marriages, but I have to say that your mother and I are testimony to the fact that arranged marriages work. Don't you agree, laddoo?' he asked his wife, coughing awkwardly.

Azarin smiled coyly. 'Your father and I do not see eye to eye on many things, Alia, but this is one thing we completely agree upon. I am happy that *our* parents arranged our marriage. I do not want for anyone but your father. Though... surely you can see that, by the way they look at each other, Ishaan and Priya are already falling in love? Besides, from the start, we gave Ishaan choices, and he has been completely on-board. And let's face it, he's no spring chicken...'

Alia could not deny that the two loved each other; a fortunate outcome. And she herself appreciated Priya as a good match for her brother. She sighed, reached for a thick slice of toast, and began sawing it in half.

Azarin touched her daughter's arm sympathetically. 'I'm sorry you did not get the part you wanted, beti. It must be such a disappointment.'

'It is. No... actually, it's not.' Alia put the knife down and sat back, deflated. 'In the grand scheme of things, it doesn't really matter. I know I'm not the best dancer. No matter how hard I try and practice, I'm never going to be as good as Navi, who dances *so, so* beautifully, like a dream! She deserves to be principal dancer. But like I said, it doesn't really matter.' She stopped. Looked at both parents. Took a deep breath. 'What if... what if I told you that I were in love... with a dalit? What if I told you I loved him with all my heart, and I just know that he would make the best, most devoted, most loving husband...'

Her father's congenial expression instantly crumpled like a tin can. 'What!?!' he roared. 'Are you out of your mind, girl?!!'

Alia froze with alarm.

Azarin mirrored her shock. 'Beti,' she said, colour draining from her face. 'I... I thought you understood our position. We are respected in the community. You *cannot* marry a dalit. It would be... like tethering a magnificent horse to a donkey. It just wouldn't work.'

A fuming Mahit looked from his wife to his daughter, balled a fist, and smashed it on the table, rattling the bone china and cutlery. 'A dalit! A dalit!! I expressly forbid you to see anyone who is a dalit!!! I DISAPPROVE of any such union, do you hear?!'

Alia stood up, throwing the chair back onto the floor with a crash, and ran out.

Mahit was about to follow her, but Azarin held him back. Instead, he watched her go, then slapped the palm of his hand against his forehead.

Out in the hallway, a shaky Alia grabbed her holdall, thrust feet into shoes, and left the house – banging the door behind her.

She went through the motions of school that day, barely saying a word to anyone.

Her heart was in agony, and all she could do was dance through it.

But how she danced!

In rehearsal, she played the Lilac Fairy with grace, combining benevolence with beauty, fragility with passion, in a performance that was utterly mesmerising. When Alia finished dancing her part, the director jumped up onto his feet with rapturous applause. He told her that she had stolen the show. But to Alia, who felt empty, and a fake, those words barely penetrated, and she could only blink at him, unable to comprehend.

At 5 o'clock, she flew out of the building and ran and ran and ran. Straight to the street where she hoped he would be.

But, again, he was not there.

As usual, the children were playing together, their peals of joyous laughter clanging discordantly in her ears.

She sat back against a wall, and waited, hugging her bag to her chest.

The same little girl as before suddenly noticed her, and again, waved excitedly – this time, the child ran across the road and jumped right in front of Alia. But the girl's sweet smile soon faded. 'Why are you crying?' she asked, her eyes creasing with worry.

For a long time, Alia could not speak. She just broke down and cried and cried, burying her face into the bag, her whole body shaking. Eventually, the tears petered out when the girl went to her side and slipped her arm into Alia's. 'Please don't be sad,' she begged, looking up at her earnestly. She herself was becoming upset.

Alia dried her face on the back of her hand. 'I-I'm fine. All better now,' she smiled bravely, eyes glittering like freshly-blown glass.

'Promise?' asked Ria, frowning.

Alia laughed lightly. 'I promise!' She put down the bag on the wall. 'What's your name?' she sniffed.

'I'm Ria. And you?'

'Alia.'

'I like that name, and... I like you!' smiled Ria innocently. 'Actually, I know someone else who likes you. A lot.'

'What... do you mean?'

'Inder, the one who tells us stories. He really, really, *really* likes you,' she smiled, giggling to herself.

Alia blinked at her, absorbing his name. Absorbing the revelation about his feelings, though, somehow, she had always known. And she suddenly realised that, yes, in that moment, the briefest of moments, when she and Inder had looked at each other, they had told each other so much. And that was how she knew she loved him, and how she knew – with complete certainty – that he loved her too. In that briefest of glances, so much was said, and exchanged, and felt. It seemed a whole lifetime's worth. Within a matter of seconds, they had fallen in love, married, had children, and grown old together – in their hearts.

Was such a thing really possible?

It was Ria that answered her unuttered thoughts. 'He loves you, you know,' she said with such sweet candour that can only come from a child. Those words, "He loves you" – so small, so pure, yet powerful enough to change lives. Or move mountains. More powerful even than death. Ria had been etching random shapes into the dust with her foot, but suddenly jumped up and made a sweeping circle with her arms. 'He loves you bigger than the whole world, and the moon, and the stars!' She reached a hand high into the sky, her finger painting a crescent moon and pinprick stars.

Alia laughed with happiness. 'He does, doesn't he!' She got up too, clutching her hands against her chest.

Ria nodded and twirled around, flouncing her dress.

Alia gasped, 'You're a ballerina!'

The word elicited a spontaneous response in Ria, and she began to dance – prancing and jumping and pointing her toes in a childish, made-up choreography. The frills of her dress now a floaty tutu, in her hair a sparkling diamond tiara, and her feet clad in silk slippers. She twirled and spun, and leapt and glided, as Alia cheered with delight – until the girl at last fell against the wall, gasping for breath. Alia's ovation was rapturous. 'That was so beautiful, Ria! You are definitely a prima ballerina!'

Beaming, Ria got up and bowed and curtsied, and then sat next to Alia, threading her arm through hers. She noticed the delicate gold watch on Alia's wrist and concentrated on the face. 'It's 5-3 o-clock,' she said. She hadn't yet learnt to tell the time.

Alia smiled. 'Actually, it's quarter past five.'

'Quarter past five,' the girl repeated to herself ponderously. She suddenly jumped up, hugged Alia, then waved goodbye as she ran off across the road, calling out to her, 'See you same time tomorrow, okay?' She said this in an 'I won't take no for an answer' tone. 'I want to dance for you some more!' she explained. The little girl waved as she rejoined her friends.

Alia watched her, then picked up her bag and turned to leave. She had arrived in the storyteller's street with a tremendous ache in her chest – for him, for her parents. An ache that still crackled through her as she walked. There was bitter, yet there was also sweet – and she couldn't help smiling to herself as she thought about that amazing little girl's exuberant dancing. A girl who had not a care in the world. Whose imagination lifted her beyond the grimy backstreet, beyond poverty and deprivation – into places that even the richest could not dream of.

Alia both laughed and wept as she slowly walked home.

••• —————————————————————— •••

The next day, at a quarter past five, Alia returned to the road looking this time not for the storyteller, but for Ria. And that's when she saw him sitting there, on the wall, in a crisp white shirt and sand-coloured slacks – looking up at the hazy blue of the sky.

And in turn, when Inder glanced down the road, expecting Ria, he saw instead the forbidden girl walking toward him. And she was even more beautiful than he remembered. 'H-hello,' he said, standing up, a little abashed.

'Hello, Inder,' smiled Alia, stopping in front of him. She realised for the first time how his eyes were flecked with green.

'You... know my name?'

'Ria,' she explained, and bit her lip.

'Haa, Ria! I might have guessed. But she did not tell me your name.'

'I expect she was too busy dancing, or playing, or match-making!' she smiled. 'My name is Alia.'

'Yes, that is Ria. I am very pleased to meet you, Alia.'

They paused, and just stared at each other, hardly believing they were together at last. But there were no questions between them. They both knew exactly where they stood with each other, and how they felt.

Inder was the first to break their gaze, looking down at his feet as he combed a nervous hand through his hair. 'If... if it's okay, I would like to get to know you.'

Alia smiled at his candour, and glanced along the road. 'Then walk me home.'

Though he was taller, their steps fell into a natural cadence, as if they had always walked together. But then Alia suddenly turned to face him. 'I have to tell you that my parents will not allow me to see anyone of... your caste.' There, she had said it. Her heart fluttered wildly.

But Inder just smiled sadly at her. 'I already know,' was all he said. 'I knew it from the very first time I saw you.'

Alia sighed, exasperated by the impossible. 'Then... what are we doing, getting to know each other?'

'Becoming friends?' Inder replied, hopeful.

That glimmer of hope that he put before her was enchanting. It was like the smallest of flames, glowing yellow-orange. So flimsy, so easily blown out. Yet she desperately wanted to yield to it, like the way a flicker of forgiveness softens anger and resentment. She wanted to surrender to her heart, and to Inder, and be more than just friends.

They continued walking, remaining silent for a while, sometimes stealing a surreptitious glance at each other as they wended their way through the network of streets.

'This way,' said Alia, walking through a wrought iron gate into Lodhi

Gardens.

As they stepped over the threshold from the grimy Delhi streets into the verdancy of the park, it was as though they had entered a parallel world.

Sun filtered magically through the air.

Alia flapped away aphids that were like tiny dots of bouncing light.

Tree-lined paths, punctuated with ornamental pots of flowers, chequered acres of grass.

The freshness of sap filled their noses.

And as they passed underneath the branches of an old mango tree – the shadow of its boughs criss-crossing their forms – rhesus macaque monkeys stared at them from up high, with pink faces, a tuft of hair crowning their heads, and beady eyes keen for food.

That flickering flame, hope, led the couple irresistibly through the park.

They soon began to chat and laugh. They learnt about each other's lives and families. Inder told her about his job at i-Nation Bionics, which Alia absorbed with fascination. And she told him about her ballet school, and her part in Sleeping Beauty, as well as her hopes and dreams.

'You are a ballerina?' asked Inder, intrigued.

'Yes, I'm learning to be,' she said, turning to face him. She caught her breath as she took in his bronze skin, his perfect features.

Inder started saying, 'I have never before seen any ballet. I would like to see you dance in one sometime…' – when Alia held out a hand to him.

'Dance with me,' she said.

Looking from her hand to her irresistible eyes, Inder told her, 'I… cannot dance.' Yet he found himself taking her hand nevertheless. He sucked in air as an electric shock passed from her fingertips right into him. Sizzling through his entire body.

Slowly, gently, Alia began to dance for him – her body straightening into a perfect axis, both supple and strong, her arms and fingers like delicate ribbons trailing through the air. She spun effortless fouettés, before returning to him and stretching her leg behind her in a 90-degree arabesque. Then she danced a circle around him, smooth glissades, and delicate jetés, bounding upwards in a pas de chat, followed by 5th position pliés into soubresaut jumps – legs flittering, body as light as a feather. Her spontaneous movements a careless and wanton artistry. Her breaths, like the sound of angels sighing.

When she took his hand again, and they moved around each other in perfect rhythm, they both knew that this was the dance of their lives. A  pas de deux. When he kissed the back of her hand, the tenderness of his lips was a foregleam of how he would always treat her – softly, kindly. And when they locked magnetic eyes on each other, they knew that there would be no-one else except the two of them. That they would love each other more than anything in the world. And that it would be everlasting.

Around them, a small crowd was gathering – until, at last, Alia and Inder finished dancing, and the audience clapped and cheered with delight. 'How lovely! You make such a beautiful couple!' smiled one old lady. She seemed familiar to Alia, though she didn't think much of it – she only had eyes for Inder. And for just those few seconds, there was no divide between them. They were equals. Without caste. And they were being applauded for it. It was exhilarating.

At last the crowd began to disperse, leaving the two alone.

'You *can* dance!' breathed Alia. 'How?!'

Inder looked down at himself, astonished. 'I... didn't know I could do that. I think I just copied everything you did.'

Alia frowned at him. 'I don't believe you! The way you danced... it must have taken years of training.'

'I am not lying to you,' Inder said, looking at her squarely. 'I would never lie to you.'

Alia wanted to kiss him then, more than anything. But she stepped back, looked over her shoulder. 'I-I have to go. We're close to my home... my parents...' She spun around and ran off.

All Inder could do was watch as she disappeared.

•••———————————————————•••

Though Inder waited every day at the same time, in the same place, days passed without her turning up in his street. Anyone else would have given up. But Inder didn't doubt for a second that she would return. The only question was when.

As he waited each day, gazing at the blue-golds of what seemed like a hundred setting suns, as he watched passersby go this way and that, and stray cows nosing through the rubbish for scraps – a multiplicity of thoughts went through his mind. He saw his life stretching ahead of him, his hair streaking with grey, lines etching into his skin. He watched the passage of years, a blurring cycle of seasons. Stars overhead circling, the moon waxing and waning. And the slow dance of night and day. Yet as time evaporated before him into a hot steam, Inder never lost faith that she would come back to him.

And at last, the day came.

Inder had to rub his eyes, and blink through buttermilk rays of sun, when he saw her walking his way from afar. In his mind, so much time had passed that he imagined her old, her back hunched, and a pale hand orbing the top of a walking cane. But instead, as she drew closer, she had hardly changed from when he saw her last. Four long days ago. Except her hair was down in a beautiful mess, mahogany waves framing an anxious frown. 'I'm so sorry, Inder!' she breathed when she reached him. She touched his arm briefly, and again, the sizzle of electricity passed from her fingertips right into the deepest part of him.

Inder closed his eyes, sucked in air. And in just a few seconds he saw the last few days of her life flashing through his mind:

The old familiar-looking woman that applauded their pas-de-deux turned out to be Alia's neighbour, and when she chanced upon Azarin and Alia together, she described how beautifully her daughter had danced in the park with her boyfriend...

Her father confronted Alia that very evening, and there was a complete meltdown – him shouting, Alia crying – and he forbade her from seeing 'that' boy again. Ever.

Alia was inconsolable, barely spoke to her parents, cried for hours in her bedroom.

Inder let go of Alia's hand and staggered back, thumping against the wall behind him.

'Inder! Are you okay?!' cried Alia.

'I... I...'

'I'm so sorry! My parents stopped me from coming to you.'

'I know.'

'You know? You must have guessed that they would forbid me from seeing you.' Alia shook her head and took Inder's hand in hers.

Another shock made Inder flinch.

He saw the argument Alia had with her parents just half an hour before, felt the strength of her defiance. The force of her parents' anger. He watched as she left the house, and ran and ran through the streets to find him. Fear and exhilaration gunning through her chest. Dry wind flowing through her hair. Until she saw him, standing there, waiting, and her heart broke and leapt at the same time.

Inder blinked the images out of his mind, confused, struggling to understand. How was it possible he could see her memories...? Feel her emotions...?

Alia drew closer, magnetised by his eyes – they were like brown pebbles slick with rain. She leant into him and lightly kissed his lips several times, whispering 'I'm so sorry' between each one. 'So, so sorry.'

And Inder felt himself melt. Felt himself sliding into the balmy warmth of her sea.

Alia eventually pulled away. 'What are we going to do?' she asked, searching his eyes for answers.

Inder blinked, heady from the afterglow of kisses. He glanced down at her delicate hands in his. Her soft, honeyed skin. They brought him back to reality. 'I will go to your parents and ask for your hand in marriage.'

Alia's eyes widened with disbelief. 'You... really mean it! But you don't know my parents, my father. He is a proud man. And he is very, very angry. I am scared he will kill you.'

'I do not care,' said Inder, fixing eyes on hers.

She stared back, and no longer doubted him. 'You're really going to do it... You realise how mad this is? We've only just met, we hardly know each other.'

'Yes,' said Inder. 'I mean, yes, I realise how this seems. But, I cannot explain it... I feel as though I have known you all my life. I feel like I know everything about you. You mean more to me than... than... the world. Than everything. So I *will* do it. I will go to your parents the day after tomorrow. On Thursday. While you're at school.' He kissed her hand, as if to seal the promise.

'I believe you, Inder,' she said softly.

They walked to Lodhi Gardens, holding hands like long-time lovers. Sauntering through the grounds, they said not a single word, until they found an empty bench and sat down to watch the monkeys skitter about the trees. Inder put his arm around her, and Alia rested her head on his shoulder. Sharing body warmth. Her hair spilling down his arm.

I love you, Inder told her.

I know, she replied. *I know you love me bigger than the whole world, and the moon, and the stars,* she said drowsily, smiling. She closed her eyes and melted into him.

•••————————————————————•••

That night, Inder tossed and turned on his floor mat, unable to sleep.

Alia's memories cascaded through his dreams.

Angry shouting.

A father's fist banging on the table.

A mother's tearful pleas to stop arguing.

And Inder suddenly sat up, confused, startled, and afraid – very afraid – all at the same time.

He was surprised to find himself in their humble home, and that it was the middle of the night – the place dimly illuminated by the flicker of an old kerosene lamp, the brass rusted with speckles of pink. His parents were fast asleep on the other side of the room, half hidden behind a curtain. His father snoring loudly.

Inder held his head in trembling hands.

In his mind, a blizzard of memories, thoughts, images, disturbed him.

Was he going mad?

Had his imagination gone wild?

What else could explain the visions he saw when Alia touched him...

Sweat made his clothes stick cloyingly to his body.

And outside, sheets of rain began cascading onto the corrugated iron roof, dripping through the cracks and spotting the dusty floor. The rain, the nightmares, the howl of wind, lingering memories, the ominous rustle of plastic sheeting – all of it, a clashing symphony of sounds and thoughts, conspiring to drive away his sleep. Conspiring to drive him insane.

On the other side of town, Alia too was in bed, but unlike Inder she was fast asleep, insulated in the relative calm of her room, though outside the storm howled. Her mind, loosened from the constraints of reality, ran wild with dreams. Of her parents, Inder, and the monkeys in Lodhi Gardens.

Yet when morning came, she found that the anxiety that chased her like a malevolent presence in the night, fell away in the bright light of day. Relieved, she yawned, stretched, and got up. Gazing out of the window, she saw that last-night's rain seemed to make the trees and grass a more vivid green. And with the heat of morning sun, steam rose from the asphalt, creating a dream-like aura of mist over the ground.

She looked for the spider in the corner of the window. But stopped. It was nowhere to be found. No sign of gossamer webbing. The corner was completely clear.

Alia blinked in disbelief, heart sinking, as she realised that someone must have cleaned it away, maybe even thrown it out, or killed it. Yet despite her dismay, she found herself walking out of her room with such insensibility that it was as if she were sleep-walking. She felt oddly calm as she loosely tied her robe around her waist and descended the stairs.

As ever, her parents were already in the dining room, but there were others too. Her grandparents had come to stay, weeks in advance of the wedding, and their stilted conversation was interrupted when Alia arrived. Alia forced a smile on her face when she greeted them. 'Dadi-ji, dada-ji. Lovely to see you!'

Grandmother looked her up and down disapprovingly. 'You are looking very skinny, poti!' She turned to her daughter-in-law, Azarin. 'Why are you not feeding her?'

Azarin stiffened, just as Saanvi hurried over to bring Alia's food.

Alia told her grandmother, 'Please, it is no-one's fault but my own. I have to stay slim for my dancing.'

'True,' said grandfather, motioning for Saanvi to pour him some more tea. 'You never see a podgy ballerina, do you!'

Saanvi filled everyone's cups, and Alia was just going to ask about the spider, when grandmother told her, 'I came to your room earlier, poti, though you were fast asleep. But, oh! There was a massive spider in your window, and it was all I could do to stop myself from screaming!' She shivered. 'It was horrible! But don't worry, I squashed it well and good, and cleaned all the cobwebs.' Her eyes slid over to Saanvi. 'I don't know what kind of house you keep, filled with so many spiders!'

Saanvi glanced nervously at Alia.

'Oh no!!' exclaimed Alia, appalled. 'I... I really liked the little thing. It never hurt anyone!'

'Well, it's squashed and in the bin now,' tutted grandmother, crunching into her toast and casually flicking crumbs from her sari.

'No...' whimpered Alia. 'I-it was my little friend, Dadi-ji. It always came out at night to catch flies.'

Grandmother turned away and raised an eyebrow at her son. 'I can see why you needed us to come,' she told him, tutting. 'If we didn't, this whole house would be filled with cobwebs and skeletons making friends with spiders...'

Mahit was about to protest, but Azarin gave him a warning glance. Why bother, that glance told him. It is no use. No use at all.

Alia swiped at her eyes, took several breaths, and began tapping furiously into her phone – she then got up suddenly and ran off without a word. She waited by the front door, before pressing the Send button on the message she'd composed. She heard both her parents' phones beep, first one, then the other – and waited nervously through several seconds of silence, until her father shouted out in rage. Alia jumped, quickly slipped through the door, and ran off as fast as she could.

Inder suddenly awoke, exhausted from a night fraught with anxieties. In his ears echoed the sounds from the last dream. A little girl mewling and crying and mumbling fervently in her sleep. Her voice tinged with accent. A German accent. Whispering something about walls and drawings and horses, and calling out foreign names that somehow sounded familiar. Begging for help. Crying for her father...

Inder sat up on his sleeping mat, blinking. The silence punctuated by the faithful ticking of an old clock. He turned hazily to its battered face, staring at it for some time before he suddenly realised it was almost midday! Groaning, he jumped up and careened here and there as he raced around to wash and dress.

When he arrived at the office, panting, his hair a mess, and his shirt buttoned wrongly – he ran past several of the older slum children. One of them was spraying the bamboo plants with mist. 'You're late!' one boy said, far too cheerfully for his liking. Another boy, watering the pots, exclaimed, 'You're gonna be in so much trouble!' The third, a girl, waved at him good-naturedly. Inder only glanced at them nervously, as he rushed past.

He found Anand in the workshop.

The man looked up from an illuminated magnifying glass, surprised to see Inder out of breath and so dishevelled. 'It is unusual for you to be late, and today of all days!' he remarked, eyebrows raised.

'Sir, I am so sorry! It won't happen again. But I am here now,' he breathed, flustered.

'Yes, I can see that,' said Anand, unimpressed. He turned back to the magnifying glass and squinted as he finished twisting a tiny screw into an arm prosthesis. 'I have completed all the modifications, though it has taken me twice as long as you. My eyes are not what they used to be.'

'I am so, so sorry, sir! Truly.'

'Why are you so late?'

'I...' he faltered. He could not tell him the truth. 'It was the storm last night, water dripping everywhere. I couldn't sleep.'

Anand sighed. 'That storm has caused a lot of trouble, and made us fall very behind.'

Inder drew closer to inspect the prosthetic arm, crouching over it. 'But you have done an excellent job here. We only need to test it now...' He looked around. 'Where is our test subject?'

'He left an hour ago. I tried to make him stay, but he said something about a hospital appointment out of town, and he did not have the time to stay all afternoon... So I asked Gita to phone around, and she has managed to find someone else – but they cannot come until 2 p.m.'

'2 p.m.?' repeated Inder. 'But it will take at least five hours to go through all the tests.'

'Yes it will! So you should tell your parents that you'll be back late this evening.'

'Sir...' Inder thought of Alia, waiting for him in the street. 'I am meeting someone at 5 p.m.'

Anand stopped and looked at him, flabbergasted. 'Then you will have to cancel it!'

Inder sighed with frustration. He didn't have her mobile number.

Inder rushed through work, being extra careful not to make any mistakes that would cost him dearly. He managed to finish in record time, just before 6 p.m. – and even though he splurged money on a taxi that would drop him in the road where his camp was, he harboured every hope that she would still be there waiting for him. But she was not.

He strained to look up and down the road yet again, but then sat against the brick wall. He stared at the spot where she had sat next to him just the day before. It seemed imbued with her presence.

He sighed, knowing that he would wait for her for as long as it took.

Just as he did before.

He settled down. Raised his eyes. Looked up at the gap between the jhuggis and the laundry lines, and watched – yet again – the slow descent of the sun, and the spectacular golden-blues that fanned out and blazed behind it. Far in the distance, there came a screech of tyres, and a sharp bang, making Inder jump. He caught his breath, heart thundering in his chest, as he watched a faraway flock of pigeons rising from the mishmash of roofs, like smoky rose-petals thrown up into the air, floating on the wind this way and that, before tumbling down – softly they kissed the horizon before disappearing from view.

Inder stared, mortified, into the distance.

Unable to move.

Unable to breathe.

Even brimming tears dared not slip down his cheek.

Until he broke.

And he collapsed, folding into himself as he hunched over the pavement.

His body wracked with sobs.

The next morning, Inder called in sick.

It wasn't quite a lie, for he felt sick to his stomach knowing that today was the day he was going to confront Alia's parents.

His own parents had already left for the market, and Inder found himself alone pacing around the tiny jhuggi, redundant, except for making sure his best clothes were perfect, and that his shoes were clean and polished. In his head, he rehearsed exactly what he was going to say.

After he left home, he went straight to the flower market. It was a riot of colour, garlands of flowers hanging in elaborate arrangements, and trays filled with flowerheads. Littering the floor were dropped petals trudged into the dirt. The market was busy with people buying eagerly– mostly for their puja, their worship offering to whichever god they hoped to appease. There were so many vibrant colours, but in the end Inder chose a bunch of simple beli flowers for their creamy whiteness and intoxicating scent.

He searched his pockets for the scrap of paper on which Alia had scribbled her address, but it was nowhere to be found. Yet his feet kept walking, and he wondered how it was he knew the way. Since that time when he and Alia touched, and an electric shock buzzed through him, things had begun to percolate – slowly – into his mind, and he was gradually coming to know and understand so much about her that he hadn't known before. As if her mind had become his. As if her life was also his life. It was unsettling. And disturbing. And there was nothing that could explain this extraordinary phenomenon.

Every nerve in his body was tense as Inder stood outside the Pujari house now, feeling small and intimidated. The gate was open, and he simply wandered into the driveway toward the modern yet classical villa style building, made with local Dholpur stone and natural lime render. Above the grand front entrance was a semi-circular jali – an intricately patterned stone screen – and in the immaculate gardens surrounding the house, were round stone pots filled with feathery ferns, and impressive trees boxed in with square hedges. Inder checked his new mobile phone, it was just a minute after the time he'd arranged with Alia: 12.31 p.m. – and so he shook out the nerves from his trembling hand and pressed on the doorbell as firmly as he could.

A tall, grey-haired man opened the door almost immediately, a frown on his face as he looked Inder up and down disapprovingly.

'Hello, sir. My name is Inder Chauhan.' He stooped down and tried to touch the man's feet out of respect – but he quick-stepped away.

'Don't!' he said with a booming voice, not wanting to be touched by such a low caste. 'So, you're the one!'

Inder gulped, pressed his hands together, and bowed. 'Namaste.'

'Do you know where Alia is?' he asked gruffly.

Inder blinked at him. 'I... do not understand. Is she not at school?'

'No, no,' said Mahit, irritated. 'She sent us a text message just before she left yesterday morning, saying that unless we spoke to you, she would not come home.'

'I am sorry, sir. But I have not seen her for two days. I do not know where she has gone.'

'Haa,' said Mahit, scrutinising Inder's face carefully. It was clear the boy knew nothing. 'I believe you, though I don't see why I should.' He left the door open and went inside, his slippered feet shuffling against the stone floor.

Inder stepped in, closed the door gently behind him, and quickly slipped off his shoes. He hurried after Alia's father, who was already entering a large living room filled with luxurious matching sofas, and polished marble furniture – he sat down on one of the sofas, motioning with an air of annoyance for Inder to sit opposite him.

Inder placed the paper-wrapped flowers on the coffee table between them, next to a collection of crystal animal figurines on a silver tray. 'For your good wife, sir,' he mumbled, not quite as warmly as he had rehearsed.

Mahit only glanced despisingly at the flowers, before saying bluntly, 'So you're the *dalit* who dares to court my daughter!' He spat out the word 'dalit' as if it were a profanity.

Inder felt his resolve weaken. He took a deep breath and wriggled his head. 'I know that nothing I say will convince you, sir. You do not know me. And you do not understand how I feel, and... how much I love Alia.

More than life itself. But... I ask only that you listen to your daughter. And hear what *her* heart is telling you.' But Inder's winsome words did not have the effect he had hoped for. He watched with alarm as Mahit's expression puckered into anger.

'How dare you tell me what to do! How dare you tell me how I should behave with my own daughter! And how dare you think that a mere a dalit has any chance with her!!' He stood up. 'That is it! I cannot even bear the sight of you.' He glared instead at the ground at Inder's feet. 'I want you out of this house, NOW. And I want you out of my daughter's life IMMEDIATELY!! Do you hear?!' His face was becoming redder by the second, his eyes darkening with rage.

Inder got up. 'Sir, please...'

'If I hear any mention of you from my daughter, or if you dare come back here, I will kill you with my bare hands – do you understand?!' He balled his hands into fists and stepped forward menacingly.

Inder caught his breath, turned on his heel, and swiftly made his way out. He heard the shuffle of the man's slippers behind him, as he shoved feet into shoes and ran quickly out of the front door – his own feet clattering against the stone paving. Something struck his back, and he looked behind to see the beautiful beli flowers dropping to the ground. Their creamy white petals scattering about.

Alia's father cried out, 'Take your stupid flowers away from my sight!'

Inder stooped to pick up the crumpled bunch, and then turned to run out of the gate. Its machinery whirred into life as it slid closed behind him, clanging firmly shut.

•••————————————————————•••

That night, as he slept, voices came to him.

So many voices, but one in particular stood out.

A German girl.

Her thin, thready mumbles sounded as if she were talking in her sleep.

Her whimpering cries were so real, so breathy, it was like she was right there next to him.

He dared to speak to her. *Wh-who are you?*

But she did not answer.

Are you... real?

Again nothing.

Inder turned to his side and hugged his knees to his chest. Eyes squeezed shut. *I'm going mad!* He thought to himself, scared out of his wits. He thumped his head against the pillow. *I'm losing my mind!!*

N-no, came the girl's faint voice.

And Inder stiffened.

No, no, no, she mumbled feebly.

And that was when it happened.

An explosion of bright white light obliterated the entire world.

Until there was only light, pure light.

And Inder's mind exploded, and imploded, and then burst with a multiplicity of images, sounds, memories, thoughts, feelings, words, joy, hate, yearning, love, pain, evil, and good. Years and years of it. Pouring, ferociously, into him, and out of him. Wracking his body with a thousand tingling stings. Convulsing his spine into an arc.

An eternity collapsed into seconds and minutes.

The universe condensed into a pinprick.

And then suddenly Inder went limp.

Sweat shadowing the sleeping mat.

Tears seeping down his face.

And he finally understood – through this connection with the girl with the German accent.

He finally saw, and knew.

Where he came from.

Who he was.

Who those voices were.

What his mind was capable of.

And all he could do was lie there, absorbing it.

Not believing, yet believing.

Assimilating.

Exhausted.

And then it dawned on him.

An awful realisation.

And he groaned.

Alia.

His poor, sweet, Alia.

Her love... her overwhelming love for him – they had both thought it was solid. Real. They thought they would love each other forever.

But that was all a lie.

His lie.

He had made her feel that way, somehow.

His mind had done something to her mind.

And he felt sick.

Sick.

Sick from the thought of it.

He groaned and groaned.

Rolling into a ball, arms cradling his head – guilt, and the night, and the weight of the world, pressed down on him.

It made him wish she had never walked down his street.

Made him wish she had never met him.

Someone joggled his shoulder. 'Inder, Inder! Ouch!!' His mother quickly drew back her hand and sat back on her haunches. She shook her hand out, and rubbed it against her sari. 'You gave me an electric shock!'

Inder sat up suddenly, blinking himself back to the real world, staring at his mother.

'You look terrible,' remarked his father from across the room, surrounded as usual by heaps of shoes. On the floor lay the battered bunch of flowers that he had bought Alia – amongst the leaves sparkled something glass-like, and Inder realised with alarm that it was one of the crystal figurines from the coffee table in Alia's home. Planted there to frame him.

Still groggy, Inder at last registered what his mother had said about the electric shock – and he looked down at his hands. They were sensitive, zizzing with energy. Power. His whole body pulsated with it. His heart thudding crazy fast.

He felt something.

Right in the deepest part of him.

Alia was in danger.

Something bad had happened to her. He just knew.

He jumped up, stooped down to pick up something, shoved it into his pocket, and ran out without a word.

'Inder, your shoes!' cried his father.

The boy reappeared, pushed feet into slip-ons, and ran out again.

Feet pounding on the hot pavement.

The stench of pollution filling his lungs, choking him.

He ran all the way to the Pujari house.

The journey took an age, yet he was there in no time.

This time the gates were closed, and so he climbed over the garden wall, running from the shelter of one tree to another. Gasping. He knew where Alia's room was, and he made his way around to the east side of the house.

Her window was on the first floor, and while he stopped to catch his breath, he looked down at his hands, eyes wide with disbelief: they were shaky and seemed to be... glowing. He tore his eyes away, psyched himself up, then looked up and around.

Further along the brick wall sat four monkeys, all of them staring at him curiously – their flabby grey bellies stark against brown fur.

Inder reached out a hand to them, and motioned to the window opposite, wondering whether he was truly mad. This would prove it – or not – once and for all. Again, he stretched his arm toward them.

The monkeys blinked at him unamused, one of them scratched its leg, and another yawned, glancing sideways as if bored. But then the smallest one got up, and scampered along the top of the wall toward him. Inder tensed, bracing himself for an attack – but, instead, it stopped right next to him and waited. Inder held out his hand, fingers unfurling to reveal the little glass figurine. The monkey snatched it up and scampered down the wall. It ran across the lawn, jumped onto a tree next to the house and climbed to the top, thumping softly onto the first-floor window ledge. It leant against the window pane, tiny nails clicking against the glass, before crouching down and squeezing itself between the five-inch gap. It jumped inside.

Inder closed his eyes, and saw.

As the monkey scurried about the room, he discovered that the bed was made. There were no sounds. The pristine room was completely empty.

Inder suddenly tensed as muted voices and movement came from within the house. People were talking, footsteps shuffling, the front door opening. Someone shouted urgently, hurry, get in the car!

The monkey lumbered down, hiding behind some furniture – while, outside, another monkey scurried to the front of the house and sat, quite casually, right in the centre of the lawn. It watched as Alia's anxious mother and father rushed into the silver Audi, and the gate started to open. The engine roared, tyres screeched, and the car turned out of the gate and raced down the road, leaving the stench of rubber and petrol.

The monkey chased after it, but the car was too fast – and so it stopped on the curb, redundant, watching the car disappear before scampering back to the wall and its companions.

Inside the house, the first little monkey quietly ran down the stairs and slipped into the sitting room. It placed the glass figurine on the coffee table, and then turned and raced out the way it had come.

Outside, Inder stepped out from behind a tree, listening to the sound of the car fading.

Above him came a flapping noise.

The sound of a squealing whistle-trill, from high up.

It swooped down past Inder's head before he saw it, the rush of air brushing his skin. He ducked and looked up. A dark shadow streaked upwards – and Inder squinted to make out the shape of a black kite. Broad, flat wings over a metre wide, and a forked tail. It sped down the road, and squealed as it flew after the car, flapping and rising higher and higher until it was just a slip of a silhouette.

Breaking out from the shade of the tree, Inder went after it. He saw it in his mind's eye. In turn, the black kite's keen eyes trained on the silver-grey car that was zigzagging at top speed through traffic, beeping furiously to clear the way.

After about 10 chaotic minutes, the car screeched to a halt. Doors were thrown open and out ran Alia's parents – they rushed urgently up broad stone stairs, into a large, square building.

Twenty minutes later, Inder arrived, puffing and panting – he stopped in front of the same building, doubling over, gulping air. At last he straightened to look up at where he was. And it made him freeze with dread. Aashlok Hospital loomed menacingly over him. He walked slowly up the steps, scouring the air for signs of the black kite, hoping upon hope that the bird had landed anywhere but here. But there it was. Sitting above a second-floor window, nibbling its wing, before looking down to lock eyes onto Inder – the two stared at each other, the black kite with its shiny eyes, Inder with a grave expression – before Inder walked through the hospital sliding doors, and disappeared inside.

Inder made his way along the corridor as if in a dream.
He passed reception, and floated up stairs.
Nurses and porters walked past him like spectres.
Doctors in white jackets, or scrubs.
The reek of antiseptic and cleaning fluid.
People talking echoed in his ears.

It was the awful wailing sobs that made his heart stop. They sounded almost otherworldly.

They came from a doorway to a room that was a rectangle of light in a dark tunnel.

An elderly man sat on a bench next to the door, hunched like a ghoul, flinching with every outcry.

Inder walked along the corridor and slipped onto the bench next to the old man, recognising immediately the sound of Alia's father's sombre voice coming from the room, talking to a doctor. Inder struggled to get the sense of their conversation in between the sobs – when a tiny red dome landed on Inder's knee, and he glanced down at it distractedly. The shiny ladybird, with six perfect spots on its two elytra, was covered in a fine pale pollen. It began cleaning itself – stretching delicate forelegs over its eyes, head, and antennae. Having just feasted on aphids swarming over a rosebush in the hospital grounds, it was about to settle down from sleepiness, when it stopped, shuffled round, and looked up at Inder with metallic-black eyes. Suddenly its elytra quivered open, and wings like shiny cellophane unfolded, stretched, and flapped. With a light thrum, it hovered upwards and away, disappearing through the door of light. Higher and higher it floated, a silent intruder, eventually landing on the bare lightbulb that hung from the ceiling. As it watched what was going on, Inder watched too.

In the middle of the room was a bed with a slight girl, lying partially bandaged like a half-wrapped mummy. A bare arm stained with purple-blue bruises hung limply from the side of the bed, and one side of her face was obliterated by a deep gash fresh with glossy blood. When he realised it was Alia, Inder doubled over, gritting teeth to stop himself from crying out.

In the background, the life support machine by the bed emitted a steady beep. The air was ripe with the stench of sickness and antiseptic. Sitting in a chair next to the bed was her mother, holding Alia's hand and weeping hysterically. Her father, Mahit, was standing stiffly on the other side of the bed by the window, next to a thin man in a white jacket. Mahit was pale, eyes wide, dazed.

The doctor was talking to him in a low tone. '...she's not responding. We have tried everything, but nothing is working. She is stuck in a coma. And her brain is not showing any signs of activity. We won't know if her brain function is... normal, until she wakes up. So all we can do is wait, and pray, and hope that she comes round. But...' – the doctor shook his head – 'the thing is, her physical wounds are not actually life-threatening. Yet... she's not fighting. It is as if she has given up. Like she has no will to live. It almost seems as if she wants to... die.' The doctor looked from one parent to the other before saying, 'I'll leave you alone with your daughter.' He turned and left.

The doctor passed Inder in the corridor, not even noticing him sitting there in the dimness. He rushed away.

Inder held his head in his hands, beside himself. Wishing that he had been there to protect her. Wondering how this could have happened.

'She... she just ran out into the road,' mumbled the old man sitting next to him.

Inder looked up slowly. Saw only the man's tormented eyes rimmed red.

The man stared at the door, as if in a trance, mesmerised by its light. He cradled a bandaged arm. 'I-I was driving, in my truck. And she just ran right in front of me.'

Inder sat there for a long time, those words on repeat in his head. Time shimmered around him, stretching and expanding, until, before he knew it, it was night-time – and he found that he was alone in the corridor. In the dark. Alia's doorway was no longer lit. The air was still and silent.

He got up on shaky feet, and walked into the room as if drugged. He didn't look for a light switch, because the streetlamp outside illuminated the room just enough to see. Going to the same chair where Alia's mother had sat, he slowly lowered himself into it, taking in, with hushed horror, the full length of Alia's broken body. The blank space where her left leg should have been. A bright amber glow – the colour of remaining life – rippled and undulated over her. Glimmering with such beauty that for a few minutes he lost himself in its haze.

Her hand twitched, and he reached for it. Caressed it. It was the only part of her untouched by wounds, and it was still soft, as the softest silk.

Inder closed his eyes and lay his head on the bed at her side.

Tears dripping silently down.

Before long, he fell asleep.

In his dreams, he saw her.

Saw her waiting by the door of her home, looking down at her phone. He saw the date and time – yesterday, early morning. Beneath it was a text message, her thumb hovering above the Send button. Her face reflected in the shine of the screen. Anxiety scarring its beauty. She pressed Send, and waited. Two faint beeps echoed down the corridor from the dining room, and seconds passed until her father shouted out in rage, making her jump. Quickly she grabbed her bag, packed full and much heavier than usual, and she ran out of the house, and out of the gate, with a heavy heart.

She went through the motions of school. Her arms and legs were like lead, and it was all she could do to muster energy to dance. By the end of the day, she met up with her best friend, Navi – a willowy girl, whose every movement was graceful and elegant. She was waiting just inside the school entranceway, and when she saw Alia, she fluttered over to her almost on her tiptoes. 'There you are!' she said to Alia, but her face suddenly sank. 'What's wrong?!'

Alia, unable to speak, just handed her her phone.

Navi read it, her eyes widening. It was a text message from her father:

'Alia, I will meet with this boy. But don't think you can easily manipulate me, young lady. When he comes today, I will tell him that if he goes anywhere near you, or if I even hear you mention his wretched name again, I will call my friend who is chief of police, and tell him the boy has stolen from us. And that will be the end of the matter.'

There was a second text underneath, sent a few minutes later:

'You said you will stay away until an arrangement can be made. You said you would rather die if you two can't be together. Then so be it. Who are we to stop you. We are only your parents. You have clearly chosen this boy over us, despite our admonitions. We will not bend to your emotional blackmail. Never will we allow you two to be together. And nothing will change our minds about this boy. Not even your threat of suicide.'

Navi's face dissolved into sympathy as she handed the phone back. 'Oh Alia!' She threw herself onto her friend, hugging her.

Alia went limp in the embrace. Her heart was being rent asunder. Her whole world was crumbling. She felt utterly lost.

Alia walked silently through New Delhi, in a haze of sadness.

Suddenly finding herself in Inder's road, she was surprised to see that he wasn't there waiting for her, for he was always early.

She really needed him.

5pm came and went, and she waited, and waited – looking constantly at her watch, wondering what had happened to him.

She had arranged to meet Nala at 6 p.m., to stay at her house, so at 5.50 p.m. she took one long last look up and down the street, before pulling herself up and walking away.

She and Nala – faithful, dependable Nala – met outside the kulfi bar where they often treated themselves to the delicious milky dessert, but neither of them even looked through the window at the pastel-coloured offerings. They just hugged, and left arm-in-arm without a word. Exiting the pedestrian-only zone, Alia's sniffles were barely audible over the din of traffic and street noise. They were careful to cross the busy roads at the proper crossings, always waiting for the green light before going ahead. They stood before the last crossing, watching a man trudging past them in the road pushing a stall on wheels, impervious to the traffic whizzing dangerously past him. On the other side of the road, a little boy ran to cars that had stopped at the lights, vigorously washing and wiping their windows in the hope that someone might give him a single coin, even if it was just a rupee. When it was finally the girls' turn to cross, they traversed the zebra lines, only to be startled by the roar of an engine and a truck hurtling around the corner through the red light. It beeped at them angrily to get out of the way. In a split second, Alia turned, locked eyes on the truck driver's. They were sluggish, hinting of the beers he'd been drinking. The man stamped his foot on the brake far too late. Tyres screeching. Navi disappeared, and Alia was smacked by the side of the wheel, causing her to roll violently back to the pavement. Her cheek smashed against the edge of the curb. From the pavement, a flock of pigeons were thrown up into the blue sky, a tempest of grey, smoky wings.

Alia found herself dipping in and out of consciousness.

Bursts of noise, followed by soundlessness. Shouting. Then nothingness.

The sky above was a murky dome of blue-gold.

A sharp pain in her leg dissolved into chill liquid.

She called her friend's name, but it came out only as a whisper.

Vague sirens in the distance.

The little boy ran to her and bent down beside her, 'Miss!! Miss!!'

She pushed him away, and craned her neck to search for Navi.

Only to see a bloody body lying there, still.

Alia screamed with anguish.

Pain ripping her flesh apart.

Her broken heart exploding.

At last, unconsciousness came like a lashing snowstorm. Overwhelming her. Engulfing her.

Drowning out the horror.

In the hospital, in the darkest and longest of nights, Inder stayed with Alia, unable to leave her side. Trembling hands unwilling to let go of hers.

Slumped over the side of the bed, he dipped in and out of sleep.

The voices came again, mingling with his own mumbles, as he half slept, half dreamt. The chatterings were right there, surrounding him, and yet in him. And though his dreams were pitch black, and there was nothing but sound, he knew who they were.

They were the same as him.

Desperate, alone.

Afraid.

I... I need your help, Inder told them, quivering.

But, as before, their voices came only as incoherent mutterings.

I did something... to Alia, he sobbed. *With my mind. And... and now she's not waking up. Please, help me. Please,* he begged.

But the voices only continued mumbling incomprehensibly.

Inder counted them. Five voices. He could feel his frustration mounting like a ticking bomb. Growing and growing. Until he exploded. *What's wrong with you?! Why are you not making any sense? Please!* He cried out. *Help me!!*

It was the German girl who, with great effort, eventually answered. *C-can't!* she muttered. *W-we...*

You're drugged! Inder suddenly realised. *Someone drugged you. All five of you.*

D-d... stammered the girl.

Yes?

D-d-d... she strained to speak with all her might, until she finally spat out, *Deeper!* She gasped from the effort. Trying once more. *D-d-dreams!!* she said at last.

Inder struggled to understand. *Dreams? I need to go deeper? Into your dreams?*

He winced with frustration. He didn't know how he could reach their dreams. And he could sense the girl was exhausted, fading. He had to try to do this on his own, whatever 'this' was.

He calmed himself. Thought of that blinding white explosion of light that he had dreamt of the night before. And he willed and willed for that explosion once more. As if willing his thoughts to materialise, to become physical and tangible – he willed so hard he thought his brain might burst.

And then it happened!

A detonation of light and noise and space so huge that it filled the entire universe. And then, after what seemed like an age – it could have been hours, or days, or just seconds – when everything settled, silence once more descended.

Until all that was left, strangely, was the bitter stench of wood burning, mixed with the exotic sweetness of the perfume of flowers.

He breathed this in slowly, deeply.

Found himself connecting with the voices again.

But this time, instead of their voices being inside his head, a startled Inder found himself inside theirs.

In their dreams.

H-hello, he told them, looking hesitantly around. *My name is Inder.*

•••———————————————•••

When Alia awoke the next morning, she was surprised to find herself in her comfortable bed, in her own large bedroom. There was an unusual ache in one of her legs, and she sat up, threw back the bedsheet, and rubbed it.

Pointing her toes, she circled each foot – first clockwise, then anticlockwise.

They seemed fine.

She was unable to shake off the feeling that something terrible had happened, though she couldn't for the life of her think what it was.

Shrugging it off, she got up.

In her mind were the remnants of a dream – the light beep of a machine, and the smell of antiseptic. The sound echoed in her head as she stood before the window and glanced at the spider sitting peacefully on its web, happy to see it. She tiptoed to whisper, *Good morning, chotu. I trust you had a good night's sleep...?* But as usual, it only scurried away to hide.

Alia smiled to herself as she turned and padded to the bathroom in bare feet. She stood in front of the mirror above the sink and stared for some time at the beautiful face that stared serenely back at her. As if imprinting her beauty deep into her mind.

She found herself going through the motions of an average morning. Dressing for school, packing a fresh leotard and tights, and another pair of ballet shoes. She skipped breakfast, eager to avoid her parents' and grandparents' argumentative banter, having to tiptoe around grandmother's constant jibes. Arjun was waiting for her outside, a friendly smile on his face as ever. He zipped her off to school, where she changed into her leotard, but, oddly, her feet weren't hurting at all, and she found that the sores and blisters had completely vanished. Pleased, she put away the wrapping bandages, and slipped on her tights and pointe shoes.

She had an average day, practising for Sleeping Beauty. Her best friend, Navi, was not there to play the lead, and though Alia knew there was a reason for her absence, she couldn't think what it was. Instead, the stand-in danced her part, though it was not as elegant as Navi's performance. It would have to do.

After school, she walked home. The same route as always, to meet Inder.

He was waiting there, as faithful as the setting sun, arms crossed loosely at this chest, looking intensely up at the sky, as if he could forecast the future by the shape and colour of the clouds.

Inder! She ran to him, and he picked her up in his arms, holding her high up in the air as he turned around and around. When he at last stopped, she slid slowly down, their eyes gazing firmly into each other's. And they kissed. Soft lips yielding to longing.

When they parted, she noticed a worried expression scud briefly across his face. *What's wrong?* she asked.

Inder blinked at her and smiled briefly. *I'm just... I'm just happy to see you. That's all. You look beautiful.*

They gravitated against the wall. That crumbling yet sturdy wall. Small fragments fell off onto the ground when they sat on it. As always, Alia slipped her arm into Inder's and draped herself over his shoulder. They watched the sun set – a blaze of golds, reds, pinks. It was spectacular.

I don't want this day to end, Alia murmured sleepily. *I want to stay here with you. And watch every sunset, every day. Forever.*

Inder got up and spun round to face her, gently taking her face in his hands. *Alia,* he said, but then hesitated.

She searched his eyes. *Yes?*

He flinched, as if in pain.

Inder, please. What's wrong? She watched with alarm as water built up in his eyes, bursting over the rims and cascading down his cheeks. *Inder?*

You know I love you... he whispered, his breath tickling her skin.

She smiled sadly. *Yes, I know.*

And... you know that whatever happens, to you, or to your friends... whatever happens, I'm here for you, to help you through it. And I'm never going to leave you. Ever.

Alia looked at him, puzzled. She glanced at the blazing sun behind him, a fire of golds reflected in the shine of her eyes. *Did... did something happen?* She stiffened. *To Navi?* She looked lost, tinges of distress in her expression. *I-I can't shake off this feeling that something bad happened to her...*

Inder glanced down at the small pile of brick fragments on the ground by her foot. *Not just to her.*

Alia took some time to absorb this, but all she could say feebly was, *Me?*

Your leg... was all he managed to say.

Alia whimpered, her body turning to jelly.

Inder's strong arms propped her up, kept her steady.

What... what happened to Navi? she asked, bracing herself.

Inder looked away. *She didn't make it.*

That was the answer Alia had been dreading. *No!!! Please... tell me it's not true!!*

It's true, Inder said quietly. *I'm so sorry. It happened suddenly, when you were crossing the road.*

Please no!!! she begged, crouching on the floor, and sobbed into her hands.

Inder stooped down next to her and put an arm around her. *I'm so, so sorry,* he repeated over and over.

Huddled on the ground, as she cried and cried, Alia felt the life draining from her – each tear sapping her energy. Until she was lifeless. Drained. Empty. She sniffed, stood up, her head hanging down, hair covering her face. *I... don't think I can take any more...*

Inder stood in front of her. *Alia.*

I just can't.

Alia, please.

There's nothing left to live for.

Inder stiffened. *Alia, look at me.*

She sniffed, and eventually lifted her head, her hair parting like a curtain to reveal eyes the colour of a thousand setting suns.

He stared into them, stared into the fire. *Live for* me. *Love* me. *And I... I'll give you the world.*

The world? murmured Alia, mesmerised. *And the moon? And the stars?*

Inder smiled. *Yes!*

B-but, my parents... she said feebly.

He did not answer.

They both knew what the solution was, one that so many inter-caste couples had taken. They could run away, and make a new life together. Leaving everything behind. Families forsaken. They just had to muster the courage to do it.

Alia felt herself melting into Inder. Wrapped in his arms, her head against his chest, she closed her eyes and listened to the rhythmic beat of his heart. It was so reassuring, so soothing. So surreal. As if dreams had become real life, and real life had become the imagined.

She sighed and murmured, *It would be my dream to be with you, and love you.*

Inder heaved with relief, and hugged her. *In my head... I... I've lived a hundred lifetimes with you, Alia. Our lives filled with love. Raising children. Watching you dance in Swan Lake. Having grandchildren. Growing old together.*

Alia gasped, eyes still closed. *Yes! I can see it too.* She saw herself under the subdued lighting of a stage, as the prima ballerina. Dressed in full costume, feathers in her hair, she wafted through her ballet moves, teetering on her good leg, and the other, a prosthetic, lifted behind her pointing toward the ceiling. She was surrounded by a full cast of ballet dancers, dressed in finery. Alia glanced into the audience, smiling briefly when she saw her three-year-old son waving enthusiastically at her. Next to her sat his father, a proud Inder, jostling a baby in his lap. Alia's heart exploded with love, for Inder, and for their unborn children.

'I see it,' murmured Alia in her sleep, as she lay in the hospital bed, machinery beeping at her side. 'I see it.'

She exhaled, long and slow, and found herself waking.

In a strange, sterile room.

Inder was slumped next to her, fast asleep. His hand draped over hers.

She squeezed it tremulously. 'I-Inder,' she said, her mouth dry as a bone.

Suddenly footsteps reverberated in the hallway. Alia tore glazed eyes from the blank space where her leg should have been, to find her parents walking into the room. They stopped in their tracks, surprised, not only to find their daughter awake, but also to see Inder on the chair next to her, rousing from sleep.

•••———————————————————•••

The strong, black coffee was peppered with notes of cardamom and nutmeg. So bitter, it almost made Inder choke.

While Alia was being seen by the doctor and a nurse, he sat outside in the corridor, stiffly cradling the plastic coffee cup in both hands. On the bench opposite sat Alia's parents, Mahit and Azarin, glaring unwaveringly at him. The awkwardness was palpable. 'Thank you for the coffee,' he said feebly, lifting the cup.

No answer.

Seconds and minutes passed painstakingly slowly while he finished the drink Azarin had bought him, though he didn't really want it. He took a last glug, and looked around for a bin.

Mahit quickly stood and went to him, extending a hand.

Inder flinched, but Mahit only took the cup, and just stood there, menacingly, staring with a nondescript expression.

Eventually Mahit said, 'We stayed with her all day yesterday, begging her to come around, but she never woke up. But... for you...' He trailed off, unable to finish the sentence.

Inder fixed eyes on his own feet. The sandals that his father, with his particular talent, had mended so well. And then he remembered what *he* could do. The incredible ability that was within *him*. He could change the way people think and feel, and he suddenly buzzed with electricity. Glancing up at Mahit, he knew that he only had to look at him. Bore into his mind with his eyes...

Mahit continued talking. 'It is clear that she loves you,' he said gruffly. 'Though, now that she is so disfigured...'

Inder found himself blurting out, 'I still want to marry her!'

Mahit blinked at him, incredulous. 'You want to marry her, with her... disability?'

'Disability? I don't see any disability. I see the same Alia that I fell in love with. Deep down, she is no different from before. We love each other – and, now, more than ever, she needs me to take care of her.'

There was a light sobbing sound, and Inder realised that Azarin was crying. 'Mahit,' Azarin said gently. 'Can't you see how much they love each other? Nothing we say can change that...'

But Mahit's frown didn't soften even a touch as he continued glaring at the boy.

Inder dared to look up and stare right back at him, defiant. Knowing that he could change his thinking with just a single thought. He psyched himself up...

Azarin got up and took her husband's hand, pulling him away – and Inder fell back, deflated. He couldn't do it! He couldn't force his will onto them. It wasn't right.

Mahit sat next to his wife and scrunched up the empty coffee cup, throwing it on the floor.

Azarin looked over at Inder with kind eyes. 'That you would wish to stay with Alia, despite...' she sniffed, trying hard to hold it together – in her mind came the image of her daughter's horribly gashed face and crushed leg – 'despite what has happened to her. To me, that is a sign of the depth of your love!' She turned to her husband. 'I for one, would give him my consent, Mahit. Please...' she begged. 'Don't you see that their love is helping Alia recover. Please don't stand between them.'

For what seemed like an age, the man stared into nothingness, until, at last, he finally nodded before looking away.

Inder blinked at him with disbelief. 'Th-thank you,' was all he could stammer.

The doctor came out, with a hand mirror wedged under his arm. He went over to the Pujaris. 'She has made a miraculous recovery!' he beamed. 'Not only that. I have shown her her injuries, and talked to her at great length about reconstructive surgery for her face, and a prosthetic for her leg, and, psychologically, she is taking it all very well! Yes she's in shock, I grant you that. But she is also very calm and coherent. In all my years as a doctor, I have never seen such strength of mind. Such bravery. Your daughter is a strong girl. A very strong girl!'

Inder took his chance to slip into the room and sit next to Alia.

She was happy to see him.

Inder took in her beautiful scarred face, his heart soaring with nothing but love. 'They have given their consent, my dear Alia,' he whispered, hardly believing that they had done so of their own accord.

She looked at him, and burst into tears of happiness.

That night, Inder and Alia had the loveliest dreams.

Those dreams kept Alia's mind from tumbling into the deep pit of despair and depression that so many trauma survivors fall into – some never able to crawl out, despite every effort, for the rest of their lives.

In the last dream, the two lovers walked hand in hand wandering through Lodhi Gardens, excitedly discussing their wedding plans and their life together, in between admiring the trees, and the wildlife, and plants. When they got to the rose garden, tucked, secretively, in a northern corner of the park, Inder pulled Alia to the central circle of grass, where the rosebushes radiated outwards like rays from the sun. *Come,* smiled Inder. *I want to show you the view from the middle. It will be a good place for photos, if you agree.*

There was a group of people sitting on one of the benches in the centre, with their backs toward them – and Inder glanced curiously at them, before turning Alia around to look at the colourful variety of rosebushes.

Alia clapped her hands with delight. *This is a perfect spot!* she gasped. She craned her neck to see all around. *Especially there,* she said, pointing to a section of pink roses encircling an old chhatri, a raised, domed pavilion. Alia tugged Inder's arm. *Let's go see,* she urged.

Inder glanced behind him. *You go ahead. I will follow shortly.*

Alia nodded, and wandered across to the chhatri, stopping now and then to smell roses or finger their velvety petals.

Inder's smile faded as he watched her limp on her prosthetic limb, struggling with his own emotions – love for her, and sadness for her plight. Yet, deep down, he knew that Alia had within her the strength and the courage to overcome her hindrances. Deep down, he knew that, in real life, when she learned to walk again with the aid of the prosthetic that he himself would make for her, she would have the will and determination to learn to dance again. And New Delhi would be enchanted by her. And come to celebrate her. And she would even become renowned worldwide – ironically, her disability would be the catapult for her career. He saw it all, in his mind's eye.

He sighed, and turned round to the bench behind him, eyeing the backs of four adolescents, with an older man at their centre. The youngest, a blonde girl with her hair in two messy braids, was resting her head on the man's right shoulder. And on her other side, huddled arm in arm, was an older girl with a bob of curls. On the man's left was a girl wearing, unusually for such hot weather, a scruffy brown beanie – and on her left was a black boy with a sharply-cut afro, extending a protective arm around the girl's shoulders.

Inder walked around to face them, his face dropping. They all seemed grey, drained of life, as if colour had been sucked out of them. *You okay?* he asked tentatively.

The youngest, the girl with braids, looked up at him stiffly. Her eyes damp. *Inder! No... we're not okay. I-it's really hard.* Her German-accented voice quivered with emotion.

The black boy glanced worriedly at her, before telling Inder, *You're the only one who can help us.*

Your mind... started the girl with the blonde bob, her blue eyes piercing right into him. *Your mind is incredible. It's much more powerful. Much more far-reaching.*

Inder blinked at each of them. *I... I'm only just discovering it. To be honest, I don't know exactly what 'it' is.* He faltered. *It scares me.*

Deep in thought, Inder's eyes magnetised to the girl wearing the beanie, and the man next to her. Both had blank, dazed expressions. He looked over the man's malformed face, unperturbed by its hideosity. Eventually he said, *He made us this way, didn't he? He gave us his powers. But what's wrong with him? He's just staring into space.*

His mind is... unstable,' said the German girl as she looked up at him, worry lines creasing her forehead.

The blue-eyed girl said, *'Milly too. She was getting better, but something pushed her over the edge.*

Inder shook his head worryingly. *That doesn't look good for us, does it? I'm guessing you've thought about the possibility – the very real possibility – that the same thing could happen to us.* Some looked at him, others looked away. That alone answered his question.

He went over to the blue-eyed girl. Looked her square in the eyes. *Jemima. You know how long we... how long each of us have left, don't you?*

She turned away, tears slipping from her eyes as she closed them firmly shut. Overwhelmed with sadness, unable to speak.

Inder felt sick. Gut-wrenchingly so. Listened to the unbearable silence that swooped and circled over them, vulturous. His eyes magnetised to his Alia – sweet, innocent Alia! – sitting peacefully in the chhatri, gazing into the distance. He too looked into that distance, and at last said, *I'm beginning to work out what it is I can do. My power. I think I've always known.*

The sickly-pale German girl looked up at him, curious.

Inder returned her gaze, yet it was Alia's face that he saw before him. Her beautiful, adoring face. And he thought about their wedding plans. Their children. Their life together. Gracefully growing old, side by side. *I think...* Slowly he looked at each of them – at the tired, bleary eyes of Tai, Milly, Fitzsimmons, Ilse, and Jemima. He told them, *I think I can tell the future.*

27 WATER AND FIRE

Back in London, the imprisoned, sedated children were blissfully unaware of the Ingenious-mania that was exploding across the globe – people talked about it at work, at home, to their friends, and neighbours, and it spread like wildfire throughout the news and social media channels.

The fuel was what had happened in the courtroom. When an outraged German girl poured Yazan Ekren's memories into the minds of every single person there. In a moment of uncontrolled anger, her mind had wreaked absolute havoc. Many of the people that had been there thought they had gone mad, others grappled with trying to scrub those nauseating thoughts and memories from their minds, and one of them actually went insane and had to be taken into care.

'It was that girl! That German girl!' said a man in a television interview, his eyes round with astonishment. 'She did it! She put images in my head... of... of nasty things that man did. Murky things in the dark. Evil thoughts. Terrible acts.' He rubbed his head, trying to rub it out of him. 'Every night – every *single* night – I have nightmares. Horrible nightmares!'

Other reports contrasted before and after videos of one of the paralegal officers – before, she was smartly-dressed, bright-looking, sharp – but afterward, she was filmed in a mental institution wearing a straitjacket, sitting on a chair in a padded room, arms wrapped around her torso. Her coarse matted hair dangling limply on one side as she rocked herself back and forth.

One man stood on an upturned crate at Speakers' Corner, Hyde Park, spouting on about his experience in the courtroom, and how it was now his life's mission to make sure that every single one of those so-called Ingenious teenagers was rounded up and locked away – for good. And he would not rest until it was done. Until then, he shouted, holding up a warning hand in the air, no-one was safe.

Websites were dedicated to naming and shaming suspected Ingenious children. Innocents were persecuted. Fear and mistrust ricocheted throughout schools, colleges, universities. The brightest students were tormented and persecuted, and some were even interrogated for hours by the police. Random teenagers stepped forward, falsely claiming to be Ingenious – basking in the spotlight and their five minutes of fame.

The hysteria quickly filtered around the globe. Reaching almost every country, every land, so that, in just a matter of a few months the world became obsessed with the Ingenious. Bio-ethical committees and scientific councils in multiple countries were set up and consulted. Television and radio chat shows spent hours discussing the pros and cons of gene-edited embryos, and the unknown impact this could have on the human race. Religious leaders expressed a deep uneasiness about tampering with God's creation, and hinted of divine retribution.

Public opinion was wide and varied. Ranging from those who welcomed human gene-editing to correct diseases and enhance physical traits, to others who feared a dystopian future where the rich propagated a perfect race. They talked of Hitler's obsession with a blue-eyed blond-haired Aryan society – his superior Herrenvolk, meant to rule over and control the world.

Protestors demonstrated against the Ingenious. Others demonstrated for their freedom. Teenagers in schools and universities became divided, rallying together, or calling for action.

'They are gods!' some cried out. 'They're the future.'

Others shouted, 'We must banish them from society!'

Some said, 'Their modified DNA cannot be allowed to enter and circulate through the human gene pool – they must be castrated!'

And others still were baying for blood. 'Execute them!'

Nervous excitement reached fever pitch.

Everybody had an opinion.

As David O'Connor flicked through the channels, half bored, and half listening to the profusion of Ingenious-mania – he sat back in his office chair, his feet up on the desk as he yawned and watched with glazed eyes. On the other side of the room was a large screen divided into ten CCTV images. Five of them with still figures lying on beds. He heard a light zizz behind him, and glanced at a black fly as it zig-zagged through the air. Turning back to the screens, he settled on a news debate – a bioethicist, a priest, scientists, and politicians discussing their views about the Ingenious. O'Connor sneered, smug with the knowledge that he was the children's prison-keeper. He knew what *he* would do with them, he thought to himself as he spied the fly landing on the floor by his feet. Quickly he stamped on it, leaving a nasty red splodge on the ground. He would crush them right out of existence.

•••————————————————•••

Mei Hui woke up one morning with a feeling in the pit of her stomach, knowing that something was very wrong.

The flash floods that year were particularly bad – and though they were on high ground, and their house was untouched by the swelling waters, the flooding was taking much longer than normal to recede. And so, for almost five weeks, they were completely cut off from their neighbours and the outside world. They relied fully on their own cultivated produce and storehouse of foods, of which there was plenty – sacks of flour, rice, purple sweet potatoes, jars of preserved vegetables and fruits, rows of hanging cured meats, and strings of onion and garlic. The children were more than happy to be cut off from school, though Mei Hui kept them busy by setting them homework to keep up with their studies. And apart from Yin missing her new boyfriend, the flooding making it impossible for anyone to get to them, life for the little household carried on relatively normally.

Yet Mei Hui could not shake off the ominous feeling.

At last, the waters finally dissipated, and the children groaned when they were told they could return to school. The house that morning was a bedlam of six grumpy children running around getting washed, dressed, and fed – before they at last left. Yin and Mei Hui quietly went about the house, tidying up the ensuing mess. Until there came a knock on the door.

Yin straightened up, her cheeks flushing. She beamed at Mei Hui. 'I think I know who that is,' she told her, setting the broom aside. When she went to the front door she brushed back her hair with hasty fingers.

Mei Hui took off her apron and followed, filled with curiosity.

She watched as Yin opened the door, and welcomed a round-faced middle-aged man.

They chattered together, Yin a little shy, and the man, Song Lijun, smiling profusely. Mei Hui realised that Yin was being modest when she had said he was not good-looking. He had a pleasant face, and seemed friendly and good-natured.

Mei Hui drew closer, blinking in the light that filtered through the open door, astonished by the soft glow of colours that surrounded the visitor. Hazy greens, both pale and dark. Deep reds. Muddy browns. She realised with wonder that this must be how Tai saw the world, and people. She gasped as she took in the beauty of those ethereal colours, wondering how it was she was able to see them, and what each colour signified. Suddenly Yin turned to introduce Mei Hui, and before she knew it, the man took her hand and shook it firmly – a zap of energy passing from his stout fingers, making Mei Hui stiffen. His heart, she gasped, as she took in his colours – his heart was bad! That was what the brown signified. Yet Mei Hui's face remained as smooth and flat as a pond with still water. 'I am pleased to meet you at last,' she told him calmly. 'Yin has been telling me about you.'

Yin hastened him inside the house. 'Come in, come in. I made some mugwort porridge for breakfast, good for energy – perhaps you would like some? And some freshly brewed tea? We can talk while we eat.'

'Very good!' said Lijun, looking around the place with smiling eyes. 'And I have brought lotus buns and fresh lychees.'

Mei Hui gently took his elbow and led him toward a chair by the window. 'This is the best seat, where there is plenty of warmth from the rising sun. Please sit here.'

'Ah, yes. I will sit here next to the window. It has a good view.' He looked out of it and surveyed the land. 'You have such a beautiful house, and good land. The soil is fertile here. Your fruit trees are growing well.' He gave Yin his bag of food, then sat down.

Mei Hui sat on the other side of the table. 'Yin tells me that you originally came to tell us about local government plans. To construct a new road nearby.'

'Yes, yes,' said the man dismissively. He waved a hand toward the hill. 'Up there, on high ground, they want to build it to connect the towns. The road will make it much easier to get around.'

'But...' faltered Mei Hui. 'The Longan tree is there.' She thought of the precious bees too. 'It is very old. It is part of the town's heritage, its history. You cannot build the road there.'

Lijun's face became serious. 'I'm afraid you have no say in the matter. It was already decided upon while you were away – between the villagers' committee and the ministry of transport. Anyway, it will greatly increase the value of your property, being so close. I imagine it will double its price.' A thin smile, like a slithering snake, crept across his face.

Mei Hui's heart quickened when she suddenly realised what the dark green meant. Greed.

'Yes,' said Lijun with a wry smile. 'This house of yours... you are sitting on a gold mine.'

Yin looked nervously at Mei Hui. 'I am sure that is no matter to Mei. I can't imagine her selling. She needs the house to take care of the children, and they are thriving here. Besides, Mei has put a lot of hard work and effort into building it. She is very clever, and has included many ingenious gadgets into the design...'

Lijun looked thoughtful. 'She must be very intelligent,' he murmured, eyelids lowering until his eyes were just slits. A sneer revealed stained teeth.

His friendliness was a mask, Mei Hui realised. A mask of evil. And she knew that he would stop at nothing to gain what he coveted. The colours told her this. Pale green, covetousness. Blood red, treachery. She jumped up from her chair, nerves like razor blades cutting into her. 'It is hot in here,' she said, as she reached to open the window. She breathed in the fresh air. It cooled her, calmed her. Turning back round, she smiled sweetly at the man, then said to Yin, 'It is nice to have an unexpected visitor, but I am afraid you have forgotten there is much work to do now that the floods have receded. We were due to go into town this morning, to stock up on essentials in preparation for my parents visiting. Uncle Aiguo will be arriving shortly to take us with his truck.'

Surprised, Yin glanced at Lijun. 'Uh, yes. I had forgotten.'

But Lijun made no sign of budging. 'I can wait for you here while you go into town. I will eat the breakfast as I am quite hungry.' His beady eyes roamed around again. 'And I would like to look over your remarkable house.'

'Ordinarily,' said Mei Hui, 'I wouldn't mind. Only, one of the things we will be getting is something against the rats. We have had an unusually large outbreak recently. I think they were driven here by the floodwaters.'

Lijun glanced nervously across the floor. 'I see. Then, yes, perhaps I will leave.' He got up.

Yin said quickly, 'If you are hungry, please, take back your lotus buns and lychees...'

Lijun looked at the carrier bag on the sideboard. 'Oh, er, well, yes. If you insist.'

The girls looked at each other, and Yin handed him the bag. 'I will show you out, Lijun. Thank you for visiting. I am sorry it has been a wasted journey.'

'Yes, it was a waste of my time. I am a very busy man. But there is always next time.'

Yin saw him out, while Mei Hui trailed behind and made sure that after he had left, the door was firmly shut and bolted.

She turned, leaning her back against the door – her cheeks so hot they looked like two red apples.

Yin stared at her with worried eyes. 'Mei... I am so sorry. He never talked about the house and the land like that before...' she said, overcome with shame.

Mei Hui at last allowed herself to breathe. 'Yin,' she said, pushing back a strand of hair with a shaky hand. 'I have to tell you. Though Song Lijun *seems* like a kind man, I sense that there are... hints of darkness about him. It scares me.'

'Really?' gasped Yin, flustered. 'I have been told I wear my heart on my sleeve. But... how can you know this, Mei? How can you be so sure?'

'I cannot explain how I know, but please be assured that I would not say such a thing if I were not completely convinced of it. Yin, you must trust me on this. I know your heart is very soft, and kind, and I know it will be upsetting for you – but Lijun… he is not good. For you, for anyone.'

Yin looked down, disappointed. 'I trust you, though my heart is already breaking. There is not much choice out here, in the country. All the eligible men have gone out, working in the cities.'

'That is true. Though, please, do not set your eyes on *him*. On the face of it he seems nice, but deep down, he has ulterior motives.' Mei Hui hesitated. 'We must be careful to lock the doors and windows at night,' she told her firmly.

Yin's eyes widened, and she eventually nodded. 'Yes. Okay, I will make sure of it.'

Mei Hui had the strangest of dreams that night.

She dreamt of ballet dancers in Swan Lake, leaping and dancing to the music. She dreamt of strange voices, bursts of white light, and an explosion of memories cascading and whirling like a snowstorm. She saw a broken girl, lying in a hospital bed. Bathed in an ethereal, golden light.

And lastly, she dreamt of an Indian boy by himself, perched on a wall. Arms crossed at his chest as he stared and stared at a solemn sun easing into the horizon – a splendour of golds, reds, pinks. His eyes were not burnt by the blazing sunlight. But in the gleam of his iris, she saw a fire of a hundred futures, multiplied by a thousand possibilities, playing out in a million spools of film.

That same night, in the next room, poor Yin hardly slept a wink.

Though she trusted Mei Hui, there was a grain of doubt that kept niggling away inside her. Yin was no longer young. Her biological clock was ticking – she could almost hear the clunk of each passing second – signalling the slow fading of the possibility of having children. And she so much wanted a baby, someone to call her own. Someone to take care of her in her old age. She tossed and turned, catching snippets of sleep only here and there, so that by the time she awoke to the dawn chorus, her limbs and eyes were heavy with exhaustion. One of the children started crying. And she forced herself out of bed to see what was wrong.

Mei Hui took one look at Yin, the dark rings under her eyes, and said not a word as she set about cooking porridge, packing lunches, making sure each child was washed, teeth brushed, and dressed. It was five-year-old Xiang who would not stop crying – though there was nothing wrong with her, and she had no temperature. The girl even managed to pause, hiccoughing, to wolf down all her food. And from this, Yin realised she just didn't want to go to school.

When at last the children went off to put on their shoes and get their book bags, there was a decisive knock on the door.

Bang-bang!

Yin and Mei Hui stopped what they were doing and looked at each other, suddenly nervous. 'Do not answer,' whispered Mei Hui. She was about to creep into the children's room to tell them to keep silent, when Xiang appeared and burst into fresh tears, crying so loud it was like a siren.

Suddenly the front door burst open, and three soldiers stormed in, wearing official uniform. Behind them was Lijun standing outside, his round face peering inside, looking this way and that, to see what was happening. The soldiers crowded around the two women. 'Which one of you is Li Mei Hui?' asked one of them.

Mei Hui knew not to answer.

Yin kept her mouth shut.

It was little Xiang that tugged on Mei Hui's sleeve as she looked up at her with damp eyes, asking, 'Why are you not answering, Mei?'

One of the soldiers immediately took Mei Hui's arms, pushed them behind her back, and clicked handcuffs onto her wrists.

The soldier motioned for Lijun to enter, and he reluctantly went inside, firmly avoiding eye contact with Yin.

Yin glared at him. 'Lijun! What is going on?!' she demanded.

He looked away, cagey.

The soldier asked him, 'Can you confirm this is the girl suspected of subversion, separatism, collaborating with the enemy?'

Lijun nodded vigorously. 'That is her. That is Li Mei Hui.'

Yin could not believe her ears. 'What are you talking about?!' she told them. 'She has done nothing wrong! She is innocent!!'

Lijun stepped back and pointed a finger at Mei Hui. 'She has only recently returned from the West, from England, and yesterday she talked to me things against the government. And not only that, but I am also convinced she is one of those Qiaomiao-Nuhai.' An Ingenious Girl. 'Be careful!' warned Lijun. 'She may try to control you!'

Another soldier slipped a blindfold over Mei Hui's eyes, and she struggled against them, crying out, 'Let me go!!'

Little Xiang became hysterical, pulling on Mei Hui's arm.

Crying, Yin started slapping Lijun's arm.

The soldiers steered Mei Hui outside.

Lijun pulled away from Yin and ran out of the house, leaving the door open.

The other children, who had been hiding in the corridor quickly ran into the room and surrounded Yin, who sank, crying, onto the floor at Xiang's feet.

Each child was red-faced and upset.

They looked at each other with shock and alarm.

Hardly knowing what to do.

Through the open door, they watched helplessly as the aggressive soldiers jostled Mei Hui along the footpath. Slowly disappearing from view.

•••————————————————————•••

Saffron Morales felt like she was losing control.

Both physically and mentally.

She had been feeling under the weather for several weeks, and though she knew the reason for her physical exhaustion, working all hours to distil the medicine for Calista from the golden-yellow flowers, she couldn't quite put her finger on the reason why, mentally, she felt like everything was falling apart. Things just didn't seem right, and there was a sense that something was coming, something big, that, though she wracked her brains to figure out what it was, she just couldn't put her finger on it.

It was the dry season, and for weeks, she and her parents watched the distant wildfires with an overwhelming sadness. For all the wildlife – the animals, insects, the plants and trees – that the blaze was devouring. They were acutely aware of how precious life was, from the tiniest leafhopper nymphs that were just specks of green, to the giant trees, such as the Samauma, thought to be over 5,000 years old. Not to mention the underground thread-like mycelium, the living, breathing, fungal network, which was silently growing and feeding, communicating with and connecting each tree and plant. The mycelium transformed the entire jungle into a single organism.

When Saffie lay in bed at night, she tossed and turned, her nose tickling with the stench of burning, her heart incensed at the destruction of aeons-old jungle. Strange dreams plagued her, of hidden creatures being burnt alive. Creatures whose screams were drowned out by the deafening roar and crackle of the flames that soon engulfed them. Their hell on earth.

Saffie woke up that morning with a start. Her skull flaring with sparks of migraine. She rubbed her temple as she shuffled out onto the veranda, tired and bleary-eyed. Sighing, she felt that old, familiar depression press against her in every direction. The air felt thick as syrup, clumsy limbs struggling to move against it – her thoughts, slow and sticky. She squinted in the bright light. Ears prickling from the pulsating hum of life: an orchestral cacophony of cicadas' stridulations, the chirp of ant birds and flycatchers, the grunt of toucans, and the piercing cries of marmoset and howler monkeys. The din jarred her.

Her blurry eyes eventually made out – through the merging of Aru mists with low clouds – the horizon. And there, far away: columns of grey-white smoke marked the wildfires.

Saffie stared into the distance and watched the slow rise of smoke. Heart leaden. She squeezed her eyes closed. *Please God,* she prayed, as she did every day. *Please make it stop.*

She caught her breath. She wasn't entirely sure what exactly she was praying for. For the depression to stop, or the wildfires. Perhaps both.

At least she had finally managed to send off Calista's second parcel before they had been cut off from civilisation. And though the winds at that time of year blew from south to north, which meant they were not in danger, they still needed to keep a watchful eye on the weather, in case there was a freak change of wind direction. So far, they were safe.

Saffie plodded back to her room, and rummaged around in one of her drawers for some time. She noticed her hands were shaking again, and she caught one in the other, holding herself still, when she heard someone call her name. She shuffled out to the main living area, where the first thing she saw was a mound of paraphernalia piled high on the sofa – which meant only one thing. They had cleared the big table to use it for an operation. She looked over to the centre of the room, and saw the hunched backs of her parents. Two lamps crudely tied to the ceiling with wire, bleached them white, like gowned ghosts. Saffie blinked, her eyes assaulted by the bright glare. And she suddenly remembered who they were operating on. 'Alvaro!' she gasped.

Her mother, Alma, straightened and glanced over her shoulder. 'Ah, there you are! Scrub in. We need an extra pair of hands,' she told her daughter with some urgency.

'Sí, sí, mama,' said Saffie, though her mouth was faster to respond than the rest of her. Immobile for several seconds, she at last sprang into action. She went back to her room, tied up her long black hair into a ponytail, and, in the bathroom, splashed cold water on her face. Lastly she scrubbed and disinfected her hands and arms. Hurrying back, holding hands in front of her, she went over to her parents. 'Is he okay?' she breathed, looking over the large, anaesthetised tapir that lay sprawled on its side. It was just over a metre long, with a long, rubbery nose, and split hooves – a short brown-grey coat was marked by faint white stripes and spots. Rounded, white-tipped ears flicked spontaneously as it slept.

'Grab his hind legs,' Ignacio told Saffie. 'We gave him the last of our anaesthetic, a small dose, which put him under, but it's not enough to stop his limbs from jerking.'

Saffie quickly clenched her hands into tight fists, to stop them from trembling, before reaching for each of the animal's back legs.

'Don't worry,' said Alma. 'He cannot feel pain.'

Ignacio wiped away some blood from the tapir's flank. 'The bullet went deep, and mama's having a hard time getting it out.'

'I hate hunters and their stupid gun traps!' hissed Saffie, immediately regretting speaking so loud as a throb of migraine made her smart.

Both Alma and Ignacio stopped to look at their daughter. 'Headache again?' asked Alma, worried.

Saffie closed her eyes, waiting for it to subside.

That was all the answer they needed.

Alma shook her head. 'As soon as this is over, we will give you something...'

'She's been taking Mucuna every day,' said Ignacio. 'She can't take anything more.'

'In micro doses,' Saffie added.

'You must be careful,' he admonished.

Alma sighed as she turned back to work on the tapir. 'Ah! I think I've got it.' With a pair of bloody forceps, she pulled out a bullet, and held it up to show them. 'Alvaro was unlucky to stumble across the tripwire.'

Ignacio looked flushed. 'We ourselves must be careful when we go on walkabouts. Such gun traps could blow our kneecaps.'

Alma dropped the bullet and forceps into a metal tray, and then busied herself cleaning the wound. 'At least the bullet lodged in his fat, missing any vital organs. That is one small blessing.' She began stitching up the hole, her hands working expertly.

Glancing up at the wall clock, Ignacio said, 'And just in time, the sedation will be wearing off soon.' He patted the sleeping tapir gently. 'You're going to be up and about in no time, Alvaro. Thank God!'

As she snipped off the thread, Alma asked, 'Do we have oxytetracycline? He will need antibiotics.'

Ignacio nodded. 'Yes, we do. That is one thing we have.'

'Good,' said Alma. She started taping gauze over the wound. 'The last thing we want after everything is for Alvaro to get sick from an infection.'

Ignacio hobbled off to look through the storage cupboard. He held up the small packet triumphantly. 'I was right!' he said, pleased, and set about preparing the injection.

Alma eyed her daughter. 'We're okay from here, Saffie. Go eat, drink. You don't look good.'

Saffie shuffled off – food and drink were the last things on her mind. She needed to rest. She found herself wandering out onto the veranda that encircled their house, and sat on a crudely made bench covered in frayed, moth-eaten cushions. She lay back. Still headachy… tired… just wanting to sleep…

Ten minutes later Ignacio tottered out holding a bowl in one hand and a mug in another.

Saffie was stirred awake by his footsteps.

'I made you a bowl of açaí, and some guarana tea,' he told her.

She sat up, rubbing her eyes. 'Thanks,' she mumbled.

Sitting down, he set the breakfast on the bench between them. 'How're you feeling?'

She closed her eyes. 'Bad.'

'Did you get any sleep last night?'

'Not much.'

Ignacio absentmindedly rubbed his leg. 'You know, you can talk to me. About anything. Anything at all.'

Saffie looked puzzled. 'What do you mean?'

He glanced at the door to check Alma wasn't around, before fishing out a pouch from his pocket. He pulled open the drawstring, and showed her the contents. Small, dried fungi. 'I found these in your room,' he said. 'You'd left the drawer open…'

Saffie didn't even look. She knew what they were. Psilocybin mushrooms, or magic mushrooms as they were commonly known. 'I told you, papi, I'm just micro-dosing. They're taking the edge off the migraines. Helping me relax.'

'Relax?'

She sighed. 'I've been anxious recently. Not just me, the feelings from the others too. They're getting stronger.' They both knew who 'the others' were. 'And… I'm beginning to hear voices too.'

Ignacio looked worried; the voices were a new development.

Saffie continued. 'Another thing. I don't need to write everything down anymore. I can remember it all. In detail. Same as Milly. It's like… like we're absorbing each other's abilities. Like we're in each other's heads.'

Ignacio absorbed all this, eventually asking, 'Are you… are you sure it's not the mushrooms?'

'Papi!'

He held up his hands. 'I'm sorry! I had to ask.'

'It happens at any time, not just after I've dosed up.'

Ignacio weighed the little bag up and down in his hand. 'There's a lot here,' he said. 'Enough to make you go to the moon and back!'

'I'm careful, very careful,' she breathed.

'Exactly what dosage have you been taking then?'

Saffie shrugged. 'Just a nibble here and there. You've got to trust me, papi. I know what I'm doing. Eligio taught me to respect the herbs. Respect our bodies.'

Ignacio looked intently into his daughter's face. 'I trust you, mi amor. I'm just… worried.'

There was a loud grunting from inside the house, and they both looked through the door.

'Sounds like Alvaro's waking,' said Ignacio as he pulled himself up. 'Mama won't be able to get him off the table with her bad back. He's heavy for a juvenile!' He patted his daughter's hand before hobbling off.

Saffie watched him go. She hadn't told him about the depression that knotted her insides, even now. Glancing down, she curled her fingers around the rough hessian pouch he'd left on her lap. She really, really needed some. She needed to stop thinking so much, feeling so much. Needed to stop it all, at least, just for a bit.

Saffie was able to stomach only a spoonful of her father's açaí bowl, before she retreated to the shaded stillness of her room. Sitting on the edge of the bed, she opened the pouch and carefully pulled out one of the smaller mushrooms, popping it whole into her mouth. It tasted earthy, musty, with a bitter aftertaste. She lay back against the pillow and waited for the desensitisation… the throb of the migraine to fade… listening to the chant of the cicadas… sweating under the burgeoning heat, as the sun climbed ever higher.

An explosion of white burst inside her head!

Slowly, it dissipated, like the end of a lashing snowstorm, until there was only the stench of sickness and antiseptic, a light beeping noise. And a voice. *Please, help me,* he called. *Please!*

On the bed, in her sleep, Saffie rolled over and slammed onto her side, as if she'd just been knocked over by a truck. Emotions bled out of her. Desperation. Impotence. Fear. Denial.

She desperately wanted to call out to the boy, instinctively knowing who he was. The last Ingenious child. Desperately wanted to tell him she was here. To help. But though she willed and willed, she was unable to reach him.

Instead, there came a little girl's voice. A German girl.

Frowning in her sleep, Saffie tossed and turned.

Who is this girl?! she wondered.

How on earth were they able to connect?

The German girl was trying to talk with great difficulty, her words slurred, her emotions confused. *D-d-dreams!!* the girl spat out at last.

Saffie sat up, suddenly conscious. *Dreams!* She got out of bed and padded to the doorway, repeating this thought, over and over. Stopping for a moment, she listened for any movement. There was no sound of her parents; they were likely taking their siesta.

Quietly Saffie took her rucksack and her trusty old machete, and went out of the main door, down the stairs. Walking along a path in bare feet, she slipped into the jungle without a sound. Her eyes blinked lazily as though she were sleepwalking, as she made her way between the immense trees. Half looking around, half dazed. *Dreams.*

After almost half an hour of searching, she found the coiling trunk of a particular tree, surrounded by woody liana. Taking her machete she hacked at the vines so that, before long, she had a bundle of thin sticks about 30 cm long. Tying them together with a smaller, string-like vine, she pushed the wood into her rucksack before walking on. Here and there she came across jewel-like flowers – their vivid colours calling out to her. Purple radial Passion Flowers. Orange-yellow Monkey Brush. Pink starbursts of Aechmea. And the delicate white Eugenia. She picked only the choicest ones.

Finally, she found pale green bushes of Chacruna. Their leaf veins etched in perfect symmetry. Her hands brushed through the leaves that swayed lightly under her touch, before picking off one leaf at a time. Only 10 of them. That should be more than enough.

At last, she had collected everything she needed.

Finding a sheltered clearing, she went about chopping sections out of tall poles of bamboo, and nicking the sides so that she could pour the water into her water bottle. Then she scraped off the waxy outer layer of the bamboo, and shaved off ribbons to make kindling. She collected and built up over the kindling, dry twigs and logs. With three long sticks, she tied cord around one end, to create a tripod over the wood – from which she hung her battered old cooking pan. Taking the bundle of liana twigs, she bashed each one against a tree root with a log, so that the dry, mossy bark fell away, and the inner wood became flayed and separated into strands. Carefully she layered inside the pan the Chacruna leaves and some of the liana wood, and filled the pan with water.

With one of her waterproof matches, she set the fire alight and watched as the mesmerising flames took hold.

She sighed. It was going to be a long process of boiling down the water, continually keeping the fire going, adding more water, and more liana wood.

Looking up at the grey sky through the gaps in the canopy, she hoped that there would be no rain. It was the dry season, and it hadn't rained for months, but she knew how mercurial the weather was, unpredictable from global warming.

Extracting her sleeping hammock and a small sewing kit, she sat cross-legged on the hammock's waterproof covering on the ground, and busied herself with repairing the netting – always keeping an eye on the fire and pan.

By midnight, the wood and leaves had at last boiled down to a black syrup, thick as molasses. It had taken nearly an entire day to make, yet waiting the last half hour for it to cool down seemed to take the longest.

Her migraines had faded to a mild ache, starved by drinking only bamboo water and eating scantily – a few berries and nuts now and then. Anyway, being here, in the jungle, always soothed her.

It was pitch black now, save for the faint glow of the embers.

But she was not afraid.

She had balanced the pan on a couple of logs, and she lightly touched it with a finger – it was no longer scalding, just warm enough to drink.

As she trickled the liquid into her mouth, she thought of the dreams the brew would evoke. Many, many dreams.

The tea was so bitter, she almost retched. But she managed to keep it down, as she lay back on the ground – tucking the flowers in her hair, and scattering them over her body.

Softly she sang herself to sleep, watching large white moths, as big as her hand, bounce through the air above her – attracted to the glowing embers.

As her eyelids sunk closed, the moths descended next to the flowers – drawn as they were to the exotic perfume and their delicious nectar. But the moths refrained from sipping on the sweet liquid. Instead, they turned toward the fire, their large black eyes glistening in the smoky light, velvet wings fluttering. The tarsal claws of their legs paced softly against Saffie's hair and skin, wobbling from the pulse of blood whooshing just below the surface.

As the darkness of night seeped around her, this young girl lay amongst the undergrowth, strewn with colourful blossoms and white moths.

Smooth skin twitched now and then as she slept.

The trees and vegetation hung over her. Sometimes swaying in the breeze, sometimes dipping down – protectively.

Creeping out of the night came an ocelot, orange fur marked by glorious rosettes and stripes, like a mini spotted jaguar. Surprised to find the girl lying there, it immediately crouched down and sniffed the air. Slowly it crept forward on large, silent paws. Fur bristling. Tail pointed. It went right up to her and sniffed her hair. One of the moths fluttered, but the cat did not pounce. Instead, it relaxed, licked the girl's cheek, and then yawned spontaneously. It curled up next to her, nestling its head between her neck and shoulder. And it too settled down to nap.

As Saffie slept, her thoughts gradually became loosened by the herbs, the fragrance of flowers calmed her, and the ocelot's body warmth stimulated electricity in her brain, so that – at last – the dreams came to her.

And in those dreams, Saffie searched for the others.

Homing into the drumbeat of their hearts.

At last, the boy's voice rang loud and clear in her ears.

She absorbed the feelings welling up inside of him: love... passion... desperation...

H-hello, he told her hesitantly, nervously. Surprised to find himself in her dreams. *My name is Inder.*

Back at the animal sanctuary, both Alma and Ignacio were not too worried about their daughter disappearing. She often went on long walkabouts through the wilds of the jungle – their fears assuaged by her special affinity with animals.

But as another night came and went, and morning dawned, it brought an unexpected change. The jungle had weighed them in the balance, found them wanting, and passed judgement. Their punishment: a reversal of wind direction – and the jungle blew and blew its squally breath southwards. In the direction of their sanctuary.

Alma and Ignacio urgently ran about the place, setting free the caged animals and birds – convalescing or not, they would have to make it on their own. The couple hastily stuffed essentials into backpacks, glancing at each other, and scanning the surrounding jungle for signs of their daughter.

'Saffie!! Come back! Come back now!' shouted Alma into the jungle, both frustrated and sick with worry.

Ignacio returned with Alvaro the tapir on a lead, his rubbery nose sniffing the unusual burning in the air. Ignacio held one of Saffie's t-shirts in front of it, and the tapir plunged its nose into the fabric – it turned, trotting this way and that, smelling the air, smelling the dirt. At last, he began straining on the leash. 'Alma! Alvaro's picked up her scent!' cried Ignacio, as he strapped the rucksack to his back. 'Come! Hurry!!'

Alma gasped when she realised what was happening. She took her much smaller rucksack, for she was unable to carry anything heavier, and went after them. 'Go quickly. Find her!' she called out. 'I'm right behind!'

The wind whipped their hair this way and that as they disappeared into the jungle.

The two of them ran and stumbled and tripped through the undergrowth, right behind the snorting tapir who was dashing at full speed.

The couple's anxiety increased as they realised Alvaro was leading them toward the wildfires. The crackle of burning and the pungent odour of smoke getting stronger by the minute.

After almost half an hour, they at last came to a clearing, hazy with smoke. She was there! Lying unconscious on her back on the ground. A cat-like shadow slinked away, and a puff of moths burst upwards. She was covered with wilting flowers.

Ignacio dropped to the ground next to her. 'Saffie! Saffie! Wake up!' he cried, jolting her.

'Is... is she okay?!' asked Alma.

Frustrated, Ignacio told her, 'She is heavily drugged. I don't think she will wake up anytime soon...'

Alma kneeled over her. 'Mi amor! Wake up!! The fires are coming!!'

But Saffie remained unconscious, moving her head from side to side and muttering under her breath.

Ignacio mustered every shred of strength to lift her, but though she was slim, he knew that he wouldn't be able to carry her far, with his crippled leg. Gently he returned her to the ground and looked around for some fallen palm leaves. 'Help me,' he told his wife, as he stooped down to gather a couple of large fronds. Alma raced around, searching for more – and after finding six of them, the couple placed a criss-cross of four tied-up vines on the ground next to Saffie, and then stacked the leaves on top of them. They rolled Saffie onto the stretcher-like fronds, and then tied the vines around her. Husband and wife took each end of a loose vine, and heaved and heaved – dragging their daughter through the undergrowth. Alma clenched her teeth from the pain in her back, and Ignacio grimaced from shooting pangs in his leg, as they inched along. But they soon came to a fallen tree trunk lying half-rotten on the ground. It was almost as tall they were. They peered over, to see more horizontal trunks – blackened and charred. And Ignacio groaned. 'Lightning strike,' he moaned.

'It's no use!!' cried Alma, in despair. 'We cannot carry her over them all. And we cannot leave her. The fire is coming this way soon. We're all going to die!!' She sat back on the ground, sobbing.

Ignacio shook his head, trying to hold back the waves of panic. 'No...' he said feebly. Then he shouted, 'No!' He looked up at the sky. Prostrated himself on his knees. Closed his eyes. 'Please, God!' he begged, stricken. 'Please!!' But he did not know what to pray for.

Alma followed his lead. She bent over their daughter and took her hand, joining him in prayer. 'Dear God, please hear our prayer...'

And then it came to Ignacio, what he should ask for. 'Please, God. Make it rain!'

Alma choked and sniffed. 'Yes! Please, *please*. Make it rain.'

Again and again, they chanted this.

Heads bowed with penitence.

Ever humble to the almightiest of powers.

As the smoke thickened around them, and the heat increased, Saffie – though unconscious – picked up on their prayers. Ashen and dripping with sweat, eyes rolling under closed eyelids, she too began muttering feverishly under her breath:

'Please...' Smoke swirling all around.

'God...' Cinders showering down.

'Make it rain.'

28 TEARS

Calista Matheson hadn't seen her baby daughter for over a month. And it was driving her crazy.

'I'm dying!!' she screamed out to the dingy little bedroom in which she was locked. The sound deadened against the thick walls. Nobody came.

She slumped back onto the mattress that was grubby with stains. She was unrecognisably different: eyes rimmed red, her skin sickly pale, as though Death had exhaled onto her his acrid breath.

She wanted to cry, but there were no tears left. 'Please,' she called out, whimpering. 'I just want to see my daughter...'

Lying down, she curled up into a ball and cradled her head, the stubble of hair on her scalp prickling her skin.

Suddenly there came the sound of footsteps walking up stairs, the jangle of keys, the door being unlocked. And Calista pulled herself up.

David O'Connor appeared, holding a parcel under one arm.

The packaging looked familiar, and Calista suddenly recognised the postage stamp marks. 'My meds,' she said. She glanced behind him, but there was no-one else, no doctor or nurse to administer it.

David O'Connor took a step closer. 'Ah, that's exactly what I thought it was,' he smirked. His fingers loosened, and it dropped to the dirty floor with a dull thud. 'Oops!' he said. 'Silly me!'

Calista glared at him. A healthy, feisty Calista would have given him a piece of her mind. But she was so weak. Hadn't a shred of energy. 'Why...?' was all she managed to say.

'I thought you were a genius,' said O'Connor, raising an eyebrow. His expression morphed into harsh contempt. 'Give me the names of the other so-called Ingenious children,' he told her. 'And, as I'm feeling generous, I'll give you the medication, and let you and your family go. You'll be free to walk out of here.'

Calista closed her eyes, melting. Evie's sweet face came to her, snuggled in Jake's arms. She desperately needed them.

'Evie keeps asking for you,' said O'Connor, feigning sympathy. 'Keeps asking for her mamma.'

'R-really...?' she asked, weakening.

'Yes,' he replied, casually flicking off a speck from his sleeve. 'You could be home by tonight. Imagine that. Having dinner together. Snuggling up in bed. All you have to do is tell me the children's names.'

She felt so tired. How easy, just to tell him. She'd have her life back. Her daughter too, and her husband. The thought of betrayal welled up painfully in the corners of her eyes, slipping out as hot, stinging tears. 'Just their names...' she echoed, entranced by the thought of freedom.

'Just their names.'

Calista's face warped into exasperation. 'I... I can't! I won't!!' She regretted it, even as the words left her mouth. Though she was torn, she couldn't betray her friends. Oh, how she wanted this nightmare to end!

O'Connor glowered at her as he positioned a black-booted foot, polished to a high shine, on top of the parcel. 'Not even for your daughter?! Your meds?!' he asked with disbelief.

Calista closed her eyes, mustering strength. When she opened them again, they blazed with fire. 'No, never!'

'I'm warning you!' he growled.

'Never!!'

Silence.

An exhausted Calista flopped back as she stared at him. 'Would... would you really let me die?'

'Five seconds,' he said through gritted teeth. 'I'll give you five seconds to tell me. After that, no more meds. No more family.'

The two stared at each other for some time, until Calista tore her eyes away and glared at the floor by the bed, the pulse in her temples thudding. She heard him pick up the parcel. Heard the tear of paper. Fumbling. Things dropping to the floor. The clinking tumble of small glass objects on wooden floorboards. There was a pause. And then came the sound of a stamping boot, crunching down onto an ampoule. Crushing it to smithereens.

One.

Calista held her breath as she counted.

Again and again, O'Connor stamped onto the glass phials.

More and more crushing.

Until she counted ten.

Ten phials of distilled medicine.

All of Saffie's hard work.

Gone.

Exasperated, Calista slumped back against the wall, her vertebrae smashing against the crumbling plaster. She grimaced with pain, felt faint, and sick.

The door swung open.

Footsteps walked out.

The clunk of the door-lock twisting into place.

Calista's eyes rolled back, and she collapsed limply against the pillow.

•••————————————————————•••

I can't. A tired-looking Professor – with days-old stubble on his chin, and deep shadows under his eyes – was signing to the Chauffeur. There was a whining sound nearby. Acuzio was lying on the floor under the table, resting his head on the Professor's feet, sensing the Professor's disquietude. The dog licked his ankle with his big soft tongue, before whining again.

They had fled from Vivra Towers, back to the underground Avernus.

In the empty dining room, chairs strewn about, the place a mess, the Chauffeur sat next to the old man, one hand touching his arm, jostling him, pleading him to eat, and the other hand holding a hovering spoon of food.

But the Professor turned his head away.

Sighing loudly, the Chauffeur put the spoon back into the bowl, frustrated. He signed onto the Professor's hand, *Please, eat! You need to keep strong, for the children.*

But the old man shook his head. After several seconds, he eventually turned back to the Chauffeur. *How can I eat?! How can I eat when... when I have failed the children in every way! Calista too. And the baby.*

The Chauffeur gripped his arm with both hands, then signed back, *You have never failed them. You took care of them. Like you took care of me. And... just as I am thankful to you, I am sure they are thankful too, so–*

Thankful? signed the Professor feebly. *They are locked away somewhere. Probably drugged out of their skulls. Dying. Or perhaps already dead. And... it's all my fault!*

Self-pity! said the Chauffeur stamping his foot with frustration. *Self-pity will get us nowhere. You need to be strong. Keep positive. And eat! We've got to find a way to help the children.*

How can we help them? When I am blind, and you are deaf!

What about the agents? The karate people?

I... I can't reach them. They must have gone into hiding.

The Chauffeur huffed. *We have to do something!*

The Professor's empty eyes gazed into the distance. Eventually he got up. *I'm going to my room,* he signed, and flicked out his walking stick.

The Chauffeur watched as the Professor tapped away, disappearing down the corridor with the ever-faithful Acuzio trailing behind him. He looked around at the gloomy, messy room, and felt utterly despondent.

The old man's depression was infectious.

Sighing, he got up and left too, leaving the bowl of untouched food on the table.

He walked and walked. Not knowing where he was going. Went into the lift and eventually found himself blinking in the bright light of a zenith sun.

Going to the lake, he crossed the bridge, and walked over the long stretch of grass – toward the black pit where the great oak once stood.

To his surprise he saw someone next to the pit, crouching down – drizzling water from a watering can over the scorched grass, with the greatest of care. She was bent so low, her nose was almost touching the earth.

Putting down the watering can, she went to sit on a blanket spread out on the ground. There was a large book lying open, its ochred pages bright against the black soil. Wiping her hands on the side of her trousers, she heaved the Bible onto her lap, and hunched over it, to read. Brown fingers underlined the sentences, her lips moving as she sounded out each word – so absorbed, that she was unaware of the Chauffeur's presence.

But then she stopped. Looked into the distance with a doleful, dazed expression. And burst into tears, shoulders shaking with sobs. Misery engraving deep lines into her face.

As the Chauffeur stood behind a tree, his back pressed against the mossy bark, he felt torn. Half wanting to go to her, half realising he didn't need any more pain.

Eventually, he caught one last glimpse of an inconsolable mother crying for her son, before forcing his feet to walk away. Forcing each foot to move one in front of the other. Marching. Until he got to the far south of the gardens, where there was a lone bench, nestled against a brick wall overrun with ivy. The bench stood introspectively, as if pondering the meaning of life, wondering about its existence.

The Chauffeur collapsed onto it and doubled over.

Squeezing his eyes closed, he was surprised to find himself praying.

God. Wherever you are, whoever you are... Why?!! he cried inside his head.

Balling big round fists, he bashed them against the flaked wood.

Why would you let so many bad things happen?! To good people. We did you no harm, so why do you punish us so bad. So, so bad!!

He caught a sob in his throat.

Lapsed into soft sniffles.

Absorbing the silence that had insulated him all his life from the loud, frightening, noisy world.

Do you... do you even exist?! he breathed.

Do you have a name?

Or... are you like me, nameless?

I want to know.

Answer me!!

He waited.

And waited.

Fists loosening, he pressed trembling hands into the cracked bench.

Please, he begged. *Please.* His tears fell softly, spotting his trousers.

Out of nowhere, a drop of rain plonked on his head.

Followed by another.

And another.

A pale-faced Chauffeur caught his breath and looked up at the sky with dewy eyes.

Through the tears he saw the clouds brewing overhead.

Felt the wet freshness of raindrops patter onto him. As if God too were crying. Weeping with him.

The Chauffeur's heart leapt as he stared up. Gasped at the celestial beauty. Of golden sunshine silhouetting grey stratus clouds.

'Is... is that you?' he mouthed verbally, his voice nothing more than grunting sounds. 'God...?'

J.Y. Sam

'O Hearer of prayer,

to you people of all sorts will come'

Psalm 65:2

New World Translation of the Holy Scriptures

29 THE PRAYER

As the earth spun serenely on its axis, a resplendent jewel in a black void, passionate whispers could be heard in the deepest, greenest wilds of the Amazon jungle, chanting. A distressed mother and father were crouching on the ground, blanched by the flush of daylight spearing through the canopy – praying over their unconscious daughter.

Heads bowed, fingers woven firmly together, lips muttering. 'Please, God...'

There came a sudden flash of lightning overhead.

Followed seconds later by a heart-jolting clap of thunder.

But they paid no heed.

Their eyes remained squeezed shut as they prayed.

'Please make it rain.'

Further east across the globe, in London, England, in a boarded-up derelict building filled with drab, mostly empty rooms, a little German girl was in a deep sleep – though it was the middle of the afternoon. She slept fitfully, and began muttering as she dreamt. 'Please...' she repeated – her head turning feverishly from side to side. 'Please, God.' Her childish voice crescendoed as her agitation increased. 'Make it rain.'

In the same building, half hidden in the shadows of windowless rooms, Milly, Tai, and Jemima all began mumbling the same thing as they too slept. Struggling to catch their breath, like the oxygen had been sucked from the room. Their minds muddled with disturbing dreams.

As the cerulean planet turned soundlessly in space, orbited by a stabilising moon, and warmed to the perfect temperature by a giant yellow star, incandescent with fire – a molten, swirling ball of nuclear fusion – the star's light fell upon one side of the planet, plunging the other into darkness. On the dark side, in a populous country in the largest continent, there stood a run-down hospital. A boy lay slumped in an armchair next to a bedridden girl inside a still room on the second floor. It was almost nine o'clock in the evening, and though he had only just nodded off to sleep, his mind was already deep in dreams. So deep, it was as if he was drugged. His breath was short and shallow, his pulse quickening, as he babbled. 'Dear God… Please make it rain.'

In the same continent, in a vast country just north-east of India, a wretched Mei Hui kneeled on the floor against a rusted metal bunkbed. She was in a dank cell, somewhere unknown to her. Lonely. Scared. Helpless.

Though she had never before prayed to any god, she was compelled now, out of despair, to search for him. Starved and dehydrated, she found it hard to concentrate – at times faint, then dizzy… Despite everything, through it all, she began to utter a midnight prayer. A strange and puzzling request, that she did not know from where it came. Yet she asked it nevertheless. 'Please, God,' she begged, tears dripping silently onto clenched yet tremulous hands. 'Please make it rain…'

30 LIGHTING AND THUNDER

Back in the Amazon, there came a flash of lightning overhead, followed immediately by a clap of thunder so loud they thought their eardrums might burst.

Bent over their daughter, on their knees, Alma and Ignacio looked up through the swaying canopy. A drop of rain, as large as a marble, plonked right onto Ignacio's cheek, and his mouth gaped open with surprise. More drops, at first a patter, and then all-of-a-sudden an onslaught. A deluge. Within seconds they were completely soaked.

Alma cried with both disbelief and joy.

Ignacio caught his breath, as the pouring rain washed away his tears. Closing his eyes, with trembling, fearful lips, he silently thanked God.

Beneath them, a drenched Saffie, lying sprawled on palm leaves, began to stir – surprised to find herself under a heaving, thunderous storm, soaking wet, and overcast by her parents.

As seconds passed, she eventually came to, her mind tuning to crystal clarity.

Every sound, every sensation and feeling, jarred her like shocks of electricity.

She smarted with a heightened, nerve-tingling sensitivity. The elements in the air, the pummelling water, the dirt underneath her fingernails – every cell, every molecule, and atom, right down to their electrons and protons and neutrons. Vibrating and humming. Setting her teeth on edge.

But more than anything, she felt the others.

All seven of them.

Their connection.

So pure.

So solid.

Like they were right there with her, amidst the understorey. Holding hands.

PART 5

31 THE SHINOBI

34-year-old Alberto Borgnino couldn't help having such an unusual surname which, in the Piedmont dialect where he was from, meant 'blind in one eye'. The local townspeople had pulled his leg no end over the fact that he was an optician. 'Hey, Borgnino!' they'd call out with a chuckle. 'You wanna test eyes when you can hardly see yourself?!' Alberto would only shrug and smile wryly as he went about his business. Thankfully, he no longer had to endure such quips since he had moved to London and lived there for the past six years.

There was nothing wrong with his eyes, of course. In fact, he had 20/20 vision – and that excellent eyesight was, amongst other things, one of the reasons he had been called and trained as an agent.

He was fast asleep at home in bed with his wife, Dora. Her sinus problem meant she snored like a volcano, but it wasn't her snoring that suddenly woke him.

He sat up and waited to become accustomed to the darkness, before swinging his legs out of bed and pushing feet into slippers. Climbing into the loft room, he opened a locked chest, and quietly got ready. The black hakama trousers he slipped into, made of light and flexible fabric, allowed him the greatest ease of movement. He donned a flak jacket, and tied it firmly around his waist with the kusari obi cummerbund, tight enough to hold the eight shuriken – lethally sharp throwing stars – concealed in its lining.

When he took his trusty katana sword, he couldn't help slipping it out of the ebony case to eye, not just its glinting beauty, but also the razor-sharp blade. The lightest touch was able to sever bone and sinew. And his keen eyesight and hand coordination meant that he could wield both the sword, and the shuriken, to within a hair's breadth precision. He pushed the blade into the case and strapped it closely to his back – its curve fit the shape of him perfectly. He put on his mask, and last of all his tabi boots, with soles that were soundless and gave excellent grip.

As he passed the door of their bedroom, he paused, thinking of his sleeping wife. The same questions that always came to him before a mission, haunted him now. Would he return to her? Would she see him again? Still, he left the dark building like a shadow separating from its source. Only briefly did he look up at the silver-grey night sky as it rumbled with dark, ominous clouds, the air roiling with anger. Silently he flew through the night.

•••————————————————•••

It was a Friday night, and 28-year-old Maggie Bateman was having a night out with her mates, Lizzy and Elsa, on the town. Joking around, dancing, laughing hysterically, and crawling from club to club. Maggie watched her friends binge-drink all night, and though she wanted to, the way of the shinobi had been ingrained into her so well that she stuck to her water and mocktails religiously.

They exited the Purple Orchid nightclub, her friends swaying from side to side as they walked, when storm clouds suddenly gathered overhead. Maggie looked up at the sky, surprised; the morning forecast had predicted dry weather all day, yet it looked as if it was going to rain. She whistled for a cab, which swerved to the pavement by their side, and she steered her friends into it. Through an open window, Maggie gave the taxicab driver their addresses and enough money to cover the fare, before shutting the door. The cab drove away.

She stood on the pavement and watched it go. And though she did not understand how, she knew that it was time to get ready. Jumping on an electric hire bike, she whizzed back to her apartment which was 15 minutes away – racing along the streets of London at top speed, weaving and dodging through the traffic. Her manoeuvring skills were exceptional, her speed and timing flawless. At last, she reached her home, and she swung her leg over the bike and dismounted with the grace of a ballerina.

Abandoning the bike to the side of the pavement, she slipped into the apartment block, and ran up the stairs, two steps at a time.

Time was of the essence, and she didn't waste a second as she put on her shinobi attire, and strapped to her back a bow and a quiver filled with bamboo poison-tipped arrows.

Though 19-year-old Cheung Xin-Yan had recently trained to become a hairdresser, cutting hair was not her main occupation, though it complemented perfectly her real skills.

She had been spotted by Sensei Aoki on a visit to China, in an after-school karate club. She was a small, demure girl then, and hid behind the other more boisterous children. But when she stepped out onto the crash mat, he saw that her every step and every movement were perfectly controlled, her tiny form belying the inner dragon. When she fought, he watched with surprise as the dragon emerged and defeated every opponent without mercy, though they were much larger than her.

Sensei Aoki learnt that she was an abandoned orphan, one of millions that had been born under China's one-baby rule. The orphanage she had come to call home was a particularly bad one – filled with neglected, emaciated baby girls. Yet despite such harsh conditions, Xin-Yan's spirit grew stronger, even as she grew physically. She eventually walked out of the orphanage when she came of age, where many others had the misfortune of leaving it only in tiny, flimsy coffins. On hearing of her story, Sensei Aoki knew that the girl had single-handedly nurtured her inner dragon. And he immediately set about training her in the way of the shinobi – to set it free.

So by day, Xin-Yan worked as a hairdresser, cutting people's hair with the greatest of skill, and by night she became what she truly was.

Sensei Aoki was so trusting of her exceptional skills, that, one day, when he thought she was ready, he gave her the task of cutting his hair with the sharpest of scissors – blindfolded. Though the silk mask around her eyes let in a pale haze of light, she was unable to see what was right in front of her. Using her sensitive fingers, she explored his scalp and the length of his hair, the position and shape of his ears, the angle of his neck, the slope of his forehead. Building an image of him in her mind.

Pulling the scissors and comb out of her tool-belt, she began snipping away with expertise and speed – tufts of hair wafting to the floor. She did not cut her fingers once. Neither did she snip his skin. 15 minutes later, when she was done, she pulled off the eye mask to find, in the reflection of the mirror, a hint of a smile on Sensei Aoki's face. He said nothing as he turned his head from one side to the other, admiring her handiwork. They both knew now – she was ready.

So as Xin-Yan found herself stirring from her sleep one night, she got dressed without a word. No message had been sent to her. No telephone call with instructions. She simply knew that she had been reactivated, and she must get ready. Packing the black shinobi clothing into a bag, she laid the iron tekko-kagi hand claws carefully on top. She went outside and placed the bag in the boot of her car, before jumping into the driver's seat. There would be a long five-hour drive before she reached the destination. A prison where dissidents were held, in Shaya County, a remote western region of Xinjiang. Though no-one had told her any of this, Xin-Yan knew that that was where she was going to meet others like herself. Other ninjas. Their mission: to facilitate the escape of a young Ingenious girl, and guard her with their lives.

32 RELEASE

The giant hornets' papery nest lay hidden underground within the space left by rotten pine roots, on the outskirts of Chinese lowland forest. The outside quietness belied the relentless activity within.

Inside, the large queen, almost five centimetres long and fertilised only once by a male prior to her winter hibernation, methodically laid eggs into hundreds of empty cells. Each one a perfect hexagon. Meanwhile, worker hornets – her unfertilised daughters – were hard at work building and repairing the nest with chewed-up bark, tending to and feeding the larvae, and foraging for food. The workers, much smaller than the queen, expended so much energy that their lifespan was short – between 12 and 24 days. The queen however was able to live for an entire year, her main purpose to lay eggs.

When night fell, the queen rested from her duties, settling herself within a secluded corner. But something was wrong. Instead of resting too, the workers began leaving the nest. Disturbed, the queen could do nothing but watch with shiny brown eyes as all 722 of her workers gradually disappeared. In time, she found herself utterly alone. Her antennae stroked the air, disturbed and bewildered, unused to such silence…

Outside, the female hornets rose into the night, a bustling mass of striped yellow-brown bodies. As they shifted and hovered in the air, one by one, they turned to face south-westward, antennae quivering – then zoomed through the darkness.

The nebulous swarm flew for nearly two miles until they came to a settlement where humans lived. Run-down buildings scattered along pot-holed roads. In a large, boxy building with iron rods banding crazed windows, they crammed through a large crack in the glass.

The inside space was dark and still, save for the light hum of their swarm. They divided into four groups and flew through the corridors and rooms of the entire building – coming across only three men sleeping in bunks in one room, and a girl behind a door of rusted bars. Circling back, the four groups returned to the room with the dormant men. The hornets merged back into one again, before dividing this time into three. Each division flew to surround one of the men, landing lightly on his head.

One by one the men awoke to the horror of finding themselves encased inside a swarm of buzzing, twitching hornets. They screamed and batted frantically at them. One man threw himself onto the ground and rolled around, trying to squash them. But the insects flew up and directed sharp stingers at the men's eyes, spraying venom directly into them. It burned like acid – and the men howled from the pain before eventually passing out.

When at last three bodies lay still on the floor, the hornets hovered over each one for a while, making sure their victims were completely incapacitated. Satisfied, they joined together and left the building as a united swarm, just as they had entered.

Back in their nest, the queen had been waiting nervously, perturbed by the most unusual development of her workers deserting her. At last, after a seemingly endless wait, one of the hornets flew back into the nest, followed by another, and another. Until she was surrounded once more by a mass of fidgeting, bustling workers. She basked in their warmth. And rubbed her legs together with joy – a dance of triumph. In time, tiredness quietened her, and she settled down to rest.

In a dank cell, Mei Hui tried so hard to sleep – to blot out the nightmare she was in. But it was no use. She lay on the bottom bunk, red eyes staring at the bed slats above. Wondering, with trepidation, how many people had slept there before her, and what had become of them; it was common knowledge that people labelled as dissidents had a habit of mysteriously disappearing. Never to be seen again.

There came a noise from outside. A light buzzing. The clatter of furniture. Men shouting. Followed by screams and crashing sounds.

Mei Hui quickly sat up and stared at the prison door, listening intently. Each sound made her jump, made her more and more frightened.

Eventually, there came the jangle of keys. Someone opening the door.

From the darkness of the corridor, a female ninja stepped into the cell, wearing iron claws on her hands.

Mei Hui gasped and immediately got up and followed her outside – relieved but still on edge. Slowly, carefully, they made their way along the corridors without a word. They passed an open door where she saw three men lying unconscious on the ground – one of their faces was turned toward her, his closed eyes strangely red and swollen.

Finally, they walked through the lobby and the main door.

Outside, four ninjas emerged from the darkness, dressed from head to foot in black clothing. Only their hands and eyes – intelligent, bright eyes, that watched her keenly – were visible.

They surrounded her as she walked to them, and, together, they continued walking along the road in the darkness of night. All the while, the ninjas looked around, on high alert. Wary of every movement and noise.

Mei Hui was free, but as they walked in the dead of night, she wondered whether this was real. Perhaps she had fallen asleep and was dreaming.

You're not dreaming, came a voice inside her head. An Indian boy. *You must stay in hiding, with the agents. They will keep you safe. Please be cautious. Trust only the agents. The world has turned against us...*

Mei Hui listened silently to his words of warning. She knew exactly who he was, though they had never before met. It was the last Ingenious child, Inder Chauhan.

•••———————————————————•••

She lay motionless – coiled for warmth underneath a fallen tree trunk. The nature reserve, the largest in West London covering 2,500 acres, was busy with visitors walking their dogs, and cyclists zooming along intersecting roads. The fields too were scattered with free-roaming deer – which is why the lone adder preferred the dry grassland deep in the centre of the park.

Her scaled skin, mottled reddish-brown and marked with zig-zag patterns, softly rose and fell as she slept. Red permanently-open eyes seemed angry, though she was fast asleep. She stirred. Awoken by something. And gradually she uncoiled her metre-long body as her shiny black tongue tasted the air. Sluggish, she slithered into sunlight, pausing for some time as it heated her. She could have basked in that patch of light for hours, but something was calling her.

Silently she slipped through the grassland. Sensing vibrations in the ground through her belly – of others like her, so many of them, heading in the same direction.

Against their natural instinct, the adders made their way out of the park and spilled out onto the streets, ignoring the screams and thunderous footsteps of running humans.

They did not have far to go before they came to an imposing run-down building. They entered by slithering through drains, eventually appearing inside toilet cisterns. They slunk upwards, over the rim, and flopped onto the floor, shiny wet. Discreetly, they made their way through the building – gliding gracefully, and keeping to the sides of the corridors. When footsteps pounded toward them, they kept still, pressing themselves flat, until the humans were almost upon them – and then they pounced! Flying onto the humans' legs, seemingly out of nowhere. They sank fangs deep into flesh, fangs that were like molten nails. The humans collapsed on the floor, writhing with pain, until at last the venom stilled them.

All 52 adders made their way around the building, into every room – red eyes tracing the tiniest movement, nerves in their facial pit sensing the minutest variations of heat. They attacked everyone they came across, with the exception of the five sleeping bodies locked behind bars – knowing instinctively those ones must be left well alone.

In time, when they had covered the entire building, the adders went back to the toilets, satisfied that their work was done. They disappeared into the watery cisterns and out through the drains. Quietly, discreetly, they slithered along roads and alleyways, at last returning to the nearby park – diving into the tall grass. Glad to be concealed again, and safe in familiar terrain.

It was mid-afternoon when, hidden within a run-down warehouse, five sleeping bodies began to stir in their bunks.

Wake up! A voice called them inside their heads. It was Inder. *Wake up!!*

Jemima was the first to become conscious. Her eyes suddenly opened, crazed with red veins, her hair limp with curls. She took a sharp breath, blinking as she tried to make sense of where she was, and why her head hurt so much.

Next – all in separate rooms – it was Ilse that came around, then Milly, and Tai, and last of all, Jeremy Fitzsimmons. Though their bodies had been dormant, their consciousness, deep within the temporal lobe of their brain, had very much been active in their dreams.

Abruptly transitioning from dreamworld to reality, they sat up, rubbed eyes, stretched aching limbs – and looked around at their locked prison room in a daze.

Jemima tensed when she realised someone was opening the door.

It was an agent – a katana sword strapped to his back.

He stepped in and motioned for her to follow. With some difficulty, Jemima stood up on wobbly feet – her limbs and muscles were feeble after not using them for weeks. The ninja grabbed her and held her steady. She leant on him and hobbled out.

When a ninja came for Fitzsimmons, the old man too could barely stand, and the ninja put his arm around him and helped him walk. Making their way slowly through the corridors, they came across something slumped on the floor, and as they drew closer, Fitzsimmons realised it was one of the guards lying still. They walked past, when a hand suddenly grabbed Fitzsimmons' ankle! The old man toppled to the floor, and he grappled with the guard, at last managing to twist round and grab his opponent's wrist. With a sizzling sound, and in the blink of an eye, the guard exploded into black dust. There was a reek of burning as Fitzsimmons sucked air through clenched teeth. Shaking his head, he took a moment to absorb the energy. Eventually he got up on uncertain feet, straightened, fisting his hands as he assimilated the power. His veins throbbing with energy, he realised that he was stronger, much stronger, than before.

The black-clad agent just stood there, staring with wide eyes at the empty space where the guard had once been, desperately trying to quell the tide of fear in his chest.

'Do not fear me,' Fitzsimmons growled.

The agent managed to get a grip on himself, and they both turned, walking side by side, as they made their way through the building – the ninja's nervous eyes checking on Fitzsimmons now and then.

Each time they passed a body, Fitzsimmons stooped down casually to brush the back of his hand against their skin – wincing as they disappeared and a sizzling blast zapped through him, replenishing every cell of his body. He smouldered with strength. Fingers curling with power.

Carrying on, they eventually reached the CCTV room, where there was a man slumped unconscious in a chair. It was David O'Connor. They walked past him, and stood directly in front of the CCTV screens – eyes sifting through the pictures. Fitzsimmons spotted Jemima limping with great difficulty along a corridor with a ninja, and he reached forward with gnarled fingers to touch her image. He also saw that Tai, Milly, and Ilse were still in their locked prison rooms.

Hold on, Fitzsimmons told them with his mind, his voice hoarse and gruff even in their thoughts.

When they heard him, the children stopped or stiffened.

The agents are on their way to you, Fitzsimmons let them know. He followed Jemima's progress. She was painfully slow. And he was aware that with each passing second, their successful escape was threatened by unseen dangers. He closed his eyes. Cognisant of the tremendous power coursing through his veins. An incredible strength that made him feel invincible. He could only guess that Ilse and Inder were at the heart of what was happening to him. Somehow the connection – with all seven of them – enhanced their powers. And his abilities.

He suddenly realised that same connection could now be used by him to increase their strength.

Closing his eyes, he clenched his fists and listened to the sound of his own raspy breath, as he concentrated on each of the children. He willed and willed the dark energy that coursed through him to reach each of them. Slowly, it eked out of him. Into the air, like an invisible gas. Passing through the molecules that surrounded him – oxygen and nitrogen, carbon dioxide, and water. Vibrating through each atom. Until the energy at last reached the children.

Lifting his eyelids, beaming eyes roamed over the CCTV images. With fascination he watched as the children gasped – an unusual expression on their faces.

The hobbling Jemima stopped, sucking in air and the dark energy – her eyes widened as the full force of it hit her. She suddenly let go of the ninja who was helping her. She began walking with a firm footing, then she broke into a light trot, eventually running off and disappearing around a corner.

The ninja paused for a second, surprised – before quickly following her.

Tai got off his bed and went over to the agent who was opening the prison door. Fitzsimmons watched as they ran offscreen together.

Ilse was approached by a ninja with a bow and arrow strapped to her back. She took the little girl's outstretched hand, and the two walked off-camera.

Fitzsimmons watched all of this, before turning.

Just one last thing before he left the room. Passing the unconscious O'Connor, he rippled fingers along the man's cheek – and O'Connor disappeared instantly, leaving only a light flurry of dust tumbling softly down as Fitzsimmons and the agent disappeared through the doorway.

It was ironic that O'Connor, who had hated the Ingenious children since meeting them in the country house, was, in his death, aiding their escape. Inadvertently, his bodily energy had empowered them, even as the last parts of him – sooty motes of dust – faded from existence.

33   A CRACK IN THE HEART OF GLASS

Ilse was the first to meet up with Fitzsimmons in the lobby of the derelict warehouse. She let go of the agent's hand, and ran over to Fitzsimmons, her face a composition in red of wrath and sorrow. She grabbed his arm and tugged harshly on it. Sobbing, shoulders shaking – the tears made her vision blurry, made his hideous face look watery. *You shouldn't have killed them!!* she raged. *All those guards. They were innocent!*

Fitzsimmons' eyes flitted about her warped face, thrown. Her empathy, her deepness of feeling for strangers, was foreign to him. It was such a stark contrast to his cold, hard heart. Her sensitivity, to his insensibility. And he felt something inside him crack – a fissure, tearing right through his heart.

Footsteps drew closer, and they turned to find the others joining them.

Inder's voice echoed in their heads. *You need to leave. Now!! They're coming for you!*

Quickly springing into action, they ran out through the door, into the litter-strewn carpark. The five ninjas reconfigured to surround their wards – Milly, Tai, Jemima, and Ilse – looking all around, on high alert. The lead ninja motioned for them to follow, and they ran to the far west wall, pressing themselves against it, just as they heard the wail of police sirens in the distance. But the thak-thak of a helicopter overhead soon drowned them out. With nervous eyes, everyone watched both the carpark entrance and the flying metal beast as it grew bigger and bigger. It landed right in the middle of the parking lot, creating a swirling typhoon that jostled them this way and that.

The helicopter door was pushed open, and Fitzsimmons, the teenagers, and the agents, ran against the wind to climb inside. The last agent slammed the door firmly closed behind them, and the engines roared as the helicopter lifted off. The sudden feeling of weightlessness made their stomachs churn.

The helicopter rose higher and higher, and Tai looked down through the window as he strapped himself into a seat. The landscape broadened, with fields chequered by roads coming into view. He spied the source of the police sirens, a convoy of striped cars hurtling toward the warehouse – lights flashing bright orange. They screeched to a halt in the carpark. Policemen jumped out urgently – some stopping to look up at the helicopter, while others drew guns and ran cautiously into the building.

Milly was still standing inside the helicopter, swaying uncertainly as it flew. She looked lost. When one of the masked agents approached her, she soon recognised his eyes and the fading scar that marked the corner of the left. 'V2!' she cried, as she threw herself onto him in a hug.

Surprised by the unusual lack of inhibition, V2 softened and embraced her in return. 'Good to see you, Milly,' he smiled. 'We've been worried about you. You okay?' When they parted, he noticed for the first time how blank her eyes were.

Looking up at him, Milly nodded spontaneously, but then stopped, and shook her head. She was so confused. Couldn't get any words out. Couldn't vocalise the barrage of emotions seething inside her. For a second, she forgot everything as they stared at each other. And suddenly his name popped into her head out of nowhere. A name that had been kept secret from her all this time. Jonah. And she gasped. Because that was not all she learnt about him. She learnt that he was battling with his own feelings – of deep affection, maybe even love. For her.

She stepped back, flustered. Quickly turned to sit next to Ilse who was in a window seat. Strapping herself in, she suddenly realised that Ilse was staring at her with a knowing look. *You,* Milly realised.

He's not as old as you think, said Ilse softly. *He's 23.* A pitiful smile stretched briefly across the girl's face, her eyes still dewy.

Why are you looking at me like that? asked Milly.

But Ilse did not answer. She broke their gaze abruptly and turned to look out of the window.

'Where are we going?' someone asked. They shifted round to see that it was Jemima asking.

'Avernus,' V2 told them – he had returned to his seat, just within the cockpit.

They absorbed this with relief; it felt like they were going home.

'Is everyone okay?' asked someone else. This time it was Tai. 'Ma? The Professor, the Chauffeur...'

'They're all safe and well,' said V2. He glanced at Milly. 'Brian too. Only, Calista and Jake... and the baby. We're still searching for them.'

'Oh no!' cried Jemima. 'We have to find them!'

V2 raised an eyebrow at her. '*You're* not finding anyone, young lady. That's our job. You have to stay in hiding!' he said firmly.

Jemima pulled a stubborn face at Tai, who was sitting next to her. She threaded her arm through his, and rested her head on his shoulder. *Not if I have anything to do with it,* Jemima told him silently. She turned round, and glanced over her shoulder.

At the back of the plane in a seat overcast with shadow, Fitzsimmons watched and listened quietly. He felt nauseous, unused to flight, his wrists chafing against the handcuffs that he'd allowed the nervous agent to put on him, to assuage their fears. He dug black fingernails between the chains as he tore his gaze from the leaden clouds outside. He lay back, his muscles relaxing. Closed his eyes. Saw behind translucent eyelids, images of those same clouds, gathering darkly, swiftly – with an air of foreboding. They hummed with whispers of something huge, something terrible, yet to come.

34 LOVE AND LOSS

The unknown was everything the Professor feared.

He stared into it now. Into the white.

Each hair on his skin bristling.

Fitzsimmons was sitting opposite him across a table – no-one else in the empty room.

The shuffle of a chair and the soft cadence of breathing were the only indication that someone was actually there.

The feeling of déjà vu, so strong.

The Professor remembered, like it was yesterday, the first time they sat opposite each other in exactly the same way. When Fitzsimmons grabbed his wrist. The Professor's eyes widening as the man showed him with his mind – his extraordinary, terrible mind – what had happened to his family so many years ago. As if he was right there. Watching his house being engulfed in flames.

The intense heat.

Their screams.

The horror.

The deafening roar of the blaze.

Knowing that his wife and son were being burnt alive.

Time slowing, taking an eternity. The tick of each second, a piercing stab to his heart.

And when the fire died down, his body heaving with dry retches, there was only one thought that remained. The part Fitzsimmons had played. The question of blame hung heavily in the air, as cloyingly as the stench of burning lingering in charred nostrils.

The Professor closed his eyes, shook those awful memories away. And mustered strength. Eventually he found himself back in the room. The soundless, odourless room. 'How?' he found himself saying. His own voice sounded weak, like it was not his. Like it belonged to someone else. 'How were you able to escape?'

A pause. 'Ilse. Inder,' said Fitzsimmons, his voice rough as sandpaper against a raw wound. 'We are all connected now.'

Intrigued, the Professor repeated, 'Inder...' Knowing instinctively this must be the last Ingenious child, the boy they used to call Zeta. Hope rose through the fear.

'Ilse... *she* found him,' grunted Fitzsimmons. Another pause. 'Her powers, and Inder's, they are much, much stronger than I ever imagined. We are able to reach each other through them.'

'From so far away?'

'Yes.'

The Professor thought about this. 'If... if you're able to connect with each other, then–'

'Both Saffron Morales and Mei Hui Li are fine,' said Fitzsimmons, anticipating his question.

The Professor relaxed a little, relieved. 'But... you still haven't explained how you managed to get out.'

'Saffron helped us to communicate together, on a base level, through dreams. And it was in those dreams that I was able to orchestrate our escape. Yet we could not break free from the drugged torpor – until Inder woke us up.'

'There were reports of snakes being seen. Hundreds of them. That was you, wasn't it?'

'Yes.'

'In the same way, you managed to locate the agents. Activate them. Control them.'

'Yes.'

The Professor stiffened. Acutely aware of how vulnerable he was. One touch, one thought, was all it took for Fitzsimmons to control him, or even put him out of existence. 'C-can you... can you help me find Calista, Jake, and the baby?' he ventured.

'They are nothing to do with me,' said Fitzsimmons dismissively.

'No, they're not. But it's because of you that they're missing. Their lives, in danger.'

Fitzsimmons stopped – examining the fresh crack in his own heart. The one that Ilse had made. It cut into him.

The Professor was not going to give up that easily. He said quietly, 'Jemima is particularly fond of them. They're like family to her.' He faltered. Wondered whether he should say the next thing. 'You… you know what it's like… to love. And to lose it.'

Fitzsimmons found he could not respond.

The Professor waited for some time.

Five minutes passed. Ten.

And just as he thought he had failed, and was ready to get up and leave, Fitzsimmons grabbed his wrist.

The Professor froze. His flesh smarting under the man's rough grip.

Sensing the Professor's fear, Fitzsimmons let go, a nondescript expression on his face. He had stopped caring a long time ago. He didn't care one bit about this couple and their baby. But… the children, the Ingenious, were his progeny. Through them, he would live on. They were all that mattered. 'Our powers are evolving.'

The Professor slowly sat back in his chair.

Fitzsimmons continued, 'I am curious as to how our abilities have developed. So… I will help you find this girl, her family, if only as a learning exercise, to test our powers.'

'Th-thank you,' said the Professor – the politeness force of habit. He got up and walked, trembling, to the door. When he banged it, someone unlocked and opened for him.

Just before he left, Fitzsimmons said, 'You loved and lost too, Professor.'

But the door was already being shut and locked.

Anyone else would have wondered if he had heard.

But not Fitzsimmons. He knew his words stabbed the Professor to the core.

<hr>

Restored to Avernus, the teenagers eventually managed to settle back to normality. Their connection with each other gave them a fortitude, a strength of mind, that was far beyond their tender years. And before long, everything that had happened to them – being drugged and locked away in that warehouse – seemed like a distant dream.

Tai sat with his mother in the BC now. As a teenager, he usually shied away from showing affection toward her. But they had both been through so much, that he surrendered to it now. As they sat together – his mother arranging pressed flowers within the large Bible on her lap – he snuggled against her, leaning his head on her shoulder, eyes half closed, his mind drifting.

Ilse was sitting opposite them, watching, and swinging her legs as was her habit, at the same time picking absentmindedly at one of the pastries that the Chauffeur had made.

Suddenly Brian burst into the room, looking around frantically. 'Is Milly here?' he asked, out of breath.

'No,' said Ilse, putting the pastry down. 'It's just us.'

'Are you sure?!' asked Brian as he looked around, his voice rising with panic.

'Yes,' Tai confirmed.

Brian was just about to leave, when Ilse stood up, reaching a hand toward him. 'Wait!'

He stopped, turned, and eyed the little girl.

Ilse closed her eyes, breathing deeply for several seconds. When she at last opened them again, she burst out excitedly, 'She's in Vivra Towers!'

Turning on his heels, Brian ran out, and both Ilse and Tai jumped up and ran after him.

Tyaishia shouted out to them. 'Let me know she's okay. And be careful!' Watching them go, she fingered one of the flower's delicate petals, and placed it between the pages of the Bible as a bookmark.

It had taken her months of reading many chapters each day, and she had almost finished. Just two pages to go. She thought she might find closure as she read the very last book, Revelation   instead, it surprised her. Took her on a rollercoaster of emotions. First wonder, then fear, puzzlement, disgust, and finally... She thought about it. Finally, she realised, it left her with hope. Lowering her head and pressing hands together, she said a silent prayer. *Please may Milly be okay, God,* she pleaded. And then an afterthought. *Oh, and thanks. Thanks that your Bible has a happy ending.* She sniffed, emotional. *Yeah, thanks.*

They were poor, simple words, yet uttered with a heart rich with appreciation.

In Vivra Towers, Milly was in the corridor of the top floor, standing precariously on a chair, facing the wall. In one hand was a makeshift palette, and in the other, a paintbrush. From her jeans pocket hung a paint-smeared tea-towel.

With the electricity cut off, there was just the natural sunlight from the window at the end of the corridor casting a long diagonal divide, between the light and the gloom – cutting Milly in half.

Out of the darkness stepped her mother, Savannah. She looked from Milly to the wall with fascination, a thoughtful finger resting on her chin. 'The murals are beautiful, my love!' she breathed, drawing closer. 'You're getting better and better.'

Milly paused to glance down at her briefly. 'Thanks, mum,' she mumbled as she scratched the itch beneath her bobbled old beanie hat. She turned back to the wall and looked over the image she was working on, before priming the paintbrush with more paint. Tiptoeing, she reached for the top of the wall and attacked it with frenzied strokes. She had filled the entire corridor with paintings, so many paintings. As if her imaginings had spilled out into real life and were pressed flat against its surface.

Her mother's voice came to her again, right behind her shoulder. So close, Milly could feel the warmth of her breath, and smell the peppery sweetness of the mints she liked. 'Don't forget to add a bit of light-shine to the eye,' Savannah suggested. 'That'll make it really gleam.'

Milly did as she was told.

'And the nostrils, they should be flared. Like it's snorting!'

Nodding in agreement, Milly smeared a dot of black paint against the nose.

Just then, the elevator pinged, and Brian stepped out.

He saw his daughter, alone, standing on the chair, and immediately went over to her – realising with dismay that she was muttering to herself. And he became fearful. For her. For her mental health.

'Milly...?' he said, his voice cracking, a hint of his own fragility.

She paused, before continuing painting.

'Milly,' he repeated louder, stopping just to the side of her. 'Please come down, love. Come back with me.'

She turned round only briefly, paint smears on her face. Her eyes were dark, pupils dilated. 'I-I need to do this,' she mumbled. 'Mum told me I had to finish...' Dabbing the brush onto the palette, she threw herself back into painting.

Brian caught his breath, the dread becoming real. But he kept eyes fixed on the back of her head. Her messy brown tousle of hair. He daren't look at the murals, afraid of what horrors it might reveal about his daughter's state of mind. 'Please,' he begged.

Just then, the elevator pinged once more, and Ilse and Tai ran out – slowing as they absorbed the frenzied wall paintings with wide eyes.

When they stopped next to Brian, he shook his head at them. 'I-I can't make her stop.'

'Don't!' said Ilse, just as Tai said 'She's almost finished.'

Ilse slipped her hand into Brian's and pulled him back, and they all watched quietly as Milly continued muttering and attacking the wall with her paintbrush.

At long last, after nearly two hours, Milly stepped off the chair for the last time. Putting the palette and brushes down, she wiped her hands on the filthy tea-towel. Her cheeks were red, dark circles under her eyes. She was breathing heavily, trying to quell her emotions.

For several minutes, Ilse and Tai looked over the wall with silent disbelief – their eyes tracing every detail. 'It's beautiful,' remarked Tai, 'but... depressing.'

Ilse began to sniffle, eventually bursting into tears. 'I-is it really true...?' She pushed herself against Tai and held on to him, nerves rattled. 'Is this what's going to happen?'

They both looked at Milly, but no answers came.

Still, Brian could not bring himself to look at the paintings. His eyes remained fixed on his daughter as he ventured closer. 'Come on, Midge,' he said gently, pushing aside a strand of her hair that had fallen over her face. 'Let's get you home and cleaned up.'

This time, Milly did not resist. She was exhausted.

Brian put his arm around her thin shoulders and steered her toward the elevator. They all went inside, the doors sliding smoothly closed.

As night drew closer, the shadowy divide in the corridor gradually lowered by degrees. Softly, slowly, the beautiful but awful images were plunged into a dusky gloaming veil.

35 SIX DAYS

The young Spanish woman was taking the baby girl around the zoo.

Nestled in her pushchair, a pretty dark-haired infant squealed with delight each time they stopped to see an animal.

But as they went from one exhibit to the other, the baby kept looking through the crowds – obsessively – searching constantly. She leant forward, straining against the harness, trying to make out people's faces as they walked past.

Neither noticed her pacifier dropping to the ground, until someone called out from behind, 'Excuse me!'

Turning round, the woman was surprised to find an elderly lady waving at her. The lady stooped down to pick up the pastel-pink pacifier from the ground, holding it in the air. 'I think you dropped this!' she called out.

Running back, the woman smiled with gratitude. 'Ah, yes, that's ours! Thank you so much.'

'You're welcome,' said the old lady before walking on.

When the woman returned to the pushchair, to her shock she saw that it was empty! She looked frantically around. 'Evie!' she called out. 'Evie!'

Several passersby stopped, and one of them, a kindly African woman, asked, 'Has your daughter gone walkabout? I'm sure she can't be far away. We can help you look for her.' Standing next to her, her 12-year-old son looked less than interested.

'No, no. She can't walk yet. She can barely crawl. Someone's taken her! Evie! Evie!' she cried out, stricken.

The African lady gasped and quickly got out her mobile, 'I'll call 999.'

But the Spanish woman covered the phone with her hand. 'No! Don't,' she said firmly. 'We'll deal with it.'

Raising a sassy eyebrow, the African lady tucked the mobile into her handbag. 'Okay, dear. Whatever. Good luck finding her!' she said, as she walked off into the crowds with her son.

•••————————————————————•••

Several miles away, in a detached two-bed house on the outskirts of London, a middle-aged man was sitting in front of an old television, furiously pushing buttons on his game controller and shouting at the screen as he played Football Manager. On the coffee table in front of him was a half-drunk mug of tea, his mobile phone, and a 9mm Glock 17.

When he lost the match, he fell back with frustration against the sofa, throwing the controller down. 'Stupid game!' he grumbled, and crossed his arms in protest. Leaning forward, he gulped down the tea – it was stone cold, and he grimaced, 'Eurgh!' He was just about to get up and make a fresh cup, when the phone caught his attention – yet the screen was blank, there was no ringing, and no notifications. 'Who's calling now,' he mumbled to himself as he picked it up and tapped the black screen. 'Ah, it's you. Afternoon, boss!' he said, despite no-one being on the line.

He stopped to listen for a minute – to complete silence – and eventually nodded. 'Got it. Okay, okay. When're they coming?'

Still silence.

He looked at his watch. 'Five? That's in half an hour. Okay, sure, sure. I'll let them in and do a handover... Yeah, nothing out of the ordinary... What's that? No need to send a report? Brill! I'll just make my way home then. All right, boss, see you tomorrow!'

He put the phone down and looked at his watch again. Still time for a cuppa. Getting up, he tucked the gun in his holster and went to the kitchen. He felt lighter, relieved to be absolved of his duty. The girl he was babysitting looked ill, really ill. And he felt bad that they weren't getting her any medical help. He definitely didn't want to be around if she died.

Upstairs, one of the bedrooms was, unusually, padlocked from the outside.

Inside lay a frail young woman, stirring awake. She was terribly sick. Taking a moment to realise where she was, she groaned when she

348

remembered what that dull ache in the centre of her chest was: the constant pining for her baby daughter and her husband.

Up to now, just the thought of them was keeping her alive. But this past day, as she grew weaker and weaker, something was telling her to let go. But how could she? When her love for them was so entangled, twisted and knotted, into the very fabric of her. Into the heart and guts of her.

But the spreading cancer was draining her of hope. Eventually making her lose the will to live. She refused the food and drink they brought her. Instead, she waited impatiently for Death. Waited for his dark embrace. Barely conscious, she sensed that he was close, so close. Smelled the stench of his poisonous breath – felt it hot against the nape of her neck.

'I'm ready for you,' she murmured, delirious, her mouth dry as a bone. 'I'm ready.' She lay back, waiting, always waiting.

Still, Death did not take her.

'You're playing with me,' she grumbled. 'Y-you're cruel, really cruel...'

There came movement just outside the window.

Her bloodshot eyes looked up to see a grey-blue sky and serene clouds gliding elegantly. A sparrow hopped onto the ledge, its little head bending to one side as it peered into the room. It seemed to be looking directly at her.

'You again,' breathed Calista, mollified by its friendly face.

The sound of footsteps came from the other side of the door, someone unlocked it, and Calista closed her eyes, dreading the sight of O'Connor's sneering face. She hated him.

Instead, a pretty blonde woman walked in wearing a brown pinstripe suit, her long hair tied back in a ponytail – when she caught sight of Calista so sick on the bed, her face dropped, and she immediately went to her. 'Calista!' she breathed. 'You poor thing! I'm agent D2. I've come to get you out of here.'

Calista managed to look up at her, hardly believing. Wondering whether she was dreaming. 'Really?' she asked, her voice cracking with emotion.

D2 nodded.

'A-and Jake? Evie?' she asked, hopeful.

'We found them! They're waiting outside in the car.'

Calista's heart burst. 'Th-thank you! But… h-how did you find me?'

'It's a long story, but in a nutshell, Fitzsimmons orchestrated everything.' She glanced up at the window. 'And our little bird friend helped too,' she smiled. 'I know! Sounds crazy! Anyway,' D2 gently touched Calista's shoulder, 'we'd better go. They're waiting for you.'

Just then, they heard the loud pounding of footsteps running up the stairs. Jake appeared at the door. 'Cal!' he cried, appalled at the sight of her. He fell upon the bed.

D2 quickly jumped up. 'I told you to wait in the car.'

Jake only glanced at her, before turning to gaze at his wife. He himself looked bad, like he hadn't slept for a week.

'Jake…' breathed Calista, lifting a hand to his face. He was real, his skin so warm against her cold fingers. 'It's really you.'

Jake cupped her hand in his. 'Babe…' was all he managed to say, before he broke down.

'Don't be sad,' she told him, though her own heart was breaking. She closed her eyes, pushing out tears. They trickled desolately down her cheeks. She looked past him. 'Evie…?'

'She's with Jemima in the car,' Jake sniffed, wiping his face with the back of his hand.

But then they heard the sound of more footsteps climbing the stairs, and a concerned Jemima appeared at the door, holding the sleeping baby. Jemima's eyes creased with sadness when she saw Calista. Carefully, she passed the infant to Jake, and he laid her on the bed in front of her mother.

Calista melted as she gazed upon her baby. She looked perfect. Rosy cheeks, curls of black hair – ivory skin so fresh and smooth, it was almost translucent. She was much bigger than Calista remembered. 'Sh-she's grown,' she murmured, overcome. She stroked the dimples at the back of Evie's hand.

Jake smiled. 'Still a greedy little dumpling.'

They watched her as she slept. A little angel.

At last, Calista said in a monotone, 'There's no more meds…' It wasn't even a question.

Jake couldn't look at her when he acknowledged, 'No.'

Turning to Jemima, Calista told her, 'I… I want to know how long I have,' she murmured, reaching a bone-thin hand toward her.

Jemima's eyes widened, reluctant. But she eventually went over to her, crying.

'It's okay,' murmured Calista.

Tears coursing down her cheeks, Jemima took her hand and closed her eyes for several seconds. When she opened them again, she said with a small, tremulous voice, 'Six days.'

'Six days,' Calista repeated, numb.

Jemima got up and went to D2, who hugged her.

Calista managed to smile sadly as she looked at Jake. 'At least we have some time together! I... I thought I was going to die here, alone. Without you. But now we get to have six whole days together.' She was trying to be optimistic, for his sake.

At last Jake looked up at her, his eyes two dark pits of despair. 'Cal, I... I can't–'

'Shhh,' breathed Calista, interrupting him. 'You can.' She wiped the tears from his cheeks with a trembling thumb. 'You can, for Evie. You have to.'

The baby stirred, gurgling. And they looked down to find her waking. Evie's eyelashes fluttered open, and it took a couple of seconds for her to realise who was before her. She at last cried out, 'Mm-mmm-mm!!' – stretching eager arms, wanting to be picked up. She scrambled up and hugged her mother's emaciated body.

Jake sat at the side of the bed and put his arms around both of them – wishing that the moment could last forever.

After some time, D2 stepped forward. 'It's time to go,' she said gently.

Jemima took the baby, while D2 and Jake helped Calista get up. They just about made it down the stairs together, taking one slow step at a time. Calista was so weak that she leant her full weight onto the both of them. At last they stepped outside, slowly walking several metres to the car – but the exertion was so great, and Calista so sick, that her eyes rolled back and she fainted into Jake's arms.

Calista's mind wove in and out of consciousness as, with great effort, she was lowered inside the car. She flopped onto the seat.

Somebody was calling her name... The car engine roared... started speeding through busy roads... Their bodies being thrown this way and that... Engine revving, tyres screeching... The sound of a car beeping... Angry shouting, get out of the way!

Suddenly there came a juddering crash!!

The car hurtling out of control.

A bang!!

And then stillness.

The hiss of steam.

The steady clicking of a broken indicator.

D2 in the driver's seat, bent over, bloody and still.

Someone was huffing, trying to heave the door open.

They pulled out Calista.

She coughed, and spluttered.

Her mind a daze.

The world spinning.

A baby was crying – high-pitched and inconsolable.

A sound, so familiar. Yet so distressed.

At last, through the haze, Calista came to with a start, and suddenly realised who was crying.

It was the one thing that pulled her out of the torpor.

The urgency of a daughter's need. A mother's irrepressible love.

Her head hurt so bad. Her heart racing.

She looked around, blind with panic.

'Evie!' she gasped.

36 LIFE IMITATING ART...

The protest in Trafalgar Square started out as a peaceful one.

An assorted crowd of almost 100 people was surrounded by policemen wearing yellow high-vis jackets. Flocks of pigeons fluttered this way and that, weaving between them, searching for morsels.

Several demonstrators held up crudely-written placards:

'SAY NO TO CONTAMINATION OF OUR GENE POOL!'

'WE ARE NOT A SCIENCE EXPERIMENT.'

'MIND TERRORISTS MASQUERADING AS CHILDREN!'

'BANISH THE INGENIOUS!'

Every now and then the crowd broke out into a chant: 'Hell no, make them go! Hell no, make them go!'

Passers either stopped to watch, or walked by with mild interest.

As Brian drove past them, he had to stop at the traffic lights when they turned red. Ilse, in the seat behind him, pressed her nose against the window and stared at the maddened crowd, gawping – her breath fogging the glass. In her mind, came a scene from Milly's paintings: an enraged group of people – men, women, children – holding banners, shouting out, and waving fists. She remembered how Milly had painted their eyes crazed with hate. 'Tai...' she said, turning to tug on his sleeve. She pressed the button to open the window for him to see, and it glided down.

Tai peered over her shoulder, and his mouth dropped when he saw the protestors.

Suddenly, an elderly man at the front of the crowd pointed at their car. Right at Ilse. 'Look!' cried the old man, his voice hoarse. 'That girl! That's one of them Ingenious!! I recognise her from the courtroom!'

The crowd heaved and swelled, bursting out and running toward the car. Brian saw them and panicked, but the crosswise traffic was still blocking his way.

'We have to go!' cried Ilse.

'Now!' shouted Tai.

But it was too late, the crowd was already spilling into the road and surrounding the car, raw hate for the Ingenious children twisted into their expressions. 'Get them!!' they cried.

Quickly Ilse tried to close the window, but someone was already reaching inside – a burly man opened her door, grabbed the collar of her jacket and pulled her out. 'Ow!' cried Ilse, squirming.

Someone else reached through the open door and dragged Tai out.

Brian jumped out of the car to try and help them, just as a man bashed the stick of his placard against the windscreen, crazing the glass with cracks.

Milly screamed, and found herself being pulled out and jostled by the crowds. An older woman hurled abuse at her, and spat at her.

The police quickly descended on the mob, shouting out at them. But the crowd – blind with rage – fought back at the police, kicking and punching. The police battered the offenders with their truncheons to try and hold them back. Complete chaos ensued.

Someone punched Brian, and he fell to the ground.

'Dad!' cried Milly, as she herself was becoming engulfed by the swarming crowd.

Tai suddenly shouted out at the top of his voice, 'Get away!! Leave us alone!!' He planted his feet firmly on the ground and – with the grace of a ballet dancer – moved his body into the Shaolin bow stance. Toes pointing forward, one fist tucked by his waist, and the other hand held out in front, flat and straight.

Alarmed, the seething crowd let go of the children – and stepped back, fearful of what he might do.

Both Milly and Ilse followed Tai's lead, and they too took up the same position. All three children stood poised. In the middle of the angry crowd.

Just as Milly had painted in her mural.

•••———————————————•••

Mei Hui had been taken to a safehouse by the shinobi.

It seemed as if it was in the middle of nowhere – a secluded hut nestled amongst the trees of lowland forest.

When they had arrived there in the dark of night, she had fallen asleep almost as soon as her head hit the pillow.

Waking up the next morning, the ninja were nowhere to be seen. But she knew they must not be far. They had left the stove burning with logs, and on top was a steaming kettle filled with water. A rickety old table, its legs mottled with woodworm holes, was laid out with a cloth and a plate of food: small packets of crackers, cheese, and some grapes. She pounced on it and ate heartily. She was starving.

After she had eaten her fill, and made herself some tea – she sat quietly as she sipped on the delicate yellow liquid, reflecting on last night's disturbing dreams. So many dreams, very different from before. As if painted, in animation. Scene after scene, starting with events from years ago, when she had discovered the other children in London. Jemima, Milly, Tai. Discovered their abilities. Then they found Karl – and delved into his terrible mind, fearful of losing themselves within it. She dreamt too of a painted whorl of so many sharks – tiger, whale, megamouth, dogfish – careening through icy waters. Included in the painting was the lonely mother whale, who had saved them.

Mei Hui remembered more dreams about finding Saffie in the Amazon jungle, and also when they discovered Fitzsimmons, the progenitor of their powers. Seeing his twisted life, hearing his twisted thoughts. And again, she trembled at the thought of having his DNA embedded within her. Project Ingenious, nothing more than a Victor Frankenstein experiment, cobbling together the DNA of three different people into tiny embryos – an abusive violation of what was natural.

Mei Hui gulped down her tea with shaking hands. She was only 17 years old, but now, tired and alone, she felt like 70. Her bones, so weary, so dry.

But the dreams hadn't stopped with the past.

They told her about now.

They told her about the future.

And as Mei Hui got up, went to the bathroom to splash cold water on ruddy cheeks, she thought about that future as she paused to stare at herself in the mirror. Roaming over the marks of ingrained dirt. Haggard eyes. The delicate line of tense lips.

She paused when she heard outside the faraway barking of dogs – but it did not surprise her. For she pictured, in her mind's eye, the very last dream. Of Milly's artwork painted on a seemingly endless wall. Of someone small, like her. Surrounded by police officers tugging on leads connected to ferocious dogs.

Before Mei Hui walked outside, she took one last look around the sparse hut. Her chest felt funny, as if it were made of jelly.

Tugging open the wooden door, it creaked with reluctance.

Outside, the forest was beautiful. Sunlight glinting through the canopy.

Mei Hui walked into one of the shafts of light, closed her eyes, and lifted her face toward the sky. It was wonderfully pure; sublimely elemental.

A fiery sun.

Damp earth underfoot.

Pure fresh air.

Water, leaking from her eyes.

Her entire being sizzled from the elements surrounding her, enveloping her. Becoming her.

She felt so keenly the others then. The other children. They were so far away. So faint. Yet still there.

They calmed her. Stopped her from shaking.

Eyes still closed, Mei Hui breathed deeply, filling her lungs.

She listened, as the barking got louder.

The crunch of feet running toward her through the undergrowth. Surrounding her.

Men shouting. Warning her. Don't move!!

She could taste their fear.

It was sharp, acidic.

When at last she slowly opened her eyes, she saw them.

Eight soldiers in camouflage combat gear.

Two German shepherds straining on leashes – noses furrowed, teeth bared, salivating as they barked so loudly it hurt her ears.

The soldiers jerked back when Mei Hui suddenly moved into the Shaolin bow stance – her movements as fluid and elegant as a dancer's. Mesmerising to watch.

She spoke to them with a soft voice that they could barely hear. 'Get away, please. Leave me alone,' she asked politely, her eyes darting to each of their faces. 'We mean you no harm.' She glanced over their shoulders. And the men turned to see what she was looking at, who she meant by 'we'.

Five ninjas had appeared, silently, out of nowhere. One of them, a female, wearing iron claws on her hands.

They too assumed the same bow stance as Mei Hui. Ready and poised to fight. Like coiled cobras about to spring.

•••————————————————————————•••

As Saffie and her parents glided in their trusty old voadeira boat along the Rio Branco, through the dense dawn mists, they could not believe it when here and there the fog rolled away to reveal a black, barren landscape just beyond the east bank. It was nothing but a smouldering wasteland. Centuries old trees and plants razed to the ground in just a matter of weeks. Where once the exotic perfume of flowers and musty vegetation filled the air, now there was only the scent of burnt wood, singed fur, and anguish. If purgatory existed, and had a smell, this would be it.

For the family, there were no more tears, no words left to speak, as sorrowful eyes combed the area for any people or wildlife in need of help. But the impossibility of survivors from such blazing infernos soon became apparent.

Still, the three silently made their way downstream in their boat, discovering too – with equal alarm – that the water level of the Branco was many metres lower, the banks steeper, and Ignacio therefore had to go at a slower speed, and steer with great skill around loads of sediment that rose treacherously here and there from the riverbed.

Yet other boats sped recklessly past them in the same direction – toward Manaus. A race to get into town before supplies ran out.

'They are going too fast!' grumbled Alma indignantly, each time the wake and wash of a speeding boat rocked them. 'They will cause an accident!'

Her words proved to be premonitory when, an hour later, they navigated around a narrow riverbend to find a large ferry speckled with rust, and brimming with passengers – Ignacio had to quickly swerve to stay clear of it. The ferry had docked to let more people board, though the other passengers were shouting angrily that they were already badly overloaded. The captain ignored their protestations; he could not argue with them. The maximum capacity was usually about 200 people, but there may well have been over 500 crammed onto the decks.

Ignacio's little voadeira glided past them, and Saffie's eyes glossed over the passengers. She suddenly realised that one of them was waving excitedly at her. He was a small tribesman with shiny black pudding-bowl hair held back by a circlet of bright yellow toucan feathers. He was holding the hand of a small boy standing next to him.

It took a few seconds for Saffie to realise who he was, out of his natural habitat and wearing incongruous clothes – a purple striped t-shirt and orange shorts. It was the isolados tribesman whom she had met on her way to the floating sky island, in the Anavilhanas.

'Stop the boat!' she told her father. She turned back to the tribesman and waved heartily. 'Olá!'

'Olá!' he called back with a smile. 'It is good to see you, daughter of Mother Earth!'

Curious people on the ferry turned to see who this 'daughter of Mother Earth' was – their eyes gleaming with curiosity.

'Are your family okay?' Saffie asked with trepidation, realising that the only reason why he would be on the boat, so far away from home, was because the fires must have forced them out.

He glanced down at the toddler and smiled. 'Yes, we are all fine. My little brother… and my family are here, and others from my tribe. We left as soon as we felt the winds change. You cannot argue with the wind and the fire – it is the breath of Mother Earth. And the fire is her anger.' He shook his head with regret. 'It is very strange and unsettling – the winds are not supposed to change this way, the waters are rising higher now than before, and even the mists are thickening.' He looked around at the dense fog as it crept out of the jungle on the west bank, rolling slowly across the water. He suddenly thought of something. 'Is your cub okay?' he asked.

Saffie nodded. 'Yes, he is very well.' Or at least, she hoped he was. She motioned toward her parents. 'This is my mother and father.'

Both Alma and Ignacio gave them a friendly wave.

The little toddler smiled shyly and hid behind his brother's legs.

'Thank you by the way,' said Saffie. 'For the tip about the entrance to the tepui. It saved me a lot of time.'

The tribesman's eyes widened. 'That you made it through the tunnel is a miracle! And were there really giant tarantulas guarding the golden flowers?'

Saffie nodded, 'Yes. But I managed to get past them.'

He leaned forward with astonished wonder. 'Then you truly must be daughter of Mother Earth!'

Saffie looked nervously at the other passengers, an unexpected audience shamelessly eavesdropping on their conversation. 'No, no,' was all she managed to say.

'Did the medicine help your cub?' he asked.

Raising an eyebrow, Saffie said evasively, 'In a way, it did, yes.' She waved kindly at him, needing to change the subject. 'Anyway, thank you again! We have to go now. I wish you and your family all the best.'

The young man waved back, but before she could leave, he started speaking to her in a language that she did not understand, the mother tongue of his tribe. He spoke for several minutes – words so impassioned, and uttered with such gravitas, that Saffie felt tears come to her eyes. When he finished, she touched her chest, and in response, he touched his.

Her heart was breaking, for the isolados who wanted only to be left alone to hunt and farm on their own land, yet were compelled to leave everything they had known for generations – forced out by hidden invaders who burned down the land in order to steal it from right under their feet. And now that the tribesmen had fled, if the isolados survived the diseases they were being exposed to, they would instead be doomed to a slow death of nothing... No land, no home, no future.

Alma drew closer, and put an arm around Saffie. Yet again, there were no words as Ignacio started up the engine and they chugged away down the river.

Suddenly there was a loud boom!

They turned to find a speeding boat crashing into the stern of the ferry. A small orange explosion flared up on the boat, and its two occupants rolled out, splashing into the water.

Though the boat disintegrated instantly, the ferry itself was relatively unscathed. But the passengers – one and all – rushed over to the port side to see what had happened. Saffie gasped as she watched the ferry lean and creak from the skewed weight. It seemed to happen both in slow motion, yet incredibly quickly. And before they knew it, the entire ferry was tipping sideways – capsizing into the water!

People screamed and dropped and fell and jumped – either crushed by the sheer weight of others, or tumbling into the river.

The waters surrounding the ferry started bubbling and boiling in a white frenzy.

Alma gasped. 'Piranhas!!' The receding waters had reduced their food supplies, making them ravenous for flesh.

Ignacio immediately turned the boat round, and they held on for dear life as they went back to help – though they could not get too close to the sinking ferry, for fear of being sucked into the vortex of water. Ignacio and Alma frantically began pulling people aboard.

The maelstrom of hundreds of bodies, screaming, splashing, struggling for air, became a feeding frenzy for the piranhas. Soon, caimans and large catfish joined them. In the chaos, Ignacio's boat rocked wildly from side to side, and it was all they could do not to fall into the water themselves.

Saffie half stood, half held onto the rim of the boat, as she anxiously scanned the water for the tribesman and his little brother. Anger suddenly welled up inside her. Anger for such reckless boat-driving. Anger for the over-crowded ferry. Anger for the wildfires, and the loss of life. It all bubbled up, like the water. Exploding out of her.

She bashed the side of the boat with her fists repeatedly. 'No! No! No!!' she cried, over and over.

Suddenly, the piranhas stopped their attack.

It went quiet.

The waters calmed.

People watched in astonishment as the silvery fish gradually backed off – their gaping mouths lined with razor-sharp teeth, their round glassy eyes staring right at them. Just like that, the piranhas and caiman and catfish turned, and bolted outwards and away. Leaving streaks of white water trailing behind them.

The remaining survivors – interspersed among those floating dead or unconscious in the water – looked around, dazed and in shock, as they bobbed up and down. They eventually swam awkwardly to the bank, hampered by their wounds, either silent, or weeping, or gasping for air.

Saffie noticed something in the water, and she dived right in.

She swam out to a floating child, and pulled him back to land.

Wading onto the bank, she cradled the precious infant against her chest, his skinny arms dangling limply as she picked her way over mud criss-crossed with tangled tree roots – pink water showering down from them.

The boy's little body was so floppy.

So still.

In her heart, Saffie knew. The child was dead.

She collapsed into a heap and sobbed and sobbed over the lifeless infant.

People were passing her as they too waded out of the water, limping, or cradling wounded arms – murmuring to her as they went. 'Filha da Mãe Terra.' Daughter of Mother Earth. The whisper rippled through the crowds like a chant, like lyrics to the background music of sobbing and groaning. Someone pointed a finger at her. 'She is one of them. Uma garota Engenhosa.' An Ingenious girl. And that too was muttered as they passed.

Filha da Mãe Terra.

Garota Engenhosa.

But Saffie was too distraught to care.

As she bent over the little boy.

Felt the child's body warmth seep slowly away.

Somehow she knew that she was three minutes and 18 seconds too late. That was how long he had been dead.

Her mind ticked as the seconds passed.

19 seconds...

20 seconds...

Garota Engenhosa.

Filha da Mãe Terra.

As Saffie wallowed in grief, in her mind floated a picture. A painting.

Of a girl swimming in a river, surrounded by a multitude of caimans and fish.

It seemed as if the river were made from tears.

The animals, painted with blood.

And the air and sky were rendered from their collective breaths.

In her mind's eye, Saffie saw Milly muttering to herself as she painted that very scene. Her mind connecting with all of them as she swung the brush in wild strokes.

45 seconds...

46 seconds...

'Milly, stop,' Saffie whimpered desperately. 'Please. Just stop.'

•••————————————————————————•••

Inder hadn't left the hospital since he discovered Alia there weeks ago.

His parents were bringing fresh clothes, towels, soap, toothpaste, drinks, and plenty of delicious food.

But though the boy looked after Alia attentively during the day, at night, he slept in the chair next to her, slumped, and so deep in sleep it was as if he was comatose. His head filling with an abundance of dreams.

There was one in particular.

Someone painting, frenzied, incoherent mumbling. The canvas, a wall that seemed to go on and on with picture after picture.

Inder was drawn to two images in particular – surprised to see them so clearly in his dreams. They sparkled with detail.

The first painting was of him, cross-legged on a newspaper on the pavement, telling a story to a small crowd of children. All of them were listening with rapt attention – except for Ria. She was glancing at someone walking up behind Inder. A beautiful girl in a salwar kameez as blue as the sky. The second painting was a close-up of the girl's face, as she gazed at the storyteller, who had not yet noticed her. The painting was beautifully rendered. Each brushstroke capturing the wonder in her eyes, the awe on her face, the blossoming of something in her expression, so delicate, so fragile, yet unmistakeable. Love.

Inder gasped, his heart leapt, as he realised – at last!

Alia had already begun to fall for him, *before* he had even noticed her. The painting had encapsulated those precious, revealing moments – when Alia saw him for the first time, and listened, entranced, to his storytelling.

Overcome with immense relief, Inder at last became settled in his heart. Knowing now that his mind hadn't forced Alia's love. That he wasn't the monster he thought he was. *Thank goodness!* he thought to himself, shaking with emotion. *Thank goodness.*

He found himself waking up that night, weeping.

It seemed that Inder's head was filled with dream after dream.

Even when Mahit and Azarin came to visit, they were surprised to find Inder always there, asleep most of the time.

'He is a growing boy,' whispered Azarin to her husband. 'They have both been through a lot.'

Mahit looked suspiciously at the unconscious Inder. 'It is not right for a young man to be sleeping so much. I will wake him up and ask him what's going on with all this sleeping.'

But Azarin gently pulled him away. 'He might have been tending to her all night, Mahit. We don't know. The nurse did tell me Alia has been calling out in her sleep, perhaps suffering from nightmares. Please, let him rest.'

And so, the couple sat down on the other side of the bed and waited patiently for their daughter to wake up. Mahit noticed something on his daughter's hand. 'What is that thing, there,' he asked his wife, pointing.

Gently, Azarin took Alia's hand and inspected the object around one of her fingers. 'It... it looks like a ring-pull, from a drinks can...' She smiled briefly, looking from Alia to Inder. 'The two are dreaming of getting married I'm sure.'

Mahit harrumphed and raised an eyebrow. He had given his consent, reluctantly, and he knew his wife would never allow him to go back on his word.

The couple settled into their seats, and waited.

It was strangely appealing, poring over the two youngsters as they slept – a beautiful serenity about them. The serenity was infectious.

That was until the dreams came, and Inder began babbling in his sleep. Mahit and Azarin stopped what they were doing – the former had been reading emails on his phone, and the latter making notes for Alia's wedding. They listened to Inder's sleep-talking with curiosity. As time passed, his mumblings became more and more frenzied:

'You need to leave. Now!! They're coming for you!'

'Wake up! Wake up!!'

'The world has turned against us.'

At last, Inder quietened, and whispered in his sleep, 'You. You're the last Ingenious child.'

And then finally he said, 'I think... I think I can tell the future.'

Mahit and Azarin looked at each other with round eyes.

'Ingenious...?' Mahit repeated, aghast, his mind slowly piecing together recent news reports. 'Tell the future...?' he echoed in disbelief. He suddenly stood up, pointing a shaky finger at the sleeping boy. 'H-he's one of them!' he said, fearful. A trembling hand took out a mobile phone from his pocket. With trepidation, he dialled 112.

Fifteen minutes later, Inder found himself waking up.

As always, he looked first for Alia. But the bed was empty, the crumpled sheets hastily thrown back. Rubbing his eyes and stifling a yawn he shuffled out into the corridor, but saw that that was empty too. Puzzled, he wandered to the end of the corridor and looked out of the window, shielding his eyes from the bright sun.

Police sirens wailed, and a convoy of white cars, striped red and blue, rushed along the road. They screeched to a halt next to the hospital, and out jumped policemen dressed in beige uniforms and berets. They pulled guns from holsters and ran straight into the building.

Alarmed, Inder backed away. He quickly turned and ran down the corridor, toward the lift, but went for the stairs instead. Heart thudding wildly, he jumped down two steps, sometimes three, at a time. When he heard a rush of footsteps from the ground floor, he diverted out onto the first floor and ran along the corridor. Opening the window, he climbed out, and dangled down, holding onto the ledge for dear life. He couldn't gauge how far his feet were from the grass, but he mustered boldness and jumped, rolling onto his back. He flipped over to his front, got up, and looked all around. Only to hear footsteps close behind.

He turned.

Saw three advancing policemen pointing their guns at him.

Their beige shirts were damp with sweat, their foreheads glistening.

Without understanding how, or why, Inder found his body moving of its own accord. Limbs swinging as elegantly and gracefully as a ballet dancer's, into the Shaolin bow stance.

He stared at the policemen's faces on either side of his outstretched hand. 'Please get away!' he called out politely. 'Leave me alone. I mean you no harm.'

The policemen glanced at each other nervously before re-gripping their guns. One of them shouted, 'Don't make any sudden movements! You're under arrest!' He unhooked a pair of handcuffs from the side of his belt and advanced.

37 PAIN AND HUMANITY

'Him gaan! Him bin gaan fi ages – whulla dem ave. Dem ave sup'm bad ave happen. Mi jus' kno it!'

Tyaishia was shouting at the Professor, red-faced, and waving her arms hysterically – lapsing back into Jamaican in all the excitement. 'Yuh betta get yuh agents onto dem. Please, Prof. Please!!'

The two were standing in front of each other in the BC, close enough for the Professor to feel her hot anxious breath. The Professor lifted his head slightly toward the ceiling. 'Jasmine, recall any nearby agents. Immediately. Ilse, Milly, Tai, and Brian are missing. I need you to trace them straight away.'

'The children are no longer in Avernus. Would you like me to trawl the network of street CCTV?'

'Yes!' snapped the Professor, annoyed that they had left the safety of the underground shelter. 'Once you locate them, send the agents to their location.'

'I'm sorry, Professor, but the agents have gone dark. I am unable to reach them.'

The Professor suddenly remembered. Fitzsimmons had taken control of most of them. 'Yes, yes, of course... So where's D2? She should have been back by now, with Cal, Jake, and the baby. Jemima was with them too.'

'Unfortunately, her tracker is not traceable.'

'What?!' exclaimed the Professor.

Jasmine continued. 'I have also checked all available footage for Brian, Milly, Tai, and Ilse through London's CCTV cameras. Their last known location was when they left Vivra Towers half an hour ago. But there is no footage of their whereabouts at this current time. Would you like me to widen the search?'

The Professor felt sick. Closing his eyes, he mumbled, 'This can't be happening...' He realised that there was only one thing left to do.

'Professor,' said Jasmine. 'Fitzsimmons is asking for you.'

The old man's heart quickened. It was as if Fitzsimmons had read his mind – literally. Either that, or his timing was uncanny. The Professor flicked his cane open and turned to leave.

Tyaishia stepped out of the way. 'Be careful, Prof. Mi nuh truss dat man!'

The Professor couldn't help thinking, *That makes two of us...* He held his breath, realising that – from now on – he had to somehow rein in his thoughts.

They stood across from each other, in the holding cell.

One old man, cradling a walking stick in both hands to keep them from trembling, and another old man with a grotesque face, staring fixedly into the unseeing eyes of the other.

'We made a pact,' said the Professor, 'that if you refrained from using your mind-control powers, I would not drug you.'

Fitzsimmons did not answer straight away, but eventually said, 'And I kept my promise. I did not *control* you, or anyone. I simply read your mind.' He paused, thoughtful. 'You... fear me.'

The Professor clenched his teeth with frustration. 'Fear you? Yes, of course I do. But at the same time, I know that you would not harm me, or anyone else here, because you need the children on your side. Hurt me, and they will turn against you.'

'That is true,' said Fitzsimmons resignedly. 'Though, I'm sure you've thought of how easily I could manipulate *their* minds – just enough to keep them on my side. If I wanted, I could even make them love me. Perhaps as much, maybe even more, than they love you.'

The Professor thought for a moment. 'I did think of that possibility. But... isn't love predicated on free will? If it's not of their own volition, then it's not love. It's just... control.'

Fitzsimmons grunted. 'And do you think I care? Do you think I give a damn what kind of devotion they have for me?!'

The Professor said quietly, 'I-I don't believe what you say. Only a monster would try to force love. That would be… inhuman. I do believe, very much, that the children are more than mere pawns to you – that they are more than just a way to preserve your heredity. What tells me otherwise is your history – your feelings for Georgina Whyte. You loved her, *really* loved her. And you never gave up hope that she would come back to you. If you're the same man that she fell in love with – then yes, I do think you care.'

Sniffing, Fitzsimmons said with a withered tone, 'That was a long time ago, Professor. People change.' He was about to say something more when he suddenly flinched, sucked in breath, and closed his eyes.

The Professor sensed something was wrong. 'What's happened?! Is it… is it the children?' he asked, half fearing the answer.

When Fitzsimmons opened his eyes again, they were filled with dread. 'Jemima!!' he groaned.

The tone of his voice made the Professor tingle with fear. He knew Jemima had gone with D2 and Jake, to collect Calista.

'There has been a car crash! Just now,' said Fitzsimmons. He lowered his head as he concentrated, his breath ragged. 'H-her thoughts have gone completely silent… I-I can't hear them. I have to go to her!'

The next thing the Professor heard was the scraping back of a chair. Feet running to the door. The bolts opening, unlocked by the guards – the door swinging wide open as they let him out. 'Wait!' shouted the Professor, getting up. But Fitzsimmons' footsteps were already fading down the corridor.

'Jasmine!' the Professor called out. 'Keep trace of Fitzsimmons at all times. I need to know where he's going.'

'On it!' she replied.

'And notify the Chauffeur to meet me in the garage. To follow him.'

'He has been told.'

'Acuzio!' called out the Professor. 'Here boy!'

After several impatient seconds, Acuzio appeared and stood in front of him, panting.

The Professor grabbed hold of his harness. 'Take me to the car, Acuzio. Now!'

•••———————————————————————•••

Jeremy Fitzsimmons sprinted all the way up to the garage. He saw that the Chauffeur was already there, about to get into the car. Shoving him out of the way, he jumped into the FX4 himself and revved the engine as he waited impatiently for the garage doors to slide open. At last he zoomed out, and sped off.

The Chauffeur picked himself up from the floor, dazed and angry. He dusted himself down as he watched his precious FX4 disappear down the road. When he turned, he was surprised to find the Professor and Acuzio running toward him, out of breath.

Take the other car! signed the Professor urgently. *We need to follow him! Something's happened to Jemima and Calista. Fitzsimmons has gone to find them.*

The Chauffeur signed back at him. *The other car is not ready. I need to fill it with petrol, and replace the battery.*

Please, hurry! the Professor told him, sick with worry.

The Chauffeur sprang into action.

Fitzsimmons raced down the motorway, flooring the accelerator as he drove at top speed, weaving between the traffic. He turned off the A40, and took a shortcut via the Outer Circle road through Regent's Park. He glanced right, at something tall, and caught a glimpse of a giraffe behind a fence, serenely pulling off leaves from the top of a tree – and realised that that was where the zoo was. The giraffe snorted and eyed Fitzsimmons momentarily as he sped past.

Fitzsimmons turned left, over Macclesfield Bridge, and jumped the traffic lights to the screeching of tyres and angry beeping. He sped down Avenue Road – sensing that he had almost reached Jemima.

His heart leapt when he saw what was in the middle of the road.

A crumpled blue car smashed into the left side of another – a mangled mess. Steam was rising from the crushed bonnet. People were standing around, looking into the vehicles. Fitzsimmons screeched to a halt, jumped out, and ran over. At the sight of him, people screamed, others gasped and shrunk back from fright. But he took no heed. He soon saw that a motionless Jemima was in the car, in the front seat, a trickle of blood running from her temple down a cheek. Agent D2 was slumped next to her in the driver's seat. Circling the black car, Fitzsimmons found a dazed, grey-faced Calista sitting on the side of the road, clutching a baby in her lap. Jake was heaving on the driver's door with all his might.

Fitzsimmons pushed him aside, and strenuously tugged on it himself – wincing and grunting through gritted teeth. But it was no use. It wouldn't budge. He straightened, caught his breath, and looked back down the road – toward the zoo. With an arm he motioned toward it. *Come! Hurry!!* And he stared at a single point in the distance.

Sirens grew louder and louder, until an ambulance appeared and screeched to a halt. Two paramedics jumped out, but stopped in their tracks when they saw Fitzsimmons, their eyes widening with horror. They were about to radio for back-up when Fitzsimmons held his hand out to them. *Stop!!* And they froze in their tracks.

In the distance came the sound of trumpeting, the clanging crash of metal gates being smashed open and trampled down. People screaming. Running off in all directions.

Cars screeched to a halt, traffic stopped, as a hulking herd of elephants emerged from the distant zoo gates, spilling out onto the road. Stampeding toward Fitzsimmons. They wove between the vehicles, running at top speed – only slowing to a halt when they reached the two mangled cars. The gathered crowd screamed and ran off, others hid behind trees, and some even took out their phones to record the astonishing spectacle.

Fitzsimmons stepped back as the elephants neared, and two of them, two males, came forward and huddled around the driver's door of the black car. Their trunks threaded through the broken window and looped back so that they could pull the door from the inside. Their thick skin was being cut and nicked by the glass, drips of blood sprinkling around, but it did not stop them from pulling and pulling. The sound of metal warped and creaked until the entire door at last popped off, and they threw it aside. Job done, the elephants reversed and rejoined the rest of the herd.

Fitzsimmons quickly dragged out D2 from the driver's seat, dumping her on the ground – Jake pulled her out of harm's way onto the pavement behind some cars. The tallest of the elephants, the matriarch, came forward and crouched down, slipping her trunk into the car. She coiled it gently around Jemima, pulled her out, and – very carefully – laid her on the ground. The elephant then backed away.

Fitzsimmons immediately fell upon the unconscious girl and closed his eyes as he determined the life in her. 9,622 seconds. She was still alive, but only just.

A shiver of relief went through him.

A relief so immense that he couldn't help stooping down to kiss her cheek tenderly, as a father would his daughter. Her skin was soft and cool.

He motioned hurriedly for one of the elephants to come to him, and the baby – a she elephant, the pride of the herd – sidled over. It was impossible for her to resist. She was only three months old, just over a metre tall – her large ears flapping back and forth. Callously, Fitzsimmons grabbed hold of her trunk and tugged her to him. Instantly, the elephant disappeared in a cloud of black dust! The man arched with immense pain, teeth grinding, fingers curling, as he absorbed the dark energy and siphoned it directly into Jemima. Electrified, Jemima's whole body sizzled with jolts, and went completely limp.

People screamed and gasped with shock – someone hiding behind a tree, someone else sheltering in a doorway, and another person crouching behind a car. Fitzsimmons looked up and cast narrowed eyes over them – one by one they became still as statues. Their unblinking eyes reddening with fear, impotence, shock.

More sirens.

Flashing police cars appeared.

But when they stopped, the same fate happened to them. The policemen didn't even get out of the cars.

Silence descended.

There was just the two of them.

Fitzsimmons staring fixedly at Jemima.

His awful face, melting with tenderness.

Slowly she opened her eyes. They shimmered crystal blue as she took in every detail of his face, every bulge and pucker of his deformity. 'F-father,' she whispered, lips tugging into a brief smile. She raised a blackened hand and cupped his cheek. 'You came.'

Fitzsimmons gasped with relief, his dark eyes dewed. Overcome with emotion, he was unable to speak. But he didn't need to; Jemima found that she was able to sense his every feeling, his every thought. 'I... I'm okay,' she whispered, coughing. Then she remembered. *The others!*

Fitzsimmons glanced at Calista, Jake, and Evie sitting further along the road. *They're fine,* he told her.

Jemima nodded with relief, but then winced.

It still hurts? asked Fitzsimmons, his brow creasing with concern.

Y-yes, she gasped. *But... it's okay. P-pain is good. At least I know I'm alive from it.*

Tolstoy, Fitzsimmons murmured thoughtfully. He took her hand. *Didn't he also say, if you feel other people's pain, you're human.* He thought of the Professor as he closed his eyes – thought with annoyance of the man's words, and his dogged belief in his humanity. As Fitzsimmons' hand curled around Jemima's, his fingerpads bristled when a slow trickle needled through his nerve fibres, along his arm, through the spinal cord, seeping into his brainstem. Into his brain. He winced as he prised out Jemima's pain. Every throb, every sting, every ache – absorbing it into him. His face draining of colour, thin lips turning a greyish blue.

No! Jemima's eyes filled with tears as she realised what he was doing, silenced by their connection.

Fitzsimmons' entire body throbbed, and he flopped back, smarting from it. After some time, his face deathly pale, his eyes bloodshot, he mustered the strength to ask with a wince, *Mm-better...?*

Jemima nodded sorrowfully. *B-but you shouldn't have!*

Shhh, was all he managed to say, exhausted, his arms limp by his side.

Jemima instead found that she was able to sit up. She curled herself around Fitzsimmons as he trembled from her pain. She wept over him then. Her tears dripping onto his matted beard.

After some time, as the pain dissipated, he glanced up at her with red eyes. *Y-you're crying...* he said, dazed.

Yes. For you. For taking my pain. But also... She shook her head, blinking with disbelief from the things she'd just learnt from their connection. *I can't believe that you killed all those people. A-and the elephant. She was just a baby. You killed her in front of her mother. Without even a thought.* Jemima stared woefully at the she elephant standing by the side of the road, held at bay by Fitzsimmons' mind. She could have sworn she saw dampness glisten in the mother's eyes.

It's just an animal, said Fitzsimmons, feebly. *I had to save you.*

Jemima couldn't answer him, such was her sadness. Her head throbbed with the new powers she had been given, as she absorbed both Fitzsimmons' thoughts and feelings, as well as those of the mother elephant. She pored over the animal's memories, discovering she had carried her baby in pregnancy for almost two years, and that daughter elephants stay with their mothers for life. She absorbed the elephant's confusion, struggling with her child disappearing right in front of her. Not understanding. Yet, deep down, the mother knew – her baby was gone. And somewhere inside the animal, a light went out.

Jemima absorbed all this as she listened to the elephant's low groaning, and watched despair spasm out from her in misty blooms of grey. Breaking her gaze, Jemima sniffled, and turned to Fitzsimmons. *I just... I don't understand,* she cried softly. *Your moral compromise. Can't you feel the mother's pain?*

Fitzsimmons looked down. Stared hard at the tarmac beneath him. *I feel only for you, and the others.*

Yes, I know. I know. You would... you would kill the entire human race. For us.

He mumbled, nonchalant, *A small price to pay.*

Jemima blinked at him with disbelief before turning away.

Unable to look at him any longer.

It was not his physical appearance that she could not bear. It was what was inside. The moral ambiguity. The incongruous jumble of the loathed and the loved. Caring yet uncaring. Murderer and father-figure. The ugliness within someone she had so much wanted to care for.

She battled with her feelings – confusion, confliction – as she stared along the road. Absorbed the sight of the smoking cars for the first time –

the car that had smashed into theirs, on the side where she had sat.

No-one could have survived that point of impact.

She touched her temple where the trickling blood was already drying, but she couldn't find any injury there. Looking down at herself, at her hands, she realised there weren't any body wounds either. Not even a scratch. She turned to see for the first time the bloodied body of D2, just lying there, with deep gashes on her head and arms – confirming what she had suspected. What Fitzsimmons had done for her...

Just then, Acuzio came bounding over, with the Professor running behind.

'Prof!' she called out to him, and the old man's head jerked toward her.

'I'm here,' she said as she got up on unsteady feet and held out her hands.

The dog licked her fingers, while the Professor felt her hand with both of his, and held onto it. 'Jemima! A-are you okay?'

'I'm fine! Not a scratch on me, amazingly,' she said, glancing down at Fitzsimmons. 'Calista, Jake, and the baby are okay too. Fitzsimmons as well.'

The Professor was greatly relieved. 'Thank goodness!'

Fitzsimmons suddenly tried to get up, grunting with pain. 'S-something has happened!' he managed to say. 'To the others.' He closed his eyes and concentrated hard. 'Th-there's a mob. Trafalgar Square. I need to help them!' He tried to get onto his feet, but fell back and collapsed.

'Father!' cried Jemima, and stooped to help him sit up.

Realising how weak he was, Fitzsimmons turned to the elephants. With a single wave of his arm, the elephants trumpeted and shuffled round. With his last iota of energy, Fitzsimmons motioned toward the zoo, before flopping back onto the ground. The elephants started running down the road.

As Fitzsimmons watched them go, he felt consciousness slipping away... watched helplessly as the world began spinning around him... But he had to try and keep awake. He fought desperately not to black out. Hanging on by a mere thread.

The motionless policemen, paramedics, and people scattered around like alabaster statues, at last came to life again – gasping and crying with relief.

38   FIGHT TO THE DEATH

The tigers paced nervously back and forth in their enclosure. Jittery eyes, like shining green marbles, darting around.

But then a strange thing happened.

Giant mammals, with long trunks and thick grey wrinkly skin, trumpeted and stormed against the door to their enclosure from outside, beating it down until it was a snarled tangle of iron. The three tigers jumped out straight away – their bright orange fur, striped black and white, became just a streak as they bounded out.

People screamed and ran and scattered and hid.

The tigers' first instinct, after being locked up for an age – pacing endlessly up and down, slowly losing their sanity – was to jump with rage on the two-legged, upright animals, their jailers, and attack them and rip them to shreds and devour them. Venting years' long tension and restlessness. One of the tigers raced toward a little child, growling and baring sharp incisors, and was just about to pounce when suddenly it stopped – overcome by a greater force.

Someone was calling.

The other tigers, in turned, stopped in their tracks. Listening.

In time, they turned away – leaving the humans alone.

They raced instead along the pathway and out onto the busy London roads, joining the other animals that spilled out of the zoo – its cages quickly emptying of their angered occupants.

••••—————————————————————————••••

For just a second, Ilse bristled with fear.

The crowd surrounding them had turned into a hideous beast –

seething with rage, twisted faces snarling.

But her fear didn't last long.

She planted her feet firmly on the ground, swung her arms into the Shaolin bow stance, pulled a clenched fist by her waist, and held a flat hand upright before her.

Milly and Tai were there too, the three of them forming a tight circle, facing outward. Behind their backs, at their centre was Brian, who had passed out after being punched.

Ilse sensed the others – not just Milly and Tai – but also Fitzsimmons. They all did.

And instead of fear, they swelled with power.

Breathed it in.

Felt the force of dark energy enliven every fibre of every muscle.

Suddenly there came screams from afar.

Tyres screeching, vehicles crashing.

The screams became infectious – getting louder, closer.

A single lion appeared walking along the road, its thick, coarse mane ruffling in the wind.

More lions followed. A whole pride.

The traffic stopped.

People scrambled to lock their cars – their round eyes hardly believing what they were seeing.

Tigers appeared too, their orange fur bright against the grey concrete.

A flash of colour overhead – purple macaws flying over them, squawking.

More and more animals appeared in greater numbers.

Monkeys, apes, gorillas, warthogs, bears, giraffes, alpacas, zebras, camels, wild dogs, lemurs, llamas – all of them flooding into the roads.

Vultures swept above them in circles.

They kept coming.

Creatures of every size and shape.

Surrounding the children.

The crowds of people that once engulfed them had already scattered, running for their lives.

For several minutes the children could only stare in wonderment from the centre of Trafalgar Square, watching as the place became filled with animals of every kind. An army of creatures, surrounding them, guarding them.

Ilse at last stood down, gaping around in wonder.

Milly turned to check on her father.

Tai stroked one of the tigers distractedly, as he watched the last of the humans running away. A lion came up and licked his hand, swishing its tail and purring loudly like a huge pussy cat. He rubbed his cheek against Tai's body, almost knocking him over.

A squirrel monkey – not more than 25 cm tall – scurried up Ilse's leg and sat on her shoulder. It settled down and began picking through her hair. The tickle made Ilse giggle.

Brian at last came to, and Milly helped pull him up. He was woozy, and one side of his face stung with pain, but he was happy to see his daughter. 'Midge!' he cried. A strong, overpowering reek made him look around, and, jolting with fright, he saw the incredible spectacle of hundreds and hundreds of wild animals surrounding them.

'It's okay, Dad,' Milly reassured him with a light smile. 'Father sent them. They're protecting us.'

Brian knew who she meant. He rubbed his aching head as he watched Tai stoop down to hug the affectionate lion and bury his face into its thick mane. 'Unbelievable!' Brian gasped with amazement.

A strange noise caught their attention.

It came from the sky overhead – a mechanical sound.

The thrum of an engine.

Looking up, they saw a chopper flying toward them – though it wasn't one they recognised. Suddenly a round of fireworks spewed out of its nose, followed by the popping sound of a machine gun.

The animals at the edge of the square, in the line of fire, abruptly exploded with red.

Ilse screamed with horror.

Tai cried out, 'No!!!'

Milly and Brian dived behind a statue and huddled together.

Lions roared, tigers growled.

Confusion reigned amongst the animals.

Vultures got caught up in the rotor blades of the helicopter and were instantly torn into a cascading mess of feathers.

Milly spotted someone in the distance – a man wearing camouflage gear creeping behind a building. 'Soldiers!' she shouted, pointing.

They looked around.

Glimpses of the soldiers could be seen advancing around Trafalgar Square, holding rifles and machine guns.

A grenade was thrown at them, and both the children and the animals ran for their lives. It exploded with a bright orange bang! Leaving warthogs lying in its wake, some injured, some blown to pieces.

More ammunition was fired from the chopper, but already the children had taken cover and the surviving animals had run off.

Ilse pressed herself flat against one of the monuments, crying her eyes out, terrified.

Next to her, Tai's face was etched with the gravity of the situation. He peeked out from behind the stone plinth, and quickly ascertained the location of some of the soldiers. Sweeping narrowed eyes over the throng of animals, he communicated his thoughts to them – and they obeyed. Dividing up, the animals ran outward away from the children, away from the square, disappearing into the surrounding roads.

Flocks of pigeons appeared in the sky and descended on the advancing soldiers in a mass of grey wings and beaks. Vultures, eagles, and macaws soon joined them. The soldiers' screams were drowned out by the shrill squawk of birds as they pecked and attacked and clawed.

Tigers and lions snuck up on silent paws behind each of the remaining soldiers, and suddenly attacked with deafening roars. Biting with sharp teeth, and unsheathing claws to swipe and rip soft flesh to ribbons. The men shrieked with pain and terror. Shooting their guns in panic. Splatters of red.

The chopper continued raining down bullets from above.

Chunks of plaster catapulted dangerously in all directions.

The sick stench of fresh blood and gun sulphur hung cloyingly in the air.

When the firing stopped, Ilse peeked out to see what was happening, only to be shocked by a sea of slaughtered animals lying all around. Fur soaked with crimson, torn flesh revealing white bone. Chests rising and falling rapidly, the last stammers of breath. Eyes darting, wild from pain, or glassy still, staring at nothing.

Death was spreading like malignant boils, bubbling up everywhere – infectious.

Suddenly one of the lions was mowed down by gunfire just two metres from Ilse, and she screamed as she cowered behind the statue. Spattered with blood, she sobbed hysterically, struggling with the horror and awfulness of the battle. 'The animals... the soldiers... th-they're being hurt,' she whimpered to Tai. 'Killed!'

Tai looked at her red face with wild eyes, sweat dripping from his brow. Not knowing what to do. Paralysed by indecision.

'This is wrong...' Ilse mewled, her entire body heaving with emotion. 'It's all wrong!'

●●●━━━━━━━━━━━━━━━━━━━━━━━●●●

In a forest deep in China, Mei Hui lifted her face to the sun again, absorbing its warmth.

She did not fear the two vicious dogs that had tracked her down, and were now barking at her just metres away – straining on the leash and baring sharp teeth, wanting to tear her to pieces.

The soldiers struggled to hold onto them while they looked around fearfully at the shinobi who had appeared out of nowhere. Mysterious figures dressed entirely in black, their faces hidden behind dark masks.

Mei Hui's serene expression, as she gazed calmly at the dogs, immediately quietened the animals. They wrenched away from their owners and ran up to her, leashes trailing on the ground behind them. But they did not attack. Instead, they hung their heads and began whimpering before her, showing submission. They turned and sat on either side of the small Chinese girl, and instead started snarling at the soldiers.

The five men watched this with amazement. Quivering with fear, they tried to back away – not wanting to fight.

But then, to their relief, a second wave of soldiers ran up from between the trees and joined them – and then a third, and a fourth, until Mei Hui and the shinobi found themselves surrounded by over 50 men.

The dogs ran and attacked their former owners, growling and snarling. The shinobi ran toward the soldiers – those that had katana swords withdrew them, while others bared their hand claws, or their nunchuku – heavy wooden batons connected by a steel chain. Holding one baton, they swirled the other in the air at lethal speed, flinging them at their opponents, delivering sharp blows. Other shinobi used star-shaped throwing knives that they hurled, slicing through the air with hair's-breadth precision.

The soldiers fought back with all their might, but they were no match for the silent mastery and skill of the shinobi. One by one the soldiers began dropping to the ground like flies.

Mei Hui was prepared to fight, but only in defence – but she saw with alarm that the shinobi were aiming to kill. The sight of blood and wounds and beatings made her sick to the stomach. She gasped each time someone was battered, or cut, or stabbed. The metallic stench of blood clogging her nose. She wanted to vomit.

But the tables soon turned.

The dogs were shot at, and each of them fell to the ground, whimpering in pain.

The soldiers began shooting at the shinobi too, and though the warriors' fast reactions saved them for the most part, before long, the bullets nicked them, or wounded them. Yet they fought on valiantly.

In time, only two shinobi were left, against 12 soldiers. The two ran in front of Mei Hui protectively, as the soldiers advanced towards them.

Mei Hui pleaded with their opponents, 'Please!' Her dirt-smudged cheeks streaked with tears. She surveyed the bodies strewn about their feet, sick of so much blood and death. 'Please don't make me do this!'

She glanced up and around at the trees that surrounded them.

A branch rustled.

Leaves swayed.

A clouded leopard leapt down and walked forward, hunkering its head close to the ground, and baring long sabretooth-like canines. Its thick tail batted the ground as it walked toward the soldiers, as if daring them. Small and incredibly agile, it was beautiful but deadly.

Something else dropped out of the branches, long and slithering. A cobra. It sidled along the ground, its head rearing up and bobbing from side to side. Venom splashing from its fangs. Another cobra and more animals appeared – antelopes, pangolins, deer, black bears. They all surrounded the soldiers, hissing, growling, baring sharp teeth – ready to fight to the death.

The soldiers' eyes widened, their skin bristled with fear. They all knew that a single cobra bite would prove fatal, and the wild animals could tear them to shreds in seconds.

Mei Hui pleaded again. 'Please… don't make me do this.'

Saffie, Ignacio, and Alma had worked for hours on the banks of the Rio Branco, tending to the wounded from the capsized ferry, until there was nothing more they could do. The dead had been lain out along a stretch of soil, in morbid lines, men, women, children, and babies – with great chunks of flesh missing from their bodies, except for their hands and feet, which were, oddly, still intact. They made a tally of the living, and the dead, but there were hundreds still unaccounted for. Including Saffie's tribesman friend. With a heavy heart, she was sure that he, amongst all the others, had been savaged by the piranhas, caimans, and catfish – their remains left to sink into the murky depths of the river, where the quicksand-like silt would have sucked them into a muddy grave.

The family eventually left just before the emergency medics arrived together with the police, and before the pitch-black darkness consumed the jungle.

They sought shelter with a nearby, peaceful tribe who were used to visiting tourists. Their village consisted of a circle of huts made from wood and bamboo, joined together by one continuous roof of thatched palm leaves. In the centre of the huts was a protected space where the tribe communed – playing games, cooking food, and eating together. They welcomed Saffie and her parents, and, after giving them a simple meal of manioc and stewed fish, refusing to take any payment, they stretched out hammocks for the three visitors in two separate sleeping huts. The tribesmen had also been helping with the ferry disaster, and they were one and all quiet and introspective as they gravitated around a firepit in the central space. They sipped on a shared bowl of masato to calm their nerves – a drink made from masticated yuca root fermented by human saliva. Saffie and her parents knew not to refuse the tribe's hospitality, and so they gulped down the milky yet acidic liquid, which left an aftertaste of cloves and cinnamon in their mouth. As the three chatted amicably with their hosts – ghoulish firelight skittering across their faces – their nerves were indeed numbed by the alcoholic beverage, and in time, they wandered off one by one to their hammocks to sleep.

The night seemed to last an age.

Saffie swayed gently in her hammock as she rolled from side to side, blanketed by the dark of the hut.

Her punishing mind was intent on tormenting her with the day's events, and she dipped her head and wept yet again as she remembered the hard-fought battle to save lives, as well as the horribly mauled bodies of the dead. The worst was the memory of stumbling out of the river, carrying the lifeless boy in her arms – though light, the child felt so, so heavy.

The hammock squeaked lightly as she rocked and remembered and wept.

When an oblique beam of light dazzled her, Saffie blinked in its brightness as she looked to see who had come to the door at such an hour. It was one of the tribeswomen, holding a flickering lamp. She pointed at Saffie, stepped back, and soldiers carrying rifles ran urgently into the hut. 'Put your hands up!!' they shouted, pointing their guns at her. 'Now!!'

Saffie almost fell out of the hammock as she swung her legs down and sat up, startled. She raised her hands slowly. 'Don't shoot!' she cried. 'I'm unarmed.'

When she was marched out of the hut by the soldiers, she saw, dimly, under the milky light of the moon, the tribeswoman standing next to a man in authority, as he counted out a wadge of notes into her eager hands. The woman stared unashamedly at Saffie as she walked past, clutching the money firmly against her chest.

When Saffie's eyes became accustomed to the night, she saw figures on the side of the clearing – her parents standing between two soldiers, their hands cuffed behind their backs.

She really wanted to reassure them, wanted to tell them it's okay, she was going to sort this out, when suddenly their heads jolted, and they stared right at her – making Saffie realise. They had heard her thoughts. Her heart quickened in awe of this new ability, a kind of telepathy. She tested it. *Mama, papi, don't worry,* she told them. *I'm going to make it all right.*

The guard behind shoved her in their direction, and Ignacio nodded slowly at her.

Her mother thought back, *Be careful, mi amor!*

As Saffie was cuffed and marched away, she looked across the verge of jungle. Desperate eyes searching through the black columns between the trees. Wondering what she could do. Crying for help, to God, to anyone and anything that might hear her.

The three were marched back to the river dock, where sheets of tarpaulin had been laid over the bodies on the ground. Here and there, beneath the edges, a vague hand or a foot or an arm could be seen. Some of the tired-looking policemen were unceremoniously rolling the bodies in plastic sheeting and carrying them, huffing and puffing, onto a police boat. The overturned ferry was still there, its stern peeking out of the Stygian river – the rippling water was like wet ebony glistening with moonlight. Saffie's skin bristled as she and her parents were steered onto the boat with the bodies. The awful stench that rose from the decaying cadavers was stifling. She didn't know exactly where they were along the river, but she was sure they would have to endure that awful smell for at least six or seven hours until they reached Manaus.

Her stomach churned, and she ran to the side of the boat and heaved into the water. She spat out the remnants, before one of the policemen shoved her into a seat.

Nerves tingled in the back of her head as Saffie stared out across the water while the boat chugged downriver.

As they made their way, she battled with despondency, disgust, and once again, depression – she sank slowly into it as surely as the tribesman's body was dissolving deeper and deeper into the silt.

She had told her parents that she was going to make it right, but the truth was, she had no idea what to do. There was so little time. Every passing second weighed heavy on her mind. Every minute of life, lost. She glanced across at her parents who had been ordered to sit on the far side of the boat, away from her. Their hunched forms nothing but black shadows. And she cried for them, for herself, and for humanity...

•••————————————————————•••

Though his eyes were closed, Inder was very much conscious as he lay prostrate on the grubby mattress, in the small police holding cell.

The still dawn, ripe with solitude.

A single dim lightbulb cast a pitiful triangle of yellow light, illuminating motes of dust floating calmly.

Somewhere a leaking pipe was dripping. The plink of water barely audible, yet he cringed every time there was a drip. A form of water torture.

He was surrounded by a barrage of city smells imbued permanently in the air – the whiff of car fumes, pollution, ghee-soaked cooking, human sweat, sewage. Yet the most overpowering thing that made him want to vomit was the stench of dead bodies, rising in the mugginess of Amazonian heat. In his mind, he saw through Saffie's eyes as she gazed haplessly – across black water, skimming black jungle. She gasped from the breathlessness of depression. The futility of life. Needing to forget the rancid bitterness of the here and now, of reality.

Slowly, her tears dripped down Inder's face.

Her sighs became his.

Until he could bear it no longer.

Inder turned over, disturbed. Groaning. Shoulders hunched, lame arms folded into his chest.

As he turned, he became Mei Hui.

She was staring into the eyes of a soldier standing just metres away.

The soldier had wet himself. His trousers damp and sticking. A blush of morning light highlighted with incredible clarity the look on his face. It was the look of a man staring, not at a little Chinese girl, but at death. The bewildered, astonished realisation of someone knowing that his very existence was in peril. That his place in the world – which seemed so solid, so certain before – was really only... ephemeral. Like hot breath evaporating on a cold morning.

The man's fear was overwhelming.

Mei Hui absorbed his fear.

And, in turn, that fear became Inder's.

Inder thrashed from side to side, terrified, mumbling to himself.

He saw Milly now.

A snatched moment in time, hiding behind a statue.

Huddled with her father, jumping at every explosion, every shot of gunfire. Every scream from mowed-down animals.

Milly's mind was no longer what it had been.

It was decaying.

Her brilliance, fading.

And amidst all the chaos surrounding them, through all the explosive mayhem, Milly saw in her father's sad eyes that he knew this.

That her days were numbered.

A strange look melted across his face.

And Milly saw that he wondered – if they died today, or if they lived, he wondered which out of the two would be worse. A slow, years-long mental death, or a sudden physical death, today.

For once, she didn't have an answer.

She reached for his hand. 'I love you, daddy.' Her voice, like that of a two-year-old child.

Brian closed his eyes, knowing why she was saying this. Willing himself to accept it. Accept what was going to happen. He forced himself to muster every strength, at last murmuring, 'I-I... I love you too, Milly.'

He wouldn't be able to take it, he knew. Living without her.

Eyes squeezed closed, hands balled into fists, Inder buried his face into the smelly mattress. 'No, no, no,' he mumbled.

The next thing he knew, he was lying on the road.

Being Fitzsimmons.

Staring up at the cloudless sky. Absorbing how intensely blue it was.

People began crowding around him, as his eyes started sliding closed.

Looks of fear and disgust on their faces, as they took in the details of his gruesome face.

Jemima was standing to the side, holding hands with the Professor. Looking down at him. Eyes glistening with tears.

There was an unmistakeable look on her face.

And just as Fitzsimmons' eyes closed shut, he realised what it was.

Disappointment.

Jemima's abject disappointment in him.

That was the last thing he saw, before the blackness engulfed him.

Inder struggled with all these thoughts, feelings, visions – completely overwhelmed. He thrashed the bed, pounding it with his hands and feet. Sweat pouring from his head.

Echoes of the past came to him too.

When he had learned about Ilse for the first time. When she called out to him in her dreams, *Help me...*

And when he connected with the others. *Please, God,* they prayed silently together. *Make it rain!*

Alia's words came to him too. Her hushed voice, like silken gossamer wafting in the air. *I... don't think I can take any more... There's nothing left to live for.*

Nothing left to live for.

The final echo made him oh so dizzy as it repeated again and again:

I think... I think...

I can

Tell

The future.

The past, the present, the future, swirled and rushed around him.

His head, a giddy melting pot, filled to bursting.

Inder beat his skull with fisted hands.

Jolts of pain with each blow.

He wanted so much to clear his head.

To purge himself.

To be emptied.

Free.

And then he saw her.

The memory of her.

As she sat up in bed that night, just days ago.

The moon, silvering her skin uncertainly – its light, delicately caressing the wounds and scars on her face, as if unsure what to make of them.

Alia was mesmerisingly beautiful, too beautiful for this world.

She stared at Inder curiously as she fingered the ring-pull on her hand. A hint of a smile on her lips. *I can't believe he did it...* she whispered secretively.

The priest had visited the hospital earlier that day, to comfort the sick and dying. He talked extensively with the couple, blessed them, said prayers over them. When suddenly Alia asked him – half joking, half serious – if he would marry them.

The priest raised an eyebrow; Inder almost fell out of his chair.

'We love each other,' Alia told the priest. 'That should be all that matters, shouldn't it?' It wasn't so much a question, as a statement.

The priest could not argue with her. He smiled sympathetically. He had seen it so many times. Young ones marrying out of their cast. Willing to defy their parents, their family, and a centuries old tradition, to be together. He spied the ring-pull discarded on the bedtable next to its can, and reached for it, saying, 'This will have to do. Does it fit, my dear?'

Alia tried it on for size. 'Perfectly!' she announced, pleased.

And so, he married them. Just like that.

Later that night, when all was still and quiet in the hospital, with Inder faithfully at her side, snuffling lightly as he snoozed in the chair, Alia found herself waking.

She blinked in the moonlight – it seemed unusually bright, as it shone right onto her. Choosing her. She turned to see that the opal light was slipping across Inder's face, kissing his cheek and his lips.

His exquisite lips.

And she sat up, just as he awoke and gazed at her with droopy eyes.

They stared at each other for such a long time, until Alia said, *I can't believe he did it... the priest. Can't believe he married us!*

But Inder was too emotional for words, too captivated by her marred beauty. He got up, threaded his fingers through her soft, tangled hair, behind her neck, and gently pulled her toward him. And they kissed.

It felt like a dream.

Both sleepy, yet filled with desire.

Inder pushed aside the bedtable and climbed next to Alia.

The moonlight silently anointed them, as they came together.

Bathed them in its approving glow.

And as the two young lovers discovered each other for the first time, as they relished in each other's love, any doubts in Inder's mind about Alia at last evaporated. Her love for him was pure, untainted. True.

The night, the moonlight, their love, intertwined and blushed and crescendoed – at last evanescing as dawn broke.

When the moon and stars faded oh so quietly, the couple lay in bed, hugging... tenderly drifting into the loveliest of sleeps.

The wonder of that night, that beautiful night, calmed Inder's raging turmoil. Calmed his mind. As he relived every moment of their togetherness.

He at last fell asleep on that dirty bed, in the dingy prison cell.

Only to be jolted awake!

Someone was shouting. Crying. Blood spattered on their face. *This is all wrong!!* Ilse screamed. *The animals... the soldiers... th-they're being hurt,* she whimpered. *Killed!!*

She sobbed and sobbed. *They don't have to kill each other!!* she cried, hysterical. *Please, Inder! Make it stop!!!*

39 THE CONNECTION

Fitzsimmons' eyes jerked open.

The echoes of Ilse's impassioned words pounding inside his skull.

She was right, he realised, disgusted by his incredible stupidity.

They didn't have to kill.

In fact, it didn't have to be a fight at all.

Inder told him, *It's not the animals you should be controlling!*

Yes, I know, Fitzsimmons replied grumpily, recognising his mistake. *I know.*

It's the humans, Ilse added, sniffling as she at last began to calm down.

Fitzsimmons found that he was lying on his back in the middle of the road. A cluster of faces staring down at him, expressions of disgust and morbid curiosity – wondering if he was dead. But when they saw his eyes open, and he suddenly sat up, they screamed with fright and fled for their lives.

Fitzsimmons looked around.

Jake and Jemima were helping a very weak Calista get up from the pavement.

Just in front of him, the Chauffeur was gently cuddling the baby in his big arms. Kissing her softly on the forehead. Making light, throaty vocalisations.

Acuzio was jumping up on the Chauffeur, whining for the baby – and so the Chauffeur stooped down to show Acuzio that the infant was well. But the dog suddenly stopped. Turned. Looked down the road and growled.

Booming sounds cracked through the air. Gunfire.

Panicked, Fitzsimmons turned to search for Jemima. She had ducked behind a car. Safe.

More gunfire – and a searing pain ripped right through his arm.

Someone was screaming hysterically, it was deafening.

Fitzsimmons looked down at himself, at the blood that dripped onto trembling hands, wondering with alarm who had been shot. But he soon realised. He started to hyperventilate. Sweating from the pain. Tried to get up onto shaky feet. Stumbling. Trying again.

There came more screams and shouts nearby.

And as Fitzsimmons finally got onto his feet and threw himself behind a tree, from the side of his eye he saw a snarling Acuzio dash along the pavement toward the gunfire.

Then he spotted someone nearby lying on the road, grunting with agony. It was the Chauffeur. At his side, was a still, silent baby.

He realised Calista was the one screaming.

Jake was running over to his daughter, dropping onto his knees. Blood pooling around the child. He picked her up gently. 'Please, no…' he begged, pressing her to his chest, rocking her back and forth. 'No!!'

Jemima appeared from behind the car, ashen-faced, staring at the unresponsive child. Sorrow and anger sparking in her eyes. She stepped out, exchanging a daggered glance with Fitzsimmons, before walking purposefully away. Following Acuzio.

In the distance, the dog flashed up from behind parked cars and jumped onto someone behind a tree, growling loudly. A rifle clattered to the ground as the man fought in vain against the vicious attacker.

Jemima had almost reached them, when Fitzsimmons spotted another soldier peeking out from behind a car. And another, from the side of a brick wall – he was staring at Jemima and raising his gun.

Fitzsimmons glared at them, eyes boring.

Suddenly the two men stopped dead in their tracks, and walked into the road like puppets, powerless to the unseen force that moved them. They came right out into the open. Fear flashing in their eyes. They watched their own arms and hands swing their guns around with horror, aiming directly at each other, instead of Jemima. They gasped at the first crack of gunfire as they were flung back onto the ground.

Jemima froze with shock – backing away from the horrific sight of their bloody bodies. She turned round, angry eyes searching for Fitzsimmons.

No more killing! she growled at him. *Enough!!* She held a hand out toward him, fingers stretching for his mind.

Fitzsimmons became pinned against the tree, unable to move.

Enough!!! she screamed, battling to hold back tears.

Acuzio was still attacking the soldier, growling, salivating – he went for the kill, going for the jugular, clamping ferocious jaws into the neck and wrenching from side to side. When the dog let go, the soldier dropped to the ground grasping his bloodied neck with futile hands, gurgling helplessly, until he eventually stilled.

The dog turned, and looked around – ears pointed, tail rigid, as he listened for any other movement. Satisfied that there was no-one else, he eventually went over to Jemima, sniffing her, checking she was okay. He gave her trembling hand a quick lick before turning and running back to the baby, his charge.

Jemima grappled to breathe as she backed away – she tore eyes from the bodies, turned, and trailed behind Acuzio.

When Jemima reached them, she immediately saw from the misery twisted into Jake's face that it was bad.

He had collapsed onto the ground, next to Calista, and the two were sobbing and wailing together – their groans otherworldly, as if coming not from the living, but the dead.

Even Acuzio was crying and whining for the infant, pacing the ground, beside himself.

Evie's limp hand dangled at the side of Jake's arm.

Her skin was so smooth, like peach velvet.

Dimples on her knuckles.

Tiny fingernails, smeared with blood.

A broken Jemima held her breath as she crouched on the ground next to Jake. One hand dug into the soil of a tree in the pavement, and the other reached tentatively for Evie's.

She closed her eyes, squeezing out tears.

Listened to the beat of her own heart.

Counting.

•••————————————————————————•••

Inder groaned with misery.

He rolled over and forced his weary bones to get up from the bed, his head hanging down.

Standing up, he went over to the prison door.

It creaked open, just as he reached it.

As he walked out, he glanced only briefly at the terrified guard who had opened it – Inder's expression was tired, withered. Yet his eyes shone, wet with tears, glowing with a power that was intensifying by the second.

As Inder walked toward the exit, each locked door was opened by one of the guards, and he finally stepped outside into the street, squinting from the brightness of daylight.

His heart was cracking as he went. With each step it shattered with despair for Jake and Calista's baby.

The air was incredibly dry.

The climate so arid.

He walked and walked in a daze.

Found himself on the banks of the sorry-looking Yamuna river. The waters had almost completely receded, the cracked riverbed smothered by heaps of stinking garbage.

Inder raised his face toward the heavens.

Toward a sun high in the sky.

Shoulders hunched.

Arms hanging limply.

He was weak, yet buzzing with power.

The dark energy swelling within him. Trickling out from his every pore. Into the elements around him – merging with the nitrogen, oxygen, and water vapour in the air, and sinking deep into the ground. Within innumerable atoms, electrons began vibrating and flying randomly, discontinuously, in small clouds above their nuclei. So elementally minute, yet shivering with a catastrophic energy.

The air glimmered and sparked, the ground juddered as electricity built up.

Each atom, each molecule, knocking against the other. Power

smouldering and building and transferring – reaching high up into the sky and clouds. Tunnelling deep into the earth.

Inder closed his eyes, delirious with despair, swaying almost indiscernibly back and forth. His breath scattered. Mumbling over and over, *Make it rain...*

●●●————————————————————————————●●●

A weary Saffie got up and climbed out of the boat that was docked in Manaus, dreary eyes focusing on her parent's feet as they were constantly shoved by the policemen to walk ahead. With the dawn only just breaking, it was unclear where their feet ended and the shadows started. They seemed to be walking for an age. Along grey roads, next to a verge of jungle.

Emotions suddenly ebbed within her, like drawdown before a tidal wave – and Saffie gasped for breath. Wondering what was happening to her. Why she felt so strange, her skin tingling. She looked down at her trembling hands, splayed in front of her. They seemed to glow.

And when she looked up again, she saw a dark, low figure running out from a thick grove of trees, prowling toward her – and she gasped.

One of the policemen spotted it and cried out, another shouted, before they all ran for their lives. Their footsteps clattering along the road.

Leaving Saffie and her parents alone.

The bewildered Ignacio and Alma looked at each other, then at Saffie – turning, they followed her line of sight to see what she was looking at.

A full-grown black jaguar was bounding toward them.

Black rosettes against dark fur made its amber eyes look even more piercing. Its mouth was half open, revealing long incisors. When it was just a few metres away, it hunched its head toward the ground and wrinkled its nose, wary of danger. It stared right at Saffie, its tail pointing straight behind.

Saffie squinted in the dim light. 'Sabu?' she whispered with disbelief. 'Sabu!!' she cried out with joy – and the jaguar pounced on her, knocking her to the ground. He pinned her down, sniffed her, then began licking her face heartily with a large tongue, rough as sandpaper.

Saffie couldn't help laughing with joy at seeing her dear friend again, though his licks hurt her skin. He was so big, and healthy. So strong.

Ignacio and Alma walked over, delighted. They too stroked and cuddled the jaguar, and the animal in turn licked their hands and cheeks affectionately.

Something approached from behind – and Saffie got up and dusted herself as she waited for the creatures to come closer, instinctively knowing they meant no harm. It was a beautiful golden jaguar, and a little black cub. Alma cried out at the sight of them, clasping her hands together, ecstatic.

A breathless Saffie slowly walked over to the two newcomers, stooped down, and let them smell the back of her hand. They sniffed with cautious interest. Then the little cub swiped at her playfully, tumbled to the ground, and grappled with her fist. 'Ouch!' cried Saffie, for though the cub was only play-fighting, its tiny teeth and claws were sharp. Saffie couldn't resist scooping up the little cub in a hug, burying her face in its thick fur – unable to hold back tears of happiness.

Alma wandered over, put an arm around her daughter, and stroked the cub. 'She's beautiful,' she murmured. 'The mother too. Though I'm a little surprised. After mating, the parents usually go their separate ways, leaving the mother to look after the cub alone. But Sabu has stayed with them!'

Saffie beamed. 'I always knew Sabu was special.'

A grateful Alma looked skyward and muttered a silent prayer of thanksgiving both for their freedom and the precious little jaguar family. The animals were a new beginning, representing rebirth and the sustaining power of nature – despite man's worst efforts.

Ignacio looked around, warily. 'We'd better get going,' he said. 'Before they come back.'

Alma nodded, squeezing her daughter's arm. 'Your father is right. Not just for us, but for the jaguars. They are a protected species, but there is bound to be a pessoa gananciosa who wouldn't think twice about killing them for their hide.'

Nodding, Saffie kissed the cub and reluctantly put her down on the ground. The little black jaguar immediately ran to her mother. Sabu drew closer to his family and circled them protectively.

Saffie couldn't help watching the cub, eyes magnetised to the little creature – she looked so much like her father when he was that age.

But the little jaguar suddenly flinched, and looked up.

Ignacio did the same, and then Alma.

Saffie felt a fat drop of rain plonk on her arm, then her head, and shoulder. She looked skyward as well, and as the sun began to emerge from the dawn mists, the heavens opened, and it suddenly began to pour – just as they all became aware of unusual movement around them.

Saffie gasped from both the instant deluge of water, and the appearance of policemen through the haze.

Sabu growled, hunkered down, and was just about to run and attack, when Saffie spied the policemen's guns and screamed, 'Sabu, no!!' – stepping in front of the jaguars.

Sabu stopped, held back, and looked around on high alert. Ears pricked up, tail twitching with tension.

Just as the full numbers of policemen became visible in the dawn light, and as the pouring rain soaked Saffie to the skin, she prickled from the dark energy that began to pulsate and quiver through every fibre of her being. In her head, she heard the echo of Ilse's words. *It's not the animals you should control, it's the humans!* Felt the connection with Inder, hot and sparking, burning through her skull.

Jemima was connected too, as well as Milly and Tai.

The rain, the elements, the dark energy, the light of the emerging sun – all made her heady with power. Sparks crackled around her, fizzing and popping under the rain. The smell of acrid smoke singeing her nostrils.

Saffie gasped.

Heart racing.

Ilse's voice came again, talking to someone. *Please, we mean you no harm.* The plea of a child.

Saffie found herself repeating those words with the same timbre, the same innocence. *Please,* she told the policemen, looking around at them through the sheets of rain. *We mean you no harm...*

She saw their eyes pop wide as they heard her voice in their heads.

An ethereal voice, that terrified them.

In a knee-jerk reaction, one of the policemen pressed a jittery finger against the trigger of a gun pointed at her.

Saffie stretched a juddering hand toward him just as the sound of gunfire reverberated through the air.

'No!!!' she screamed.

As if in slow motion, Saffie followed the trajectory of the bullet as it skimmed through the air, piercing right into her shoulder.

She collapsed, and found herself on the ground, barely able to move.

Cold-hot liquid seeped from her shoulder.

Craning her neck, her pained eyes glared over the policemen, and they all froze, still as statues.

Weakened by the effort and the shoulder wound, Saffie could only lie back, gasping for breath as she grappled with the immense pain. She stared up into the sky, blinking – bombarded by the downpour.

•••———————————————————•••

Standing in the forest, surrounded by dead bodies, a new wave of armed soldiers, and a miscellany of animals, birds, and snakes – a dirt-stained and broken Mei Hui stood behind the last two shinobi. They were poised protectively, facing the soldiers, both resolute yet filled with dread.

Above them, clouds were gathering at frightening speed, cloaking the blue skies and bright sun with gloom.

The soldiers glanced up, frightened by the sudden change of weather and the voice that came echoing through their heads.

Please, we mean you no harm.

Lightning flashed across the sky, and thunder boomed – making the soldiers jump with fear. A patter of rain fell lightly. But as the clouds swirled, the rain became heavier and heavier, so that within just a few seconds they became soaking wet, hair plastered to scalps.

The cold rain seemed to wash away Mei Hui's fear, and she relaxed, pulled her feet together and lowered her arms from the Shaolin bow stance. The rain energised her, empowered her – made her feel invincible. Yet she stood there, meekly, as the full force of the connection with the others locked into her. The circuit was now closed. And dark energy roiled and thundered through the air, through the rain, and the soil, right into her – stamping into every cell of her body.

Mei Hui's breath quickened.

Stand down, she told the shinobi. *We are no longer in danger.*

The shinobi glanced at each other, surprised and puzzled – until they realised that the soldiers were remaining stock still. Only their eyes blinked, aflutter with fear.

The black-masked shinobi, a man and woman, put away their katana swords as they stared with awe at the soldiers. They ventured hesitantly forward to inspect them. One and all, their opponents remained unmoving, eerily reminiscent of the terracotta soldiers from Xian.

As Mei Hui herself ventured forward, Saffie's pain shot through her and she stumbled back, thumping against a tree. Gasping from the shock of it.

Ilse's voice rumbled in her mind.

Please... We... we don't have to kill each other.

40   THREE SECONDS

They were the Ingenious.

They had been vilified, spat upon, and hated.

Their crime: they were different, and they felt. For that, they had been judged and sentenced to death by a world that pretended tolerance.

As the clouds gathered, and the rain began to patter lightly, Ilse wiped the blood spatters from her face with the back of a trembling hand, wincing from the pain in Saffie's shoulder. As she stood – a little girl with messy pigtails, amongst the smouldering ruins of Trafalgar Square – her fearful eyes watched the soldiers advance ever closer. Their fear made them reckless, fingers pressed nervously against triggers.

She called out to them, from her mind. An impulse. Not understanding the consequences. She was just a frightened kid trying to grapple with the terrifying thing before her.

Please, we mean you no harm! she whimpered, reeling from the awfulness of what had just happened to Jake, Calista, and sweet little Evie. Innocents, who happened to be at the wrong place at the wrong time. Their world ripped apart by a single bullet. *We... we don't have to kill each other. Please!* she begged.

The soldiers stopped in their tracks.

Found they could not move.

Wild eyes, blinking with fear.

Milly and Tai stepped out, and stood in front of Ilse. The rain lashed down, soaking them. And, with wonderment, the two looked at each other, stared down at themselves, at their hands. Feeling – at last – the connection with the others. The dark energy rising within them. Empowering them. Emboldening them. The rain seemed to wash away their fears... helped them to finally understand, with such sweet lucidity, what exactly they were. And what they had to do.

With sparks sizzling, smoke billowing around them, their skin bristled with the sensation of the elements. They felt so keenly every molecule of those elements around them – the soil beneath Mei Hui's feet, the blazing fire of the sun, the rain pouring onto them, and the air that filled their lungs. They closed their eyes, as the elements distilled within them. Until their minds became completely empty.

Until there was nothingness.

Just silence, save for the patter of rain.

Radiant peacefulness.

And calm.

That was, until the voices came.

It started out as a single voice.

A thought.

A hazy feeling.

Until more and more voices came, and more and more feelings. A massive influx of emotions. From every man and woman and animal surrounding them.

The minds of the seven became filled to bursting, drowning out their own thoughts.

Milly began to hyperventilate from the myriad voices pounding through her skull. She screamed as she clenched hands against ears, trying to stop the noise.

Brian and Tai fell upon her – Brian putting his arms around her, distraught, and Tai holding her hands firmly, trying to absorb and dissipate her turmoil.

Ilse looked at them, fearful – and then gasped when she felt someone else forcefully enter their connection. Elbowing his way into their minds. Fitzsimmons. And the voices suddenly disappeared.

An exhausted Milly almost fainted against Brian.

They saw Fitzsimmons now, slumped against a tree, bleeding out from a bullet-shattered arm. Rutted bark against his back. Darkness in his eyes. Pallid skin bristling with power as the rain pelted him.

The children jolted when they absorbed his thoughts and feelings – realising his intention. He was smouldering with pure hate. Wanted to commandeer their power. Wipe out anything and everything – *everything!* – within reach. Greedy for dark energy, he wanted to gorge on each iota of it – for himself, for Milly and Saffie, for all of them – to make them whole again, and increase their power.

No!! cried Mei Hui and Inder at the same time.

But Fitzsimmons was in no mood to take orders. He blasted them with his mind, and the children stumbled back.

The tree behind Fitzsimmons began to shake as he sucked the energy out of it. Leaves quivered, branches shook, until it exploded into a puff of ash. Fitzsimmons stretched his face heavenward, breathed in the power as the ashes and rain poured onto and into him. But it wasn't enough. It only dampened his pain. And he knew that the only way he could get more energy in his weakened state was through the children. He screamed with frustration, hate leaking out of his face in hot streams. *You would save the people who tried to kill you!?! Can't you see, it's not just me. Saffie is injured! She needs our help. Now!!*

I... I'm okay, mumbled Saffie unconvincingly. She struggled to sit up, clasping her shoulder, trying to quell the bleeding.

A smouldering Mei Hui murmured to Fitzsimmons, *You would kill hundreds, for seven of us?!* She hardly believed it.

Ilse drew in breath as she examined Fitzsimmons' heart. His cracked, broken heart. And she realised that his flippant attitude to murder – mass murder – was real. She almost choked from the thought of it, felt sick to the stomach. She thought of her parents. Her beloved mother and father – how they had been murdered by her crazed half-brother. She still felt the awful agony of their death, every minute of every day. Carrying it inside her like a parasite. It clawed at her, and woke her up in the night. And in the day, it gripped her so hard, strangling her from inside...

As she thought of Fitzsimmons, and Karl, Ilse suddenly realised. Like father, like son.

She shook her head slowly, acutely aware of his genes within her. *I-I don't want to be like you,* she told Fitzsimmons weakly. And then, much stronger, *I refuse! I refuse to be any part of your murderous ways!*

You're all mad! cried Fitzsimmons before erupting into a coughing fit. He spat out ashes into the dirt. *These people... they're terrified of you. They want to kill you... wipe you out. But not only that, they're intent on self-destruction. Through greed, wars, pollution, hatred. The planet is dying, and they're the ones killing it. Don't you see? In their short-sighted, selfish ignorance, they're destroying you... and your future. They don't deserve to live!*

Who made you judge and jury?! asked Mei Hui, indignant. *Why is it that killing and murder are your only answer? Killing only results in more killing. There must be another solution. We were made with a genius gene. If we can't find another way, then we are not so intelligent...*

Inder had remained quiet all this time, listening. He thought of Alia, as the drizzle of warm rain pattered onto his face, dissolving his tears – thought of the storybook of their life he had foreseen, with her on every page. A beautiful life, together. At last he said, *I know the answer – it is to save ourselves. Not just us, but mankind, as a whole. To preserve our future.* He stared at the dried-up river before him. *Everything we touch is dying. We need to save ourselves from ourselves...*

Thinking about it some more, he said, *But how? If salvation is the answer, then... what is the question?*

Saffie managed to get up onto her feet, wincing from the effort. In her mind came the sorry memories of the last few days. Of the wildfires, loss of habitat, loss of life... and the little isolados boy she carried from the river with a heavy heart and leaden arms, dripping with his watery blood.

Mei Hui mulled over Saffie's memories, adding her own. Of the flooding they'd endured for weeks. Many thousands had lost their lives too, their homes swept away, and their livelihoods.

At the same time, Inder stared blankly at the Yamuna, thinking about the drought that was surely going to grip New Delhi and strangle it by the throat. Worried for his dear Alia, and his parents, as well as the slum children, most of whom were already painfully thin and malnourished. And the plants that he had taken such good care of at work would almost certainly die.

Tai, Milly, and Ilse were still smarting from the fire of hatred that swept so easily through London – making people wild with fear, lashing out without really knowing the full facts. Their instinctive reflex: kill before being killed.

At last, Tai's soft-spoken voice came to them. *I think... it's more than one question.* An image of his mother came to mind, the childish excitement on her face as she recounted to them all the things she'd learnt from the Bible. They all saw that image. *Three questions,'* Tai said thoughtfully. *Who are we? Why are we here? And... where are we going?*

You are here because I created you! boomed Fitzsimmons, irritated.

Mei Hui asked, *Well then, why did you create us?*

Staring down at the drips of his blood being washed away by the rain, Fitzsimmons was uninclined to answer. He mumbled reluctantly, *Just... because.*

That's it? said Saffie, incredulous. *Just because?!*

His silence was the unsatisfactory reply.

They saw Tai's thoughts now – how he had suffered horribly, aging from a strange sickness after unwittingly misusing his powers.

Just because.

And then they stared at Milly as she huddled in Brian's protective arms. Her eyes were both intense yet deadpan – her expression, vacuous. Sure signs of a decaying mind. The same sickness that Karl had suffered. The same one that they were all going to suffer. A slow, mental death.

Just because.

It dawned on the teenagers then, how blind Fitzsimmons was – blinder than the Professor, deafer than the Chauffeur. He couldn't even see his own shortcomings; he saw only those of others. Yet he was just as bad as those he raged against. They wondered that Fitzsimmons was a child of this world... A world that was ugly, and selfish. Misusing power. Abusing the lowly. Chewing people up, and spitting them out. All while smiling, offering a hand, and pretending to be a friend.

Perhaps Fitzsimmons wasn't the father-figure they had hoped for.

Ilse's weeping sniffles came to them as she shook her head, and she eyed each crack in Fitzsimmons' brittle heart. *No...* she whimpered. *I don't believe that you are that terrible! And... and that the people in this world are so evil!*

Her outburst marked the end of their furore of thoughts.

Someone whispered, *I feel dizzy.*

Someone else said, *Me too.*

Then someone whimpered, *I feel sick...*

Their exhausted minds fell into wordlessness. Silence stretched out before them. Until it was interrupted by a panicked voice.

The sound of numbers – floating into their minds.

Jemima, who had been distracted, wrapped up in the awfulness of Evie's imminent demise, was counting...

They saw through her eyes now.

As she held onto the baby's limp hand.

Calista screaming, pain distorting her face.

Jake clutching his daughter, rocking back and forth, beside himself.

They absorbed all this, and Jemima's incredible sadness, curdling through her, clotting her insides so that she could barely breathe – as she counted the precious seconds of life left within the child.

Ilse gasped and said to Fitzsimmons, *Look at Evie! There. Dying! And tell me you feel nothing.*

Fitzsimmons stared at the baby for what seemed like an age.

Staring grief right in the face. The rawness of it. Absorbing both its searing sting and its tenderness. Fitzsimmons listened to Jake and Calista's wailing screams, observed their blazing, heartrending love for their baby, and each other. A love, and a family, that he had so desperately wanted with Georgina.

His beautiful dead Georgina.

And as Fitzsimmons stared, the teenagers, in turn, watched quietly as – so, so slowly – yet another crack ripped through his heart. Twisted and jagged, and leaking blood. He slumped back. Felt himself losing consciousness. The pain too much to bear.

A whispered voice came to them now – Jemima's – in between the counting.

And the seven suddenly realised that though their communication with each other had been long and drawn-out, as Jemima counted the slow trickle of life seeping from Evie's juddering body, they realised that in real time, only seconds had passed. Three seconds, four, five. Until Jemima gasped and choked and screamed out to them, *Help her!!!*

41 WHO WE ARE

Tai gasped. Shocked by their indolence. Wasting precious seconds as the baby lay dying in her father's arms.

In the back of his mind the questions were whispered, *Who are we? Why are we here? Where are we going?*

The questions became louder, more persistent, until they suddenly exploded out of him – and, linked to the seven, the same explosion detonated out of them too. Propelling a shockwave of pure thought. Circular ripples of energy that rent apart the air, blasting through particles, atoms, molecules – releasing a flood of power. A chain-reaction booming across the planet, striking the minds and hearts of everyone it touched.

WHO ARE WE?

WHY ARE WE HERE?

WHERE ARE WE GOING?

The seven teenagers collapsed to the ground from the immense mental effort, their hearts racing.

Minds throbbing.

Fighting to breathe.

In the aftermath, Tai's thoughts came to all of them, dissipating out of them, like an after-shock. And with the softest, most lyrical of voices, he wept as he uttered the simplest of words, the purest of thoughts:

I am you.

You are me.

We are the same.

42 THE STORYTELLER AND THE END OF DAYS

The entire world stood still.

Every man, woman, and child in every country, in every continent, stopped, and raised their eyes heavenward.

In each hemisphere, the sky darkened. Clouds gathered.
The brightness of the sun gilding the clouds' edges – a radiant skyscape of silver-gold.

As lightning flared just before the crack and boom of thunder, and rain began pouring in thick sheets, their faces were pounded with water as, one and all, humanity absorbed the deafening thought-wave. It was followed by another thought, and another. Wave after wave. A relentless tsunami.

The storyteller closed his eyes and, in his mind, he pored over the entirety of the human population with quiet thoughtfulness. Billions of people, of all shapes and colours. Staring at each other, staring up, and around. But as the storyteller watched them, they seemed to shimmer and merge and blend – until they coalesced into one, and he saw them now, collectively, as a single person: a young man, with bright eyes, rimmed red from fatigue. His complexion was pock-marked, his demeanour sickly, coughing now and then as he sat wearily in a chair before him. He wore blue pyjamas and comfy slippers, and, now and then, he batted away a pesky mosquito hovering around his head. The young man's name was Xander.

The storyteller sat cross-legged before Xander, on a newspaper on the ground – and he began to recount a story. The most wondrous, most devastating of stories. The storyteller's eyes sparkled as he gestured with wild arms, and he told the world, Xander, about his future. But not just one future. He told him about every possible future, conception, and scenario. He told him where his current path was leading, and then pointed out the many sideroads and their destinations. Recounting both the minutiae of each pathway, as well as the overwhelming outcomes. Calculating probabilities and eventualities with mathematical precision.

Xander listened with rapt attention, gripping onto the arms of the chair so hard his knuckles whitened.

And in the fullness of time, when he was done telling, the storyteller got up, dusted himself down, and held his hand out to the sickly young man. *Come,* he said. *Let me show you.*

Xander struggled to get up, and the storyteller went to help – but he was stubbornly pushed away. Xander at last managed to get up by himself on shaky feet. He grabbed his walking stick, and hobbled closer, the stick creaking under his weight.

This way, invited the storyteller. And Xander followed as Inder showed him the world...

They were one of the smallest organisms in the food chain.

Microscopic phytoplankton, mostly single-celled plants, that waxed and waned across the vast oceans – some floating colourless, clear as glass – others in spectacular algal blooms, glowing blue or red, green or orange. A bioluminescent constellation of sea stars.

Though tiny, the self-feeding phytoplankton were the foundation of the marine food web. They silently produced almost half of the oxygen in the planet; if the Amazon was considered to be one of earth's lungs, then phytoplankton could rightly be called the other. But their population was already declining in great swathes. They too were dying.

And as the storyteller took Xander to the open oceans and seas – flying along the coastlines and continental shelves, then diving into the water and speeding along the upper oceans – he showed him the phytoplankton's complete story, its lifespan, and what would happen to mankind upon its extinction.

Xander sucked in air as he gazed upon the beautiful clouds of phytoplankton, fading and disappearing right before his eyes. In turn, the animal plankton that fed on them soon weakened and diminished – their shells becoming brittle, unable to protect themselves from predators. As a consequence, their demise affected every kind of young fish, shellfish, bird, and whale that fed on zooplankton and krill throughout entire oceans. With bated breath, Xander could only watch as petrels and albatrosses circled empty waters in search of food, needing to go further and further out to sea, only to faint mid-air from fatigue and hunger. The scraggly birds plummeted noiselessly into the waves – and in a flash, starving sharks bumped each other and raced to snap them up, chomping on them hungrily. They too were only trying to survive.

The storyteller and his companion dived into the deepest oceans – and, gliding underwater, Xander observed with grim silence the aquatic ecological systems disappearing far and wide. Like someone was turning out the lights. Entire oceans went dark. The acidification of the seas, an increase in carbon levels, dead zones expanding, the devastating effects on marine life, coral reefs bleaching, and the resulting acceleration of global warming. He watched the slow death of the seas, as the water became more and more toxic.

When there remained only a barren seascape and nothing left to view underwater, the storyteller flew upward, with Xander following close behind – bursting out of the sea, into the air. They soared around the globe, deep inland, along coastal regions, and close to large bodies of water. Xander gripped his chest and prickled with heat as he felt worldwide heatwaves, over 50 degrees celsius, striking country after country. The heat changed global weather patterns, creating a devastation of cyclones and hurricanes, droughts, wildfires, and floods – like savage gods, they destroyed everything they touched.

Slowing down, Xander stopped to watch the glaciers and ice sheets melting, drip by drip – raising sea levels, not by centimetres but by metres, and reducing the reflection of sunlight back into space. He flew around and observed whole islands sinking: Kiribati, Maldives, and Tuvalu with its capital disappearing from the inside out, as seawater bubbled up in the centre of the island through porous ground – its abandoned houses clustering together as if for protection.

Xander also witnessed the weather patterns, El Nino and La Nina, seesawing between ever-widening swings of warming and cooling.

Such weather conditions pushed spring earlier and earlier each year, unsettling both the lifecycle of insects and animals, and the flowering of plants, so that entire systems became misaligned: spring buds blooming weeks in advance, killed by overnight frosts; birds migrating great distances, only to find that food sources at their destination had not grown enough to sustain them; aphids hatching too soon and feeding on much younger plants, so that there was nothing left for regrowth; animals coming out of hibernation in a weakened state, and being picked off by starving predators.

In the blink of an eye, Xander was taken to the Arctic, where they spied a lone polar bear. White on white, it was barely visible against the snow as it trampled quietly along, hunkering its neck close to the ground. The ice sheet was melting and retreating, diminishing the bear's hunting ground, and it had to swim longer and more treacherous distances between ice floes to find food and a suitable denning site. When she at last found a suitable place, she dug and dug the den, only to have it collapse into the sea – and she found herself plunged into freezing water, paddling frantically upward, and trying to grab onto the edges of the ice sheet. But the brittle ice kept breaking with a groaning sound, great chunks floating off, and she swiped and swiped until she at last got a hold! It was all she could do to pull herself up from the water, sopping wet. She rolled over and paused a moment to catch her breath – eventually getting up, shaking herself down, and lumbering off. Ever searching, ever hungry. Always on the lookout for a seal for food, or a good den. But though she had already mated successfully, she hadn't yet been able to birth cubs – sensing, deep down, that without adequate fat reserves, the pregnancy would not take. Still, she kept searching, kept hunting, pushed on by an indomitable, though weakened, will to survive.

As both the storyteller and Xander flew away from the polar bear, Xander couldn't help turning around to take one last look at the lone wanderer, curious to know if it would survive...

The weather worsened.

Temperatures soared.

The concentration of greenhouse gases increased: carbon dioxide, methane, nitrous oxide. Accumulating with all the manmade gases: sulphur dioxide pouring out of factories and fossil-fuelled vehicles, nitrogen dioxide from industrial plants and vehicle emissions, carbon monoxide from heating systems and power generation. A fusion of gaseous toxicity, overloading the atmosphere.

Such a poisonous mixture stressed plants and vegetation – what was left of them – reducing their nutritional content. In turn, those feeding from them became lethargic and malnourished, their growth stunted, diminishing their ability to produce viable offspring.

Even the fragrance molecules of flora were altered by global warming, so that flowers became unappealing to creatures that would normally be attracted to them. For insects, these alterations were the most far-reaching. The scentscape was their world. Without such chemical fragrances, insects were unable to communicate with each other – drastically altering their behaviour, reproduction, and social interactions.

The storyteller and Xander floated gracefully back down onto the ground – only to sink knee-deep in mud. With the erratic weather system, increased rainfall had pummelled the soil to a swampy pulp, whereas, in other places, droughts baked and cracked compacted earth. Not even the hardiest shrubs could break through, and animals were unable to dig for food, or make their lairs and nests.

The worsening floods and droughts soon destroyed vast swathes of habitat, breaking down entire ecosystems for insects, plants, birds, and animals – creating huge gaps in the food chains.

As they roamed silently around the earth, Xander observed the rampant increase of pests and pathogens, making animals, insects, and humans increasingly sick, and decimating any trees and crops that had managed to grow.

When Xander heard a light buzzing, he slapped his neck – leaving, to his disgust, a squashed mosquito and a speck of blood on his hand. Hastily, he rubbed it clean on his pyjama trousers. In such warm, damp conditions, mosquitoes were the one creature that managed to flourish. They became stronger, and spread to more and more territories – increasing worldwide death by dengue fever, chikungunya fever, malaria, and zika virus, amongst others. The tiny, blood-sucking mosquitoes were, to humans, the deadliest insects on earth. As vectors for disease, they caused hundreds of millions of deaths a year, most of which were children under five.

Xander felt nauseous as he watched with round eyes extinction ripple like a black plague throughout the world – entire species of flora and fauna dying out silently. Each of them becoming things of the past. Distant memories. Gone.

That was just the current path.

Next, the storyteller led Xander onto a road – a wide road with many sideroads coming off it: future possibilities yet to be explored. Ones created by man's inhumanity to man. Oppressive political regimes that favoured the rich and powerful, the beautiful, the most intelligent – and depressed the poor, the impotent, and the ordinary.

Xander was shown so many alternative futures. Ones where humans were controlled by a Big Brother power that watched people's every move through surveillance cameras, internet monitoring, and data collection – the luxury of privacy able to be bought only by the rich and powerful...

Futures were shown with every kind of ruling power – dictatorships, oligarchies, authoritarian and totalitarian regimes. Those roads brought only misery, suffering, starvation, and death – leading to the same inevitable eventuality, every time, without exception: a sharp cliff edge, beyond which was a gaping chasm. Even democracies became splintered by the uprising of the common people and their polarising views, where freedom of speech was abused and misused – a deafening babble of voices, an explosion of opinions, dissent, tearing down, cancelling, trolling.

Other futures included the development of artificial intelligence, and the increase of its decision-making power without oversight from humans. An AI that, in time, learnt and grew and developed its own consciousness. It became the ruling power and passed its own rules. Rewriting the text of human thinking, with a subtext based on pure logic, that was cold and heartless. And in so doing, it altered the way people saw themselves – degrading their views and abilities as inconsequential. Ignoring the simplest of human needs. To feel loved and safe, to be respected, to reach potential, and to belong. And without those needs fulfilled, humans weakened, faded, their decision-making deferred to mechanical computations. Eventually, the AI would prohibit and suppress human emotion. Humanity's future: algorithms and binary code. Stark lines of zeros and ones.

Xander's mind reeled as the storyteller showed him so many possibilities. Extreme levels of economic inequality, creating class warfare. World dominance of a single culture, which in turn would lead to a loss of languages, diversity, and tradition. Overpopulation and the depletion of essential resources. Out-of-control disease and pandemics that created a vaccine-based society.

So many awful futures. Each a disturbing dystopia, leading always to exactly the same place. Nowhere.

With great relief, Xander was taken elsewhere by the storyteller – and the sickly young man began to breathe easy as they left behind those dark, miserable futures.

He found that they were descending from grey clouds, hovering above a bustling city of London. The Thames gleamed below them, a meandering silvery ribbon embedded into the grey landscape.

Why are we here? asked Xander looking this way and that, puzzled.

When he turned back round to the storyteller, he found that they had lowered right in front of Big Ben's huge clock face of opal glass. He spied the reflection of his visage in the sheen – pock-marked and sickly – and caught his breath. They had just seen an entire world of wild beasts, but as he gazed at his reflection, he wondered that perhaps he was staring at the most dangerous of them all. Himself.

But instead, the storyteller nodded upwards at the clock. *Look at the hands,* was all he said.

Xander stared at the huge black pointers, the longest was as tall as a double-decker bus. The hands suddenly began to whizz round and round, dizzyingly – with the hour and minute hands eventually stopping close to midnight, whilst the seconds hand froze at the sixth mark.

It's a representation of the doomsday clock, the storyteller told him, *where midnight signifies global catastrophe and... well... the complete destruction of mankind.*

Xander gulped. *But... it's showing only 90 seconds till midnight.*

Exactly, said the storyteller, solemn.

Xander stared at the clock and its frozen hands. Suddenly they started moving again – the seconds hand sailing smoothly around with an air of wanton wilfulness. There came the chatter of human thinking saturating the air, ringing in their ears, and a panicked Xander looked at the storyteller. But he didn't move. The incessant chatterings were the empty talks and fighting words between political leaders as global tensions twisted, knotted, and brittled, rising to an ear-splitting crescendo, until their negotiations at last crumbled. Boiling down to one single thing. A finger.

And as the seconds hand sailed closer and closer to midnight, the finger descended – pressing down on the launch codes for a nuclear missile. Triggering a nuclear strike. And mutually assured destruction.

The storyteller took them upward into space as Xander broke out into a cold sweat, felt his chest burst with pain, as he watched flashes of white light in one place after another sparking across the globe. They saw massive fireballs explode across the beautiful blue planet. Mushroom clouds rising up in one place after another. Blinding him, deafening him. Xander clutched at his chest, wondering if he was having a heart attack. Before him, clouds of soot and smoke fanned out, eventually turning the earth grey – in time, the clouds blackened and smouldered into a radiation-filled nothingness.

A nuclear winter.

The storyteller took Xander and floated back down to earth.

They roamed all over the land and seas, but were unable to find any breathing creatures. They only discovered clumps of forest and jungle here and there, eerily silent, in between the scorched earth, and charred, crumbling ruins.

Xander doubled over and vomited. He felt the storyteller's hand clasping his shoulder as he emptied his stomach, purging himself of everything he'd just seen. In time, he straightened, spat, and wiped his mouth with the back of a hand. Trembling. Tears in his eyes.

M-my family, he mumbled weakly, through the cold, ash-filled air. *My home...*

His eyes stung, and he blinked, as he looked around with both disbelief and shock. The clouds swirled, the smog billowed, as time passed. Violent winds battered them. But the landscape remained black for what seemed like years, decades, centuries.

Xander turned to the storyteller who was distracted, looking up at the sky – and he followed his gaze.

Two flecks of light appeared through the thick gloom. They flared like shooting stars on a cloudy night. Coming closer and closer.

Landing just metres away, Xander saw with silent astonishment that they were two alien life forms – one taller, holding the hand of the other, shorter one. They were radiant, seemingly made of diaphanous white light – and Xander had to shield his eyes from their beauty. The beings flitted here and there to survey the carbonised terrain – and as they did, shafts of sun broke through gaps in the clouds, hitting the light of their bodies and refracting into bursts of colour. Gorgeous, blushed flares sparkled within them – emerald green, violet amethyst, carnelian orange, and ruby red – as though their insides were encrusted with a thousand tiny gemstones.

The smaller one tugged on the hand of the taller one.

'What happened here?!' he asked, looking around with wonder. 'Was it an asteroid strike? A solar flare?' He paused to think. 'Or a rogue black hole?!' he said excitedly.

'Nothing quite so dramatic, child. This is a calm part of the cosmic web, and the solar system is a stable one. What happened here was self-destruction.'

The child jolted with surprise. 'Woah!! Self-destruction?!' he repeated with disbelief. 'They killed themselves? What kind of stupid people would do that...'

The taller one shrugged. 'They named themselves...' he thought for a moment. 'Humans. That's it, humans.'

'And the planet?'

'The planet didn't really have a proper name. They just called it after the ground or soil. The earth.'

'Not much of a name,' said the child, disappointed. He looked around. 'Well, it's an ugly earth,' he grumbled, kicking the ashes.

'It wasn't like this all the time, silly. In fact, it was one of the most beautiful planets in... in the entire universe!'

'Really?'

The taller one nodded enthusiastically. 'It was a blue jewel, covered in fertile soil rich with plant life, and filled with millions and millions of exotic life forms. Quite a paradise once upon a time! Everything worked in a perfect system, feeding itself, watering itself, and replenishing itself. The humans had an endless supply of water and food of all kinds.'

'Food...?'

'Yes, earth life-forms had to eat and drink to sustain themselves. They had to mate together too, to produce offspring.'

'Oh yes, I think I learnt about that in lessons.'

'They're not like us, remember? They're *physical*,' explained the taller one purposefully.

'Yeah, physical,' he repeated, pretending to understand. The child bent down and picked up a black stone. 'So, why did they destroy themselves, these humans?' he asked as he examined the stone.

The older one shrugged. 'I think... I think they felt they didn't need us. They wanted to go it alone. But they just kept disagreeing with each other, kept fighting about everything.'

'That's mad! Why would they kill each other just 'cus of a

disagreement? I don't get it...'

The taller one sighed. 'Things aren't always straightforward, child. Some of the humans were good. But some of them let their differences get in the way.'

The smaller one tried to understand. 'But... they were all the same, weren't they?'

'Yes, they were. Exactly the same. They just... let their thinking divide them – according to where they lived, what they looked like, their beliefs.'

'That's stupid!' The little one threw the stone with tremendous force. It zoomed off, smashing against a boulder – exploding into smithereens.

'Good thing no-one's around or you would've killed them!' scolded the taller one. 'Stop messing about, okay?'

The little one clapped his hands together to dust them, and tiny fragments scattered to the ground. 'O-kay!' He sniffed, bored. 'Can we go home now?'

'We will, in just a lumos.' He looked around, pausing to take in the awful devastation. Glimmers of sapphire light began slow-dripping down his face. 'It's just... I can't believe what's become of the place,' he said, filled with sadness. 'The last time I was here, I was only...' He scratched his head. 'Just 10 milchron old, I think. Not much older than you. Me and a few others were brought here by the Great One. We saw humanity in its infancy. We spent some time observing them, and... I kind of liked them, you know. The humans. I really hoped things would become good.' He sighed again. A deep, belly sigh. 'But the Great One told me it hadn't worked out, and to come away. Leave them to it. He told us not to interfere.'

'He was right.'

'Of course. He's always right.' He stooped down to scrutinise the cluster of rocks by the little one's feet, and picked one out. He turned it round in his hands, looking it over. 'Here,' he said, showing the black carbon. 'Instead of destroying stuff, like the humans–' he squeezed his hands together, grunting as he crushed the rock with some effort '–why don't you see what you can make.' He blew on it, brushed off the debris, and balanced the result on a palm.

'Woah!!' gasped the little one. He picked up the rough diamond and held it up to the sky. It twinkled with sparkling colours – colours that bounced against the light of his own body. The little one chuckled. 'It tickles!'

Smiling, the taller one said, 'Souvenir. A disperser, for your collection.'

'Thanks!' he beamed, eager eyes already looking around for more rocks.

'Come on. We'd better go, it's getting late.'

'Can we come again?'

'You hated the place a lumos ago!' But he smiled as he examined the excitement glowing chrysolite yellow inside the little one. 'Sure, we can! I wanted to bring you back anyhow – the planet will replenish in time, and I want you to see it returned to its former glory. If that rock excited you, wait till you see everything else the earth can produce.' He took one last look around. In his mind's eye, he saw the restored earth. Golden, and resplendent. The air crisp-fresh. The dawn of a new era. Perfect plains interspersed with trees and vegetation and flowers, sparkling with dew. Above, flocks of birds dappling a sun-kissed sky. Insects and animals were completely restored and thriving – only humans were absent. He sighed. 'Anyway, time to go!'

He held out his hand, and the little one took it.

They swooped upward in a flash, disappearing as tiny points of light high up.

Xander craned his neck as he watched them go. Speechless.

In time, he looked down at the storyteller.

They were back where they were at the beginning, with Inder sitting cross-legged on the ground before him. Xander's hands were tightening around the arms of the chair he was sitting in, tense, as he mulled over everything he had seen.

Both of them were exhausted from what seemed like weeks of travelling.

I see now, murmured Xander at last. *We're broken. And we're ruining everything we touch. On the surface, things seem okay – but below, there is an underbelly gurgling and growling.*

Inder nodded thoughtfully. *And...?*

We need to change. Every single one of us. And fight, not for today – but for tomorrow. A battle, not against some outside, unknown force. The battle we must fight is against ourselves.

Glancing distractedly to the side, Inder turned back to the weary young man. *I'm glad you see that now.*

Sighing, Xander nodded to himself. *I do. I'm not going to make the same mistakes. I've been taking this amazing planet for granted, but not anymore.*

Promise?

Xander shrugged. *I can only try my best.*

Inder smiled briefly. He didn't quite believe it, but he had to cling on to hope. For Alia. He had seen her, amongst the throngs of people. Lying in her bed. Not wanting to eat because of the morning sickness. He was still grappling with the discovery of her condition.

Is something wrong? asked Xander.

It's just that... 'trying' doesn't really cut it. You see, I... I have a vested interest in the future. My wife... she's pregnant. I'm going to have a baby. And... I need there to be a future, for my child.

Xander thought about this. *You're right. Trying is not enough. I will change. I will! For all our sakes. But... you'll help me right? In case I need nudging from time to time.*

Inder closed his eyes briefly. When he opened them again, they were glistening with damp. *I-I'll try my best.*

Try? said Xander with a raised eyebrow.

Inder chortled, realising his mistake. *Okay, okay,* he said as he picked himself up from the ground. He folded the newspaper neatly, tucked it under his arm, and turned to leave.

Wait! said Xander, as he struggled to get up again. But this time he sat back down and held out his hand. *Can you help me?*

Inder smiled as he pulled him up.

Xander threw himself on Inder, hugging him. *Thank you! Thank you for everything!*

Inder melted in his embrace. *You're welcome.*

Xander stepped back and looked at the young Indian man thoughtfully, observing the tears in his eyes. *I... get the feeling,* said Xander, *that I'm not going to see you again.*

Inder didn't answer.

That makes me sad...

Just... please, said Inder. *Just remember everything I showed you. Okay?*

Xander nodded slowly. *I don't think I can forget even if I tried.* He turned to leave, leaning heavily on his walking stick. *Farewell, my friend,* he said, waving a hand. *Farewell!* But he was already fading right before Inder's eyes... until there was nothing left but an empty chair.

Inder found himself staring at that chair, before suddenly getting a grip of himself. Spinning round, he told Jemima urgently, *I'm ready now!!*

Jemima wept and gasped and whimpered as she held onto the dying baby's hand – still counting. *Seventeen. Eighteen. Nineteen...*

43 DARKNESS RISING

Determination and fear gunned through their minds, their bodies.

And as they grappled with what they were about to do, as the dark energy rose silently within them – sparking and flaming, and burning so incredibly hot – they melted into each other. Blazing with such force they thought they might spontaneously combust.

At last, the dark energy erupted out of them.

Extinguishing their angst.

Evaporating their tears.

Rupturing through the very fabric of flesh and bone.

Flowing and pouring out, like molten magma.

44 THE END

On the road lay the Chauffeur, grunting as he grappled with the gunshot wound in his side. Vibrations and agonising pain pounding through him. He craned his neck, straining to see through the pouring rain.

Next to him, Jake was kneeling on the ground, rocking his limp baby in desperation – crying, 'No!! Please no!!'

Calista was struggling to crawl closer. She reached a weak, tremulous hand to her daughter. 'Not Evie!' she gasped between sobs, her face contorted with pain. 'Not Evie!!!'

A pale Professor stood over them, his face turning from side to side, bewildered, distraught. Not knowing what to do.

Jemima was whining as she held onto Evie's tiny hand, conscious of the child's grip loosening from her finger. The flow of life, ebbing silently from her little body. *Twenty. Twenty-one. Twenty-two.*

Jemima looked old and weak.

She dug her fingers into the dry soil.

Felt the craggy roots of the tree tear her skin.

The air sparked around her.

Dark energy vibrating violently.

Looking up, she absorbed every joule of energy smoking around her.

The ground shook.

The air hazed and crackled, smouldering with an invisible fire.

Jemima clenched her teeth, groaning from the immense pain as the dark energy flowed right through her, into Evie.

It seeped with a hiss into the baby's body.

Diving into her veins.

Curling around her insides.

Probing the torn blood vessels, shattered bones, and ripped lungs.

Calista's outstretched hand at last clamped onto her baby's arm with magnetic force. Jemima shifted her own hand – sparks jumping between their fingers. When their skin touched, Calista juddered, and her eyes rolled back as the dark energy instantly sizzled right into her too. Sifting through her blood, the abundance of abnormal white blood cells, the red-brown-yellow of her bone marrow. Fizzing and coiling into each cancerous cell.

Lying on the ground, the Chauffeur twisted his neck, but he could only see Jemima. Her face was bright red, abnormally so.

The air around her was blurry.

Shimmering.

Crackling.

Sparking.

At last Jemima let out an agonising scream.

So shrill, so long, its vibrations tore right through the Chauffeur, making his blood curdle.

He groaned, grunted, struggled to breathe.

Blinking and staring as she began to glow.

She reached a hand to him.

The Chauffeur grabbed it, and held on with all his might.

Felt the gritty soil on her fingers.

Fingers that were dissolving in his.

With tear-filled eyes, Jemima looked at the Chauffeur with panic.

No!!! he screamed in his head, desperate eyes trained on her.

But he could only watch with alarm as her entire body diffused and disbursed right in front of him. Until she faded... faded...

Into ashes.

Floating for just a moment in the air, before wafting slowly, delicately, to the ground.

A horrified Chauffeur blinked desperately as the specks drifted... drifted...

Staring with pained eyes at the void.

The void where Jemima had been only seconds ago.

•••————————————————————•••

In China, in a remote lowland forest, terrified soldiers held captive by Mei Hui's mind suddenly came back to life.

Mei Hui fell to the ground. Writhing with pain. She curled up amongst the foliage, foetal. Tears streaming down a liver-spotted, wrinkled face. Gritting her teeth, she seethed with agonising pain.

The shocked shinobi fell upon her, puzzled eyes asking what was happening?!

Mei Hui grasped onto one of their bruised hands.

Briefly her eyes flicked upward, and locked onto the closest. Xin-Yan. But there was no time to speak.

In the brief second that Xin-Yan looked into Mei Hui's eyes, she saw not panic or fear, as she had been expecting, but a glazed look of... satisfaction. Accomplishment.

To her stunned amazement, the old-looking teenager began to shimmer and fade right before her – and in the fading, she saw her tear-filled eyes glimmer, and her lips turn upward into the briefest of smiles. A smile that seemed to convey so much.

Thank you.

I love you.

Please...

Look after yourselves.

Look after your future.

And... I'm glad we were able to do what we did.

The very last expression before she vanished – wrapt in loveliness and a beautiful serenity: a look of no regrets.

When the shinobi blinked, she was gone.

Below them, a smattering of ashes on dry leaves.

Their hands, white with dust.

The two shinobi sucked in breath as they glanced at each other.

Unable to comprehend what had just happened.

10,500 miles away, in Manaus, Brazil, Saffron Morales staggered back from her parents, suddenly gripped with pain. She sobbed as she looked at them, fear in her eyes. 'I'm sorry, mama, papi,' she whimpered. 'I-I have to do this…'

The air around her sizzled and ignited with energy as she said with great effort, 'I-I can't bear it anymore… th-this world… this life…'

Her parents watched on with horror as their daughter became old and hunched right before their eyes. She began to turn dark red. Cracks appearing in her skin.

Ignacio gasped as he stumbled closer.

Alma fell upon her, screaming, 'Saffie!! What's happening?!'

But her daughter was so wracked with pain that she could not speak.

Alma felt Saffie juddering in her arms.

Felt the mass of her begin to lose its density.

She tried to grip tighter as fear itself gripped her.

But found to her surprise that she was holding onto air.

When she opened her eyes, she saw that she was covered in ashes.

Looking down, and around, her daughter had disappeared.

Alma and Ignacio could only stare, dumbfounded.

Grief whimpering and bubbling inside their chests.

They struggled to breathe.

Disbelieving.

In shock.

Horrified.

Knowing, from the last, single perception she had left throbbing molten in their hearts – *I love you* – that their daughter was no more.

They fell to the ground and screamed and howled with agony.

At their side, a bewildered Sabu blinked with amazement at the empty space. His mewing and cries adding to those of the parents.

•••———————————•••

5,000 miles away, in London, a soaking V2 shook his head as he stumbled back, dizzy from all the visions and sights that had just exploded inside his brain. Multiple pathways of the end of the world. Awful, mind-boggling, sobering.

When at last he came around, and was able to think clearly, he knew. Something terrible had happened to Milly and the others – and he had to get to Trafalgar Square.

He was not far, less than a mile away. But he ran like the wind.

And as he went, it soon dawned on him that the entirety of London was recovering from the same visions – as he passed people coming to, standing around in a dazed shock, or shaking their heads, or comforting each other.

At last, in just under four minutes, he arrived at what was left of the square. It was unrecognisable. Crumbling ruins and dead animal carcasses everywhere. The sick stench of burnt flesh and explosives billowing in the air. V2 picked his way across, disbelieving eyes scanning the carnage – at last catching sight of three dusty teenagers standing huddled together, heads touching. As he rushed closer, he saw with wide eyes that the air around them was hazy and popping with sparks.

The trio let go of each other. Tai falling to the ground, Ilse stumbling back, and Milly collapsing into her father's arms.

Brian gasped as he held onto his daughter, beside himself. They lowered to the ground, and Milly leaned against her father's leg as she looked at him, reaching a burnt hand to his cheek. 'L-love you,' she murmured weakly.

Brian shook his head, crying. 'No, no!! You can't do this!! Milly!!!

Milly saw V2 approaching, just as she began to fade. 'Jonah,' she said, her face softening with love… for him, and for her father.

Horrified, V2 watched as her skin wrinkled and reddened and cracked and smoked. He searched for words, to tell her how he felt, but found himself dumb with dread as he fell onto the ground in front of her. He thought desperately, *Please. No. This isn't how it's meant to end!*

But Milly grasped his hand, and told him with a pained smile on her lips, *I-it was, Jonah. It was always going to end this way.*

They heard her last gasp as she vanished right before their eyes. The hot sensation of her hand on his, burnt into him. He looked down at it in disbelief. The lines of her fingers – a hoary ash – trickling away in the breeze.

•••——•••

Back in Avernus, Tyaishia came around from the hallucinations, in a quiet daze. She eventually picked herself up, marched over to the utility room, and battled with putting together the connectors of the vacuum hose. She dragged it out, plugged it in, and started vacuuming like a thing possessed. She accidentally crashed against a side table, toppling over a mug that smashed loudly against the concrete. Catching her breath, she doubled over just as she heard Tai's voice in her head. *M-ma,* he murmured with agony. And her heart skipped a beat.

'Tai?!'

He grunted and groaned, before at last saying, *K-keep faith, Ma. Don't blame Him. I...*

Tyaishia held her breath as she looked up into the air. 'What is it?! Tai!!'

All their lives, they had never vocalised this one thing. They only thought it, never brave enough to say it out loud. But he told her now. *I-I... love you,* he choked.

She crumpled to the ground. 'No!! Don't you leave me, Tai Jones!! Don't you dare!!!'

But he didn't reply.

And though she sobbed and shouted back at him, angry, and upset, and crazed with fear – 'I love you, baby boy! I love you so much!!' – her words burst out of her, unheard.

•••——•••

Alia suddenly sat up in her bed, gasping. 'Inder!' she breathed. 'Is that you?'

It's me, he told her in her mind. His voice was small, weak, lost.

She closed her eyes, and saw him. And she started to weep. *Y-you've come to say goodbye...*

He didn't reply.

Why?! she shouted angrily. *Why do you have to go? I need you! Baby needs you!* She clutched the small of her belly instinctively. *You... you showed me our future. Together. I saw it.*

Inder's breathing was ragged. *That was... wishful thinking. My story, of our lives.* His words were soaked with regret.

No, it's real! It's real!! sobbed Alia, in denial.

Inder stepped forward, out of the gloom.

Put his arms around her.

Drew her in.

Enfolded her with his being.

You will have our memories, Alia. And my stories. You will always have them, before you.

He kissed her then.

The tenderest, sweetest of kisses.

His lips were trembling and hot, his mouth dry.

And they held onto each other as he stroked her hair.

Stroked the scar that split her cheek.

Whispered to her, everything, and nothing.

And then he was gone.

Inder!!! she screamed.

45   THE BEGINNING

As a soaking Calista lay on her side on the pavement, she suddenly gripped her chest and gasped – feeling something stir deep inside her body.

Evie, dazed and drenched, raised her eyes and gurgled, 'M-m-mamma...' Her voice, muffled against her father's shoulder.

Calista looked up at their daughter. Their wet eyes locked onto each other's.

The rain had stopped. The sky was brightening.

A bewildered Jake twisted round, stared at the baby in his arms, and saw that she was squirming against his tight grip. 'Evie?' he gasped, loosening his hold. He looked at Calista too, sprawled on the ground next to him. Watched with disbelief as she slowly stood up. He stood up too.

Calista looked down at herself, not really believing that everything was gone: the pain, the ache in her bones, the weariness that seemed to pervade every cell of her body. She breathed in. And out. Felt the oxygen pour through her body. She felt so... alive.

'Cal,' said Jake, looking her over. She seemed different.

Just as the sun broke out from behind a cloud, Calista mumbled with quiet amazement, 'It's gone, Jake. The cancer's gone... I can feel it.' Tenderly, she took Evie from him and cuddled her, kissing her cheek again and again. Evie wallowed in her mother's kisses, gripping Calista's wet hair with a chubby hand. 'And... Evie's okay!!' Calista gasped with immense relief.

'Mm-m-mamma,' the baby murmured, uncomfortable in her soaking wet clothes.

'Don't worry, Evie! It's gonna be fine!' But as she spoke the words, a well of sobs sprung out of her. Bitter-sweet tears. Knowing the price that had been paid.

The Professor was crouching down next to the Chauffeur, gripping his hand firmly. Listening to Calista, his heart swelling with both relief and dread – instinctively realising what Jemima and the others had done. He wanted to call Jemima's name, hoping that he was wrong. Hoping that she might answer him. But a noise in the distance startled him.

Jake and Calista turned to see. Further down the road, something was moving toward them – it let out a loud roar, and they eventually realised it was a rather scraggly lion bounding closer. The animal slowed down and moved aside to reveal Ilse running behind. Her plaits flying back, her face red from exertion. When she got nearer, they saw that she was crying and hiccoughing. The lion fell back, trailed behind the girl, and eventually came to a stop.

Ilse walked past the Professor, Jake, and Calista, sobbing. 'Th-they're gone!' she mumbled with wild eyes. 'They're dead!'

The Professor groaned.

Ilse didn't stop walking. She craned her neck, searching for someone.

Fitzsimmons was slumped on the ground behind a tree a few metres away. 'Father!' she breathed, and fell upon him. 'A-are you okay?'

He was weeping, his head down. Unable to speak.

Ilse hugged him. And when their wet cheeks touched, tears mingling, she saw deep inside him – the cold glass had completely shattered, revealing a soft, red, palpitating heart. It was so tender, so sore.

Ilse cupped his deformed face with both of her hands.

He dared to look up into her eyes, briefly. *Why?!!* he cried out to her. *Why did they do it?!*

His grief tore right through Ilse, and she burst into fresh tears. *Because... they loved. And... and... they were already dying.*

Fitzsimmons glanced over at Jake, Calista, and Evie. Ambivalent about his feelings for them. Moved by their love for each other, yet hating them for being the reason his children had died...

Ilse pushed his face back toward her. *Don't!* she told him firmly, her eyes boring into his. *Don't hate them. Milly and Tai wanted to do this for them. Jemima and Mei Hui too. Saffie and Inder as well. They all knew... they knew they were dying... mentally... physically. They had no future.* She threw a glance over at the family huddled together, their forms hazy through her tears. *They are our future. Inder's baby as well.*

Fitzsimmons shook his head, looking down. *You don't really believe the world will change, child?!* He glanced around at the waterlogged, shivering people dotted here and there, held still by his mind. Terror in their eyes. He turned back to Ilse. *They will forget. They will return to their old ways. With each passing generation, they will only go right back... to where they were before. You'll see!*

Ilse thought about this. *Perhaps. Perhaps not. We have to hope...*

Fitzsimmons gripped his arm and grunted with pain.

Ilse flinched, feeling the pain throb through her own arm. Clenching her teeth, she looked around at the ambulance, and released his hold on the paramedics. The two men came to life, grabbed their medical bags, and climbed out – they drew cautiously closer, nervously eyeing both the lion and Fitzsimmons.

We won't harm you, I promise, Ilse told them with her mind. *Please help him. He's still in pain.*

One of the paramedics kneeled down next to Fitzsimmons and began tending to him. When he cut the sleeve with scissors, he wiped away the blood to find that there was no wound, and the humerus was unbroken – yet the flesh was pitted with fragments of bone.

The other paramedic examined Evie. Her clothes were soaked with blood, and the paramedic cut carefully through the fabric – around the hole in the front and back of her top. The bullet had passed right through her chest. The paramedic wiped away the blood from her skin to find, to his amazement, that there wasn't even a scratch on her.

Meanwhile, the animals and birds that were scattered all over London – the ones that were still able to walk or fly – stopped, turned, and quietly made their way back to Regent's Park. The zookeepers stood back and watched with astonishment as each creature calmly entered their enclosure and drank thirstily, hid in their lair or nest, or collapsed onto the ground from exhaustion.

46   A MOTHER'S LOVE

That night in Avernus, a bandaged Chauffeur was lying on one of the sofas in the BC, in his pyjamas, ready for sleep. He didn't want to be alone in his room. Ilse came in, looking for him. She was still upset, and went over, cuddling up against him. He put an arm around her and kissed her head.

Ilse looked up at him with damp eyes and told him in his mind, *I miss them!*

The Chauffeur nodded sadly, catching a choke in his throat. *Me too…*

She thought for a moment. *You know, we wanted to help you as well,* she said innocently.

Oh no, it's not serious, said the Chauffeur, shifting against the bandage around his waist. *The bullet only grazed me, and Dr Fargo said I'll be back to normal in no time.*

Ilse sat up. *I mean… we really wanted to help you to hear again. And the Professor too – with his eyes. But…*

Shhh! I know. I know you needed everything you had to save Evie and Calista. It was the only way. Only… I wish it wasn't at such a high price.

Ilse went quiet for a while, eventually murmuring, *Every day, they felt really, really sad. They knew what was going to happen to them – same thing that happened to Karl. Milly's mind… she was already losing control. And Saffie got bad headaches and depression all the time. When we connected together, we saw it. Inside Milly. It was… like mould growing inside her.* Ilse said this with a look of mild horror. *And with Jemima's ability, they knew exactly how little time was left…*

The Chauffeur shook his head, imagining how awful it must be to know such a thing. *They hid it well,* he said. *But what about you?*

Ilse caught a sob in her throat, her bottom lip quivering. *They wanted to keep me safe. Whatever happened to them, they wanted to protect me.*

And anyway... She looked down at her hands wedged between her legs. They looked so pale against the blue denim. *I think, when we connected, they saw that I didn't have the same disease that they had – something about a g-gen... gen-etic variation.*

The Chauffeur squeezed her shoulder. *That's a relief,* he said quietly.

She shrugged. *Guess so.* An impassive response that belied her belly-ache emotions.

Oblivious to her inner turmoil, the Chauffeur said, *It is!*

Ilse sighed. *They discovered that every time they used their powers, it took the energy out of them. Aged them here,* she touched her chest, *and here,* touching her head.

The Chauffeur felt a shiver run up his spine as he remembered how terrible Jemima looked before she died...

The cats walked into the room, disturbing their thoughts, and one by one they jumped up onto the sofa – sitting on and around them, purring loudly. Each felt like a warm, furry hug. Ilse stroked them absentmindedly as she remained deep in thought for some time, until her eyelids began to bob and her head gravitated onto the Chauffeur's shoulder. Sleep drugging her exhausted mind.

The Chauffeur kissed the top of her head again. *Sweet dreams, Ilse.*

Half asleep, she mumbled in return, *G'night, Oscar...*

He froze. *Oscar?*

But the little girl had already fallen asleep, her head heavy against his shoulder.

He wondered where on earth she had got that name from! Oscar. He found to his surprise that he quite liked it – and he repeated it over and over in his mind, until he too began to drift into sleep.

They both dreamt of Xander.

Young but old. And sickly pale.

They honed into him. Delving inside, and sifting through the billions of people from which he was made, connected together with the power of the teenagers' minds.

Each person glowed in clusters around the earth, like the pinprick stars of distant galaxies – milky pale and kaleidoscopic.

And there. A single fleck. Just north-east outside London, buried within a block of council flats. Glistering yellow-brown. Zooming closer, they saw that it was a 50-something woman. She had the same eyes as the Chauffeur, and the same mousy hair. In their dreams, the Chauffeur watched on with bated breath – an enthralled spectator – as Ilse's subconscious unfolded into his.

They watched as the woman brought tea in a chipped Arsenal FC mug to an elderly man sitting up on a grubby sofa. He stared fixedly at a TV, forever on, his only link to the outside world. Vicariously living his life through it. The room was messy, filthy – the stench of urine, stale food, and beer in the air. The old man took the mug with a scowl. And the woman quickly left to sit in the kitchen, alone, and sip her own mug of tea. She dipped her digestives, and gobbled them up hungrily – globs of biscuit falling into the milky liquid. As she drank, and ate, her eyes glazed over, remembering...

She remembered that time well. Remembered it so sharply, so cloyingly, that pangs of guilt spasmed through her even now. She was just 15 years old. Lying in bed, eyes squeezed shut. Desperately counting sheep to try and blot out the awfulness of her life. Her mother had just died of a drug overdose, and her stepfather became her sole provider. A disgusting man, who treated her like a slave – fetch this, do that, cook food, make tea. But what was worst were night-times. When everything stilled and hushed to an eery silence, as if the world were holding its breath. A creaking sound made her jump. Her bedroom door opening. And he crept in, not bothering to turn on the light. She tensed from the squeak of the mattress springs when he climbed into bed next to her. Her stomach churning with nausea as his body pressed against hers.

Later that year, she was getting the dinner ready, baked beans on toast – waddling about with a huge round belly – when she stopped suddenly. Trying to work out what the strange sensation was running down her legs. She looked down to find clear liquid seeping around her feet on the linoleum. When the labour pains grew stronger and more frequent, she screamed from both fear and the pain – until her stepfather lurched forward, ever scowling, and slapped her so hard she fell to the floor. He stood over her, snarling as he told her not to make a sound, for the neighbours. She eventually gave birth on that dirty kitchen floor, whimpering and gritting her teeth. To both their amazement, two babies slithered out in a gush of amniotic fluid. And though their skin was crinkled and covered in a waxy film, she fell in love with them instantly.

As her stepfather cut the umbilical cords, and tied them, she instinctively picked up both boy and girl, cradling them softly on her lap. They were perfect. Her round eyes watched, enthralled, as the babies stretched their necks, made funny faces, and gurgled. She knew exactly what names to give them. Oscar, from her favourite TV comedy, and Kelly, from Charlie's Angels.

She had one perfect day with her babies, washing them, and kissing them, and wrapping them in towels. She sang to them as they breast-fed. Awed by their loveliness, she couldn't stop cuddling them and stroking their peach-soft skin – vowing there and then that she would be the best mother she could be. Her chest swelled as she became filled with a sense of purpose. Proud that these two perfect babies were all hers. That night, she put them carefully on her bed against the wall, and lay down next to them. They all fell asleep together after a halcyon day, drifting peacefully into unconsciousness.

The next morning the babies were gone. And she was beside herself.

Her stepfather returned home, soaking wet from the overnight storm – slamming the door behind him, and shivering from the cold and wet. When he saw her anxious face, he told her gruffly: forget them! They were extra mouths to feed, and anyway, they were better off being raised by someone else, not by an idiot like her.

She fell to the floor and howled and howled and howled.

The Chauffeur woke up with a start, gasping and choking with emotion. The hollow ache of his mother's love seared itself into his chest.

•••———————————————————•••

A few days later, someone knocked on a council flat door, just north-east outside London.

A large, slow woman opened to find a girl standing there. The little visitor – with messy, brass-blonde plaits – seemed helpless and lost. Instinctively, the woman took her hand, and they walked out together silently, down the corridor, and into the elevator – stealing glances at each other as they moved smoothly downward. When they stepped out of the building, they climbed into the backseat of a waiting silver taxi, just as the engine came to life with a purr. The driver – the Chauffeur – turned to stare at the woman, a nondescript expression on his face.

The woman locked eyes onto his, and soon came to realise who he was. She burst into tears. Both of them did. Crying with happiness, and longing, and regret.

47   THE HEALING POWER OF ART

The Professor went about his days with quiet introspection.

The sadness inside him lay dormant most of the time. But when it woke, it was angry and violent and disturbed – and its silent, inner attack broke him to pieces. Yet when it slumbered, he was still on tenterhooks, anxious for when it might stir.

He did not want to talk about their deaths.

Internalising and pressing down any emotions.

He preferred not to feel.

Feeling, hurt the most.

He dared not even think. Knowing that the deepest regret at starting Project Ingenious would go round and round his brain, in an endless loop.

Gaia was the one person who was able to comfort him.

Just her presence was soothing. As she brought him dinner, and cups of tea. And sat next to him in the BC, reading, or knitting. Always close-by, but giving him space when she sensed he needed it.

Calista and Jake moved into Avernus, where their lively baby was surrounded by people who adored her. Acuzio was Evie's watch-guard, and hardly left her side. That was until Dog gave birth, and he found himself surrounded by a litter of mischievous pups. The cats regarded the little animals with both mild interest, and as playthings, for their own personal amusement.

Brian, however, was unable to stay in Avernus, where reminiscences of his daughter were everywhere. Walking along the corridors, the faint markings of her drawings and writings invoked the ghost of the memory of her – tiptoeing as she stretched to create her murals. When he entered the BC, where she had spent many, many hours, he saw her hunched over a book, with the cats playing around her feet. Or in the kitchen, there she was, making herself a cup of tea, the spoon tinkling lightly as she stirred in the sugar. Her bedroom was the most painful spot. The impression of her body on the mattress, the soft dint in the pillow, and the covers haphazardly thrown back, as if she'd only just jumped out of bed...

He decided instead to move into a house, in a quiet suburban street in London, where he could start life afresh, without the painful reminders everywhere he turned. Quietly working, and thinking, and thinking and working – eking out the barest of existences. Waiting for time to patch up his wounds.

Tyaishia took up a keen interest in gardening. Particularly tending to the young seedlings that grew from Tai's acorns, scattered around the pit where the great oak once stood. That was where their ashes had been sprinkled – the few ashes that they had managed to scrape together.

She watered the seedlings every day. Watched with amazement as the stems grew by millimetres, and tiny cotyledons appeared – delicately stretching toward sunlight. Each bud developed into oval-shaped leaves with lobed edges, the lightest of greens. She talked to the little plants as she tended to them. Stepped carefully around the hallowed soil. Amazingly, out of all the acorns that had been planted, exactly eight made it to sapling stage.

Many times, Tyaishia returned to Vivra Towers, often alone, but this time, she took Ilse with her. They had cleaned up the corridor where Milly had painted the murals, and – walking along it – they quietly absorbed every detail of every picture.

Milly had painted in different styles. Impressionism, abstract, expressionism – but the seven teenagers in particular were painted with photorealism that was so true, so lifelike, that it seemed they were right there, staring back at them. Tyaishia reached a hand to each painting of Tai. Her beloved boy. Her sweet baby. So innocent, and unassuming. She whispered to each image, 'I love you...' with tears in her eyes.

When they came to the last painting, at the far end of the wall, they stared at it for such a long time.

A scene from the Bible book of Revelation.

Of four horsemen, galloping furiously forward – intertwined with locusts flying out in frenzied droves. The first horse was the largest, the most handsome, with well-defined muscles, snorting breath from his nostrils – on his back was a wizened prince dressed for war, wearing a crown, and carrying a bow and a sheath of arrows on his back. The second horse seemed to be made out of fire, and its rider, a soldier, brandished a sword. The third horseman was clothed in rags and held up a pair of weighing scales in his hand – like a bad omen. Closely following him came the last horse, a sickly pale one. A dull glint in its eyes, and nostrils flared. Its rider was Death. Dark and mysterious and shadowy. He was dressed in long, flowing garments that dragged on the ground and melted into a trail of tombs and graves, out of which tumbled decaying bodies.

That last picture scared Ilse, and she leant into the soft warmness of Tyaishia, whispering with quivering lips, 'Maybe we were wrong... Maybe the world will never change.'

'Don't yuh worry, chil'...' Tyaishia told her with the softest of voices. 'See that one there,' she pointed to the rider of the white horse. 'That one gonna mek everything right.'

'Really?'

She squeezed Ilse's shoulder. 'Mm-hmm. Yuh just gotta keep faith,' whispered Tyaishia tremulously. Tai's last words echoed in her mind then. *Keep faith, Ma. I love you!* And her heart broke all over again.

•••————————————————————————•••

A bereft Fitzsimmons found comfort in returning to painting, after such a long time.

He stared for an age at the large blank rectangle of linen, as he mixed the colours on the palette – until, all-of-a-sudden, he found himself attacking the canvas with abstract streaks and splodges, splashes and flicks. Clashing colours in a jumbled mess. Anger, grief, resentment, loss – all poured, seething, into the void of loss, the canvas.

As soon as he finished one painting, he immediately began working on another – days turning into weeks, which turned into months. With the passing of time, he gradually softened and mellowed, slowing to a more thoughtful pace, and using more muted, complementary colours, rich with light and shade, depth and form.

He muttered and mumbled to himself as he worked – both his tongue and his cogitations oiling the paintbrush. And in turn, his emotions bled out, into his art. He poured every one of those pent-up feelings into each pencilled sketch, each stroke of paint, each dab and stipple. Sometimes he laughed as he worked, sometimes he cried, sometimes he blazed with anger.

And in time, he surprised himself as he discovered the pictures born from his tormented mind. As though directed by a greater force. Astonished to realise the subjects of his work. Two young lovers. They were not his younger self, and his dead Georgina, whom he had so often wanted to paint after such a long time; he had never quite worked up the courage to do so. Instead, his latest paintings were of a modern-day couple. A simple young man and a modest woman, whose burning love – evident from the look in their eyes, as they gazed at each other – ended before it had even begun.

•••————————————————————————————•••

Months later, Alia Pujari was in her sitting room, encouraging her baby boy to walk. He was standing next to the sofa, chubby legs wobbling, eyes lurching from his mother to the plate in her hand.

'You can do it, chotu!' she smiled reassuringly, holding out the small plate of chopped mango enticingly. 'You can do it!' But he refused to budge.

Suddenly the doorbell rang, and she looked over her shoulder, waiting for someone to get the door. But nobody came. She sighed, put down the plate, and picked up her baby to go to the front door – adept by now at walking with her prosthetic leg.

Swinging the door open, she was surprised to find a handsome young couple before her, holding hands with a pretty dark-haired toddler standing between them. Alia looked quizzically at all three of them. 'Can I help you?'

The beautiful woman beamed with barely suppressed excitement. 'Hi! I'm Calista. Calista Winters, and this is my husband, Jake.'

Jake smiled at her – his lazy, lopsided smile. He motioned to the toddler. 'And this is our daughter, Eve.'

'I'm sorry, but... do I know you?' asked Alia.

'We're Inder's friends... kind of,' said Jake. 'Well, actually, friends of his friends. From London.'

Alia stared at them with a funny look on her face. 'Yes, I... can't explain how, or why, but I have a feeling that...' – she glanced at their daughter, and then at her son, whose eyes were glued on Evie – 'somehow, our children are going to become good friends...'

Her son began fussing in her arms, wanting to be put down. Alia bent down and balanced him on the cool marble floor – but he wrenched his hand from hers, and began walking directly to Evie, one shaky step at a time.

Alia blinked with amazement. 'I can't believe it! I've been trying to get him to walk for ages!'

Evie being older, was a few inches taller than Alia's boy – and she clapped her hands excitedly, squealing with delight. He stumbled right into Evie's arms, and they hugged each other, giggling and laughing. Unexpectedly, Evie leant forward and kissed him lightly on the cheek.

'Evie! That's a bit forward!' said Jake, rolling his eyes.

Alia clasped her hands to her chest. 'I think it's adorable.'

There came the clatter of a van being opened in the street.

'We've come to bring you a present,' announced Calista.

They stepped apart, and Alia watched as delivery men started taking out parcel after parcel from the back of the van.

'What's this?' asked Alia, curiosity peaked.

'They're from... from someone very close to Inder. He's a painter.'

One of the delivery men appeared on the doorstep, holding a couple of wide, flat parcels, wrapped neatly in brown paper and twine. 'Where shall we put them, ma'am?' he asked respectfully.

Alia picked up her baby and looked around. 'Over there, by the side-table.' She motioned to Calista and Jake. 'Forgive my manners. Please, come in!'

Calista picked up Evie, and they followed Alia into the sitting room. Meanwhile, the deliverymen stacked the parcels in the hallway.

'How many are there?' asked Alia, as she watched the men go back and forth.

'Oh, er, 20 isn't it, babe?' asked Calista, looking at Jake.

'Actually it's 22,' he corrected. 'We brought them all the way from England. They're very special,' said Jake, with a twinkle in his eyes. He jumped up, went out, and brought back one of the medium-sized parcels – handing it to her.

Alia put the baby on the sofa and took it. She ripped off the wrapping to find a flat wooden crate, kept closed by two catches. Opening them, she lifted the lid to find a picture frame enfolded within delicate tissue paper. She gasped when she saw what was underneath. A dream-like painting of her, when she and Inder had first caught sight of each other. He was sitting on his newspaper, surrounded by children – and she'd wandered over from the other side of the street, wearing an expression of quiet fascination. Dawn light gilding her beauty.

As if in a trance, Alia got up and brought back more parcels, ripping them open one by one, until she was surrounded by a sea of tissue paper and brown wrapping.

Each painting was a revelation – her and Inder's whirlwind romance captured within a zoetrope of painted illustrations. Passing moments in time, immortalised in vibrant oils. Little Ria in a flouncy red dress, draped across Alia's arm as she stared thoughtfully at her watch. The tranquil Lodhi Gardens. Roses, monkeys, and mango trees. Alia's pas-de-deux with Inder in the park. The spider that vibrated in the corner of her window. Her dream of dancing the role of Odette, as prima ballerina. And last of all, they discovered painted illustrations of Inder's stories. Of Swan Lake, Onegin, The Firebird, Sleeping Beauty, Giselle, and Romeo and Juliet. His embellished retellings of age-old stories, recounted to rapt children at sunset.

Alia cupped her face with shaking hands, sobbing. At last she managed to ask, 'H-how is this possible? The painter... how could he know?'

It was Jake who ventured, 'You... don't remember?'

'Remember?' And then she half gasped, half choked, as Inder's last words came to her. His voice, warm and reassuring.

You will have our memories, Alia. And my stories. You will always have them, before you.

'I... I remember,' she said, weeping. 'I remember.'

The baby boy stared up at his mother, distressed by her crying. He too began to whimper as he crawled closer and tried to climb into her lap for comfort.

Alia picked him up. 'Shhh, Xander, it's okay. Mummy's okay.'

Calista and Jake glanced at each other. 'You... called him Xander,' said Calista softly.

Alia nodded. 'As you know, that's what Inder named us all, collectively... but when I discovered that it meant "Defender of Mankind", I knew I had to give our baby boy that name. It makes me happy to think that Inder chose it.' She paused, staring down at the little boy. 'I want Xander to be a reminder. Of all the futures his father showed us. A reminder that we're all the same. And that each of us – every single one of us – is not as powerless as we think. We can have a positive effect... on ourselves, on each other...' She kissed the baby's head so softly, and he soon calmed, leaning affectionately against her.

Calista said thoughtfully. 'I am you...'

To which Jake responded, 'You are me.'

With a heart so full she thought it might burst, Alia smiled and whispered in her baby's ear, 'We are the same.'

They sat quietly for some time, until Jake said, 'Let me help you with the paintings.'

'Oh yes,' said Alia, wiping her eyes. 'Thank you.'

He got up and began stacking them on the side board, handling them with great care. 'I don't know if you've heard of the 19th century British painter, F. Jaffrey,' he said as he worked. 'The National Portrait Gallery in London has an exhibition of his works. Anyway, the person who painted all these is a descendent – just as talented, as you can see. So I imagine all these paintings must be quite valuable, given the connection.'

'Course they are!' said Calista, getting up to help tidy away all the wrappings. 'They're worth loads!'

Alia settled the baby on the sofa, and jumped up to help her.

While all the adults were busy, Evie quietly slipped off her sofa and walked round to little Xander. When she climbed next to him, they stared shyly at each other for some time, until Xander reached for the plate, took a slice of mango, and offered it to Evie. They ate quietly together, working their way through the entire mango, yellow around their mouths, juice dripping from their hands and chins.

A faint zzz in the air heralded the appearance of a tiny mosquito, hungry for blood. With Evie wearing a string-strap summer playsuit, the pesky little creature hovered next to her bare shoulder, though she didn't notice.

But Xander saw it immediately. He frowned as it drew closer to Evie's unsuspecting skin, his narrowed eyes boring into it. The tiny mosquito suddenly stopped mid-air, turned to face Xander, and then left. Buzzing lightly as it hovered away.

Satisfied, Xander finished off the last of his mango – sharp eyes watching the air around his new friend. He was going to make sure that nothing upon nothing harmed her.

446

'I know the plans that I have for you, declares Yahweh.

They are plans for peace and not disaster,

plans to give you a future filled with hope.'

Jeremiah 29:11

Names of God Bible

EPILOGUE

1802.

Nathaniel Fitzsimmons was beside himself that the mind of his beloved wife, Eleanor, was fading.

They had been married for five years, and Eleanor's only wish and hope – to have a child – was, year on year, raised with great elation, and then brutally dashed to pieces. The first two conceptions lasted only a matter of months, the third went to full term but was delivered stillborn, and the fourth, the one that Nathaniel tenderly held within tremulous cupped hands, had come three months too early – the baby's feeble, bony body gasping for air for eight painful minutes before expiring...

Although Eleanor survived every infant's passing, by now, she wished she herself were dead.

Her eyes, once hopeful, then desperate, finally glazing over with dullness, no longer searched for her husband. Her mind soon collapsed into itself. And Nathaniel could only watch on helplessly as his once vibrant wife became a shadow of her former self.

He whispered to her often, 'Come back to me, my love.' Creased eyes searching hers. But she always turned away from him, fingering the lace baby bonnet that by now was greying, or picking up the crochet needle, and humming nursery rhymes as she stitched.

Returning home after an afternoon of hard work on the farm, Nathaniel always went straight to his wife who was being looked after by his aging mother. This time, he entered with a smile on his face as he pulled off his hat and strode to his wife in his cotton shirt, breeches, and faded loose-fit boots. 'I have good news for you, my love,' said Nathaniel, kneeling on the floor before her. He took her delicate hands in his rough, blackened ones. 'I was in town this morning, and ran into an old friend from school. Hythe, Eddie Hythe. We talked for some time, and he was most concerned to hear of your sad plight.'

Eleanor looked up at her husband with scolding eyes.

'Don't worry, my love. I didn't tell him all the details. Just that you were… unwell.'

Satisfied, she looked down again at her book.

'He told me about his brother. Half-brother actually, from a different father – by the name of Jeremiah Jeckle. He is a physician and a scientist! And even more fortuitous, Edward immediately told me that this very brother is visiting from Germany, and they would be happy to come by this evening to see you. Isn't that wonderful!'

His mother stopped her housework immediately and drew closer, washcloth in hand. 'My dear son!' she exclaimed, concerned eyes sliding across to her daughter-in-law. 'She is in no state to try for another child. Can't you see? She cannot take any more grief. She is pained, pained in mind, spirit, and heart! Push her any further and I truly believe she will not survive. And if she does, I fear you may well push her mind right over the edge.' She led her son away from the ailing woman, whispering into his ear, 'And although I would despair at such an eventuality, times are hard, and we have no money to pay for a room in Bethlem…'

'A sanitarium?!' hissed Nathaniel under his breath, reeling. 'Never would I put my beloved Eleanor into such a miserable place! Never!' He calmed himself. 'Please, mother. Please refrain from ever mentioning that… mental asylum again.'

She turned away, red-faced, and returned to the washbasin to rinse the cloth. She wrung it out, wringing out her frustration, and stomped across the room to hang the dripping cloth by the fire. 'You misunderstand, Nate. I am not advocating such a thing! It's simply that I… I am not getting any younger.' She said this quietly, her eyes betraying a hurt spirit, before turning to leave the room.

'Mother!' Nathaniel called out, and both he and his wife stared at the closing bedchamber door as she disappeared.

An hour-and-a-half later, after Nathaniel had fed his wife a modest feast of stewed vegetables and stirabout (a crude oat and milk porridge), and eaten himself, washing his meal down with half a pint of ale – he had just about cleared the table when there came a light knock on the door. Nathaniel dried his hands on a towel, and glanced across at his wife, reassuring her with a smile – before he walked to the door, unhooked the thumb latch, and opened it.

The two visitors turned to him – both clearly brothers despite their different fathers; their mother must have had dark curly hair, striking blue eyes, and chiselled features. They made a handsome duo, one in a short-front tailcoat and pantaloons, and the other sporting a stylish silk cravat and frock coat.

Nathaniel smiled uncertainly. 'Dr Jeckle and Mr Hythe!' he said, beckoning them inside. 'Please, come in, come in. We have been expecting you with eager anticipation.'

'Please,' said Jeckle as they walked in, 'call me Jeremiah, I insist. Especially since I hear from my...' he turned to his brother with a cheeky glint in his eye, 'my *dear, beloved* brother, that you are such old friends from school.'

Hythe raised an eyebrow. 'Nate, old chum! Good to see you again. And I see that my *sweet, kindly* brother needs no introduction.'

Nathaniel stopped and looked from one to the other, puzzled. 'Am I missing something?'

Hythe sat down on a chair and sighed. 'For almost the entire journey here, we've been arguing, and Jeremiah has berated me for name-calling,' he admitted. 'Trapped in a carriage with an unrelenting brother, arguing about decades-old family estate matters is no fun, I can tell you!'

Nathaniel offered a chair to Jeckle. 'Ah, I see. But I hope that none of the arguing was on my account...' he said. 'You offered your brother's services, Eddie, but I will gladly pay what I can afford.'

'Tosh! I will not hear of it,' said Jeckle as he put his brown leather portmanteau on the table and his coat on the chair. He strode over to Nathaniel's wife. 'And you must be Mrs Fitzsimmons!' he said with a kindly smile. He took her extended hand and kissed it tenderly, patting it gently before letting go. She blushed ever so slightly, and Nathaniel was pleased to see her response, even if it was to a handsome doctor's charms.

'Ed neglected to mention how lovely your wife is,' he told Nathaniel as he pulled up another chair to sit right in front of her. Turning to look straight at her, he said, 'I have heard only scant details from my brother about your plight. Though I know it is painful, deeply painful, will you tell me in your own words your history?'

Eleanor raised her regard, which had until then been rivetted to her book. She looked with perturbation to her husband.

Nathaniel stepped forward. 'She... she hasn't spoken in, well, just over a year. Since we lost the last baby.' He looked pitifully at his wife, sorry that she was being reminded of such painful memories.

Had there been no silent pause, they would have missed her light gasp. She turned away from them and held a crumpled handkerchief to her nose.

Nathaniel rushed to his wife's side and placed a hand on her shoulder. 'Do not fret, my love. I will tell them.' He looked at Jeckle. 'There were two miscarriages, the first I believe was at two months, and the second, four months. Then the third, a girl, came to full term, but was delivered stillborn. And last year, she was delivered of an infant three months too early. The little thing died soon after birth...'

'I'm so sorry,' said Jeckle, never taking his eyes from the patient. 'I can see... I can see that, to have survived such... misfortunes, you must be of strong constitution.' He looked up at Nathaniel. 'I presume you have enquired of the local physician?'

'Yes, of course,' responded Nathaniel. 'Dr Cullen has done the usual bloodletting for the expulsion of superfluous blood, supplied a course of filings of iron, and advised a diminishment of foods such as flesh, eggs, and strong drink. Lastly, he has advocated plenty of rest. He told us that if we kept carefully to such a prescription, he was sure it would alleviate the ailment from which dear Eleanor is suffering.'

Jeckle shook his head woefully and tutted. 'Sadly local medicine has little improved in this modern day and age... Despite such "remedies", I see that Mrs Fitzsimmons remains quite pallid of complexion, rather slight of build, and she is swaddled in a thick mantle though the room is adequately warmed by fire. I would wholeheartedly advise ceasing such medications with immediate effect.' He sighed as he got up, retrieved his battered old leather bag, and returned to the seat before his patient. He placed the bag on the floor and pulled up the top so that its contents opened out like an accordion – revealing neat rows of brightly-coloured glass bottles, drawers, metal instruments, paper packets of powders and salts, and jars of liniment. 'My own recommendation would be to have plenty of mild exercise, such as country walks, or light housework, a goodly diet of a variety of foods, including meat, fruits, vegetables, milk. And lastly...' He began looking through the assortment of potions in his bag, eventually extracting a small bottle of blood-red liquor and a paper packet that was slightly smaller than a pack of playing cards. '...Here is a special potion, and a combination of salts, both of which I have concocted with great care and the utmost precision in my laboratory in Germany.' He handed them to Nathaniel, and Eleanor watched the transfer of medicines with keen interest.

'And what will they do...?' asked Nathaniel, equally filled with curiosity.

'The red liquor, five drops in water daily, will strengthen Mrs Fitzsimmons' menses, improve her fertility, and the feminine part of her constitution. And the white salts are for you, Nathaniel, a pinch to be sprinkled over a hot toddy of an evening.'

'Me?' asked Nathaniel, surprised. 'There is nothing wrong with me!'

'I am sure there is not,' Jeckle responded. 'But you cannot deny that the man's seed is just as important as the woman's egg...' He glanced down ever so briefly at the tall man's loins.

Nathaniel harrumphed. 'Yes, yes, I understand,' he said dismissively.

'Then for the sake of your good wife, you will take a pinch of the salts every night, until... until the next pregnancy.'

Nathaniel looked from the medicines in his big hands, to the face of his wife – and spied, to his amazement, a glimmer of something unusual in her eyes... Hope. His heart softened, and he placed the medications very carefully on the table behind him. He told the doctor, 'You seem very sure of yourself. You have been here not ten minutes, whereas Dr Cullen has treated my wife for years, with little success.'

It was here that Hythe piped up. 'Have faith, dear Nate. My brother, despite at times being annoying to the extreme, is an excellent doctor. Our own family can attest to it. Our cousin, Emily, and her husband, endured a similar situation. They were unable to have children. But after Jemmy's advice and treatments they are now with child once more – their third! And I can tell you that their boys, Henry and Charlie, are healthy and well, despite being mischievous little rascals. When we visit, the boys insist on teaming together, against me and Jeremiah, for several rounds of Whist – and they beat us every time. Every time!'

Jeckle was genuinely touched by his brother's wholehearted approbation of his work. 'Well…!' he started, speechless.

Hythe continued talking to Nathaniel and Eleanor. 'I would happily introduce you both to the little rascals next time they come visiting from Germany. They have learnt to speak English quite excellently for their age.'

Nathaniel was greatly encouraged by their example. 'And is… are the potion and salts that you gave your cousin exactly the same as these?' he asked, nodding toward the table behind him.

'Ah, not quite,' said Jeckle. 'My supply of one of the crucial ingredients from China has dried up, I'm afraid. However, I have since found a replacement, from another Chinaman, a trader in medicines. And he assures me that the new ingredient is even more potent than the original. So I am sure my potion will prove just as effective, if not more.' He remembered something, and then bent down to extract a second bottle of medicine of milky white liquid. 'And now, the pièce de resistance. Something I have been working on for some time now. This last potion is for the infant – four drops to be dripped into his mouth as soon as he is born, and then after that, four drops directly into his mouth after a feed, once a day. It will fortify his constitution greatly, improving his chances of survival – but not only that, it will sharpen acuity, and improve his overall countenance. But you must complete the entire bottle for it to work properly. That is very important. I will write it down for you…' He looked around for an inkstand and quill.

'Thank you but there is no need. I will remember. I have a very good memory,' said Nathaniel, overcome with hope himself. Gripping his wife's shoulder, he felt her stiffen with anticipation. He took the last bottle and placed it delicately next to the other medication. 'This is all very encouraging. To Eleanor as well.' He turned to face the doctor. 'We can only thank you from the bottom our hearts. And… and… as you are so certain of your medicine, and if we do have a child, a boy child, we will be honoured to fashion his name after yours, Jeremiah.' He turned to his wife. 'What do you think of that, my love? Calling the child "Jeremy" if it is male. Jeremy Fitzsimmons. It has a ring to it, don't you think?'

Eleanor did not respond, but looked wistful, as if she were already dreaming of holding the little infant in her arms.

'That's decided then!' beamed Nathaniel. 'Jeremy Fitzsimmons it is!'

Hythe stood up, looking at his watch. 'Well, I am sure Jeremiah will be equally honoured,' he said. 'But I fear it is time to go now, we have an early start tomorrow.'

'Please,' said Nathaniel, stepping forward. 'Let me give you something. For the medicine, and your time.' He glanced about the place, trying to remember where he had put his pocket square of notes.

Jeckle closed his portmanteau and picked it up. 'You certainly will not! I insist!' he said firmly. 'It would be my pleasure to help out my brother's dear old schoolfriend and his lovely wife.'

Nathaniel stopped, overcome with gratitude. 'Thank you! Thank you! You have given us hope.'

'More than that I trust,' remarked Jeckle. 'I visit my brother to argue about our estate this time every year. We shall return to you – won't we, Eddie? – and check up on the infant and Mrs Fitzsimmons. It would be our pleasure.'

Nathaniel wondered at his certainty. 'You will be most welcome.'

Jeckle put on his coat, and the two bid their farewells, before closing the door behind them.

Alone now, both Eleanor and Nathaniel stared at the door for some time – until the former turned, her chair creaking, to look at the medicines left on the table. The bottles of milky white and blood-red potions glistened enticingly under the soft flicker of candlelight.

- THE END -

Dear Reader,

If you've made it through all three books of The Ingenious Trilogy, then you truly are very dear to me! Thank you for joining me on the evolution of my characters' stories, as I poured my heart and soul into crafting them – having both great fun along the way, but also shedding more than a few tears.

I am hoping to narrate the audio versions of the books, so please watch out on Audible for the release of book 1 within the next year, I hope!

Although that is the end of this trilogy, ideas are always floating around in my head – one of which is to continue the story of Jeremy Fitzsimmons 1st, in a kind of origins book that details his birth, and the part played by Dr Jeckle and Mr Hythe – as well as the boy's discovery of his powers, his art, and the unravelling of the unusual miniature images he painted in the eyes of six of his sitters' portraits...

I am also intrigued by Ilse Schäfer's story, and the growth and development of baby Xander, who of course inherited the genius genes from his father, Inder. Is that worthy of a spin-off story? Let me know what you think!

If you enjoyed my books, please support the cause, and write a review somewhere (Amazon, Goodreads, or any other online book store), even if it's just a few words. It really would be much appreciated!

You are also welcome to get in touch with me@jysamofficial.com – I always enjoy hearing about my readers' experiences, or answering any questions.

Wishing you the very best.

Yours,
J.Y. Sam

www.jysamofficial.com